THE RETURN OF THE DRAGON QUEEN

THE RETURN OF THE DRAGON QUEEN

THE AVALONIA CHRONICLES, BOOK 3

FARAH OOMERBHOY

eBook ISBN: 978-1-63489-268-1
Paperback ISBN: 978-1-63489-267-4
Hardcover ISBN: 978-1-63489-266-7
Audiobook ISBN: 978-1-63489-281-0

Library of Congress Catalog Number: 2019912244

Printed in the United States of America

First Printing: 2019

23 22 21 20 19   5 4 3 2 1

Editing by A R Editorial Solutions and Proof Positive

Cover design by Steven Meyer-Rassow

Map design by Josh Stolarz

Interior design by Kate Tilton's Author Services, LLC

Wise Ink Creative Publishing
807 Broadway St. NE, Suite 46
Minneapolis, MN 55413
wiseink.com

For my children, my Lightbringers

PROLOGUE

"I AM DISAPPOINTED, MORGANA," said a deep voice from the shadows.

A thunderstorm raged outside the Star Palace and lightning flashed, revealing a man sitting in a high-backed velvet armchair. His face was worn and darkened by the sun. A short white beard covered his face, and his hair was peppered with numerous salty strands. Rain pelted incessantly against the ornate windowpanes, which rattled in the wind. Two massive fireplaces glowed in the darkness, throwing fleeting shadows around the room.

"It's not my fault we lost Elfi," said Morgana, turning away from him and standing in front of the fireplace, staring into the flames as they danced before her. Smoke and a cloying sweet scent filled the space, making it difficult to breathe. "Lucian underestimated the girl. I will not make the same mistake."

The man's dark eyes narrowed. He wore plain black robes and no adornments on his neck or fingers. He set his lips in a thin line as he reclined with his elbows on the armrests, his fingers linked together in front of him. "You should have gone yourself. You should have taken the Dagger to Elfi and exterminated the fae once and for all. You still fear the fae queen. Now, because of your cowardice, Abraxas has returned, and they are one step closer to destroying the book."

Morgana's shoulders straightened. "I am not afraid of her. I didn't want to risk losing the Dagger in the battle. Now the Grand Duchess of the Day Court thinks to bargain with me, the High Queen of Avalonia." A feral sneer formed on her face. "I will have to give her a reminder as to who exactly she is dealing with. I will go and retrieve the book from Andromeda myself."

"You'd better. I cannot afford any more mistakes. And don't forget who made you high queen. I can just as easily unmake you."

Morgana pushed her shoulders back. "The battle at Elfi was merely a setback. Brandor has confirmed their support. We are moving the goods to the dwarven fortress of Greygate as we speak. Once we secure an alliance with the dwarves, you shall have your new weapons, and our armies will decimate the fae. Avalonia will be ours before winter sets in."

"Good!" The man clasped his hands in front of him. "Have you appointed a new archmage?"

Morgana nodded. "He is on his way to Eldoren."

He studied her, his eyes narrowed. "And the girl?"

"I will handle her," said Morgana.

"No!" The man pushed himself up slowly from his chair. "I will handle the girl."

"I can stop her—give me another chance."

He shook his head. "This has gone on too long, Morgana. I left it to you, and you failed. I told you not to kill her, that we need her alive, but you didn't listen. My plans are far too important to leave anything to chance. Not when the Dark Lord is ready to rise. I told you to capture Aurora Firedrake, but you didn't. You had a chance to stop her in the ruins and you let her go. Now she's back with powers that no one has ever seen before. But we still need her for the final part of the plan. You just do as I tell you. I want the girl in my possession before winter sets in."

A faint smile curved Morgana's lips, cruel and sinister as she looked at the man before her, the expression in his eyes identical to her own. "It shall be done, Father."

A QUEEN IN THE MAKING

THE CLASH of swords rang in my ears as I sidestepped and turned, slashing at my attacker, slicing him across his arm, and kicking him sharply in the stomach. He doubled over and shouted to his companions: rough, armed men who had been following us all day.

"Behind you!" Tristan barked, taking on three others.

I spun and ducked just in time to avoid another sword that came swinging toward my head. Sweat ran down my brow and between my breasts, and strands of loose hair stuck to my neck and face as I twirled swiftly, holding up my sword and bracing my legs. My arms shuddered as the mercenary's broadsword connected with Dawn. The smooth, polished metal of my dwarven-made sword shimmered as the burnished gold rays of the setting sun illuminated the rubies on the hilt, which glistened like the glowing embers of a fire. Using my fae strength, I pushed my attacker away and tightened my grip on my sword.

"I thought I told you to go back to Elfi, Aurora," Tristan growled as he knocked out one man with the hilt of his sword. "Why are you following me?"

"I'm not following you," I lied, adjusting my stance and eyeing my attacker. "I'm just trying to find the book, like you are." I let my fae senses take over just as the man lunged for me. Blood roaring in my ears, I twisted the weapon in my hands deftly, disarming him.

Neither Tristan nor I wanted to use our fae magic for fear of giving away our location. These were simple mercenaries, soldiers without magic. They were more of an irritation than a threat to us. We had been careful, keeping our identities glamoured while we scoured Brandor for Andromeda and the book. The Grand Duchess of the Day Court had disappeared from Elfi after the battle of Abraxas. She had betrayed the fae and allied with Morgana in the hope that Morgana would make her Queen of Elfi. But when her plan to take over Elfi failed, Andromeda took the book and ran. It was now her only leverage with Morgana.

For now, we had been lucky; we hadn't come across any Drakaar yet. They seemed to be regrouping since their defeat at the battle of Abraxas. But I knew they would be back. Morgana would not give up so easily. I was all that stood between her and absolute power over the seven kingdoms of Avalonia, and she had no intention of letting me live past my eighteenth birthday.

"I don't need you here," said Tristan, standing over two of our attackers as they bled on the ground; the others had fled. "I can track Andromeda on my own. You should leave this city."

"I can't go back, Tristan. I need your help. It is the only way to make things right." I pointed my sword at my attacker's chin. "Where is she?"

The mercenary held up his hands, fear showing in his dull brown eyes. "Who?"

"The one who sent you to kill us," I said plainly.

Shaking his head, the mercenary said, "I have no idea what you're talking about. I met a man—he gave us your portrait. They promised us a fortune for your head."

"Who paid you?" growled Tristan.

The man shook his head again, looking between Tristan and

me. "I can't, they'll kill me."

"And you think he won't?" I glanced at Tristan, who stood almost a foot taller than me, looking as menacing as ever.

Tristan and I had taken to wearing the traditional clothes of the Brandorians—loose billowing pants, a soft white muslin shirt under a short leather tunic, a turban wrapped around the head, and high brown boots. I had decided that dressing as a man was far easier and allowed me to move more inconspicuously. But somehow these mercenaries had managed to find out who we were. They had to be silenced, or Morgana would send more than just lowly soldiers my way.

I touched my sword to the mercenary's neck, just enough to draw a little blood. "Tell me who paid you, and I will let you go."

The man looked around, eyes darting back and forth like a trapped animal. But the street was darkening, and no one interfered.

"It was—"

His words were cut short as his eyes nearly popped out of their sockets, and he went still, his mouth open in a silent scream. He fell forward at my feet, an arrow protruding from his back.

Tristan bent down and pulled out the arrow. "Ash," he said, inspecting it more closely. Then, just as quickly, he dropped it and stood up. "The tip is made of blackened iron."

My eyes betrayed my horror. "How do they have arrows made of blackened iron?"

"I don't know." Tristan's voice was tense as he grabbed my hand and scanned our surroundings. "Morgana has obviously been keeping busy, arming her soldiers with magical weapons. These arrows were meant for us. We need to get out of here now."

The burnt-orange sky cast an eerie glow over the desert city as we ran through the narrow, dusty streets of Nedora, the capital city of Brandor. Built hundreds of years ago from a small trading outpost, Nedora was a much older city than Sanria, with a haphazard maze of streets in the inner section of the town, which slowly expanded over years to create the sprawling city it was today. It was ruled by the powerful Detori dynasty, a ruthless, bloodthirsty family, with lies and backstabbing an everyday occurrence in their court.

This city was quite different from Sanria on the western coast of Brandor, where my friend Santino Valasis, the pirate prince, resided. It was said that the Detoris were the ones responsible for the death of Santino's elder brother, Alfonso, the Valasis heir, although it had never been proven. The heads of these two families were the richest and most powerful emirs on the Council of Five. In recent years, it was Santino's father Roderigo Valasis, the Emir of Sanria, who had become the most influential prince on the council. But fortunes could change at any time, and the Detori family and the Valasis family were constantly vying for control of Brandor.

We ran out of the alley and into a more crowded street as we slowed to a walk. "What would happen if one of us got hit with an arrow of blackened iron?" I asked Tristan as I straightened my short tunic and adjusted my turban, which conveniently kept my long hair hidden.

"If a High Fae gets injured by a weapon made of blackened iron, especially if it was magically forged as that arrow was, the wound will not heal as it is supposed to," Tristan explained. "If it hits a vital organ, it can be deadly even to an immortal."

I put my hand on his arm. "We need to find out where that blackened iron came from."

Tristan's eyes narrowed, but he nodded. "Among other things."

The streets were still buzzing with the sounds of the bustling market—sellers shutting down their brightly colored stalls and gathering their unsold wares or haggling for the last trade of the day as twilight started to set in. Camels lazed by a fountain in the shade of a crooked palm tree as children played a hopping game by the side of the street. The fragrant smells of spiced pastries and meat roasting on open pits filled the humid air as we hurried past the dusty alleys and roads back to the inner section of the city, where we had taken rooms at a local inn. Or at least that's where I thought Tristan was going, so I followed him.

My grandmother had tricked me into agreeing to become betrothed to Tristan even though she knew Rafe was not marrying Katerina Valasis as she had led me to believe. She timed it perfectly, knowing Rafe was on his way to see me. He'd arrived just in time to watch me become betrothed to the Prince of the Night Court in the presence of all the fae nobility. When Tristan realized what my grandmother had done and that I was still in love with Rafe, he'd left Elfi.

He had been tracking Andromeda and the book for weeks now. I had followed, keeping myself glamoured and hidden, but he knew I was there—and I was lucky he knew, or I would have had to take on the attackers on my own. I probably could have handled them myself, since I was becoming good with a sword and had been getting a lot of practice. But it was always nice to know that Tristan was around. His sword skills were unmatched in Avalonia and beyond.

I had tried everything from apologizing to trying my luck and ordering him to help me rescue my granduncle. None of it had worked; he was determined to brush me off every chance he got. If only he would talk to me and let me explain what had happened.

But Tristan was having none of it. He always seemed exasperated when he saw me. "Leave me alone, Aurora. Go back to Elfi."

"Not until you talk to me."

He whirled around, stopping suddenly in a small grubby street. "There is nothing to talk about. We were betrothed out of necessity. I took an oath, and that's why I am bound to you. But that doesn't mean I have to spend every waking hour listening to you chattering."

My spine bristled as I tried to keep calm. "I'm not chattering, I just want to talk." I threw my hands up in the air. "I need your help, Tristan. I can't do this alone."

"So you keep saying." He clasped my shoulders and pulled me toward a dark corner of the street, so close his breath was hot on my face. He smelled of cloves, cinnamon, and pine trees. My breath hitched as he gazed down at me. His dark eyes were the color of the sky at midnight. "Then talk."

"I, um . . ." I hesitated, suddenly at a loss for words. "I want to apologize."

"You did that already." Tristan's gaze was pure steel, his eyes swirling with silver sparks. "But what I would like to know is what you believe you are apologizing for."

I looked down, my eyes level with the leather straps that crossed his powerful chest and kept the swords on his back in place. Tristan was a warrior through and through, with centuries of experience and a hatred for all things mage. I didn't blame him for being upset, but I could not change the way I felt about Rafe, even if I tried. And I had tried. But Rafe's face haunted my dreams every night. I kept seeing his eyes looking at me with such hurt and anger. Not so different from how Tristan was looking at me now.

"I never meant for it to be this way," I said, finally finding the words and looking up at his devastatingly handsome face. "You knew from the very start how I felt about Rafe. I never kept it a secret. Everyone knew."

"Yes, but when you agreed to become betrothed, I thought . . ." He paused and shook his head, his face going blank. "Well, it doesn't matter what I thought."

I looked away and Tristan moved back. "I have to go. There is an informant waiting for me at the teahouse by the western gate."

"I'll come with you."

Tristan shrugged. "Suit yourself."

I followed him through the narrow streets, past short, squat sandstone houses with flat roofs, to the western district of the city. Lanterns were being lit along the way as we passed Detori soldiers, their crimson uniforms trimmed with gold, standing out in stark contrast in this drab and poor part of the city. The big, bearded soldiers patrolled the streets and dark alleys at night, sporting huge, curved swords at their waists. They paid us no attention, except a cursory glance as we hurried past.

The teahouse Tristan spoke of was not what I expected at all. I had pictured people sitting around in a small shop sipping tea and nibbling on cakes like in the little cafés in Elfi or Eldoren. But this Nedorian teahouse was quite the opposite and, despite the name, quite frankly not a teahouse at all.

I followed Tristan through a door and down the rickety stairs of a deserted house in a dingy alley. The air was thick with the overpowering smells of hookah smoke and, as Tristan pointed out, opium. It was a dark, seedy place, where drunks and pirates fumbled and frolicked with veiled barmaids and stuffed their bellies with mediocre food until they were satiated. Customers lounged on multicolored divans strewn with sumptuous but incredibly gaudy silk cushions, watching gauzy-veiled women in transparent chiffon pants and revealing jeweled tops gyrate lasciviously above them.

The proprietor was a large, bearded man wearing a green silk turban, loose pants, and a jacket in the Brandorian style. Tristan dropped a few coins in his hand; he grinned as he counted the gold, revealing his hideously rotting, tobacco-stained teeth. He pointed to a garish pile of cushions in the corner of the room where a hooded person was sitting, waiting for us.

I held Tristan's arm and kept my voice low. "Are you sure about this? We can't afford to let anyone know we are here. Who is this informant we're meeting?"

Tristan looked down at my hand on his arm as if it were a leech. "You didn't have to come," he said, stopping abruptly to face me, pulling his arm away. "Go home. Or better still, go to your Prince Rafael. Go anywhere, I really don't care."

I ground my teeth together, but I didn't want to start a fight with Tristan in the middle of this hellhole, so I kept quiet as I followed him to the corner of the room.

Tristan hardly spoke to me anymore. All the progress we had made was shattered that night when he saw how I looked at Rafe. He had become cold and distant, like he was when I first met him. Our betrothal was forced upon us, and Tristan was bound by his oath to comply. I didn't have a choice but to deal with the fact that what was done was done—we could not break a royal contract without a good reason, or the fae would think I was rejecting them. Queens rarely had the option of love in marriage; it was all royal contracts and planned negotiations. Why should I think my life would be different? War was coming, and I needed the fae army's loyalty through this betrothal if I was going to take back my father's kingdom from Morgana.

We sat down on the cushions beside the stranger: a woman, but there was something strange about her. I reached out with my magic and wove it around her probingly. The woman's features changed as I broke apart the glamour that shrouded her real visage.

Her azure eyes twinkled as they revealed themselves to me. "You are getting good at this."

"Penelope!" I gasped as I looked around the room for any other High Fae she might have brought with her. But through the haze of smoke and frolicking bodies, I didn't see anyone I knew.

Tristan's frown deepened. "What are you doing here?"

"Don't worry, I came alone," Penelope answered softly.

"How did you find us?" It was a stupid question, but I had to ask. I thought we had been quite careful. Obviously not careful enough.

Penelope shrugged. "It wasn't easy, but I do have my sources. I knew you would be tracking Andromeda and the book. The trail led me to Nedora, and after that it wasn't hard to find the two of you. You have been asking about the High Fae in a city of thieves and pirates. And if I managed to find you, the Drakaar won't be far behind."

"Let them come," I said, flexing my fingers. "I am not afraid of them anymore." Ever since I discovered my true powers as the Dawnstar and Illaria Lightbringer's heir, the fears that had plagued me earlier seemed to diminish in intensity.

"Well, you should be," said Penelope sternly. She kept her hood on as we conversed, but moved closer and lowered her voice a notch. "You would do well to remember that you are not yet immortal and can still be killed. Your magic may be strong, but there is so much you still don't know. It is dangerous for you to be out here unprotected when the world is falling to pieces. Izadora just wants to help."

"I thought I made it clear that I don't want to see my grandmother. I refuse to be manipulated by her anymore. I am not going back to Elfi."

"I understand, Aurora," said Penelope. "Believe me, I know what Izadora is like and how she has to have things her own way. What she did was unforgivable. But you will need her support for the battles to come."

"She cannot force me to do anything now," I said, straightening. "After everything I did to help the fae, this is the thanks I get? I made sure she stayed on her throne, even though the Elder Council wanted to remove her and crown me instead. She knew how much Rafe meant to me and she didn't care."

"She does care, Aurora," said Penelope, softening her tone. "But the fact remains: she is still the ruler of Elfi and the only one who can keep the Elder Council in check. If you remove Izadora from the throne, there will be chaos in Elfi, the noble families will fight among themselves for power, and civil war will ensue. The generals will not go against her. If you do not do as she asks, Izadora will not send the fae army to help you regain Illiador."

My mouth dropped open. "She wouldn't do that. She wouldn't go back on her word."

Tristan's eyes blazed. "Don't be naïve, Aurora. Of course she would. It's what she does. And what makes her such an effective ruler."

It was irritating as hell, but he was right. I relented. "What does she want?"

Penelope's face softened. "At least speak to her."

I shook my head. "I will not go back to Elfi."

"You don't have to," said Penelope, getting up from the table. "Come with me and I will show you."

We left the "teahouse," and I took in a breath of hot, humid air. Anything was better than the sickening smell of sweaty unwashed bodies heavily doused in strong perfume, mixed with the heady scent of opium smoke.

The desert sky was clear. Stars twinkled like a crowd of fireflies in a stately dance as Penelope took us to a two-story sandstone structure with a flat roof, the inn where she had been staying. The arched doorway led to a small open courtyard with date palms shading a lone bench from the outside world. A narrow patio ran along the edges of the square courtyard, adjacent to the rooms. Stone stairs led to a first-floor balcony, which overlooked the inner courtyard and led to rooms on the upper floor. It was peaceful and calm and so different from the crowded, badly maintained place where Tristan had chosen to stay.

"Why didn't we take rooms here?" I whispered to Tristan. "Instead of that awful place we've been holed up in for the past few weeks."

Tristan glared at me. "Who asked you to stay there? I would have much preferred it if you'd stayed here. Then I wouldn't have had to put up with you."

"Well, if I had known this place existed, I would have," I snapped back.

"Stop it, you two." Penelope shot us an irritated look as she greeted a young veiled lady in white, who then ushered us up the roughly hewn stone stairs to the upper rooms at the inn. It was small but clean, with a lumpy bed and a chipped ornate dresser that looked like it had once graced the room of a grand house. Even with its imperfections, it looked completely out of place along the faded old wall. But the room was airy and had two large windows looking out onto the street below, with white-latticed shutters and light muslin curtains that fluttered in the breeze.

Penelope went about inspecting a big oval mirror that hung above the dresser. The gold leaf was damaged and peeling, and the mirror had dark blotches scattered within. "This will do."

I scrunched my eyebrows together. "Do for what?"

"You'll see." Penelope stood in front of the mirror. "As I said before, there is still so much more you have to learn. Spirit magic is vast, the most complicated of all fae magic, and your time in Elfi was not enough for you to learn all there is to know."

She reached out with her magic and the mirror started to swirl with a silvery mist. Slowly a silhouette and then a figure came into view. My grandmother was sitting on her throne, with Tristan's grandmother, Rhiannon, standing beside her. Penelope explained that mirror portals let spirit-fae speak to each other over long distances without having to spend the power of creating an actual portal that could be traveled through. We could speak to each other but could not pass through to the other side.

The queen of the fae looked me over but did not smile. "I'm glad you have finally put your childish feelings aside, Aurora. There is much work to be done." She threw a look at her sister. "We have been tracking Andromeda. I will let you know when she opens another portal."

My eyes widened. "You can track portals?"

Izadora shot a fierce glance at Rhiannon. "You did not teach her portal tracking?"

"There was hardly any time to teach her anything," the Dowager Duchess of the Night Court said briskly. "She was only here for a few months, so all I could teach her were the basics.

Mastering fae magic takes decades—you know that better than anyone, Izadora."

I didn't like the sound of that. I thought I had learned adequate control over my magic, but it turned out it was not enough. There was so much more to learn, and now I had no one to teach me. But I had no more time to hide away in Elfi and learn—the time had come to act.

"Morgana will soon be recruiting more soldiers to swell the ranks of her army, and we must do the same," said my grandmother. "We must make sure the other kingdoms stand with us. Breaking Morgana's hold over Brandor will be your first task. Since you are already in Nedora, meet with Emir Darius Detori and secure his friendship. If the Detoris stand with us, the other emirs will be easier to convince."

Penelope nodded. "You are right. The Detoris rule this whole area, and they have skilled soldiers which could be invaluable to us. I will set up a meeting with Darius Detori."

"Good," said Izadora. "Once you have secured the east of Brandor, I want you to go to Sanria and meet with Santino Valasis and his father. Remind them of our friendship and make sure all the Brandorian emirs and their armies stand with us against Morgana."

I tapped my foot. "The last time I was there, Emir Valasis refused to help. What makes you think he will help now?"

"The last time he met you, you were not the Dawnstar or a Dragonlord. I think he will reconsider." Izadora paused and her gold eyes glowed eerily. "If not, make him."

"But we have to do something about my granduncle too." I crossed my arms. "We can't leave Silverthorne in that dungeon. You told me you would help."

Rhiannon stepped forward. "We will help Silverthorne. But first we have to gather our forces and find out more information. We can't have you running off into enemy territory to rescue your granduncle on a whim. We have had reports that gorgoths are patrolling the skies around Eldoren, and the Summer Palace is heavily warded, so you cannot portal in. And even if you could break the wards and manage to create a portal of such distance, it will drain your power to a great degree. If you are captured while your magic is recovering, you will not be able to save yourself."

"I don't understand," I said to the Dowager Duchess of the Night Court. "I thought fae magic could never be depleted and is fueled by the elements. You told me that yourself."

Rhiannon nodded as my grandmother gave her an irritated look. "This is true for four of the five fae powers. Spirit magic is different—it comes from within and cannot be replenished by the elements. The power of a spirit-fae depends on their inner magic, and it can be very dangerous to the fae involved if it is depleted past a certain threshold. That's why Penelope nearly died in the catacombs trying to close the portal. She had to use powerful spirit magic to battle Skye and the Day Court guards until my son's forces arrived."

I glanced at Penelope and she nodded. "Even if you have other fae powers, as you do, your ability to use them will be diminished in intensity until your inner spirit magic has been replenished. It is the cost of a spirit-fae's vast power."

I clenched my fists as I tried to gather my thoughts. This had thrown me off guard. Every time I thought I had learned enough about magic and how it worked, something would be revealed to show me that I never really knew very much at all. There was so much to know and so little time to learn.

"What about Rafe?" I asked.

My grandmother's eyes narrowed. "What about him?"

"I have to help Rafe get his throne back, and I have to explain why I agreed to get engaged to Tristan."

"Then you should have gone there when you had the chance instead of following me here," growled Tristan, who was leaning against a wall near the door to the room.

I couldn't deal with him right now, so I ignored his jab and continued speaking with my grandmother. "You said yourself we will need the mages to stand with us. And now that King Petrocales is dead, Rafe is the rightful King of Eldoren. Without him we will never get the warrior-mages of Eldoren to join us in this war."

Penelope looked at my grandmother and raised an eyebrow. "She does have a point."

"Yes," said the fae queen, her lips a thin line. "But right now, we don't have enough warriors to waste our forces on restoring Rafael to his throne." Her eyes narrowed as she assessed me. "Our first priority is getting the Dagger of Dragath out of Morgana's clutches. But at the same time, we have to make sure that the *Book of Abraxas* is never opened."

"How can you be so cold?" I gritted my teeth, my hands balled into fists.

"What's done is done," said the queen of the fae. "Rafael Ravenswood is not your concern anymore, Aurora."

I put my hands on my hips and glared at my grandmother. "He will always be my concern."

My grandmother's gold eyes flashed, but she chose to keep quiet.

The dowager came closer to the mirror. "This is the way things have to be, Aurora. It is better for all the kingdoms if you marry a High Fae prince instead of a mage."

I frowned. "Says who?"

"Says anyone with a lick of sense," snapped my grandmother, obviously unable to keep quiet any longer.

Rhiannon clasped her hands together. "You may not see it now, Aurora." Her tone was sympathetic. "But soon you will come to realize your grandmother only has your best interests at heart. You are the only heir to the ancient house of Eos-Eirendil, and the last Dragonlord of Avalonia. You cannot marry a mage, and you don't need to. You are the rightful queen of the most powerful mage kingdom in these lands. An alliance with a High Fae prince is what will bring Avalonia together once more and heal the rift between the mages and the fae."

My shoulders drooped as I looked at my grandmother, suddenly feeling like a little girl who was in way over her head. "But you promised to help me."

"I did," said my grandmother. "I promised to help you save your mother and get your kingdom back. That is what I am doing. We had no agreement to help the Prince of Eldoren."

At that moment I really hated the fae queen.

Ever since that fateful night nearly a month ago when Rafe had walked out of my life forever, I had thrown myself into tracking Andromeda and the book. I had left Elfi without consulting my grandmother, but I was so angry with her, it was better for us to have this time apart. She had tricked me into becoming engaged to Tristan when she knew Rafe was on his way to see me, and every time I thought about what she had done, my blood boiled.

I crossed my arms and glared at her. "I cannot stand by and let Rafe lose his throne. It was my fault that Lilith came back from the dead as a shadow wraith in the first place. And Uncle Gabriel is still in the dungeons. Isn't securing the last key as important as finding the *Book of Abraxas?*"

"Silverthorne doesn't have his key—he must have hidden it somewhere," said Rhiannon. "So far Morgana hasn't found it, or he would already be dead, like the other guardians."

"What about the weapons she is making?" I told them about the blackened iron arrow shot at us in the back alleys of the desert city.

Izadora stiffened visibly as she turned her golden gaze to her sister. "Penelope, find out where they are getting this blackened iron and stop them," she snapped. "Dragath's forces are already stirring. Something doesn't feel right."

My heart fluttered as a great weight seemed to descend on my shoulders. "I'm not sure I can do this on my own."

Izadora's eyes softened, but only slightly. "You won't be alone,

Aurora. Tristan and Penelope will accompany you. Once you have secured Brandor, Penelope will contact me. We can decide how to proceed from there."

Tristan, who had stayed out of most of the conversation, pushed himself off the wall and came to stand beside me in front of the mirror. "And if I refuse to help?"

My grandmother's golden eyes hardened again as she stared at Tristan. "You cannot refuse. If you do, your oath will be broken." She moderated her tone. "I need you to go with her, Tristan. You are the only one who can protect her on such a perilous journey."

"I'm quite capable of looking after myself," I said tartly.

Tristan snorted but didn't say any more.

"And Penelope will be there," I added, more to convince myself than anyone else. I didn't want Tristan to know how badly I needed his help, although he must have guessed by now, after I'd been following him around for weeks, trying to get him to come with me to Eldoren to rescue my granduncle.

"Tristan knows he must do as I say," said Izadora, a dangerous smile creeping across her face. "If he doesn't, I will strip him of his title as Prince of the Night Court and exile him from Elfi forever."

Tristan's eyes blazed, but he didn't refute what she said.

"If he chooses not to come with me, you can't take away his title," I argued. I wanted him to come with me, but not at this cost. "He is the only heir to the Night Court throne. The Grand Duke Kildaren will never accept it."

"Kildaren will accept it if he finds out he has another son." She threw a glance at the dowager duchess and gave Tristan a malicious grin. "Isn't that so, Rhiannon?"

Tristan's grandmother's face tightened, but she nodded all the same.

"What do you mean, Izadora?" Tristan took a step toward the mirror. "Is this another one of your tricks?"

"If you don't believe me, ask Penelope," the fae queen said with a sharp glance at her sister.

Tristan and I turned toward her. "Penelope, is this true?"

"This was not the time to bring it up." Penelope's blue eyes flashed with anger. But she nodded. "Yes. I'm afraid she speaks the truth."

The queen of the fae shimmered in the mirror. "Take my advice and do as I say, Tristan, or there will be consequences."

I knew without my grandmother's help I wouldn't get far, even with the powers I now possessed. "But what about my mother and the Dark Dagger?"

"All in good time," said the queen of the fae.

I weighed the options, and as much as I hated to admit it, she was right. My grandmother was a master strategist, and if I wanted to win back my kingdom, I should start listening to her, even though I didn't want to. My every instinct cried out to go straight to Rafe, but running off into enemy territory on my own wasn't an option. However much I wanted to follow my heart and run back to Rafe and my granduncle to help them, I had finally realized I had a much greater purpose beyond my own happiness.

The mirror shimmered again, and Izadora and the Crystal Castle disappeared.

I turned to Penelope, my mind a beehive of possibilities. "What did she mean when she said Kildaren had another son? Who is he?"

Tristan's jaw was tense, and he stood unmoving as Penelope sat down on a nearby chair.

"Kildaren and I knew each other when we were young. He was my first love." She glanced quickly at Tristan and the corner of her lips pulled up with the hint of a smile. "My sister was already queen; she refused the match, and we needed her consent for the wedding. At the time she had her heart set on an alliance with the Day Court, so Kildaren ended up marrying Selene instead. But after Tristan's mother passed away, Kildaren came to me professing his love. Out of respect for Selene's memory and for Tristan, we thought it would be better to wait for a while before we married. Especially after the tragic way her life ended. So we kept it a secret."

"Thank you," said Tristan, his twilight-blue eyes shimmering.

Penelope shook her head. "It was the right thing to do."

I thought back to the story Skye had told me about Tristan's mother and the brutality of the mage soldiers who murdered her. My heart constricted for the sorrow and pain Tristan must have felt when he found his mother's remains. The mages still whispered about him—the Dark Prince of the Night Court, an unforgiving fae-warrior who destroyed a whole garrison of mages and burned their fortress to the ground. But I knew why he'd done it, and I couldn't say I blamed him.

"What happened between you two? Why did he hate you so much when you came back?"

Penelope looked out at the moonlit street beyond the window, her gaze far away. "When Izadora decided to send me to Illiador to look for you and gather information on Morgana, I could not refuse. She was distraught after having lost her only child, and she was certain that Elayna's daughter was alive somewhere. She felt the magic of the portal that sent you to the other world. I was forbidden from telling anyone where I was going."

I raised an eyebrow. "You didn't tell Kildaren you were leaving? I'm sure he would have understood."

"I had no choice," Penelope snapped, turning back to me. "Izadora warned me not to tell anyone. But I loved Kildaren, and I couldn't leave without seeing him one last time. I went to him the night before I left so we could be together just once." A single tear slid down her cheek. She hurriedly brushed it away and said softly, "It was only once."

My eyes widened, understanding dawning. "Kalen is Kildaren's son! Isn't he?"

"Yes," Penelope nodded, looking at the fae prince who stood beside me, expressionless. "Kalen is the son of the Grand Duke of the Night Court and Tristan's half brother."

A CITY OF SLAVES AND THIEVES

"I HAVE A BROTHER?" Tristan said finally.

Penelope nodded. "A half brother, yes."

Now that I thought about it, they did look similar, but I had never made the connection because of Kalen's silvery blond hair, so much like his mother's. But his chin and the shape of his face were similar to Tristan's—a lighter, younger version of his darkness.

"I have tried to keep him safe," said Penelope, wringing her hands together. "He doesn't know about his real heritage or the powers that he may come to possess."

"You have no idea." Tristan gave Penelope a dark look as shadows seemed to form around him. "He must be trained properly, or he will become a risk to himself and others."

Penelope nodded. "He is still young, and his powers have not manifested yet. I intended to tell him when the time was right."

The shadows surrounding Tristan flickered and dissipated as quickly as they appeared. "My father needs to be told."

"Not yet," said Penelope, expelling a relieved breath as Tristan calmed himself. "At the moment it is better we keep this information to ourselves. Morgana thinks he is insignificant, and

I would like to keep it that way. It is better that no one knows who he really is, or his life will be in danger because of the magic that he may or may not possess."

Tristan nodded. "Where is he now?"

"In Eldoren with Rafael," said Penelope.

Swirls of silver started to form around the edges of Tristan's twilight irises.

I quickly tried to change the subject. Tristan's mood went from surly to downright dangerous whenever Rafe's name was mentioned, and I needed him to be cooperative right now. "So, how do we organize a meeting with Darius Detori?"

"I will set it up," said Penelope. She turned to the fae prince. "Tristan, can you find out where those arrows came from?"

"I will make inquiries," Tristan replied abruptly, and left the room.

Penelope sighed and sat down on the window seat. "Once we get to Sanria, we will be able to better assess the situation. Santino's spy network is even more intricate than mine. He has people stationed all over the seven kingdoms, in every court. I want to set up a meeting between you and all the rulers. Not many people really know you—they have only heard stories about you, and you have been away from this world for so long, most of them think you are merely a myth. They need to know that you are a real person, a leader who will be able to protect them from Morgana and the Drakaar. They need to have faith in you, or they will succumb to Morgana's threats because they have no one else to help them."

"Do you think they will agree to meet with me?"

"I hope so. We need to gather more forces to go up against Morgana and the Drakaar. The Brandorian cavalry consists of highly trained soldiers and is a force to be reckoned with. Once we meet with the Detori emir and assess where his allegiance lies, we will make haste to Sanria and meet with Santino Valasis and his father."

"What about the Silver Swords? Santino said they want to help."

"I'm sure they do. But the fact remains that they are not enough, even with the support of the fae army. We still need Brandorian soldiers, not to mention Santino's mercenaries and pirates, and we need the Eldorean mages as well."

"So I was right? We do need Rafe's help as King of Eldoren?"

Penelope nodded. "Yes, but that will come later. We must secure Brandor so the fae army can march unhindered through their territory. If Brandor joins with Morgana, the fae army will be effectively cut off from the rest of the world. At the moment, Morgana's army is the greatest force in the seven kingdoms. When united with the Drakaar and their demonic armies, their numbers far exceed our own. The army Lucian brought to Elfi was only a small part of their actual force. And we don't even know how many more creatures they have hiding behind the Silverspike Mountains and in the farthest reaches of the Darklands. In open battle we will be sorely outnumbered."

I wiped my sweaty hands on my pants. "But Emir Valasis, Santino's father, has already refused to help. He met me and he doesn't think I am capable of taking my throne back and defeating Morgana. I'm not so sure the other rulers will agree to follow me into battle."

"Then we must convince them," said Penelope, standing up and smoothing her skirt.

"How?"

"Leave that to me."

THAT NIGHT I slept very little and was awakened by a sudden shrill wail that sent a chill racing down my spine. It was coming from outside.

The sun had not yet reared its head, but it was making

progress. A light pink glow had started to form on the horizon, heralding its advent across the Brandorian sky. The moon, still unaware that its light would soon be rendered useless, shed an eerie glow over the foggy courtyard outside the tavern as I ran to the window. Penelope and I were sharing a room; she hurried out of her bed, following me.

I froze at the scene unfolding outside.

A young mahogany-skinned slave girl was shackled and kneeling on the cobblestones. A black-turbaned slave master wielded a whip, cracking it down on the girl's back, tearing through tender flesh and drawing blood. She cried in agony as the lash hit her.

The fog shifted, and the light of dawn illuminated her form. I noticed patterns on her body, tattoos marking her from the tribes of Rohron.

My fingers clenched and opened as I moved forward and grabbed the windowsill. It was a few feet to the ground, and I had jumped much farther than that during my training sessions in the forest with Tristan.

Penelope grabbed my arm. "You cannot interfere, Aurora. Slavery is an age-old custom here in Brandor. You cannot do anything for the girl."

I twisted out of her hold and put my foot on the windowsill. "Let them try and stop me."

The slave master raised his arm, poised to bring the whip down upon the girl's bleeding back once again.

My fae senses took over as I landed in a crouch between them.

He raised the whip above his head, and it lashed out toward me.

I moved swiftly before the weapon struck, the blood roaring in my ears as my magic awoke. My fae senses guided me as I dodged, avoiding the blow and catching the whip in my hand. I wrapped it firmly around my arm and pulled. The slave master flew forward and landed face-first in the mud at my feet.

He pushed himself up, sputtering through the mud. "Guards!" he croaked. "Guards! Arrest her!"

I raised my arms and unleashed my magic, flinging the slave master clean across the courtyard. His head cracked on the stone wall, and he fell to the ground.

There was silence.

A young nobleman stepped out of the shadows. Oval eyes studied me from under his lavender turban. He had a round face with skin the color of honey. His eyes widened when he saw me. "What is the meaning of this? How dare you interfere with my slaves?"

My hands balled into fists as I pushed my magic back down. "Is this the way you treat the people who work for you? This girl is barely conscious."

The nobleman lifted his chin. "She must be punished for daring to try to escape." His beady brown eyes flashed in warning.

But I could not let this go. "A few more lashes and she could have died," I ground out between clenched teeth.

The nobleman waved his hand, dismissing the thought. "Who cares what happens to her? She is of no consequence."

Even though I knew slavery was rife in Brandor, I had never paid attention; I had allowed myself to be blind to this until now. It wasn't my problem and I stayed out of it. But after seeing this girl and the suffering she'd endured, I realized that Illiador was not the only kingdom I had to save. I was the Dawnstar, the light that filled the world with magic. I could not let anyone—man, woman, or child—in any kingdom endure such cruelty as long as I could help it.

"Every person is of consequence," I growled. "Your worth is not determined by your fancy clothes or the color of your skin. It is the choices you make and the way you treat people that show who you truly are." I moved closer to the girl to shield her from his glare. "I suggest you let her go."

"Never!" the young nobleman snarled, his hands on his hips.

The empty streets had started to fill up as the Brandorians woke to another day and started going about their business. Onlookers who had gathered were whispering among themselves.

I ignored him and moved to break the chains that held the girl. I could heal her back, but the internal scars would not fade so easily.

"Don't touch my slaves," the nobleman shouted. "Guards!"

Before I could free her, the guards moved toward me, their swords out, wariness flickering in their eyes.

I had had enough. I stood up slowly, my hands lighting up with silver fire. My eyes flashed with fury. "Try it and you're dead."

They stopped in their tracks. But the girl was not afraid of me; she stayed behind me as I faced the guards.

Tristan appeared beside me, twin swords blazing in his hands. "I thought we were going to keep a low profile, not announce to the whole city where we are," he muttered under his breath.

The guards took a few steps back.

"I'm handling it," I snapped.

"I can see that," Tristan ground out, the muscles in his jaw clenching.

I shrugged. "We were going to leave this city soon anyway."

The nobleman moved backward and stood behind one of the guards, shouting over his shoulder. "I said, seize her!"

"That is enough for today," said a deep voice from somewhere within the crowd.

The onlookers parted immediately as another nobleman entered the fray. People started to bow and move out of the way for the crimson-turbaned nobleman. He was tall and well-built, towering over the red-faced shorter man. He had a sharp nose and deep-set brown eyes, slightly upturned at the corners. His short beard and mustache were clipped and neat, enhancing his full lips. His crimson robe was heavily embroidered with gold thread, and jewels twinkled on his fingers and on chains around his neck.

28

"But Prince Shiraz," sputtered the lavender-turbaned nobleman, pointing at me. "She was interfering with my slaves."

Prince Shiraz turned his eyes on me. "Was she now?"

"Aurora!" Penelope hurried over and whispered under her breath so only I could hear. "It is not your place to interfere with the internal workings of the kingdoms. Prince Shiraz is Darius Detori's son. Izadora is going to be livid."

"How could you condone such a barbarous practice?" I snarled at Penelope.

"It is the way things have always been in Brandor," said Penelope softly. "I don't condone it, but now is not the time to interfere and go around freeing slaves."

I tried to keep my cool. "So when would it be a good time to free slaves, Penelope? After they have been beaten to death?"

Penelope looked straight at me. "You know that's not what I meant."

One of the crimson-clad guards whispered in Prince Shiraz's ear, and I could see the fear in the guard's eyes as he spoke to the emir's son. I could tell some of them had recognized me. I had forgotten my turban and glamour when I leapt out of the window to help the girl. I had acted impulsively and knew my actions would have consequences, but I didn't regret standing against slavery and saving the girl's life.

More onlookers and guards had started milling around to get a better look. Shiraz Detori's eyes widened as he looked me over, assessing me.

"My lord," said one guard, terror showing plainly on his young face. "That's Aurora Firedrake, the Shadowbreaker. They say she can kill a hundred Drakaar with one blow."

I snorted and shrugged my shoulders. "True," I said, and gave them all a wide grin. If people wanted to exaggerate my powers, I wasn't going to argue. This was the way legends were created, and I needed to be larger than life if I was going to get people to follow me against Morgana.

"I don't care!" The lavender-turbaned nobleman stomped his foot like a spoiled child. "My slave is mine to punish," he screeched, picking up the slave master's fallen whip.

Shiraz Detori caught the whip and flung it to the ground. "This slave doesn't belong to you anymore, Berzaan." His voice was low and calm, but his tone was one that was used to being obeyed.

"No!" Berzaan's face was getting redder by the minute. "You cannot take away my slaves, Prince Shiraz."

"I just did," said Shiraz Detori, dismissing Berzaan with a wave of his hand. He looked at the guards. "Release the girl."

But I didn't let them near her, and they didn't even try. I turned and broke the girl's shackles with my magic, severing the cold cuffs away from her raw bleeding wrists. I pushed a little healing magic into her to ease the pain. I could have healed her back completely, but there were too many people watching, and Penelope had warned me about using my healing powers in front of others.

"She belongs to you now," said Shiraz Detori, as if he were giving me a gift.

"I don't keep slaves. She is a free person," I snapped.

He held up his hands in front of him as if it would calm me. "It's up to you. She's yours to do with as you wish."

Berzaan glowered at me, but I could see fear in his beady brown eyes. He lifted his chin and stalked away into the crowd.

Prince Shiraz cleared his throat. "As a gesture of good faith, I would like to invite you—" he paused and looked at Penelope and Tristan, "—and your companions to stay at the palace for a few days. My father is out of the city at the moment, but he will be back soon, and I know he would love to meet with the Shadowbreaker herself." The way he said my title was not with awe as others tended to do. I was sure he meant for it to sound as such, but it sounded like an insult when he said it.

From the corner of my eye, I saw Penelope nod once. This was the perfect opportunity to find out where the Detoris' loyalty lay. My grandmother had instructed me to convince the Detoris to ally with us and gain their support before I secured the rest of Brandor—and what better way to do it than staying at the palace as Shiraz Detori's guest? The Detoris were the most powerful of the emirs after Roderigo Valasis, Santino's father. If the Detori and the Valasis families were with us, the rest of the emirs would follow.

I turned to the girl I had rescued. She was a little thing, barely thirteen years old. "What's your name?" I asked gently.

"Rhea," she said between sniffles.

"Would you like to come with us?" I inquired. "It would be safer for you until we find a way to get you back to your family."

Rhea nodded.

I looked at the Prince of Nedora. "Rhea comes with us."

"Of course," he grinned, showing me his pristine white teeth. "I will have our best physicians tend to her back. She will be better in no time."

I nodded my assent. "Thank you."

Penelope's eyes softened, and she took off her cloak and put it around the girl. "Come, Rhea, you are safe now."

Rhea huddled under the warm blue cloak, which seemed to swallow up her small form.

Shiraz Detori called for palanquins to take us to the palace, and I got into one with Rhea, to make sure she was not scared. Tristan rode beside us on a proud chestnut stallion, brought over for him by one of the guards.

The dusky pink sky had turned to fiery gold as the sun made progress across the sky. I gazed out of my palanquin curtains at the hot dusty streets. Honey-colored sandstone houses with flat roofs spread out in a circle around the palace, all the way to the shores of the Sea of Shadows. Every little street and alley eventually led up to four main avenues that divided the city into districts.

The Detori guards whom I had seen all over the city walked beside us and behind the palanquins, their curved swords and hard looks a deterrent to any citizen who chose to come too close to the Detoris or those in their company. The subservience in this kingdom was to a far greater degree than I had seen in the western kingdoms.

For one thing, slavery had been abolished in Illiador and Eldoren many years ago. It was only in the eastern kingdom of Brandor that slavery was still practiced. In Sanria, the other big city on the western coast of Brandor, the slaves were better off than the ones I had seen here, but it was slavery all the same. I decided I would have a talk with Santino about getting the emirs to finally end slavery in Brandor as well.

As we passed the main market square, hunched women with baskets on their heads trudged beside us, while bearded men with heavy sacks laden with goods set up stalls for the day. Huge clay pots filled with fragrant spices lined the shaded area near a busy trader with a new supply of animal skins and leather goods. The smells of the market filled the palanquin as we passed, an unpleasant mix of dung, spices, and cooking meat.

Tall palm trees spread out sporadically through the city, providing inadequate shade to the hot, sweating citizens who traversed the dusty streets. The rest of the nobility moved around in palanquins and on horses, while camels were escorted into the city laden with wares for trade.

"Where are you from, Rhea? How did you end up as a slave?" I turned at the sound of Penelope's voice.

"A few months ago, I was captured from my tribe in Rohron and brought here on a ship. It was horrible—days of never seeing land; hundreds of us crammed into the bowels of the ship. There was little food, and so many people died before we even got to Nedora." Her sobs interrupted the story.

Penelope held her hand. Once she calmed down, she continued, "I was kept as a slave in Lord Berzaan's house. He wanted . . ." Her breath hitched in her throat. "He wanted me to come to his bed. I had no other choice. That's why I ran away."

"That was a very brave thing to do." I put my arm around her, my blood boiling. I remembered the smug face of the lavender-turbaned nobleman Berzaan and felt sick to my stomach at the degraded state of Brandorian society.

"I was caught by the guards. They were going to send me back when you found me." She looked at me with such gratitude in her eyes I couldn't help thinking about the others I couldn't save. What must their lives be like with no hope of ever seeing their families again? What about the families who had lost their children? What hope was there for them?

"I was trying to get to a ship that would take me back to Rohron." She shook her head and started to weep again. "My family has no idea what happened to me. I was visiting a friend when I was taken."

I balled my hands into fists. "He will be punished for this. I will speak to Prince Shiraz."

Penelope shook her head. "You cannot interfere any more than you already have, Aurora. We are lucky Prince Shiraz did not take offense from your actions. This is not the time to go around changing policies."

"But—"

She held up her hand. "Let me finish. Once you are queen of Illiador, you will get the opportunity to change the world for the better. But until then you must think of the bigger picture. If anything happens to you, there will be no world left to change."

I crossed my arms and stared out of the palanquin curtains. She was right, of course. My hands were tied. I had to get the Detoris to join us. Securing the way through Brandor for the fae army had to remain my first priority.

THE PINK PALACE

THE PALACE of the Detori emir was a colossal monument, a testament to the power and wealth the emirs enjoyed while the rest of the city lived in poverty. The Detoris were even wealthier than the Valasis family, effectively controlling all the mines and trade routes in the eastern lands as well as the ships that traversed the Sea of Shadows.

The Pink Palace, as it was called, was famous in Brandor and beyond for the brushed pink sandstone from which it was made. The Detoris owned all the pink sandstone quarries in Brandor, along with gold, copper, jade, and iron mines.

Surrounded by a massive sandstone wall, the great golden domes of the palace could be seen from every rooftop in the city. Similar domes spread out over smaller buildings on a reduced scale, which made up the rest of the palace, accenting the great center dome.

The Pink Palace was beautiful and more ornately decorated than the Red Citadel in Sanria. The flooring was made of a rare pink marble, with shades of dusky rose veins slithering inside the stone like snakes. Massive jade pillars carved to look like palm trees held the immense domed ceiling of the entrance hall up. The ceiling itself was intricately carved with flowers made of shimmering rose quartz and leaves of jade set on a light mesh of pure gold. It was an ostentatious display of wealth, and I wondered how many slaves it must have taken to build this monstrosity.

Prince Shiraz led us through great silver doors to a courtyard with terraced lawns, shaded by towering cypress trees, where our rooms were situated. A light breeze drifted through the gardens, and the birds had awoken to fill the palace with song. The air was thick with the scent of jasmine flowers and frangipani as we navigated the garden paths to our rooms. Beautiful pavilions and lotus ponds graced the interior of the palace, creating a sprawling oasis within the hot dusty city of Nedora.

"I hope you will be comfortable here," said Prince Shiraz, showing us around the suite of rooms that Penelope and I were to share. Great marble arches hung with soft muslin curtains led out to a private walled garden with a cascading fountain spouting fragrant rosewater.

Rhea had been taken to the infirmary to see to her wounds and would join us later. Tristan's room was situated in another wing, as all the rooms in this part of the palace were reserved for women only.

After Prince Shiraz departed, crimson-veiled servants entered silently and drew a bath for me. I was eager for it. It had been a while since I had bathed properly, and the hot dusty streets of Nedora seemed to cover my skin with a layer of grime and sand that required a good scrubbing.

The bathing chamber was a bright room with big arched windows that looked onto a small private garden. A great white onyx sunken tub filled with rose petals lay in the center of the room, surrounded by luxurious silk cushions. I removed my clothes and waded into what was more of a pool than a tub. Rose oil had been added to the steaming water, and I washed myself from head to toe with the scented soaps and scrubs that lay beside the pool in small crystal bowls.

I felt much better after the bath and changed into the clothes the servants had left for me. They were similar to the clothes I had worn when I came here but made with a much more expensive fabric and bordered with exquisite gold embroidery on the short tunic and loose pants.

When I was ready, I met with Penelope in the common room. Tristan was already there waiting for us, and we tried to figure out how we would approach the emir when he returned to the palace. While we were discussing our next course of action, a servant came to our rooms to announce that Prince Shiraz had invited us for a private dinner in the magnificent inner terrace, which was reserved for the emir and his chosen guests.

I inquired about Rhea and when she would be joining us, but the servant did not have any information. She just bowed respectfully and withdrew from the room. I frowned at the thought of Rhea alone somewhere in this vast palace, and decided to ask Shiraz about her when I met him. We left the room to find guards waiting outside to escort us to dinner. We followed them through many walled courtyards and inner gates to the innermost terrace of the gardens, where a massive tent had been set up with a long, low table piled high with sumptuous Brandorian cuisine.

"We must speak with Darius Detori and leave Nedora as soon as possible," Penelope whispered.

I nodded as I glanced at the fluffy silk cushions heavily embroidered with gold thread and embellished with precious stones around the edges, spread out around the table for the guests to sit on. A few chosen courtiers were already lounging around the table, inhaling smoke from flavored hookahs. The ladies that accompanied them were beautiful and unveiled. Dressed in billowing chiffon pants and small beaded tops, they had eyelids dusted with gold powder, heavily kohled eyes, and reddened lips the color of fresh cherries.

Prince Shiraz looked less imposing reclining on a cushion, his short dark hair uncovered. He had changed into an even more ornately embroidered robe of crimson and gold, with four rows of emerald beads slung carelessly around his neck. The jeweled rings on his fingers flashed as he gestured for us to sit beside him.

The Detori prince grinned, showing his pristine white teeth again, which for some reason had started to irritate me. When I asked him about Rhea, he gave me a vague answer about not being a physician.

"When will your father return?" Penelope asked.

"He is due home tomorrow," said Shiraz before biting down on a crisp pigeon pastry. "You may meet him at your leisure and are welcome to stay as long as you like." He flicked his hand and gestured for a serving girl to present me with a tray of bite-sized morsels.

"Thank you." I eyed the tray of pistachio-covered pastry squares, caramelized almonds dipped in rose syrup, and honey-glazed apricots stuffed with clotted cream. I couldn't resist.

I ate quickly as Penelope tried to get him to discuss the upcoming war, but Shiraz Detori didn't seem to have any interest in anything but the scantily clad women who had draped themselves around him.

After a few hours of the prince wasting our time, Tristan escorted us back to our rooms. Rhea was still not back.

"That was a completely useless meeting," said Penelope, exasperated. "Prince Shiraz doesn't have a head for war and politics. If we want answers, we will have to wait for his father to return."

Tristan shook his head. "We should go back to tracking Andromeda and the book."

"Prince Shiraz said his father will be back tomorrow," Penelope stated. "But he didn't sound all that sincere when I asked him about it."

"We should leave this place," Tristan insisted, keeping his voice low. "I don't like this Detori fellow. And I don't think he's trustworthy."

Penelope started pacing the room. "I know we are pressed for time, but it is important for us to meet with Darius Detori and make sure he stands with us. Without Brandor's support, we will not stand a chance against Morgana's army. And even then, the odds are against us. But I agree we shouldn't stay too long. We will wait until the end of the day tomorrow. If he doesn't return by then, we will proceed to Sanria to speak to Santino and Roderigo Valasis."

I crossed my arms. "I can't leave Rhea here."

"I asked one of the maids about Rhea," Penelope offered. "They said she is being cared for and recovering in the infirmary."

"I have a bad feeling about this," I said, going over to the window. "Why won't they let me see her?" I felt very protective of Rhea. And I had promised to help her; she trusted me, and I couldn't let her down.

"Get some rest," said Tristan, his tone low and serious. "I will find Rhea. I have a lead on where the blackened iron is coming from that I need to check out anyway."

Penelope put her hand on my shoulder. "Tristan is right. Get some sleep, and I will make arrangements with my contacts to locate Rhea's family and see her safely back home."

I nodded. "Thank you."

THE NIGHT WAS QUIET, and a soft breeze entered the room through an open window as I lay down on my soft bed and thought of Rhea. She was so young and scared, and she reminded me a little of myself when I was first dragged into this world. It was a terrible fate to be taken from your home and to never see your family again.

I felt something move in the room, and my fae senses snapped to full alert.

Tristan couldn't be back so soon.

A shadow descended into the room. My blood turned cold as my eyes adjusted to the dark and met a pair of burning red eyes flickering like hot coals in the darkness. Its leathery obsidian wings blocked out the moonlight that shone through the open window.

A gorgoth!

The hideous half-bat henchmen of the Drakaar, men transformed by dark magic into wretched beasts. The nightmarish creature perched on my windowsill growled, razor-sharp claws and serrated teeth glinting in the moonlight.

I reached for Dawn, which lay beside my bed. Magic infused my sword, lighting it up with silver fire.

The gorgoth hesitated, but just for a second. With a terrifying growl, the creature pounced.

A second was all I needed. Letting my fae senses guide me, I sprung out of the bed and landed in a crouch in front of the creature.

Adjusting the grip on my sword, I moved swiftly as the creature lunged at me. Its bat-like wings made it difficult for it to move in an enclosed space. I raised my sword to block its blow, slicing at its arm. The gorgoth screamed and moved back, but I knew from experience it would not stop until one of us was dead.

I could not risk using a blast of fire magic here—releasing uncontrollable silver fire inside the palace was probably not the smartest thing to do. My hands started to shake as fear rushed in. My mind scrambled for options. I reached within as I had done before in the battle against the Drakaar. Calling on the mighty power of Illaria Lightbringer, I braced myself.

But nothing happened. I could not call on the light of the Dawnstar.

The gorgoth leapt, and I slashed at it again. My sword tore

through its chest. Black blood sprayed my arm. The creature shrieked in fury and stumbled farther backward.

I didn't have time to hesitate as I raised my left hand, created a knife burning with silver fire, and threw it. It sank into the gorgoth's chest. Its flashing red eyes burned through me as it stopped, clutching the dagger to pull it out. I lunged forward, gripping my sword with two hands, and swung it in an arc, severing the gorgoth's head from its body.

Another growl sounded behind me. I turned swiftly, clutching my still-flaming sword, to see two more gorgoths fly into the room.

Before I could lift my sword, one of the gorgoths pounced, catching me off guard. I sidestepped just in time to avoid a direct blow to my head, but its talons slashed across my arm and my sword fell to the ground, clattering away from me.

The second gorgoth sprang at me from the other side. I flung out a push strike in a circle around me as I ducked, throwing them back while I created a glamoured sword and swung it, slashing one gorgoth across its wings, tearing through the leathery blackness. It screeched and reached out its talons, lunging at me.

I lost my footing and fell backward, hitting my head as the gorgoth landed on top of me, its serrated black teeth inches from my face. Black drool dripped onto my cheek. It smelled acrid, the stench of its evil unbearable.

The ring on my finger glowed as Abraxas spoke to me. *"Use the magic of the Dawnstar, Aurora. It is more formidable than your fae-fire,"* the deep voice said. *"There is no dark creature that can withstand its power."*

I held the ravening creature away from my face. My fae strength was the only reason I was still alive.

"I can't," I screamed in my mind. "It's gone."

"The magic of the Dawnstar has always been within you, even when you didn't know what it was. It was what saved you in the ruins when Lilith tried to possess your body. The light that pushed her away

and did not let her enter was the Dawnstar." The great dragon's voice rose. "*Fear and doubt veil the light of the Dawnstar. You must believe, Aurora—how many times do I have to remind you? Without faith in yourself and your abilities, your Dawnstar powers will not work.*"

I held off the vicious gorgoth and turned my mind within, shutting out all fear and doubt. I could do this. I had done it before. A massive force raised its head as the light of the Dawnstar arose within. Calming my racing heart, I concentrated the power in my hands and directed it, fashioning it into beams of pure white light.

The gorgoth above me screamed as my magic pierced its body like a lance, destroying the darkness from within. The gorgoth crumpled to dust, but when I stood up, three more flew into the room.

But I was no longer afraid. I was the Dawnstar, the heir of Illaria Lightbringer, and this was what I was born to do.

I lifted both my hands and the whole room lit up. White light —more powerful than any gorgoth could withstand—burst out of my hands, piercing the darkness in a blinding ray. Screams and terrified squeals filled the air as the gorgoths shrieked in fury and dissolved into ashes.

"*Good,*" said Abraxas in my mind. "*You must practice calling on your Dawnstar powers when faced with a threat such as this. The power that makes you the Dawnstar is light magic, which is deadly to demons and dark creatures alike. But light magic will not help you against mages or human soldiers. Therefore, the ability to assess what type of magic is needed in each situation is something you still have to master. You will learn with experience.*"

The door opened, and Penelope rushed in. "What happened?" She eyed the lumps of ash littering the room.

"Gorgoths," I spat, picking up my sword.

"We have a problem," said Tristan, entering the room and shutting the door with a dark look.

"Obviously." I whirled on Tristan. "Where were you? I had to take on five gorgoths on my own."

Tristan raised an eyebrow and crossed his arms as he took in the piles of ash in different parts of the room, then shrugged his broad shoulders. "You seem to have done an adequate job of it."

"No thanks to you."

He lifted a dark brow. "You seem to have forgotten who trained you."

My face heated.

He turned to Penelope. "I was busy finding out more about that jeweled toad you call a prince."

My brow furrowed. "Prince Shiraz?"

Tristan nodded. "Darius Detori isn't coming back any time soon. It seems he's already on his way to Sanria for a council meeting of the five emirs."

"What?" Penelope frowned. "Shiraz has been lying to us?"

Tristan's eyes narrowed. "I'm sure there are quite a few things he hasn't told us." He scowled. "He's left the palace too."

"He's been buying time." Penelope paced the floor with her hands clasped in front of her. "But for what? What are the Detoris up to?"

Tristan shrugged. "Your guess is as good as mine. No one will reveal that piece of information. He obviously wants to keep us away from Sanria."

Penelope rubbed her temples. "We should leave immediately. We must speak to Santino before the Council of Five meets."

"And Rhea?" I asked. "Did you find her?"

Tristan nodded. "She's still here, along with a bunch of other slaves. From what I gathered, they are going to be moved out tonight."

My heartbeat sped up. "Moved! Where?"

Tristan's eyes started to swirl with silver sparks. "I only found one old worker who was willing to talk, and that's because his granddaughter is one of the slaves."

I shook my head. "This practice of slavery is abominable. Something has to be done about it," I ground out through clenched teeth. "What did the old man say?"

"Apparently the Detoris have been collecting them to send to the mines."

I took a deep breath and tried to keep calm. "We can't let them take her to the mines. She will die there." I gathered my things and put on my short jacket and sash. I retrieved a dagger from a corner where it lay in a pile of gorgoth ash.

Penelope came up to me and put her hand on my shoulder. "Calm down, Aurora, we will get her out."

I nodded, trying not to think about all the horrible things that could happen to the poor girl. She was my responsibility, and I had let her down.

Penelope's eyes flashed as she slid a look at Tristan. "Tell me more about the mines."

"The old man told me they are being sent to the largest of the Detori mines, situated just outside the city," Tristan answered. "He said lately more and more of the slaves working in the city are being sent there."

Penelope went over to the window to gaze at the houses that spread out before her and to the desert that lay beyond the walls of the city. "The only mines around this area were shut down decades ago." She turned to face Tristan. "Are you sure?"

Tristan nodded and gave Penelope a dark look. "It doesn't look good, Penelope. There is only one thing the Brandorians could be mining in this time of war."

"I agree. I have a bad feeling about this," said Penelope. "Those mines you described were shut down for a reason. If they have been opened again, that doesn't bode well for the fae."

"Why, what are they mining?" I interrupted. What was going on here?

"In the old days when all the kingdoms were at war with each other, before the treaty, Brandor kept stores of blackened iron in case the fae ever threatened their borders," Tristan explained.

Penelope clasped her hands together. "And the largest mine always belonged to the Detori emir. It is situated just outside the city of Nedora."

My eyes widened. "So that's where they are getting the blackened iron."

Penelope's blue eyes flicked to me. "I believe so. It is only in the past few decades that those particular mines have been shut down to ensure peace. But now that all the borders are closed, the already fragile peace between kingdoms has been broken. No one knows where to turn for help. The mages distrust the fae and the fae return the feeling. And the ones without magic don't trust any magic user."

"And you think the Detoris are working for Morgana?"

"That's what it looks like."

Tristan rubbed his chin. "Morgana must have already gotten to Darius Detori."

Penelope sighed and nodded. "Darius Detori is a snake. I wouldn't be surprised to learn he is helping Morgana. The emirs of Brandor have always feared the fae. But I am more concerned with how many other mines have been opened so far." She picked up her bag from the bed. "Get your things. It is imperative that we get to Sanria immediately and inform Santino about the mines and the Detoris' hand in it. Emir Valasis is the only one who can help us now. Santino's father was the one who had a hand in shutting down the mines the first time, and he rules the Council of Five. The other emirs will listen to him."

Tristan's eyes narrowed, and he folded his arms across his chest. "We hope."

I looked at both of them incredulously. "I'm not leaving without Rhea. We have to save her. We can't leave her to die in the mines."

Penelope twisted her hands together. "Aurora, if Morgana gets her hands on that much blackened iron and makes weapons out of it, then the fae army will be helpless against her forces."

I calmed my racing heart and tried to make them see reason. "Then we shut down this mine ourselves."

Penelope's face tightened. "No! Absolutely not, Aurora. I'm not letting you anywhere near those mines. It is too dangerous. Your magic will weaken when surrounded by so much blackened iron, and Tristan will be completely vulnerable without his silver fire. If the gorgoths are here, then the Drakaar won't be far behind. We need to get to Sanria now and warn Santino—he is the only one who can convince his father and the other emirs that the mines need to be shut down."

Abraxas interrupted, his voice clear and clipped in my mind. *"Penelope is right. Your Dawnstar magic is tied to your fae powers. Even if you can access your light magic in there, the rest of your powers will be stifled. I have seen the mines you speak of, and they are heavily guarded. You will not be able to destroy them without the cost of many slave lives."*

My stomach dropped to the floor. That was not an option. We would do it Penelope's way. I knew that stopping the Detoris was as important as freeing Rhea, but I could still do both.

"Okay," I conceded. "But we get Rhea out first. Then we can go straight to Sanria and tell Santino what has happened, and he can deal with the council."

Penelope nodded and threw a glance at Tristan. "Take us to the girl."

We ran down the ornate pink marble corridors, through the courtyards to the kitchen wing of the palace. We met no opposition along the way, which was strange.

Uncertainty took hold. "Where are all the guards?"

Tristan shrugged, but I could see his senses were on full alert. He was experienced enough to know not to let his guard down. He led us down the side stairs to the infirmary, where he had been told Rhea was being held.

It was empty, except for a crumpled dead body on the floor, lying in a pool of blood.

Tristan turned the body over with his boot. "It's the old man from the kitchens who spoke to me. He must have tried to get his granddaughter out before they took the slaves."

I clenched my fists and could feel my magic rising up within me. Slave lives were discarded so carelessly, and no one seemed to bother. My resolve was clear: I had to put an end to this practice once and for all, or I was not worthy of the title of the Dawnstar. I whirled around in the empty room. "Any idea which route they have taken?"

Tristan bent down and ran his hands over the old man's eyes to close them. "His body is still warm—they must have just left."

We ran back through the palace to the eastern gate, where the servants' entrance was located. The corridor was filled by a line of Detori guards blocking the way to the courtyard, where slaves were being herded into wagons.

"You are supposed to be dead," spat one guard upon spotting me.

"Sorry to disappoint you." I created a ball of silver fire in my hands and bounced it up and down impatiently. "You'd better get out of the way, soldier. I don't have the time or inclination to play today."

The guards shouted for others to join them and charged at us.

Tristan's swords lit up beside me.

I flung the ball of silver fire at the guards. Many of them jumped out of the way, but a few were not so lucky and ended up bursting into flames. I had no mercy for soldiers who would treat poor defenseless people the way they treated the slaves. They may have been following orders, but they enforced them all the same.

I drew my sword and infused it with silver fire. Some of the guards scrambled out of the way, while a bunch of others blocked my path. "Prince Shiraz said you were to stay within the palace walls. You can't leave."

"Oh, really!" I snorted. "Tell Prince Shiraz the Dawnstar can leave whenever she wants."

Tristan cut through them like a knife through butter. Penelope and I ran to untie Rhea.

I hugged Rhea quickly and ruffled her hair. "I'm glad you are all right." Glancing around quickly, I realized there were more than twenty slaves with her, and they were still bound. I shouted to Tristan, "Get the other slaves too!"

"We can't, Aurora. We cannot risk angering the Detoris any more than we already have," Penelope cautioned me.

"Those snakes are already working for Morgana, I'm sure of it," I growled as I gathered my magic and started breaking chains around the slaves' ankles and untying their hands. "I think freeing some of his slaves is the least of his punishments."

Tristan cut down two guards who tried to stop me from freeing the slaves. "Let's go. There will be more coming."

Penelope and I gathered the slaves, leading them to the gates as Tristan dealt with the remaining guards. But as predicted, more arrived. It seemed Shiraz Detori had left a whole legion to make sure I didn't leave the place. Well, it was going to take more than a legion to stop the Dawnstar.

I closed my eyes and reached out with my magic. "Abraxas, I need you."

I got an abrupt answer. *"Are you in mortal danger?"*

My eyebrows scrunched together. "No."

"Can you manage without me?"

"I think so," I muttered as I turned back to help Tristan.

"Then there is no need for me to assist you in this battle," said the great dragon. *"Summoning me drains a great amount of magic from this world."*

I paused as I tightened my grip on my sword and took in the positions of the guards running at me. "I didn't know that."

"You and Tristan are more than capable of taking on these guards yourselves." With that, Abraxas was gone.

I gathered my magic and let it build up inside me. I unleashed a wall of fire that spread toward the guards and prevented them from following us. The slaves shrank back, cowering behind me.

Tristan burst through the flames, his blades flashing as he joined me. A faint smile curved his lips. "Shall we leave?"

I grinned and ushered the slaves out through the now unguarded palace gates. Once we were out of the palace, no one tried to follow us. I guess it helped that there was an enormous wall of magical fire making sure they didn't. It would die down eventually, and I had put boundaries on it so it wouldn't spread to the rest of the palace. There were still innocent servants and others that resided there.

Penelope led us to the docks where she had made arrangements the night before for a merchant vessel to take Rhea back to Rohron.

"I will speak to the merchant about the rest of the slaves," she said, then strode off while Tristan ushered the slaves onboard.

There was a shout behind us. "Stop!"

It was Berzaan, the nobleman who had enslaved Rhea in the first place. He had a retinue of guards with him, all of whom were running at full speed toward us.

I faced Berzaan and his guard and let my magic rise inside me. Tristan's swords relit, and he was ready to pounce on the approaching warriors.

My eyes narrowed as my senses sharpened. "Stay out of the way, Tristan. I've got this."

I braced my feet on the wooden docks and called on my magic, careful to draw the water out of the sea in droplets. I knew creating a wave of water, connecting to the ocean itself, was folly. It was possible, of course, and I had done it before, but it took too much magic. The lessons I had learned during my time in Elfi were invaluable, and I finally realized what Uncle Gabriel had been trying to teach me. Control was the most important element of magic: the ability to use your powers in the best way possible and at the right time.

I fashioned the droplets of water, molding them into ice knives, freezing them in midair.

Hovering.

Waiting.

With a flick of my wrist I let them loose. The guards went down like flies as the small ice daggers embedded themselves strategically in their legs. I left only Berzaan standing amid his fallen guards, who groaned and tried to stand up.

The insufferable nobleman grinned at me. "You missed."

"I never miss," I snarled as I gathered more magic from the air around me and shaped it into a tiny tornado that spun in a frenzy, lifting Berzaan up within it. "And if you ever whip or harm any of your slaves again, Berzaan, I will return. And next time I will not be so forgiving."

Berzaan screamed, cried, and flailed as the tornado flung him around and around, carrying him out to sea.

Rhea ran up to me, her eyes wide as she watched her tormenter carried away in a funnel of air, screaming until the night wind swallowed him up. "What will happen to him?"

"The air funnel will eventually die out, and it will drop him somewhere in the middle of the Sea of Shadows," I said, shrugging. But from the corner of my eye I could see Berzaan's lackeys getting into a boat to rescue their little lord. The air funnel would drop him into the sea once they got close. Berzaan would be fine—a little wet, but I was sure he would think twice before he mistreated any of his slaves ever again. "I hope he can swim."

For the first time since I had met Rhea, the little girl grinned, her eyes lighting up with mischief. She clasped my hands in hers. "Thank you for everything you have done for me." She looked around at the other slaves Penelope was busy tending to and getting settled onto the ship. "For us."

My eyes moistened. "Anyone would have done the same."

Rhea shook her head. Her fierce little chin jutted out with determination, and she spoke with conviction. "No, not everyone would have risked their own lives for a group of slaves, Aurora Firedrake. You are truly worthy of the name Dawnstar. Because of you there is still hope for this world, and I will make sure everyone knows it."

THE PIRATE PRINCE

Dawn was already showing its light as we readied for our journey ahead. The merchant agreed to take Rhea and the freed slaves to Galdor, the only permanent city in Rohron. Penelope did not know the merchant well, so she also sent one of her spies with them to make sure they got there. But I wasn't taking any chances with Rhea's life. I spoke with the captain myself and explained in no uncertain terms what I would do to him if anything happened to Rhea and the other freed slaves. I think he got the message, especially when I showed him who I would send to hunt him down if something happened to go wrong.

The captain gulped visibly and scurried back to his ship when Tristan turned his icy gaze on him.

Cade arrived with two griffins.

"Where's Snow?" I asked as I hugged him and then climbed on a griffin behind Tristan.

Cade swallowed. "I couldn't find her when Tristan sent the summons. There was no time."

I wondered where Snow was. Usually she knew when I needed her and she turned up.

Nedora was just a speck in the distance as we left the eastern coast of Brandor. The hot dusty city gave way to a vast desert that stretched all the way to the city of Sanria on the western coast of Brandor. Penelope and I concealed our group with glamour as we flew lower than we had before. The griffins' keen eyes scanned the landscape for threats, and Tristan was on high alert. The wind whipped through my hair and battered my face as I gawked at the glistening sand dunes that shifted and sparkled in the midday sun, giving way to a massive canyon that stretched out into the distance.

We crossed a wide river with a few farming settlements and villages along its banks. I spotted high walls rising on the other side of the river near the lake as we passed the town of Bron. Most of Avalonia's cotton was grown in this area, and the Brandorians took full advantage, setting the prices for trade across the realm. Brandorians were famous for being ruthless traders, the emirs obtaining most of their wealth in this way. They were a community of merchants, rich in resources and controlling all the trade routes between the east and west. The Brandorian mines were famous for copper, jade, quartz, and most importantly gold, making them one of the richest kingdoms in Avalonia.

The enormous fortress of the Emir of Sanria rose up as we neared the city that lay on the western coast of Brandor, nestled in a cove on the eastern shores of the Stardust Sea. The Red Citadel towered over the port, perched on a cliff like a huge bird of prey overlooking the deserts that stretched out behind it as far as the eye could see.

We removed our fae glamour as we flew over the city and landed in the courtyard of Santino's home. The pirate prince was already there to greet us as we appeared in their midst. Standing beside him, looking radiant as ever and dressed in a sheer chiffon gown, her golden hair cascading down her back, was my aunt, Serena Silverthorne.

Familiar scents of orange blossoms and wild myrtle wafted

toward me as I jumped off the griffin and ran to my aunt. She clutched me in her arms as I hugged her. It was so good to see her again. In the short time I had known her she had been like a mother to me, and it had been so long since I had seen my family. My time in Neris and at the Academy of Evolon seemed like a lifetime ago. But somehow, wherever I went, it was always Silverthorne Castle that felt most like home.

"Aurora, thank the gods you are safe." She held me gently by the arms, her blue eyes twinkling as she looked me over. Serena Silverthorne was older than Santino but still a beautiful woman. Married at an early age to the Earl of Elmsdale, she became a widow soon after her son Erien was born. She had been courted by noblemen from far and wide, but it seemed the pirate prince was the one who had finally caught her attention.

I looked over at Santino and he smiled, his amber eyes crinkling in the corners as he flashed an indulgent smile toward his new bride and came over to hug me too. "Glad to have you back, Princess Firedrake."

I grinned at my friend. "It's good to see you again too, Santino."

The pirate prince's eyes glanced behind me and his eyebrows shot up. "I see you brought your betrothed with you."

I grimaced as I turned to see Tristan standing behind me, his arms crossed and his signature scowl on his face. "So you heard about the engagement."

Santino nodded, his smile gone. "Rafael stopped by on his way back from Elfi. He told us you were betrothed to the Prince of the Night Court."

My heart sank as I thought of Rafe's face the night I saw him in the grand hall at the Crystal Castle. We never spoke, but the hurt in his eyes spoke volumes as to his feelings. If only I had trusted him and waited, we could have been together. I had been betrayed so many times I had begun to believe I could never be happy. So when my grandmother told me Rafe had married another, I believed her. I had been a fool, I saw that now. Rafe was the only one who would never betray me, but it was too late. He was gone, and I knew he would never forgive me for what I had done.

Santino greeted Tristan, and Serena hugged Penelope, who quickly explained her change of appearance to her old friend. For the past two decades, Penelope had disguised herself as an ordinary fae healer living in Illiador. When I first met her, she'd looked different, and I had no idea that she was really my grandmother's sister. But now she had reverted to her original appearance of a tall and statuesque High Fae of the Royal Court and resumed her role as the fae queen's most trusted emissary. But her true identity as Elfi's most effective spy was a secret only very few of us knew.

Aunt Serena looked astonished, but she took it in stride. "Come," she said to her guests. "It has been a long journey. I shall see you to your rooms and have refreshments sent over."

After settling Penelope, Cade, and Tristan in their rooms, she linked her arm through mine and walked with me to another section of the palace. "I want to hear everything—don't leave anything out."

Santino walked beside us as we traversed the rosebush-edged pathways that connected different parts of the vast complex of the Red Citadel. Even though I had been here before, the incredible architecture of the Brandorians never ceased to amaze. Marble pillars inlaid with gold held up the vast ceiling, intricately carved with crowns and stars ensconced in a latticed web of flowers and vines. The floors were inlaid with a spectacular mosaic of white, blue, and gold tiles, and the smell of roses wafted through the palace's many gardens and orchards, filling the space with a fragrant breeze.

I lowered my voice as we entered a vast reception room. "Santino, have you had any news about Uncle Gabriel?"

"No." Santino shook his head, leading us to another row of rooms where I would be staying. Huge arches with billowing muslin curtains that fluttered in the breeze led out into the flowering courtyard beyond. A fig tree shaded the marble fountain, which spouted rosewater into a marble-rimmed lotus pond, and creamy white bougainvillea climbed one side of the walls.

Santino frowned and turned to face me. "In this case, no news is good news. As far as we know, he is still in the dungeons at the Summer Palace in Neris. But we have heard the Blackwaters are getting desperate; after Lucian's death they are scrambling to stay in power. Now that Elial Dekela is dead, there is a new mastermage of the Academy of Evolon, and the mages of Evolon have joined the Blackwaters. Lilith has been recruiting her own army to add to the forces of Eldoren, and they are completely allied with Morgana. Rafael managed to make it back to Silverthorne Castle, but they are backed into a corner. Rafe does not have enough men to take the capital."

"You can help him, Santino," I said quickly. "He just needs more warriors."

"If only it were so easy." Santino held my gaze without blinking. "My father will not agree. He will not help Rafael regain his throne, especially after he rejected Katerina so publicly."

I froze. "He did?"

It was Aunt Serena who replied, "Rafael loves you, Aurora, we can all see that."

I hung my head and shuffled my feet. "Not anymore."

Serena put her arm around my shoulders. "A love like that doesn't just go away, Aurora. But now that you are engaged to Tristan, why does it make a difference?"

I told her and Santino everything that had happened in Elfi, as well as how my grandmother had tried to force me and then tricked me into getting engaged to Tristan.

"I see," was all Aunt Serena said as she sat next to me while Santino paced the room. "So Tristan is not in love with you either?"

I shook my head. "I don't think so. We are friends, that's all. Well, we were. But I'm not even sure about that now."

Santino raised his eyebrows. "You are probably going to have a hard time convincing Rafael of that."

I looked down at my feet. "I know." My voice broke slightly. "But I have to try." *If I ever see him again.*

⁓⁓⁓

SANTINO SENT a flock of maids to help me get ready for my meeting with the emir. Penelope had requested to meet him immediately. The situation with the Detoris was not something that could be put off. We needed to get Emir Valasis on our side and convince him to shut down the mines. Once he was convinced, it would be easier to get the other emirs to agree.

I welcomed the bath and the pampering, but this time I refused to wear the flimsy Brandorian clothes and veil I wore last time I was here, and instead remained in my High Fae training leathers, with my sword and daggers strapped in place and a black cape that was embroidered lightly on the borders with silver stars. With glamour I created a silver diadem, twisted to look like ivy. I placed it on my head for effect. I would not cower or hide anymore. I was a queen and a warrior, and that was who the emir would meet this time.

I pecked at the trays of delicious Brandorian delicacies laid out in my room while I got ready. The clotted cream, topped with fresh whole honeycomb and sprinkled with pistachios and apricots, was my favorite dish and just too good to resist.

Penelope came to get me from my room as I finished the last piece of walnut bread generously daubed with white butter. She had changed into a simple green chiffon dress, over which she wore an emerald-green sleeveless robe lined with gold-embroidered flowers. Her hair was plaited and woven with gold thread and fell to her waist. She always looked so regal and calm, and I wondered how she managed to pull it off.

Tristan was waiting outside, his weapons strapped in place.

I rolled my eyes. "No one is going to attack me in my room, Tristan."

"Have you forgotten last night?" he said, walking beside me. Cade appeared suddenly on my other side.

I huffed and strode ahead as I attempted to traverse the blue-and-white mosaic walkways that connected the different parts of the citadel. I knew my way around the emir's fortress to a degree, but it was still confusing. I let Penelope lead us through courtyards of orange blossoms and fragrant rose bushes until we came to the massive silver doors of the throne room, which were guarded by the emir's big, spear-wielding warriors. I definitely remembered them. Dark-skinned, massive, and trained to be killers since birth, the emir's guards were not to be trifled with.

"I presume you don't need me in there," said Cade, stepping to the side. "I'll just wait out here with these big guys." He threw a charming smile at the emir's guards, who didn't smile back.

Penelope gestured me forward before her. "You need to walk in front—it is protocol."

I shuffled my feet as the massive silver doors opened. I wasn't a politician, so how was I supposed to convince the emir I was worth aligning with instead of Morgana?

The emir was seated on his throne in the vast reception hall, and beside him stood a short, squat man with a round pockmarked face under his massive green-and-gold turban. He was dressed in the opulent manner of the Brandorian nobility in an emerald-green robe lined with gold thread. Santino was already there, standing at the foot of the stairs that led to his father's throne.

"That's Varian, chancellor of Brandor and military advisor to the emir," whispered Penelope as we walked the long plum-colored carpet toward the emir. "He was away on a diplomatic mission when you were here last, and he just recently returned."

I did not bow to the emir, nor did Tristan, but Penelope did.

"So we meet again, Princess Aurora," said the emir, his amber eyes studying my attire. "Looks like you are a High Fae warrior now. We heard you defeated the Archmage of Avalonia. That is no small feat. It seems you are not as weak as we first perceived."

At least he got straight to the point.

I was a queen in my own right and refused to cower before him to earn his sympathy. "You could have denied them entry through Brandor, yet you let the Drakaar come to Elfi." The accusation was clear in my voice.

The emir shook his head. "What could we have done? The Drakaar would have laid waste to all our lands in their effort to get to you. We never expected Izadora's wards to fall. If even the fae queen's magic cannot stop Morgana, what chance do any of us have? We had no choice."

"You always have a choice," Penelope said, stepping forward. "Aurora stopped Morgana from getting her hands on Elfi, and she can do the same for you if you will let her. We can protect Brandor from Morgana and the Drakaar, but we need your support."

The emir turned his gaze on Penelope. "You also need my ships and my mounted cavalry, not to mention supplies for your army." His words were sharp. It was a statement. He knew at this moment he had the upper hand—we needed his troops. His eyebrows rose. "I did not expect to see you again, Countess Penelope. Santino has only recently informed me you have been in Illiador for the past fifteen years. That was quite an accomplishment, to remain undetected by even Santino's men. But you are Queen Izadora's sister, so we would expect nothing less."

Penelope inclined her head in response to the praise and

cleared her throat. "The problem is much larger than we first believed."

The emir gestured for her to continue. "Go on."

"The mines outside Nedora have been opened." Penelope's gaze was laced with steel as she glanced between the emir and the chancellor.

Varian took a sharp breath.

"That is not possible." The emir shook his head. "I had those mines closed decades ago. The other emirs would not open them without informing me first."

"Darius Detori just did," I said plainly.

Emir Roderigo Valasis turned his gaze on his chancellor. "Varian, did you know about this?"

Varian shook his turbaned head. "No, Your Excellency. I will make inquiries."

"You must make sure those mines are closed down," said Penelope. "I don't need to remind you of the conditions of the treaty between Brandor and Elfi."

Varian made a snorting noise. "These are probably just rumors. The emirs of Brandor have always adhered to the treaty. Even though not all the fae have done the same." He stole a quick look at Tristan.

"I will speak with the other emirs," said Roderigo Valasis, tapping his bejeweled fingers on the arm of his silver throne. "We have all heard the stories whispered around the campfires at night; fantastic tales of the legendary Dawnstar who will rid Avalonia of darkness. And now that the warriors of Elfi follow you—" he shot a quick glance at Tristan, "—I am prepared to support you in your quest to restore your throne. If the other emirs agree, of course." He paused. "If the Detoris have broken the treaty and opened the mines, I will make sure they are punished. I have called a meeting in a few days, so you can address them yourself, and we can make our preparations."

But the little chancellor's eyes narrowed as he stepped

forward. His dark, beady glare flashed as he looked down his bulbous nose at me and addressed the emir. "I am inclined to believe these stories are exactly that—mere stories, Your Excellency. No one can be so powerful. You know how stories spread and distort into something they are not." Varian flashed me a sly smile. "Morgana has proven time and time again how much power she has, and we have seen that she has the resources to follow up on her threats."

Penelope clasped her hands in front of her and addressed the emir, ignoring the chancellor. She got straight to the heart of the matter. "Izadora was betrayed, and that's how Morgana found a way into Elfi. Now the *Book of Abraxas* is gone. Once she opens it, she will free the Dark Lord from his prison." She paused, and Varian's eyes darkened considerably as they stared each other down. Penelope did not flinch. "When Dragath is free your only hope will be to stand with us. The High Fae follow Aurora, and so should Brandor."

Varian tore his gaze from Penelope and smiled at his emir, but the expression did not reach his eyes. For a second, he reminded me of Lucian, with a dangerous darkness lurking beneath the surface. I would have to be careful of Varian.

"Dragath is a myth," the chancellor replied. "Everybody knows that. You come to us with stories of mythical weapons and demon lords and expect us to blindly follow you into battle?"

Emir Valasis rubbed his bearded chin as he glanced at Varian. His eyes were wary and distrustful as always, and a shrewd grin emerged as he chose to keep quiet and let his chancellor speak.

"The last time you were in Brandor, the Drakaar nearly destroyed the whole citadel. If it weren't for the fae queen's warriors, they would have." Varian stole a wary glance at Tristan. "Now you are back with nothing more than empty promises. Where is your fae army? Where is your dragon? All I have seen so far is one High Fae warrior. Formidable as he may be, he is not an army."

My eyes narrowed as I flicked a glance at Tristan. "That's what you think."

My ring glowed faintly as Abraxas spoke in my head. *"Do you need me?"*

"Not yet," I said through our bond. "But thank you. It's good to know you are around."

"Now, now, Varian," said the emir placatingly. "I'm quite confident that the Drakaar will not be foolish enough to attack the fortress while Prince Tristan is in residence."

Varian walked slowly down the steps toward us, his big green-and-gold turban perched precariously on top of his head, and stopped before me. "Morgana promised to leave the citizens of Brandor alone, and she has kept her promise."

Santino stepped up to stand beside me. "She did not keep her promise, Varian." He snarled the name. "Three villages were completely destroyed along their route."

Varian paused and his dark eyes narrowed. "An unfortunate occurrence," he said finally. "But those were small outlying villages, and most of those who died were commoners and slaves, so it doesn't affect us much. That is the cost of war."

I pushed my shoulders back as he mentioned slaves. "That is another issue that needs to be addressed."

Penelope came closer and whispered in my ear, "Not now."

I brushed her off and stepped closer to the throne. "The practice of slavery in your kingdom is barbaric." I glanced at Santino, who kept quiet and let me continue. "Something must be done to stop this."

"And what do you want us to do?" said Varian with a sneer. "Send all the slaves home and tend to the work ourselves?"

"You could pay servants to work for you, like in the other kingdoms," I said, crossing my arms. I wouldn't let him faze me. "There are other ways to tend your needs. Business and otherwise."

"Half our livelihood and trade depends on the work slaves do.

If we were to abolish slavery now and ask the merchants to *pay* them—" Varian spat out the word as if it were dirty, "—the people would revolt. You would reduce our economy to nothing."

"Varian," said the emir sharply, ending the topic and getting up from his throne. "I'm sure we can discuss this another time. The princess and her companions are our guests. I think we should consider what she has to say." He looked at me. "I will investigate the issue of the mines further, and I assure you if the Detoris are working against the Council, they will be punished. The matter of slaves is more complicated, but we can have a meeting to discuss it further. Until then, Varian—" he looked at his chancellor, "—they are our guests here at the citadel. Make sure they are treated as such."

Varian nodded, shuffling from one foot to another. "Of course, Your Excellency. I will see to it that they are well looked after."

The emir eyed his chancellor. "See that you do."

———✦———

"THAT WENT WELL," said Penelope as we walked back to our rooms, Tristan and Cade in tow. "I'm glad the emir has called the Council of Five. It makes our job easier than visiting all the other emirs' holdings and trying to convince them separately."

"Yes, the emir did seem to want to hear us out." I lowered my voice. "But I got the distinct impression that Varian doesn't want us sticking around."

Penelope nodded. "He's a snake, that one. We will have to be careful. Go back to your room and get some rest. I will speak with Santino and figure out how we should handle Varian."

I took her advice and went to my room. I was quite tired and a nap would help. I lay down on my bed and looked out at the trees in the walled courtyard outside my room. I wondered what Rafe was doing right now and if he even thought about me anymore. I had to get to Eldoren at some point so I could explain everything to him. But first I had to secure an army from Brandor and find out what Andromeda was up to. Why hadn't she taken the book to Morgana yet? Where was she?

I heard a scuffle outside my room and hurried over to the courtyard to look outside.

The courtyard was bathed in a dusky glow as the sun began to set over the Red Citadel, the leaves rustling slightly and an evening breeze sauntering through the trees.

Tristan had a man locked in a stranglehold, and Cade had his sword pointed at the man's throat.

"Tristan?"

Tristan's sapphire eyes caught the last light of the setting sun. "I found this man trying to get into your room." Tristan's arm was still locked around the hooded man's neck.

The man glanced up as Tristan pulled back his hood. A familiar face looked back at me.

My eyes widened. "It's all right, Tristan, I know him."

Tristan released him grudgingly, but Cade didn't put his sword away. The man bowed as I strode toward them.

"Marcus Gold," I said breathlessly. "I thought you were dead."

"I would have been if your friend Delacourt had his way," said Marcus, shifting away from the big fae-warriors who were still scowling at him.

My spine bristled at the thought of Brandon Delacourt. "He's no friend of mine. He gave me up to Morgana the first chance he got." I told him briefly about what happened when I was last in Brandor.

Marcus nodded. "Delacourt knew I was onto him. And just as I was about to warn Rafe, he tried to have me killed. He would have succeeded too, if the innkeeper hadn't warned me first. So I ran, and when I came back to find you, I heard you had left on Santino's ship. Calos is still recovering from their docks burning down." He raised an eyebrow at me.

I looked down. "That wasn't one of my best moments. But I've been in Elfi all this time, Marcus. Everybody knew that. If you wanted to find me, why didn't you contact me sooner? Why wait until I came back to Brandor?"

"Because," said Santino, entering the courtyard with Penelope, "he now works for me."

"Is this true?" I asked sharply, turning my gaze on Marcus.

Marcus nodded.

"Then why were you lurking outside my room like a spy?"

Santino raised an eyebrow. "Marcus, what did I tell you about sneaking around the citadel? You don't have to anymore."

"Sorry!" Marcus shrugged, but he did look a bit sheepish. "Old habits die hard, I guess. I have news, and I thought Aurora should learn of it first."

Santino moved to stand beside me. "Let's hear it."

Marcus hesitated for a moment, then looked me straight in the eyes. "Silverthorne is dead."

The blood drained from my face. I grabbed on to Santino's arm for support as my legs turned to jelly. I couldn't breathe; I needed to sit. My head was spinning. No! No! It couldn't be.

"Dead," I repeated dumbly, sitting down on the soft earth as I tried to process what he had just said. "How?"

Marcus stroked his wispy beard, his eyes troubled. "The new archmage decided to make an example of him. He was beheaded, executed in front of all the nobility of Eldoren."

Penelope came to kneel beside me and put her arm around my shoulders. "You need to be strong, Aurora. Without Silverthorne, Eldoren will be chaos. Rafe will need you now more than ever."

But the tears wouldn't stop as I thought of Uncle Gabriel. I was too late. I should have been there to help him, I should have rescued him. I should never have listened to my grandmother. She said Silverthorne would be released eventually. But he wasn't, he was dead, and there was no way to bring him back. It was all my fault for not taking matters into my own hands.

"Where is Rafe now?" I sniffed at Penelope through tears. I didn't dare look at Tristan.

"Back at Silverthorne Castle, I suppose," Marcus offered, "but I haven't got confirmation about that yet."

Penelope patted my shoulder sympathetically. "Yes, that seems likely. The rebels have been using it as a base for some time now."

I finally gathered myself, dried my eyes with a handkerchief Penelope gave me, and eased to my feet. "If Rafe can get the other nobles to follow him, he may be able to take back his throne." My mind whirled with the possibilities.

Marcus shook his head. "Without Silverthorne, that will be impossible. Prince Rafael has no allies. The Blackwaters made sure the other nobles did not dare join him."

"How can they do that? Surely there are some nobles who can stand up to them and the Dark Queen. The Blackwaters are not that powerful."

"No, but the new archmage is," said Marcus, wariness creeping into his eyes. "He has Morgana's complete support and has imprisoned the children of all the noble families. If any of the Eldorean nobles are found supporting Prince Rafael, the children will meet the same fate as Silverthorne."

My hand flew to my mouth as dread pooled in the pit of my stomach. "He has taken their children?"

Marcus nodded, his face grim. "One from each of the noble families of Eldoren. The nobility are scared—they will do whatever the archmage asks of them. As long as he holds the children, the nobles and their armies are under his control. The only thing standing in his way to the throne is Prince Rafael."

"Then we have to help him," I declared, looking around at the dismal faces around me, my hands balled into fists. "If Santino cannot give us an army, we must go alone."

Tristan's eyes narrowed and a ripple seemed to go through him. "There is no time to help the Prince of Eldoren, Aurora. We must find Andromeda and go to Illiador to retrieve the Dagger of Dragath before it is too late."

"Not to mention saving the kingdoms from Morgana," Cade interjected. I glared at Cade and he shrugged. "Just saying."

My stomach twisted. "We can't leave Rafe and the rebels to fend for themselves. And what about those children? Someone must find them. What if they're hurt? It is my fault that Lilith is on the throne in the first place. Without her, the Blackwaters would have never been able to take Eldoren."

Santino stepped forward, looking concerned. "I wish I could help, but with the way things are in Brandor, I cannot do any more. Just getting my father to agree to have you meet with the other emirs took all my persuasive power. And with Varian trying to oppose me at every turn, that has proven to be even more difficult than I expected. My father will not allow us to send troops to Eldoren. He is only negotiating with the emirs to give you assistance to take Illiador, and even then, he hasn't decided for sure. You know why he won't help Rafe."

I knew the reason only too well. Rafe had rejected the emir's offer to wed Katerina, and the emir did not take kindly to rejection. The emirs of Brandor were rich beyond belief and commanded all the trade routes in the east. Their private armies were formidable, their ships fast, and their mounted cavalry were some of the best-trained warriors in Avalonia. Even without magic, the Brandorians were an important ally to have, and Morgana knew that. But we also needed the Eldorean mages.

Penelope seemed to agree. "Aurora is right: something needs to be done about Eldoren. If they are forced to follow Morgana, we will be completely outnumbered, even with the Brandorian army. The Eldorean warrior-mages are just as important to have on our side. And without Rafael on the throne and now that Silverthorne is gone, they will never come to our aid."

I knew we had to do something, but what? I couldn't help

thinking about those poor children who must be so scared to be taken from their families.

"I will speak with Izadora," Penelope finished. "Without Silverthorne, we will have to reassess our plans. But we cannot leave Brandor until we have secured an alliance with the emirs."

I knew I had to be patient—running off to Eldoren without a plan was not a mistake I planned on making. But I still had questions. "If Morgana can put anyone on the throne, why is she still supporting the Blackwaters?"

"The new archmage is not taking any chances," said Marcus. "Devon Blackwater and his sons Zorek and Damien were also executed."

"What!"

Marcus nodded. "Now that her father and brothers are dead, Calisto is next in line to the throne after Prince Rafael, and she is due to marry the archmage."

My blood chilled at the implications. Damien and the rest of the Blackwaters were now dead. And even though I knew they hated me, I couldn't help but feel remorse for what had become of them, simply because their uncle, Archmage Lucian, got on Morgana's bad side. No one was safe from her evil web, and she was starting to close her grip around Avalonia. This new archmage seemed to be as bloodthirsty and ambitious as she was. He had to be stopped.

My eyes narrowed as I gave Marcus a contemplative glance. "Who is this archmage who thinks he can take over Eldoren?"

Marcus stiffened, his lips a thin line. "The latest Archmage of Avalonia is none other than our old enemy, Brandon Delacourt. Once he marries Calisto, he will be the Duke of Blackwater in addition to his other titles. And if he can get rid of Prince Rafael, he will be Eldoren's new king."

ENEMIES AND ALLIES

I WAS GOING *to kill Brandon Delacourt!*

That was all I could think about as I played with the food on my plate. Dinner in the grand hall at the Red Citadel was a lavish affair as usual, but I had no appetite for all the sumptuous food and had tried to decline the emir's invitation; he insisted, however. Gold-leaved tables spread about the room, flanked by silk-covered divans, with massive brocade cushions where the guests reclined in sumptuous elegance, watching the gauzy-veiled dancers spin and gyrate to the music.

I picked at the exotic dishes laid out in front of me, my thoughts all over the place. Ever since we had heard of Uncle Gabriel's execution, Aunt Serena had locked herself in her room, weeping for hours and refusing to eat. I tried to see her, but she wouldn't see anyone, not even Santino, who had taken to pacing outside his wife's bedchambers, alternating between looking distraught and looking angry.

But I was not allowed to hide in my room, when all I wanted to do was get under my soft blanket and shut myself away from the world. According to Penelope, queens didn't have time to mourn—they took action, and they stood firm in the face of all adversity. At this moment, I didn't feel like a queen. I was just a young girl who had lost her favorite uncle and staunchest supporter.

Brandon Delacourt had ensconced himself properly with Morgana. That snake! Every time I thought of him my blood boiled. He had tricked me into believing him a friend and betrayed me to Morgana. Now he had procured the most powerful post in the land. How he had managed to get her to appoint him archmage, I didn't know. But I knew he was clever, and combined with Lilith, they were a formidable enemy. I would have to be very careful if I wanted to help Rafe and those children. If I managed to return them to their families, then I knew at least some of the nobles would switch sides and join Rafe, and he needed all the support he could get. Even with Tristan and Cade, going up against an army of warrior-mages, the odds were not in our favor. I had to figure out how to do it, but doubts about my ability to do the impossible were slowly creeping in.

Tristan and Cade sat on the opposite side of the table, a swarm of serving girls attending to their every whim. Cade seemed to be enjoying the attention of the scantily clad girls, but Tristan looked like he didn't even notice them fawning over him. Ever since I expressed my desire to help Rafe, Tristan had hardly spoken to me. He just kept throwing me fleeting dark looks from across the room while Penelope was engaged in a lengthy discussion with the emir.

Marcus suddenly slipped into the hall from God knows where and whispered in Santino's ear.

Santino's eyes narrowed and he nodded. Leaning over, he spoke softly to me. "Marcus has news. A High Fae lady matching the description of Andromeda was seen near the city a few days ago."

"Do you think it could be her?" I whispered, and moved to get up.

Santino shook his head and put his hand on my arm, sitting

me back down. "I don't know, but you must stay here. If you leave, Varian will definitely get suspicious. I don't want him to know what we are looking for. I don't trust him. I will take Tristan and check it out."

Santino got up and gestured to Tristan and Cade to meet him outside.

All throughout dinner I tried to nod and answer in monosyllables to some irritating nobles while my mind was elsewhere. I saw Varian whisper to the emir and excuse himself.

Where was he going? I would find out.

I pretended to feel unwell, excused myself from dinner, and followed Varian as he scurried through the courtyard, shrouding myself in shadows. I crept through the darkness after him; he was heading toward the barracks. Looking around once, he pulled on his hood. He was definitely up to something.

I felt a presence brush up behind me and I whirled around, my hand beginning to light up.

"It's just me," whispered Marcus, his hands up.

"Stop sneaking up on me, Marcus," I ground out. I looked back, but Varian had disappeared.

"But it's okay for you to sneak around?" Marcus asked, scrunching his eyebrows and stroking his wispy beard.

"I was following Varian; he's up to something. I think he left the citadel through the barracks."

Marcus's eyes sparkled at that piece of information. He put on his hood. "I'll follow him and let you know what I find out."

I put my hand on his arm. "I'm coming with you."

"It's too dangerous in the city, Aurora. Santino would have my head if anything happened to you."

"Well, then, we mustn't get caught," I said, creating a cloak out of glamour and pulling up my hood. When others saw me now, they would only see an old lady in a worn brown cloak.

Marcus's eyes widened. "Impressive! Your magic has really grown since we last met."

"You have no idea," I said darkly. "Let's go."

Marcus knew the way out of the barracks into the city. It didn't take him long to find Varian—the short, shuffling figure was hard to miss. Protected with glamour, we traversed the smaller alleyways into numerous by-lanes when we spotted Varian entering a wide archway into the main town square.

"Where's he going?"

"The Night Bazaar," whispered Marcus as we turned into the archway.

I stopped and couldn't help but stare.

The square had been transformed into maze-like streets winding in and out of bright-tented stalls. Crowds of people flocked to the elaborate market selling everything from jewelry and trinkets to lengths of brightly colored fabrics and handmade crafts. We passed sellers of leather goods, which lay next to weapons and armored headgear in the style of the Brandorian cavalry.

I couldn't help stopping at one stall, which sold brightly dyed sandals, wonderfully detailed and studded with glittering gemstones.

Marcus grabbed my arm and pulled me away. "Come on, we will lose him."

We followed Varian to the middle of the bazaar, which was a whirl of sounds and activity. The smells of spice stalls and grilled meats wafted toward me as customers sampled savory pastries and sweet confections sprinkled with sugar and cinnamon from the next stall. A snake charmer entranced customers, who looked horrified at what he was doing with the snake.

Honey cakes and frothing, creamy drinks were being enjoyed all around, as the citizens of Sanria laughed and chatted in the marketplace. I was struck at how different this city was from Nedora, which was more gloomy, unkempt, and dangerous. I had a feeling the rulers of each city had something to do with it.

Varian moved toward a wall between two tents; he looked around once, then turned and vanished.

My eyes widened. "Where did he go?"

Marcus fondled his beard, and his eyes twinkled. "I know exactly where he went." He walked to the gap between the tents. "Follow me."

The wall behind looked ordinary enough—made of stone and separating two houses—but I could see it was no ordinary wall. The people in the market would not give it a second glance; my fae senses and spirit magic could pick up what others could not, and to my eyes, the wall shimmered with magic.

Marcus stepped forward through the wall, and I followed, entering a massive open-air courtyard. The sounds from the outside market disappeared, replaced by the bustle of a completely different bazaar. Dozens upon dozens of stalls, all draped in a deep, unyielding black, lined the four sides, selling objects and goods I had never seen before. Enchanted lanterns floated silently above, enhancing the moonlight that shone over the market.

"The Black Bazaar," whispered Marcus. "Only thieves and pirates know about this place. It is where they come to buy and sell magical goods that cannot be found anywhere else." He pulled his hood securely around his head, his eyes twinkling. "I wonder what our esteemed Chancellor Varian is doing here."

Three sides of the courtyard had big stone arches leading out into similar courtyards, and Varian hurried along the cobbled courtyard to the farthest arch and disappeared into another space. Marcus and I followed him, winding our way between the stalls and bustle of shady-looking people, all of whom had their hoods up and preferred to remain anonymous.

I paused to stare at one of the stalls, which was selling enchanted amulets for protection against demons.

"Enchanted by druids, supposedly." Marcus pointed to the

amulets. "But unreliable. I wouldn't want to face a demon wearing only that."

I arched an eyebrow. "There are druids in Avalonia?"

"Not anymore." Marcus gave me a quick look as he pulled me away from the stall.

"I've never heard anyone mention them before."

"That's because the druids haven't been seen in Avalonia for decades now."

In the next stall was a squat, balding man selling a variety of colored gemstones. "Portal witchstones," said Marcus. "They are enchanted to work only once and only to the place they are enchanted to take you. But they are very expensive and difficult to get hold of. I doubt those are real at all. There are not many witches powerful enough to make those anymore. That man is probably a fraud. Be careful here, and don't touch anything."

I could feel the magic in the air, pulsating like a beating heart. All the courtyards were warded by magic and so were many of the stalls, preventing anyone from stealing. I spotted Varian moving toward a large black tent in the corner of the courtyard, and we followed.

I extended my magic to glamour both of us, enclosing us within a cocoon of air that rendered us invisible. Just as we were about to follow him in, another man entered and left his two guards outside.

"That's Darius Detori," whispered Marcus.

My eyes widened. "But he's not expected for a few more days."

Marcus nodded.

I followed Marcus, staying close to the wall and making sure our glamour was intact, before we slipped into the tent, carefully brushing past the guards who stood at the entrance. We hid ourselves inside the tent behind a cloth-covered table, still protected by my powerful glamour. I infused more magic into it to make sure it was secure.

The tent looked much bigger from the inside than it did on the outside, like the tents at the fae market in Pixie Bush. Varian sat across the table from the infamous Darius Detori.

The Detori emir adjusted his robe, an exquisite crimson fabric embroidered with gold thread. He had an air about him that screamed nobility. Dark lashes framed his amber eyes, and his chiseled cheekbones were partially covered by a trimmed beard. "A new shipment of slaves was captured by pirates on its way to Mist Falls." Darius regarded Varian with a cruel scowl. "I thought you were going to take care of the problem, Varian. You are supposed to be the biggest slave trader this side of Brandor. You should have more soldiers on your ships. Or are you just too cheap to hire good ones?"

The Chancellor of Sanria tried to say something, but Darius Detori held up his hand to silence him. "Have you found out who is behind this?"

Varian looked down, wringing his hands. "It's Santino's men, Lord Detori, I am sure of it. His pirates are a sneaky bunch. If I can prove it, the emir will stop trusting Santino and listen only to me."

"I can't wait until you find your proof," said Darius Detori. "There is no more time. We need more slaves to finish the mining."

Varian cleared his throat. "There is something else you should know."

Darius Detori sat back in his chair and crossed his arms. "Tell me."

"Emir Valasis knows about the mines and plans to have them shut down."

Darius Detori stroked his clipped beard. "I wouldn't worry too much about Roderigo Valasis. You just make sure I get my slaves to finish the work. Once we give Morgana what she wants, she will make me Sultan of Brandor. It's time we had a real king. The council is weak, and Emir Valasis has ruled it long enough.

Santino has been a thorn in our side ever since he replaced his elder brother. Get rid of him."

I suppressed a gasp. Marcus shot me a warning look. They were plotting to murder Santino. And Darius Detori was without a doubt working for Morgana.

"Once the pirate prince is gone there will be no one who can oppose us. Roderigo Valasis is nothing without Santino and his army of pirates and mercenaries."

"But—" Varian cleared his throat, his beady eyes darting around the tent. A thin trickle of sweat dripped down his fat cheek. "But my lord, Santino is not an easy man to get rid of. Wouldn't it be better to wait until the mining is finished? The Firedrake princess is here in Sanria, along with her fae prince, and they are staying at the citadel. She and Santino are friends. If I—" He paused, rephrasing. "If we try anything while she is here, I fear there will be retaliation."

Lord Detori banged his hand on the table. "I'm not afraid of some upstart princess. If she gets in the way, get rid of her too. The new archmage has assured me as long as we keep providing him with blackened iron, I have Morgana's blessing to take over Brandor and become sultan of all its territories."

"What about the fae army?" said Varian. "If the Firedrake princess calls them, we will be destroyed."

Darius Detori shook his head and leaned back in his chair. "Varian, Varian, haven't you heard the latest news? The Drakaar have taken the dwarven fortress at Greygate. The dwarves have already started forging weapons from blackened iron from our earliest shipments and mining efforts. Those weapons will equip Morgana's army and our own. We have no need to fear the fae anymore."

Varian's eyes narrowed. "Greygate is still only one fortress. There are not enough dwarven smiths or forges to make the required weapons. We will need the forges at Stonegate. And

Stonegate is impenetrable. King Ranthor will never surrender to the Drakaar. He has always been allied with Silverthorne."

Darius Detori leaned forward, his voice soft but laced with steel. "Silverthorne is dead," he spat. "Morgana will make his supporters see the folly in their resistance. Once the fae are defeated, there will be no one to stand in our way. The Detoris will rule the east without fear of Izadora and her army. Soon all kingdoms will be under Morgana's rule. It is useless to fight her, and the other emirs must be made to see it is a useless proposition to support the Firedrake girl instead of a real queen."

He pushed back his chair and got up, his jeweled fingers, long and slender, resting lightly on the rough wooden table. "You just make sure I have enough slaves to finish the work, Varian. Remember who you really work for. Once we get rid of that bastard Santino and his father, the Detori family will rule Brandor once more."

Marcus gestured for us to move. They would be leaving soon, and it was best we were far away when they did. We slipped out the way we came, barely slipping past the guards who stood at the entrance to the tent.

"We have to warn Santino," I whispered as we headed out of the Black Bazaar through the magical wall and hurried through the brightly colored stalls of the main market square.

"We will," said Marcus, turning down an alleyway leading back to the citadel.

"Do you think it's true? That Morgana has attacked the dwarven cities, and Greygate has fallen?"

Marcus shook his head. "I don't know, but I have a bad feeling about this. Greygate is the southernmost fortress of the dwarves, guarding entrances to their mines and forges. But Stonegate is the capital, where the king resides, with over a hundred forges. If Greygate is already in Morgana's hands, it is only a matter of time before they go after Stonegate as well. If they get access to those forges, they will be able to create enough weapons to equip their whole army."

We hurried back to the citadel, entering through the barracks. "Go to Penelope's room and stay there. Tell her what has happened. We have no idea how many people Varian has working for him in the palace. I will find Santino and let him know."

"Come," Penelope said to me after I recounted everything that had just happened. "We must speak with Santino at once."

I followed Penelope through the mosaic corridors to Santino's private rooms.

The suite was massive, light, and airy, done up in the Brandorian style with carved ceilings and beautiful mosaic and marble flooring. The reception room contained huge marble pillars creating arches that led out to a private courtyard through white muslin curtains, which fluttered in the summer breeze. A large lotus pond and a marble fountain adorned the center and dispensed water in graceful arcs. Marcus was already there, speaking to Santino in hushed tones.

"Find Tristan and bring him here," Penelope ordered Marcus.

He nodded and was out the door before she finished.

"You need to take charge of the situation in your kingdom, Santino," Penelope said, turning to face the pirate prince. "It is imperative you convince your father to close the mines and support Aurora. You cannot let the Detoris come to power."

Aunt Serena came out of her room. She studied our faces and her eyebrows shot up. "What's going on here? What is she talking about, Santino?"

"Varian suspects Santino is involved in the recent attacks on his ships," I elaborated, "and Darius Detori wants him killed."

Santino's amber eyes blazed with fury. "Yes, Marcus has informed me of the threat."

Aunt Serena's hand went to her throat. "They want to kill Santino?" She moved closer to her husband.

Santino's anger waned as he beheld his wife and put his arm around her. "I'm glad to see you are feeling better, my love," he spoke softly.

"You need to strike before they do," Penelope stated.

Santino started pacing the floor. "The Detoris have been trying to kill my family for decades. It's nothing new."

"But they succeeded with your brother, Santino," said Serena. Fear for her husband's life showed clearly in her eyes. Santino had told me himself about the bloody civil war that plagued Brandor for decades, and the assassination of his brother Alfonso that caused Santino to return and take up the mantle of his father's heir, uniting the Brandorian council.

Marcus and Tristan entered with Cade. "The problem is much worse than we thought," said Marcus as Tristan swiftly shut the door behind him.

Santino's eyes darkened. "Has there been more news?"

"It is too dangerous to talk here," said Marcus, looking around. "Varian's spies are everywhere. And we still have to ascertain who we can trust. For now, that is only the people in this room."

"I can create a barrier so no one can hear us." Penelope gathered her magic and hardened the air around the room and courtyard. The sounds from the palace stopped as we were cocooned in a bubble of air.

Marcus wrung his hands. "We have another problem." He turned to look at me. "I have just received word from Eldoren."

Aunt Serena got up. "Is Erien all right?"

Marcus glanced at her and nodded. "For now." He looked like he wanted to say something more but didn't.

"What happened?" I asked.

"After Silverthorne's execution . . ." said Marcus.

Aunt Serena made a small distressed sound.

Marcus hesitated a moment and looked at Santino, who nodded. "Go on." He put his arm around his wife.

"The archmage has moved the whole court to Caeleron Castle because it is better fortified, and the children are now being held in the castle dungeons."

I started to pace in front of him. "There must be something we can do for those children. We can't let them remain there. What if they're hurt?"

"There is nothing we can do for them from here," said Penelope.

"There is more," Marcus said.

I stopped pacing.

"Brandon Delacourt has already married Calisto in a private ceremony, and now he intends to have a coronation and crown himself king."

My eyes widened. "Already?"

"And the best place to do it is Caeleron Castle," Penelope interrupted. "Eldoren's true seat of power. Every King of Eldoren has been crowned there."

Marcus nodded. "Exactly."

"Clever bastard," said Santino, his face hard as stone.

"Yes, he is even more diabolical than we thought," said Marcus, his face grim. "Delacourt has given Prince Rafael an ultimatum: surrender himself before the coronation and voluntarily give up his crown, or the archmage will have the children executed. One every day, from the day of the coronation until Rafael gives in."

I paled, dread pooling in my stomach. "When is the coronation?"

"Three days from now," Marcus answered.

"We have to do something. We must help them. Help Rafe. We can't let Delacourt take his crown, and we cannot stand idly by and let him hurt innocent children."

"You will never get there in time," said Marcus, defeated. "If

Prince Rafael gives up his crown voluntarily, no one can dispute Brandon's claim to the throne."

Penelope strode over to me and put her hand on my arm. "There is nothing you can do, Aurora. Rafe will not let anything happen to those children. He will have no choice but to surrender."

"That is hardly reassuring," I snapped.

"Delacourt has promised to let the children go back to their families once Rafael is in custody," Marcus offered.

"How do you know Delacourt will keep to the bargain?" I inquired, my hands on my hips. "He will have Rafe killed once he gets his hands on him. Delacourt is never going to let him live."

"Your grandmother has forbidden you from interfering in the affairs of Eldoren, Aurora," said Tristan pointedly. "Our first priority has to be finding Andromeda, getting the book out of her clutches, and retrieving the Dagger."

I glared at Tristan. "I don't care what my grandmother said. I have to do something." My mind was made up, and I would not let them sway me to the road of caution again. Sometimes the only answer was to take a risk. I could not turn my back on those children. I might not be able to help the slaves in Brandor, but I knew I could help the children of Eldoren if I could find a way into the castle without getting caught.

It was easier said than done, but I had to try. I gathered my courage and pushed my shoulders back as I faced Tristan, staring him down. "I can't go with you to find Andromeda."

Tristan's sapphire eyes narrowed, swirling with silver sparks. "What do you mean?"

I held his gaze and hoped he understood why I had to do this. "Cade, Penelope, and you are far more capable of tracking and finding Andromeda and the book. But who is going to help the poor children that have been taken hostage by Delacourt? I cannot allow Rafe to lose his crown. I owe it to him to make things right. I'm sorry, Tristan. I have to go to Eldoren first."

"Of course you do," Tristan sneered, his lips curling up in a snarl I hadn't seen in a long time. "You need to help your precious Prince Rafael."

"That's not why I am doing this." My hands balled into fists. I wasn't entirely sure he was wrong. I hated being in this position, and I didn't like what it was doing to our friendship, but there was nothing I could do about it right now.

Tristan crossed his arms. "And how do you plan on getting there? The skies around Eldoren will be swarming with gorgoths. Your pegasus might be able to outrun them, but she isn't even here. It takes just one to catch you off guard, and you will be dead."

"Better dead than a coward," I said tartly.

Tristan stalked up to me, so close that our noses were almost touching. "You think I'm a coward?" he growled softly.

My heartbeat sped up, but my voice was a whisper. "I never said that."

Penelope held up her hand and stepped between us. "Stop it, you two." Her eyes flashed dangerously as she looked from Tristan to me, and he moved away.

"Izadora has forbidden any of us to help Rafael. But I agree with you, Aurora. Delacourt has gone too far—he must be stopped. I think we should speak to Izadora together and see what we can do to rescue the children," Penelope suggested to my surprise. She turned to Serena. "Do you have a mirror I can use?"

Serena led us to her room, where a large gilded mirror lay along one wall.

Penelope warded Serena's room with magic as well, so we couldn't be overheard, and opened a mirror portal. My grandmother came into view.

"So," said the fae queen. Her eyebrows rose. "We have an audience."

Santino bowed. "You honor us, Your Majesty."

Izadora's eyes flashed, flickering like golden flames as she surveyed the group. Her gaze settled on Penelope. "Do we have a problem, sister?"

Penelope nodded and quickly recounted what we had learned so far.

Izadora listened patiently until Penelope finished. "And of course my dear granddaughter wants to run off to Eldoren to rescue the children."

Penelope gave me a slash of a smile.

"A fine sentiment," said the fae queen. "But not why I am giving my consent."

My eyes widened. "You are?"

I had expected my grandmother to forbid me again and even threaten me. I was ready with a retinue of arguments which I apparently didn't need.

"Circumstances have changed," said the fae queen. "If the new archmage becomes King of Eldoren, that will be one more kingdom joining Morgana's growing army. He must be stopped, and Prince Rafael put back on the throne where he belongs." She turned her gaze on Santino. "I assume the pirate prince can handle the Detori problem?"

Santino gave the fae queen a wary, considering look and nodded once.

"Good," said Izadora, turning her golden eyes on me. "Because until the mines are shut down, the Elder Council has refused to give their consent to send the fae army to your aid."

I clenched my hands into fists and tried to keep calm. "But you said—"

"I know what I said," my grandmother snapped, cutting me off.

"What about the alliance? Without the fae army we will be completely outnumbered."

"I know," she answered, completely stone-faced.

"But I'm still a descendent of the house of Eos-Eirendil," I argued. "I am the rightful Queen of Elfi and your heir."

Izadora nodded and her eyes softened, ever so slightly. "Yes, but on matters of war, the Elder Council rules and has decreed they will not send the fae army to follow you into battle until you retrieve the Dagger of Dragath and shut down the mines."

This was unbelievable. After everything I had done for the High Fae, they were going to abandon me to my fate.

"I didn't expect it to go so far," my grandmother continued. "Now with Silverthorne gone—" her gaze flicked to Serena, who flinched at the sound of her father's name, "—it is up to us to make sure the mages of Eldoren follow you, and not Morgana."

Tristan spoke up. "What about Andromeda and the book?"

"I have dispatched Aiden to retrieve the book. He will liaise with Cade, and together they will track Andromeda."

Tristan nodded and so did I. I did not like Aiden, but he was one of the most powerful High Fae. If anyone could take on Andromeda, it was the insufferable Prince of the Day Court, her own son. He was unwaveringly loyal to his queen, even if it meant stopping his own mother from going ahead with her plans.

My grandmother's golden gaze turned on me. "You concentrate on growing your army and retrieving the Dagger." Izadora waved her hand and closed the mirror portal.

Penelope clasped her hands together and turned to face us. "We will portal into the closest town, but we will not be able to portal into Caeleron Castle itself. Lilith can detect that kind of spirit magic, and the castle will be warded with powerful spells. If Andromeda is tracking our portals, she will think we have lost her trail. She may let down her guard and slip up. It will be easier for Cade and Aiden to pick up her tracks."

Tristan raised an eyebrow and glared pointedly at Penelope. "You can create a portal over such a distance?"

"I can't," Penelope clarified. "But Aurora can."

"No one but the queen of the fae can do that." Tristan's tone was low and serious.

"The queen of the fae and the Dawnstar." Penelope's eyes were pure steel. "Or have you forgotten who she really is and what she is capable of?"

I nodded eagerly. This was my one chance to help Rafe and those children. I could do this.

"You don't know how much of her magic it will drain," Tristan argued. "You know as well as I do, Penelope, when her spirit magic depletes past a certain threshold, it affects her other fae powers as well. She will not be able to defend herself should you encounter one of the Drakaar or their minions."

"That's why we have you, Tristan." I smiled sweetly.

Tristan was not amused, which was glaringly apparent from the scowl on his face.

Penelope shook her head. "I know the risks, Tristan. But we will have some time for Aurora's magic to recover while I figure out a way to get the children clear and stop Delacourt from crowning himself king."

"And how are you going to manage this grand feat of espionage?"

Penelope's mouth twitched slightly. "Leave that to me."

She turned to the pirate prince, who was standing quietly, his keen mind absorbing everything. "But if we leave right now, my other concern is what to do about the council with the emirs. We need this alliance, Santino. And we must make sure Morgana doesn't get her hands on all the blackened iron."

"I will handle it." Santino's shrewd eyes flashed. "Soon the streets of Sanria will be a battlefield, and it is better if you are all far away from here when it happens. Once I have brought the council to its knees, they will do as they are told. I have waited too long for this day to come. Varian has given me an opportunity. If I don't use it now, the Detori family will have its chance to take over Brandor. I will send word once it is done."

Penelope nodded and looked at Tristan. "Did you find out anything else about Andromeda and her whereabouts?"

"Yes, we heard she was in Sanria a few days ago and was seen boarding a ship to Orion."

Penelope looked at Marcus. "Orion is near Mist Falls, is it not?"

Marcus nodded. "It is also the simplest route into Illiador. You bypass the Cascade Mountains and take the main caravan route to Nerenor."

"The mines around Mist Falls are the largest in Brandor," said Santino.

"Andromeda must be involved with moving the shipments to Morgana," said Penelope. "That's why she has been in Brandor for so long. She must be in league with the Detoris. If we find Andromeda, we find the rest of the blackened iron."

Tristan crossed his arms. "And we destroy it."

"Exactly," Penelope confirmed. "If Cade leaves now and meets Aiden, we may have a chance to catch her before she reaches Illiador."

"Why do I have to track Andromeda while you go and have all the fun?" Cade grumbled.

Penelope's azure eyes turned stormy. I had seen that look before.

I took a step back, glad her anger was not directed at me for once.

She marched up to Cade and poked a finger at his chest. "Let's get one thing straight, Cade Windchaser. This is not fun! In fact, it is the farthest from fun I have ever seen. Do you think I enjoy running around the countryside?" She jerked her chin in his general direction. "The whole of Avalonia is on the brink of destruction, and we cannot afford any mistakes." Her words were terse, clipped, and brooked no argument from anyone. "Is that understood?" She looked around, her gaze boring into us.

Everyone nodded quickly, including me.

Although I didn't like to admit it, I was relieved Tristan and

Penelope were coming with me. I had made so many mistakes along the way; I had a lot to learn, and I was still unsure of myself at times. I needed to make things right. I knew now not everything that happened was my fault. But I had been gifted with all these powers, and I had to use them to help people, otherwise what was the point of having them in the first place? I was the only one who could do this, and whether I succeeded or not, I had to try my best.

CAELERON CASTLE

WE GATHERED our belongings and congregated in Santino's vast reception room. It was almost dawn, and the golden glow of the morning sun was starting to announce itself.

"Now," said Penelope, "since you have never been to the town of Caeleron, you must portal to the nearest place you have been before—in the woods outside the town of Roth."

"Near Brandon Delacourt's castle?"

Penelope nodded. "From there we will journey on foot to Caeleron. We cannot portal directly into the castle as it is heavily warded. As you know, portal magic cannot be shielded by the Amulet of Auraken, but it will shield your glamour."

Tristan stood beside me, his swords strapped on, looking very skeptical about this whole mission. "And then what?"

"I know someone who will be able to get us into the castle." She turned to me. "You have to rest after you do this. Do not try to use your magic until you are ready."

"How long will it take to recover?"

"That depends on you," Penelope answered. "You have never created a portal outside of Elfi before. Everyone has a different reaction to using great amounts of spirit magic. It must only be used when we really need it. Try to remember that."

I pressed my lips together. "I will."

"Be careful," said Aunt Serena. "And look after Erien."

I hugged Serena, Santino, and Cade and nodded farewell.

I gathered my magic and projected it outward, imagining the small glade in Eldoren where Rafe, Kalen, and I had camped when we ran away from the palace. It seemed like a lifetime ago. It took less of an effort for the spark of a portal to form this time, but it was much harder to grow it into one we could pass through because of the distance. I kept drawing on my magic until the portal was open.

"Good," said Penelope, "your concentration has improved considerably. Now regulate your magic to hold it. You need more magic to hold the portal than you needed to create it."

"I will go first and make sure it is safe." Tristan stepped forward and disappeared into the portal.

Penelope glanced sidelong at Santino. "Be careful. And send word once you have spoken to the council. I don't need to remind you how important it is that Brandor stands with us and not with Morgana."

"I will take care of it." He gave her a slash of a smile.

Penelope nodded and stepped into the portal.

It took a lot of power to hold the portal open. I could feel a bead of sweat form on my brow and trickle down my cheek. My magic was weakening, and I wouldn't be able to hold it open for much longer. I had to go.

I stepped forward into the void and felt the familiar rush of timelessness as I crossed through space in the blink of an eye. Landing on my feet, I closed the portal behind me. Lightheadedness hit, and I fell to my knees as my magic started to fade.

Penelope came over and crouched down beside me. "Are you okay?"

I took a deep breath and nodded as she gave me her hand to pull me up. I slowly got to my feet, a little unsteadily at first, but it was only momentary. Once I got my bearings, I felt better and looked around. The clearing was just as I remembered it, although this time the leaves were sparkling emerald-green, lush with the colors of spring. A carpet of bluebells bloomed beneath our feet as we made our way through the woods to the main road that led to the market town situated at the base of the hill on which Caeleron Castle was built.

I tried reaching for my magic, but it made me feel unsteady, and I had to sit down again. I started to panic, even though I had been warned this was likely to happen. I had never considered how vulnerable I would feel without my magic. It wasn't gone completely, I could still feel it, but it still felt strange not to be able to call on it at will.

Penelope came over and put her hand on my shoulder. "Don't try to access your magic so soon after opening the portal, Aurora. It needs to replenish. It will return, but give it time."

"Okay, give me a moment." I gathered myself and adjusted the straps that held my sword in place. I now understood what Penelope and Tristan were so worried about. This was the first portal I'd had to create over such a distance, and I hoped I didn't have to do it again.

"For now I will glamour all of us, but to get into the castle you must be able to work your own glamour. Only the amulet you wear will be able to mask your presence from someone as powerfully magical as the Dark Queen." Penelope wove her magic around us, so anyone who noticed us would only see three weary travelers en route to the bustling market town of Caeleron.

The surrounding country gradually got loftier and greener as we passed an abandoned monastery on the hillside and derelict farms that dotted the area. It took half a day of walking, skirting the woods and mountains to get to the king's road that led to the town of Caeleron.

As the day wore on, we hitched a ride with a farmer on his wagon. "This was once a small village," said Penelope as we bumped our way down the dirt road on the back of the wagon piled high with sacks of turnips. "But when Dorian the First—more commonly known now as Dorian the Great—built Caeleron Castle almost a thousand years ago, slowly the village below grew to service the needs of the castle whenever the king or queen were in residence." Penelope lowered her voice. "We must be very careful—no one must know we are here. It is our one and only chance of getting into the castle."

What started as a beautiful spring day turned dark and foggy as we approached the town. Above us, rising on a rocky hilltop, lay the great fortress of Caeleron Castle, the ancestral seat of the Ravenswood dynasty, which dominated the valley beyond. Caeleron was located at a crossing of trade routes and situated at the base of the hill. I peered up through the mist that had settled on the massive fortress looming over the walled town as we crossed a narrow stone bridge and passed over the river.

We thanked the farmer as we got off the wagon and entered the town through the western gate into the outer section, where the workers, shopkeepers, and artisans lived.

Caeleron bustled with life as traders and travelers from all over Avalonia traversed the four town gates. Guards were everywhere, dressed in black uniforms with the symbol of the black rose rimmed in gold, milling about the town gates and checking everyone's papers as they entered the town. It was distressing to see so many of Morgana's soldiers here in Eldoren. Delacourt must have called for assistance; his soldiers were also there in dark blue uniforms, eyes ravenous with the promise of riches now that they had the run of the land.

"Name?" said one guard, glancing at the papers Penelope held out to him.

"Lady Sonia Lockhart," said Penelope without hesitation, dropping a few coins into the guard's hands. I knew this was the way things always worked. A little money passed over and the guards wouldn't ask many questions. Of course, it helped that because of our glamour we looked nothing like the wanted posters plastered throughout the town. "We have traveled all the way from Fenth to see the coronation."

The guards looked at Tristan and me. "And these two?"

"My daughter and our guard," said Penelope imperiously.

The guard handed the papers back to Penelope and ushered us along, counting his coins unashamedly before slipping them into his pocket. The greedy guard had no idea he had allowed a Firedrake to walk through the front door.

We hurried through the narrow, cobbled streets and closely packed stone houses, while flickering light from candles and hearths streamed onto the streets, partly illuminating some areas and reducing others to shadow. We passed street vendors who had started packing up their wares and heading out of the town, while shop owners closed wooden shutters and locked up. I spotted numerous black-uniformed guards carrying oil lamps, inspecting the streets, and calling out a curfew. The town was crawling with them. Delacourt really wasn't taking any chances. I pulled my hood closer around me and hurried on past them.

I clasped the medallion around my neck and made sure it was hidden. It was safer to keep the Amulet of Auraken on when surrounded by so many magic users. At least now, no one would be able to detect my magical presence, not even the Drakaar.

Penelope ducked into a small street, and we followed quickly, our cloaks and hoods pulled tightly around us. It was a much darker part of the town, where hooded figures traversed the arched pathways, and the stench of rotting garbage and clogged sewers made me feel nauseous. Narrow alleys wound around an unplanned maze of houses, crammed together in close proximity. We made our way to a small wooden door at the back of an alleyway, and Penelope knocked once. Tristan stayed in the shadows, scouring the dark streets for any sign of trouble.

The door opened and a squat old lady in an old brown dress, scanty gray hair tied in a bun, stepped outside. "Yes," she said, furrowing her brow. "What do you want?" Her tone was sharp.

Penelope removed her glamour, but only from her face, so that the old lady could see clearly who she was.

"Elsa, it's me," Penelope whispered. The old lady's eyes grew wider, and she ushered us in immediately, glancing down the darkening street quickly and shutting the door.

Penelope clasped the old lady's hand. "Is he here?"

Elsa nodded. "He came for the coronation."

"I thought he would."

"Who's here?" I asked, unable to contain my curiosity.

Penelope removed the veil of glamour from all of us. "Someone who can help us get into the castle."

"And how are we going to manage that?" Tristan said. "Even with glamour, we need a reason to go into the castle. It is crawling with soldiers."

"You will simply have to walk through the front door," a deep male voice drawled from the doorway. "With my help, of course."

The speaker stepped forward and removed his hood.

I already knew who it was, and my heartbeat sped up. "Rafe!"

Tristan moved closer to me.

Rafe leaned against the doorframe, his gray eyes indecipherable as he studied me from a distance. "You shouldn't have come here, Aurora."

I took a step forward. "We are here to help, Rafe."

His gaze flicked to Tristan. "I don't need your help. You have done enough already." His tone was stiff, his voice gruff.

I froze.

I hadn't expected to see him so soon. And I thought when we finally met, he would be at least a little happy to see me. But I had not anticipated the way he spoke to me now and the coldness in his eyes. Maybe I had caused irrevocable damage to our relationship and there was nothing left to repair. Maybe he had already moved on.

"I told you this was a waste of time," said Tristan, scowling. "We should go."

"No!" I held up my hand, then turned to Rafe. "If you don't want our help, Rafe, that's fine. But I came here to help those children, and that is what I am going to do. With or without you."

"Why do you insist on interfering in my kingdom?"

I held his stare. "Are you saying that I am not welcome here anymore, Prince Rafael?" I said, using his title for the first time.

Rafe crossed his arms and gave me a wary glare. "That's not what I mean, Aurora."

"Then what do you mean, Rafe?" I said tartly.

Penelope stepped between us. "I asked Rafe to meet us because if we are going to do this, we need to work together."

"Aurora! You're back." I heard a sudden soft shout before Kalen came racing out from the room behind Rafe and hugged me so hard I nearly fell over.

I laughed for the first time in months and hugged my friend back. "Kalen! I missed you."

Penelope cleared her throat and Kalen looked up. "Sorry, Mother," he said sheepishly, letting go of me and going over to hug his mom. "It's good to see you too."

She hugged him fiercely and patted him on his back. "I'm glad you are all right," she said softly.

Kalen pushed his shoulders back, pulling himself up to his full height, which was now considerable. He had grown a lot since I last saw him. "Of course I am, Mother. Rafe has been looking after me as usual."

Penelope glanced at Rafe. "Thank you."

He inclined his head. "You know I will always look out for him, Penelope."

Kalen gasped when he finally noticed Tristan. "Is this . . . ?" He looked at me and then his mother. "Tristan Nightshade," he said in an awed voice.

I smiled at Kalen and flicked my chin at Tristan. "You know who he is?"

"Of course!" said Kalen, grinning from ear to ear. "Everyone knows the dreaded Prince of the Night Court."

"Of course they do." I rolled my eyes.

Kalen bounded over to Tristan and clasped his forearm in greeting, shaking it vigorously. "It is an honor to finally meet you, Prince Tristan. My mother raised me on stories of you and Izadora's Elite Guard of Elfi."

"Did she now?" Tristan smiled for the first time since he got here, flicking a glance at Penelope.

Kalen nodded, his eyes lighting up. "Are you here to rescue Erien?"

My hand flew to my mouth. "Erien!" I spun to face Rafe. "What's happened to Erien?" A chill went down my spine. If anything had happened to Erien, I would never be able to live with myself.

"Erien was taken by Brandon's guards," Rafe said, running his hand through his brown waves. "He's imprisoned in the dungeons with the other children of all the noble families who oppose the archmage."

"How did this happen?" I breathed, looking at Penelope. "Why didn't I know about this?"

Penelope shook her head. "We didn't know. Marcus tried to get as much information as he could, but not all spies have reliable information."

"I told Erien to stay with the Silver Swords while I was away." Rafe's voice was low. He looked tired, with day-old stubble on his chin and shadows under his eyes—he probably was as worried as we were. I had to be more understanding; after all, it was his kingdom and his people we were trying to save.

But Erien was my cousin, one of the only family members I

had left. Aunt Serena would never forgive me if I let him rot in a dungeon or, worse yet, got him killed. I had let my granduncle down, and I wasn't going to make the same mistake twice. This was my war as much as it was Rafe's, and I would tear apart the castle before I let Delacourt take anyone else I loved from me.

"So, are we going to work together?" I asked Rafe, coming back to the point. "Or should we make other arrangements? Because if Erien is in there, there is no way I am going to let you keep me from trying to get him out. Even if I have to burn the castle down around us."

Rafe raised his eyebrows and gave me a small smile, but the hurt in his eyes didn't go away. "I would appreciate it if you didn't," he said formally, but there was humor in his voice. "I would prefer to have my family's ancestral home still standing, if you don't mind."

I smiled back at him. "Then it's settled." I clasped my hands together. "What's the plan?"

Rafe sighed, resigned to the fact we were there to help. "I think you'd better come with me."

He led us through a back door of the small house and down a flight of steps. We came out into a large, dimly lit room with wall sconces that provided light and warmth, as well as a small hearth around which a bunch of people were huddled, trying to keep themselves warm. A few cots and bunks were propped up against one wall in the corner, where the men and women could rest.

They all looked up when we entered.

"Welcome to the resistance," said Rafe with a flourish of his hand. There was a large table in the center of the room, around which another group was huddled, poring over maps and pieces of parchment.

I recognized a few of them. The Earl of Rothguard came forward to greet me, as did Lord Fenton, Marquis of Greystone. According to Penelope, they were my father's oldest friends, but I hardly knew them at all. Captain Raingate, Silverthorne's captain of the guard, was also part of the Silver Swords. I wasn't surprised to see him there. If Erien was a prisoner of the archmage, I knew Captain Raingate would do everything he could to get him out. He was a capable soldier, and my granduncle had trusted him. I was glad Rafe still had some people he could depend on.

I looked around the room. The others were strangers, but I didn't have time to get to know them right now. I noticed some food laid out on a table in the corner. I was famished, and the food was fresh and warm. Small, flaky meat pies and fresh bread with white creamy butter accompanied a hearty vegetable stew. Rafe invited us to eat while he gave others instructions and sent them away to carry out their orders, until there were only a few of us left.

I picked at a meat pie while Kalen chattered away with his mother, telling her everything that was going on. At some point in the conversation he put his arm around my shoulders. I couldn't help but notice all the similarities he had to Tristan. He wasn't as tall as Tristan yet, but he had really grown and filled out since I had last seen him.

"I'm so glad you are back, Aurora," he said, a half-eaten pie in his hand.

I eyed the others in the room. "It seems you are the only one."

"Give them time," said Kalen, trying to smile. "They are all loyal to Rafe, and they know how he felt about you. Now you are here with your fae prince, and they don't know how to behave."

I looked around at all the people Rafe had gathered. I couldn't explain myself to each of them, and frankly I didn't feel the need to. Rafe was the only one who I needed to speak with, and I wondered when I could get him alone to talk. I darted looks over at him from the corner of my eye, but he was busy giving instructions to two men and writing something on a piece of parchment he then sealed. I wanted to explain why I agreed to become betrothed to Tristan before we went into the castle, but I couldn't seem to get him alone for one moment. I had a sneaky feeling he was purposely avoiding me.

"We don't have much time," Rafe announced after we had eaten and he had finished with the others. He glanced over at Tristan and me. "We need to disguise you and get you both into the palace before the coronation. It is the best time to stage the rescue while everyone is busy with the parade and festivities."

"Once the children are out, are you sure the other nobles will join you to take the castle?" Penelope asked.

Rafe shot a glance at Rothguard and Fenton, who both nodded. "I believe so. My army is hiding in the woods around the castle, as well as Silverthorne's and the other nobles' individual armies. But they will not make a move until they know the children are safe."

The plan sounded simple. We would disguise ourselves and infiltrate the palace. Then when the archmage was busy with the coronation, we would slip into the dungeons and get the children out through a portal. But as I had learned on more than one occasion, plans rarely ever went the way they were supposed to. And to top it all off, there was a catch. Rafe was going to give himself up to Delacourt before the coronation.

I shook my head. "Rafe, this is too dangerous. It's exactly what Delacourt wants you to do."

He ran a hand through his dark, wavy hair and rubbed the base of his neck as he scoured the maps on the table. "What choice do I have? If I don't surrender before the coronation, Delacourt has promised to kill Erien first. And after what happened to Silverthorne, I can't take any chances."

My face paled. "But how will you get out? Once he knows the children are gone, he will have you executed."

"He won't." Rafe's stormy eyes narrowed. "At least, not immediately. He will want to make a spectacle of me at the coronation, surrendering the crown to him in front of all the nobility. If he doesn't, his rule will always be in jeopardy. As it is, his claim to the throne is slim. Calisto may be next in line to the throne after me now that her father and brothers are dead, but she is not a Ravenswood."

A young woman with dark hair came into the room and walked straight up to Rafe.

His eyes softened when he saw her. "Is it set up?"

She nodded. "Yes, Rafael." She put her hand on his arm, and I couldn't stop my eyes from fixating on their touch. "Don't worry, I have taken care of it."

Rafe smiled at her and put his hand on her shoulder, giving her a slight squeeze. "Thank you, Danica. You have done well."

Danica looked up at him through long lashes and gave him a sultry smile. I felt a sinking sensation in my stomach. Who was she?

Rafe turned back to Tristan and me, and his smile disappeared. "The castle is hiring part-time servants for the coronation, as it will be full of guests and their retinues. I will get you a job in the kitchens—I still have people in the castle working for me. Danica will meet you at the gates and get you in."

Penelope nodded and clasped her hands together. "You and Tristan will disguise yourselves as servants. As long as you are wearing the Amulet of Auraken, the wards will not detect your glamour. If there are Drakaar in the castle, make sure you stay far away from them. Be vigilant and keep your glamour strong. Don't drop it even for a second. Brandon and Lilith will be busy planning the coronation; they will not be expecting you."

Danica looked over at me and smiled, but her smile never reached her eyes. I could see a calculating gleam behind her sweet façade, but Rafe obviously didn't. I could tell this one was going to be trouble.

Rafe looked down at the map on the table. Danica was still standing close to him, but he didn't seem to mind. In fact, the way they looked at each other suggested they were already pretty close. Jealousy rose up and threatened to clamp itself around my heart. I tried to ignore it, tried to brush it off, but it wouldn't go away. I had to remind myself Rafe was free to do as he pleased. It was stupid of me to think he would wait for me and forgive me for what I had done. He had obviously moved on.

"You must find your way into the dungeon on the day of the coronation. Retrieve the children and get them out," Rafe said finally.

"What about you?" I asked.

"That's where you and your fae prince come in." He glanced momentarily at Tristan, who was standing beside me, eyes scanning the maps. "If you really want to help, then once you get the children out, you can release me from the dungeons before Brandon decides to execute me."

The nonchalant way he spoke about his execution set me on edge. I didn't even want to think about it. But as long as Tristan and I were in the castle, there was a good chance we could prevent it from happening.

I nodded. "Then what? How do we get out?"

"Then," said Captain Raingate, stepping closer to the table and resting his hands on it, "you need to get to the main gates of the castle and let our forces in. We will take care of the rest."

"That's quite a distance," said Tristan, looking at the maps. "We cannot simply walk out of the castle with the prince. We won't be able to get out the same way we came in."

"We won't have to," said Rafe. "There is a secret passage here." He stabbed his finger at a point on the map. "It leads from the dungeons to a small alcove in the main corridor of the palace, close to the Grand Hall where the festivities will be held. If we can slip past unnoticed in the crowd of guests, we might make it past the main bailey to the gates."

"There will be guards everywhere," said Rothguard. "Rafael, are you sure you want to do this? There must be some other way we could find to get the children to safety."

"I've studied all the options and there is no other way." Rafe shook his head. "It is my duty to put my subjects first."

"Not at the cost of your life," said Fenton.

"It is the only way," Rafe insisted and glanced at me. "And with Aurora, we might just have a chance."

My uneasiness subsided—maybe all hope at repairing our relationship was not lost.

"Then it's settled," said Penelope. "I will make a potion to put the guards outside the dungeons to sleep. But you can only do it on the morning of the coronation when the rest of the guards are busy with the parade. It will only work on three or four guards for a short amount of time. If I had my other ingredients, I could have made a stronger brew, but unfortunately there is no time."

"It will have to do," Rafe said. "We only get one shot at this."

Tristan came closer and bent his head to talk to me softly. "Are you sure you are ready to do this?"

"Yes." In truth, I wasn't so sure. But we were out of options. I had to do it now or we might never get another chance like this again.

"You will have to open the portal somewhere close so you don't use up too much of your magic," said Penelope. "I will wait for you in the town. I know a place close by there where we can hide the children."

I nodded.

"You can stay here for the night." Rafe put on his hood and looked at Tristan and me. "Meet Danica at the main gate of the castle as the sun rises. I will have secured your posts by then, so she will be waiting there to confirm your credentials."

Danica joined him, her cloak and hood fastened in place. Without a backward glance, he left us in the small house in the alley and disappeared into the misty night with her. Kalen gave me a pitying look, hugged me quickly, and hurried after Rafe.

Tristan turned to me. "Get some rest. I will stand watch

tonight. We are not safe here, and the sooner we are done with this and get back to finding the Dagger, the better."

I nodded, too exhausted to argue. Rafe might need me here, but it was quite clear he didn't want me. Nevertheless, I had to do this. Erien and those children were not to blame for anything. I could not let them suffer for mistakes I may have made along the way. It was my job to make things right, or I would never be the queen my people needed me to be.

I sat on one of the small cots in the corner of the room and tried to glamour objects, but the glamour would only hold for a few moments before flickering and changing the object back to its original form. I flexed my fingers and tried to summon a ball of silver fire. My hand started to glow but never ignited. I frowned and studied my hand as if I could will it to burst into flames, but it didn't.

"Oof!" I huffed in frustration and lay back down on my bed.

"What's wrong?" asked Penelope.

"Nothing."

Penelope got up from her cot and came to sit beside me. "You just need to rest, Aurora. Your magic will return to full strength by tomorrow."

"What if it doesn't?" I whispered. "What if something goes wrong tomorrow in the castle?"

"Don't worry so much. Have faith in yourself." She put her hand on my arm. "I have faith in you. Your spirit magic needs time to recover. Once it does, all your powers will return to normal."

I looked over at Tristan, who sat in the corner looking alert. "Doesn't he ever need to sleep?" I asked Penelope softly.

"I can still hear you," Tristan muttered.

"The High Fae don't need much sleep," said Penelope in a low voice. "Immortals rarely do."

"Then why do I get so tired?"

Penelope smiled through the flickering light of the candle and lay back down on her cot. "You are not immortal yet, my dear," she said gently. "Your immortality will only set in sometime in your twenties, when you are at your prime. That is why you must be extra careful until then. You are not invincible, and you can be killed. Best keep that in mind tomorrow when you go to the castle."

THE CASTLE DUNGEONS

As DAWN ROSE over Caeleron Castle, we made our way through the deserted alleyways of the town toward the gates. I glamoured myself and Tristan, changing our features and hair to suit the disguise. Penelope was right—my magic had returned after a good night's sleep and was stronger than ever.

Caeleron town was different in the sunlight. Lemon-colored stone houses with thatched roofs were joined together by vaulted stone archways that spanned the tiny cobbled streets. We passed a few small artisan shops which were still shut, but blacksmiths were already at their anvils banging away. Some bakeries were open and had fresh bread cooling on their windowsills. Penelope got us a few hot bread rolls as we followed her to the northern gate of the city toward the massive fortress perched on top, like a colossus surveying its kingdom.

Danica was waiting for us outside the castle gates. The guards were inspecting credentials, and in the meantime I checked that we were sufficiently glamoured. Rafe had produced some false papers, and the guards, after speaking with Danica, raised the portcullis to let us through the main gatehouse. The massive vaulted entrance, which served as the only way into Caeleron

Castle, was decorated with intricate carvings. It was fortified by two towers filled with a whole garrison of archers. I took note of all their positions.

The entryway was like a tunnel. The walls must have been over twenty feet thick. According to Penelope, Caeleron Castle could hold over forty thousand warriors and had survived countless sieges. The portcullis itself was massive and would need at least two people to raise it. This was in no way going to be easy, that was for sure.

Once I was inside the massive castle, I could only stop and stare. I had been in fortresses before, but I had never imagined anything of Caeleron Castle's sheer enormity and scale.

As Danica led us through the outer bailey, a gigantic courtyard within the main curtain wall of the castle, black-clad soldiers roamed the battlements and barracks. Tents and market stalls were set up near the stables to service the growing number of guests that would be visiting for the coronation. I looked around —there didn't seem to be any Drakaar here, just ordinary soldiers and warrior-mages. If we were lucky, we could get in and out without causing too much damage. I could not take the chance of calling in Abraxas; burning down Rafe's ancestral home was not part of the plan. And as Abraxas had explained, summoning him drained a lot of magic from this world. He was only to be called when we had no other choice. We would have to do this alone.

We came to another walled gate within the main castle, and a pot-bellied man with a pockmarked face and short white hair was waiting for us with the guards. Danica spoke to him for a second, and he ushered us through the second gate into the inner bailey of the massive castle.

Within the inner walls stood a magnificent palace. Enormous towers spiked through the morning sky, and massive latticed windows lined the newer structures of the east and west wings. We traversed shaded walkways surrounded by beautiful landscaped gardens with fountains of exquisitely carved statues spraying water into ponds in graceful arcs. Snowy lilies and rose-tinted peonies, fragrant and delicate, provided bursts of vibrant color in the midst of the bright green lawns. Charmingly dressed noblewomen in swirling silk day dresses with crisp taffeta skirts, draped in velvet capes and cloaks and dripping with rows of pearls and sparkling gemstones, strolled along the garden paths on the arm of many a well-dressed gentleman. They had all come in from different parts of the kingdom for the coronation.

It was disturbing to see the nobility of this kingdom behaving as if it was Brandon Delacourt's right to take the throne from his king. I knew they were all scared of the archmage, mainly because of Morgana's backing and the presence of the Dark Queen by his side, but they didn't have to act like everything was as it should be.

Disgusted with the fickle nobles, I followed the little man through the opulent gardens to the kitchen gardens, which were growing every vegetable and herb I could think of. I had read about this castle in my books at the academy. Dorian the Great built this palace within the fortress as a royal residence. Then, a few hundred years later, it was Dorian the Second who went on to rebuild the palace, expanding on it and hiring artisans from Brandor to create an even grander set of buildings.

"Come on, come on. I don't have all day." The little potbellied man led us to the side entrance of the main palace, and we entered the kitchens. Immediately a heady concoction of delicious aromas and warmth from the numerous fires wafted toward me.

I could hardly believe the level of bustle in the castle kitchens. A huge hearth and several fireplaces surrounding six wooden worktables dominated the cavernous, vaulted room. These led out into a maze of smaller rooms joined together by huge stone archways. Broad wooden beams the size of tree trunks held up the structure. Kitchen helpers chopped, and kneaded, and stirred steaming hot pots of stewing vegetables and bubbling soups, dropping herbs and spices into them. Whole pigs and other meats roasted on spits in massive fireplaces, dripping hot fat into the fire that crackled and hissed as I stood by the warm hearth and rubbed my hands.

The cook gave Tristan and me instructions on our role for the next few days. As far as he knew, we were just some of the many slum children Danica had taken under her wing and helped get jobs. We were only temporary helpers and would have to leave as soon as the coronation was completed. We had to get to the dungeons and get the children out before then, or we would lose our chance.

The cook was still speaking. "Just because Danica got you this job doesn't mean you get paid if you don't work. Your main responsibility will be to help clear the dining room after the guests have left. For now, there are dishes to wash and utensils to scrub, so get to it." He pointed to a big stone basin piled high with cooking utensils.

I scrubbed and washed until my hands were red and raw. I healed them slowly so I would not draw attention. Tristan, as stoic as ever, finished his work as if it were just another mission he'd been ordered to do. Seeing the powerful High Fae prince reduced to scrubbing dishes in a kitchen made me smile. He looked so much more approachable when he didn't have swords of silver fire blazing in his hands. It also helped that the glamour I put on him dulled his strikingly handsome features, although it could do nothing about his height. The main problem had been regarding his swords. He had refused to give them up, of course, so I'd finally relented and glamoured the swords and let him keep them.

Once we had helped scrub the kitchens, we were given a simple warm meal of meat stew and crusty bread and sent to our quarters. I had to share with three girls who insisted on giggling and chatting, when I needed them to fall asleep so I could explore the palace to get my bearings. Tomorrow was the coronation and the wedding feast to celebrate the now not-so-secret marriage of Brandon and Calisto.

Once the coronation parade started, Tristan and I could sneak away into the dungeons. There would be a few guards, but Penelope's potion should take care of them. Getting into the dungeons would be the easy part—getting out, not so much. The main thing was to find the children and portal them out.

I hoped Rafe knew what he was doing. His plan seemed adequate, but there were so many things that could go wrong. What if Brandon decided he didn't need him and executed him on sight? I had seen what Brandon was capable of, and it was hard to imagine a friend doing all these terrible things.

"The new archmage is so handsome," one of the girls said, staring up at the ceiling. "That Calisto Blackwater is one lucky lady. She gets to be queen and gain a handsome husband all in one day."

"There is no one as handsome as Prince Rafael," said one of the other girls, sighing deeply. "He's a real prince. Archmage Delacourt is just an upstart."

"Shh, Amanda, it's treason to talk like that," the first girl said. They glanced hurriedly at me, but I pretended to be asleep.

"Prudence, your father is an archer in Delacourt's army. There is talk in the kitchens—is it true that he is holding the nobles' children prisoner in this very castle?"

"We are not supposed to talk about it, but yes," said Prudence, lowering her voice. "My father says Archmage Delacourt is even more dangerous than the Blackwaters."

"I don't believe Prince Rafael will let those children be executed," whispered Amanda.

"There is nothing he can do," said Prudence. "He has to surrender or the archmage will kill those poor children."

As soon as they fell asleep, I slipped out of my bed and snuck out of my room. I hurried through the dark, deserted hallways of the mist-shrouded castle. The passages that connected the fortress were lit sparingly with burning torches held in brackets on the walls at regular intervals.

We would have to go past the main corridors of the castle to get to the dungeons, which were situated deep under the great hall. I turned a corner to a brighter-lit corridor. The royal residence was huge and opulently designed, with stone paneling, intricately carved statues, and extravagant tapestries lining the passageways. I glanced into an open doorway where a massive ornate fireplace completed a luxuriously decorated chamber. I wished I were back in my warm bed at Silverthorne Castle, the only place I would call home. Instead I was sneaking around the castle of my enemy at night, hoping I didn't get caught. Tristan was scouring all the routes to exit the castle, and I had to make sure I knew the whole layout as well. Rafe had shown us the map, but we would only get one chance to do this. If we failed or were caught, those children could die.

A door opened behind me, and I froze in my tracks.

"You," said a female voice I recognized instantly. "Get me a glass of warm snowberry milk. I can't sleep."

I turned slowly to face the voice. I knew who it was, and I knew she couldn't recognize me, but my heart had started galloping in my chest. If I were caught, this would be the end.

I prayed my glamour was sufficient and turned. "Yes, my lady," I said to Leticia, bobbing a small curtsy and keeping my head lowered, when what I really wanted to do was walk over to her and slap her smug face. Penelope told me she abandoned Rafe as soon as he lost his crown and married Zorek Blackwater instead in her quest to become queen. But in a twisted turn of fate, she was now a widow, and it was her sister-in-law Calisto who was poised to take the crown.

Leticia's eyes flashed. "Well, what are you waiting for?" She crossed her arms, tapping her bejeweled-slippered foot. "Hurry up. I need my beauty sleep. I don't want that slut Calisto to get all the attention tomorrow." She dismissed me with a wave of her imperious hand.

My blood boiled, but I held my tongue and turned to go back

down to the kitchens. At this rate I would never be able to scope out all the castle routes.

I got Leticia her glass of snowberry milk and continued my rounds, barely making it back to my warm bed before the sun rose.

The bright morning sun streamed in through the small window of the room above the kitchens. I got up and washed my face with the little jug of water that had been given to us. It was almost empty, but the other girls had not gone down to the kitchens yet. They were sitting on one bed, huddled together and whispering fervently.

"Aren't we supposed to go downstairs?" I asked, eager to get on with it. But my curiosity was piqued.

"Haven't you heard?" Amanda said, her eyes wide like bright blue saucers.

"Heard what?"

"Prince Rafael surrendered this morning," said Prudence, adjusting her dress. "He's being held here in the dungeons."

My heartbeat sped up, but my relief was wholehearted. At least Delacourt hadn't killed him.

"Maybe Cook will let me take his food down to him in the dungeons," said Amanda in a dreamy voice.

"Don't be silly, Amanda," said Prudence. "None of us are allowed down there. Only the guards are. And in any case, he's as good as dead. He shouldn't have surrendered; the archmage will never let him live now."

Amanda covered her mouth with her hand to stifle her gasp. "Why? He's already surrendered, so why kill him?"

Prudence shook her head. "How naïve you are, Amanda. This is the way of the nobility. They kill and cheat and lie to get to power, and when they get there they kill and cheat some more to stay there."

I didn't want to hear any more of her rants about the nobility in Eldoren. It was quite clear the people were dissatisfied with the way the kingdom was run. But with Delacourt in power it would not get any better. The only way to improve the situation was to put Rafe on the throne where he belonged. He genuinely cared about the people and would be a good king. I just hoped when he was king, he would put aside our differences and help us defeat Morgana and her growing army. I was worried about him. We had to get down to the dungeons, and there wasn't much time left. The coronation parade would begin soon, and we only had about an hour before the procession got back to the castle.

Down in the kitchens, preparations for the coronation feast were in full swing. Whispers about the Prince of Eldoren surrendering to the archmage had reached every corner of the castle. Most of them spoke of him as a hero who had sacrificed himself and his crown for the sake of the imprisoned children. I smiled. So this was Rafe's plan. He knew how the people would react if he gave himself up. They now loved him more than ever. Delacourt would never gain the support of the people now, whatever he might do.

The kitchens were even more bustling this morning with fresh produce brought in from farms all around the valley and fragrant herbs freshly picked from the castle gardens. Fluffy golden-brown bread and flaky pastries baked in big wood-fire ovens while the cook frosted beautiful small cakes with a delicious buttercream. I couldn't resist tasting it before the cook slapped my hand away and continued his work. I quickly got back to my chores; I didn't need to give them a reason to throw me out, especially today. But I couldn't stop thinking about Rafe in the dungeons. I hoped he was okay.

The morning went by in a flash, and I heard trumpets blare in the outer bailey, signaling the coronation festivities were beginning. Traditionally, the coronation parade was to begin in the town and make its way up to the castle so the citizens of Eldoren could cheer their new king. But this time the procession began at the entrance to the castle in the outer bailey—an environment that Delacourt could control. Only a select number of people were allowed inside the castle walls to see the splendor of the coronation parade. Delacourt knew the people of this kingdom disliked him, and he didn't want to take a chance on being in a hostile crowd.

Now we had very little time to complete our mission. The procession would take about an hour to reach the throne room in the main palace, and we had to be gone before then.

"Back to work, everyone, the feast is nearly upon us." The cook clapped his hands hurriedly. "Faster, faster."

I looked over at Tristan and he signaled me. It was time. I snuck into a corner and glamoured myself to become invisible. Tristan came over and I did the same for him. We slipped out of the kitchens and ran through the castle corridors to a set of stone stairs that led down to the palace dungeons.

The main palace was basically deserted except for the kitchen staff and a few guards, since everyone was outside watching the procession.

We descended the dark stone stairwell to the dungeons in the easternmost tower and came to a landing where four palace guards in blue-and-white uniforms were passed out on their chairs. Two were sleeping soundly with their heads on a table, their weapons limp at their sides. Tristan had taken the guards their breakfast that morning and had slipped Penelope's sleeping potion in it.

"How did you manage to convince Cook to let you take the dungeon guards their food?"

Tristan shrugged. "The boy who usually takes it hurt his leg."

I raised an eyebrow.

"With a little help, of course," Tristan added with a half smile.

I rolled my eyes. "Of course."

Tristan bent down, took the keys from the guards, and opened the dungeon door—a slab of heavy wood over a foot thick. It creaked and groaned as it opened, a dank musty smell wafting out. We descended the rough stone stairs, slick with moss in places, into the bowels of the castle. Penelope had told me about these dungeons, a place of horror and brutal torture in the time of the old kings. Now they were mainly dimly lit prisons with torches attached to iron sconces along the wall. These dungeons were a part of the old structure of Caeleron Castle built nearly a thousand years ago. They ran in a series of maze-like caves twenty feet below the castle.

We kept to the shadows and moved by the dim light of the torches, which were recently lit. As the shadows from the flickering torches settled, I could see ragged figures huddled in corners as we moved past. I checked all the cells, but I didn't want to call out Rafe's name in case there were more guards down here. When we reached the last one, dread raced down my spine.

"He's not here." I spun around. "Maybe we should go back and recheck all the cells."

"There's no more time," whispered Tristan, proceeding farther into the darkness of the dungeons. "Maybe they have put him where the children are being held, in the last cells beyond the ruins of the ancient vaults."

I nodded, my heart hammering in my chest as I followed Tristan. The maze-like corridors darkened. There were no more torches on the walls as we reached the end of the prison cells. We didn't want to use magic until it was absolutely necessary, so Tristan held back his powers. I only used a smidgeon of mage magic, creating a ball of light in my hand, one of the first things I had been taught when I discovered I had magic.

We entered a high-ceilinged room, the remnants of a vast vault where the old kings used to keep their treasure. Now, of course, it was empty, but I could picture what it must have looked like with chests of gold and jewels heaped all over the place. Impressive pillars rose above us, branching out into gothic arches and lined with rows of decaying statues devoured by time. I gasped and moved closer to Tristan when I spotted a pile of bones at the base of one of the statues.

A chill had seeped into the very stone around us, and the damp air was putrid with the stench of blood and decay. I thought of the children and Erien, who must be so scared to be trapped here for who knows how long. That thought made me press on. The map Rafe had shown us was stamped into my brain. If he was right about the layout of the dungeons, then the children should be imprisoned in cells that lay just beyond this hall.

We were nearly there.

Through the stillness of the dungeons, I heard voices, the sound of someone crying. "They are here," I said softly, moving toward the sound.

Tristan had to bend as he followed me through an archway and into the tunnel at the end of the hall. There were no torches burning here, and we were plunged into pitch darkness. I removed my glamour and held up my palm, the mage light shining on the rows of iron bars lining small cave-like cubicles in which the children were held.

Dirty hands grasped the bars and peered through. "Aurora! Is that you?"

"Erien," I gasped and ran toward my cousin. His face was drawn and pale, dark circles shadowing his once-bright blue eyes. My blood boiled. I could kill Delacourt for putting them here in a state not fit for animals.

Suddenly there was a sound behind us. I spun around as Tristan yelled a warning and dashed toward the mouth of the tunnel. But it was too late; a heavy iron portcullis came crashing down over the arched entrance, sealing us in.

Tristan's eyes narrowed. "Create the portal now." He held up the keys we had stolen from the sleeping guards. "I will release them from their cells. We need to leave now."

I took off my amulet, willing my magic to awake, but it didn't. "Tristan, something's wrong."

Tristan drew his sword, but it didn't light up. "Something is blocking my magic as well."

Increasing the mage light in my hand, I looked closely at the walls lining the tunnel, touched them, and gasped as realization took hold. "Blackened iron."

I spun around. The blackened iron was everywhere—the bars were made of it, and it was hammered into the very stone that lined the cramped tunnel. My fae magic would not work in here, and neither would Tristan's.

We were trapped.

THE END OF THE ROAD

"I TOLD YOU SHE WOULD COME," said a voice I recognized immediately.

A light emerged in the dark hall behind the blackened iron portcullis as Calisto and Brandon came into view.

"Aurora Firedrake behind bars at last," sneered Brandon, stepping forward into the light, his hands clasped behind him. "My predecessor swore it couldn't be done. I guess that's why I am archmage now." Delacourt was wearing his coronation robes, cloth of gold and purple adorned with ermine and studded with amethysts the size of duck eggs. His light blond hair was styled elaborately; upon it rested a gold crown that he would soon replace with the more ornate and heavy state crown of Eldoren during his coronation. That was something I didn't intend to let happen.

At least that was the plan—until now.

"Did you think I wouldn't know what you were up to?" Brandon's eyes glittered at the sight of me. "I know your kind only too well. You and Prince Rafael are so predictable and noble. I was sure one of you would come for the children. Imagine my surprise when he surrendered and you walked straight into my grasp as well. With Silverthorne's grandson in my custody, getting rid of you all was almost too easy."

My hands balled into fists as I tried to call up my fae magic, but it wouldn't respond. "Where is Rafe?"

Delacourt laughed. "Oh, our little prince is not down here. I decided to let him join the festivities." His eyes narrowed. "Heavily guarded and in chains. You and your fae prince are not invited, of course." He pouted. "Don't feel bad—you can understand why I had to do this."

"You already have Rafe in custody. Let the children go."

Brandon raised an eyebrow. "I don't think I am going to do that just yet. I quite enjoy having all the nobles loyal to me."

"They are not loyal to you, Brandon," I spat. "They are only doing what you tell them to because they're afraid for their children's lives."

Brandon chuckled. "Isn't that the same thing? Everyone needs some incentive to ensure loyalty."

I tried to keep him talking. I needed to find out more about his plans. "Loyalty is not demanded—it is earned."

Brandon's blue eyes narrowed. "Like you and Rafe earned the loyalty of that raggedy group, the Silver Swords." He burst out laughing. "Your dear prince is so trusting, he doesn't even know you have a traitor in your midst."

My eyes darted to Tristan and my mind scrambled to recall all the faces I had seen in the safe house. Any one of them could be the traitor. Delacourt had known we were coming.

"At least my way is foolproof," Brandon continued. "The nobles will never go against me openly. The only thing that ensures complete and unwavering loyalty is fear."

Tristan snarled and moved forward, but I shot him a warning glare. We had to keep Brandon talking if we were going to figure a way out of this mess. He seemed to be one step ahead of us, and I had to find out more information on what he and Morgana were up to. Taking Eldoren was clearly only a part of the bigger plan.

Penelope would soon realize something was wrong. She would find a way to get us out.

"Where are the Drakaar?" I crossed my arms in front of me, hoping to look defiant, but I was trying to keep myself from trembling at the thought. I had to find out what was going on with Morgana. What was she planning?

"Why? Did you miss them?" Brandon smirked. "The Drakaar are making sure your little princeling Rafael doesn't get up to any of his tricks."

My blood chilled at the thought of what the Drakaar could do to Rafe. Mage magic was no match for them.

I gave Brandon a pointed look. I wasn't going to let him know he fazed me. "And you came down here with only ordinary soldiers for protection." I raised an eyebrow. "I would think that Morgana would have her best minions here if she knew I was coming."

"You think too much of yourself, Princess. Morgana knows I am more than capable of dealing with you myself."

I cocked my head to the side. "Like you dealt with me in Brandor the last time we met?" I didn't want to push him too far, but I still needed to goad him to reveal more of his plans.

Brandon frowned. "Morgana made me archmage for a reason," he said tightly. "I gave her what no one else could."

I smirked. "I highly doubt that."

Delacourt lifted his chin. "I have given her an army of mages. I have taken Eldoren."

"And you killed my granduncle and the Blackwaters to do it," I spat, looking over at Calisto in the shadows. "I don't know how Calisto even looks at you after you murdered her father and brother."

Calisto stepped closer, her hair shining gold in the fiery light of the torches the soldiers behind them carried. But her eyes—

I took a step back. Her eyes were no longer her own. They

were the color of obsidian, and darkness seeped out of them, covering the whole iris until no white could be seen.

"Lilith!"

The Dark Queen had taken over Calisto's body. She gave me a cold, thin smile. "Calisto is gone. She did put up quite a fight, though." Lilith flexed her fingers and dark shadows swirled from her fingertips toward me. There was nowhere to run, so I stood my ground as the shadows moved through the bars of the portcullis and encircled me like thin ropes, tightening around me until I couldn't move. "Did you really think we wouldn't know you were here? Did you really think it would be so easy to rescue the children?" She smiled, as cold and sinister as a snake.

"You should have stayed dead, Lilith," Tristan snarled, stepping forward. The shadows around me recoiled instantly, recognizing the dark prince even without his magic. "But it does give me the opportunity to make sure you do this time."

"Prince Tristan." Lilith inspected her nails briefly as the shadows dissipated completely. "It has been a while."

I stood beside Tristan, putting up a mage shield. Blackened iron only worked on fae magic and didn't affect mages. My mage powers weren't going to get us out of here, but it was something. "You two know each other?"

Tristan's eyes darkened. "We've met."

"Briefly." Lilith laughed, but her voice was filled with contempt. "Who doesn't know the infamous Prince of the Night Court? Put down your swords, Prince Tristan. The shadows may fear you, but your silver fire will not work in here."

"We know about the mines in Brandor, and we will stop you," I said, sounding more confident than I felt. Without my fae magic I felt vulnerable, weak.

"You have been a busy little bee, haven't you?" Brandon gave me a sly smile. "I heard about your exploits in Brandor. I hope you said your goodbyes to your friend, the pirate prince. Plans are already in motion to remove Santino and his father from power.

The Detori family will rule Brandor, and our supply of blackened iron will never run out. Soon, Izadora and her whole fae army will be rendered useless." He gave me a dry look. "But you already know this." He turned his eyes on Tristan. "Your only choice is to join us. If you do not, the High Fae will be wiped out from Avalonia forever."

"The dwarves will never agree to help you," Tristan said. "Creating weapons of blackened iron is forbidden by the treaty."

Brandon grinned and flashed his white teeth. "Greygate has already fallen, and I'm sure we can persuade them once we have the *Book of Abraxas*. And now we know where the last key is. Resistance is futile, really."

"You're lying," I snapped, but my gut twisted. "My granduncle would never give up his key."

"Well, he did give up its location," Brandon said simply. "With a little persuasive deception, of course," he added, looking over at Lilith. "After that he was of no use to us. The Drakaar are on their way now to retrieve the last key. So you can see why they are a little busy at the moment. And now that I have you in custody, Rafael will have no choice but to kneel to me. Torturing you before his very eyes will be exquisite. I will be able to make him do anything I want." His eyes brightened at the prospect.

"Rafe doesn't care what happens to me," I said with a shrug. "You're wasting your time."

"I think not." Brandon grinned. "Your days are numbered, Aurora Shadowbreaker."

I raised my hand and summoned my magic. I was the Dawnstar. Abraxas had said in Elfi the cuffs of blackened iron could not hold me. But this was more than just cuffs. The blackened iron of the Drakaar was blanketing my magic like a shroud. It was everywhere, even below my feet, embedded into the very stone floor on which I stood. My fae magic would not awake. In anger I sent a mage fire strike at Brandon and Lilith, which he deflected easily.

Brandon chuckled at my failed attempt to summon my fae magic. "I told you your fae powers won't work here." He put his hand to his chest, making a show of looking hurt. "Didn't you believe me?"

"Convince your daughter to give up this foolishness, Lilith," said Tristan. "Morgana will never be strong enough to bend the Dark Lord to her will, even with the Dagger and the *Book of Abraxas*. Once he is free, he will kill her and take over Avalonia."

Lilith smiled, her eyes cold and cruel. "He might if it is Morgana who wakes him." She laughed loudly. "You really have no idea who is actually behind this, do you?"

"What do you mean?" I asked, furrowing my brow.

"Fools!" said Lilith. "Morgana is only a front. There is someone more powerful in the shadows. And you cannot stop him. These plans were set in motion long before you were even born."

Brandon's eyes darted from me to Lilith. "Enough," he said, stepping forward. "They will find out what they need to know in due time. By then it will be too late."

"I could summon the dragon," I ventured, stumbling over the words, clawing for an answer in my mind. "Abraxas would destroy all of you."

Brandon gave me a sardonic smile and raised an eyebrow. But it was Lilith who spoke. "Maybe he would, if you could summon him, Dawnstar. But the great dragon cannot hear you; the blackened iron will take care of that. The codex was very specific about the effects of blackened iron on High Fae and Dragonlords."

"You have the Fae Codex?"

Her twisted smile showed me a set of sparkling white teeth. "Who do you think helped Andromeda steal it?"

"You were the one who gave her the blackened iron cuffs to subdue my magic in Elfi," I stated, finally understanding.

"You are a clever girl," Lilith said. "But not clever enough. At first I thought the cuffs would hold you, but your magic is too strong. The codex has shown me you need to be completely surrounded by it so that its effects work on High Fae as powerful as the two of you. Soon Morgana's whole army will be equipped with it, which will render your fae army utterly useless."

"Over my dead body," I snarled, staring down both of them, my spine stiff and my arms crossed before me. I looked strong, but inside I was panicking. If Morgana's army wielded weapons of blackened iron, the fae would fall like flies.

Lilith shrugged. "Have it your way. I'm sure the archmage can oblige."

Brandon laughed. "See you later, Aurora. I will leave you to say your farewells. I have a coronation to attend. I hope you said goodbye to your dear Prince Rafael while you were busy plotting against me. This kingdom can only have one king. I want him to see my triumph before I have him executed in front of all his so-called loyal supporters, who will not raise a hand to help him—as long as I have their children, of course." He turned to leave but stopped for a moment. "Once the feast is over tonight, Prince Rafael will be dead, and there is nothing you can do to stop me."

I waited until the light of their torches had retreated into the passage to release the breath I didn't even know I was holding. I had to find a way out of this. But Lilith was right; I couldn't summon Abraxas even if I wanted to. I had tried, but he hadn't responded. My ring sat cold on my finger, its magic veiled by the evil-infused iron.

Tristan and I released Erien and the rest of the children from their cells. Erien and I hugged while the others shuffled together in a corner of the tunnel and eyed me warily.

There was one figure who remained in their cell. I moved past Erien, holding up my hand for light. It was a girl with long dark hair wearing mage robes from the Academy of Evolon.

"Vivienne," I gasped. It had been months since I had last seen my best friend. I stepped closer, but she moved back into the shadows, out of my reach.

I froze.

"Viv," I said in a small voice. How could I explain the past few months and why I'd never said goodbye when I left?

"Why did you come?" Vivienne said, suddenly stepping into the light. "We don't need you here. Haven't you caused enough damage as it is?"

"Viv, I . . ." I stumbled over the words. "This is not what I intended."

"You never intend to do anything, do you? It just so happens that every time you come near us, someone ends up dead. First Professor Dekela, then the king, and now . . ."

I shook my head. "This is Brandon and Morgana's doing, not mine, Vivienne. Please just hear me out."

"Brandon is a monster, but he hates you. It's because of you we are here. And it's because of you they are gone—" Her voice broke off and she started to cry.

Erien brushed past me to put his arm around Vivienne, looking at me sharply. "She lost both her brothers in the fight when Brandon's men came to take her. Give her some time."

Vivienne looked at me with bloodshot eyes. "Do you know why they came for me and not for one of my brothers, Aurora?" Her voice was sharp and pained. "Do you?"

I shook my head. I knew what she meant, but I didn't want to believe this was my fault too.

"They came because I was your friend," she said softly. "The Foxmoor family is not important. It's because of you I'm in here and my brothers are both dead."

Tears welled in my eyes for my friend's grief. "I didn't know. I'm so sorry, Viv," I said, my voice small, broken. What could I say? I couldn't bring them back.

She glared at me, her eyes still red and full of anger. "No, you never know, do you? You never know what a mess you leave behind. Everything is about you and only you. The rest of us could fall off the end of the world and you wouldn't give a damn."

"That's enough, Vivienne," Erien said finally and turned to me, his arm falling away from Vivienne. "I am glad to see you, Aurora. I'm sorry you got dragged into this mess."

I hugged my cousin. "I'm here to help."

"I know," said Erien, running his fingers through his beautiful blond hair, which was now crusted with dirt and grime. "I know I shouldn't have, but when Vivienne was taken, I . . ." He cast a quick glance at Vivienne, who smiled faintly.

Tristan came over to me and put his hand on my arm. "We will find a way out of this, Aurora. We always do."

I nodded as I went through all the options in my head, trying to be optimistic. Maybe Penelope would realize something was wrong and send help, but by then it might be too late. I sent out a silent call to Abraxas again, but he didn't respond.

I tried not to let my anxiety show. There had to be a way out of here. Tristan was right, I had been in situations like this before, but I'd always had my magic to fall back on. This time was different, and I had never realized how vulnerable and useless I felt without my fae powers. But I still had my mage magic.

I gathered what power I had left and sent a fire strike at the iron bars that held us in; mage fire enveloped the iron in a blaze of golden flames, and for a moment I thought it was working. I tried to infuse more power into it, causing the fire to burn hotter, but it was not enough. The blackened iron bars stood strong. The only thing that could melt blackened iron was silver fire, or fae fire, which burned at a much hotter temperature than the fire created by mages. It was what made Tristan and the fire-fae warriors of Elfi the most feared in the seven kingdoms and beyond. But Tristan's magic refused to surface, and my mage magic had already started to weaken.

I slid down the wall and sat on the floor. I was so tired. It had been days since I had slept properly, and all the worry and anxiety weighed heavily on my shoulders. I had been so sure I could get these children out, and now I was imprisoned here with them.

Not to mention Rafe was going to be executed in a few hours and there was nothing I could do.

Suddenly a deep voice spoke in my head. *"What are you doing sitting in a dungeon, Aurora?"*

I jumped up. "Where have you been?" I practically shouted out loud. The others looked at me like I had gone mad. But Tristan's eyes sparkled—he knew who I was talking to.

"There was a patch when I couldn't sense you," said Abraxas, *"but I heard your call. It was faint, so I came to see what was happening. Are you hiding from someone?"*

"No, I'm not sitting down here because I want to," I snapped. "The whole tunnel is lined with blackened iron. I'm trapped."

I proceeded to tell him what had happened.

"So, break down the door and go stop Brandon," he said matter-of-factly.

"I can't." I threw my arms up in exasperation. "That's what I'm trying to tell you. My mage magic can't burn through the blackened iron, and my fae magic doesn't work in here. I've tried."

"Well then you haven't tried hard enough," the ancient dragon snapped back. *"Haven't I explained to you before that there is no dark power that can contain the Dawnstar?"*

I frowned. "But that was just two small cuffs. Lilith said the codex told her this much blackened iron can contain High Fae magic."

"You haven't been listening, Aurora," said Abraxas, exasperated. *"You are not just a High Fae, just as you are not just a Dragonlord. If this blackened iron could really contain your magic, you would not be able to speak to me. Lilith made you believe that you can't, so you didn't try hard enough. You lost faith. And what have I told you about losing faith? Do I have to say it again and again until it gets into that thick head of yours?"*

I held up my hands. "I know, I know. Nothing is impossible."

"Exactly," said the great dragon, satisfied. *"The magic of the Dawnstar only appears when you have complete faith in who you truly*

are. But you go on doubting yourself despite the many instances where you have been shown the truth of your powers. Remember, the magic of the Dawnstar is different from all other fae magic, although it is inextricably tied to it. The light you produce when you access that particular power is a culmination of all the five powers of the fae directed by your will, your innermost being. With magic like yours, you can do anything. You just need the will to do it. Now let us begin."

TO TAKE A CASTLE

ABRAXAS DIRECTED me to place my hands on the walls of the tunnel, fingers spread out flat against the stone. Within it I could feel the blackened iron surrounding me on all sides, pulsating with an ancient evil that sucked the magic from the High Fae. But I was not going to let it get the better of me. I was the Dawnstar. I could do this.

The festivities had begun. I could hear the noise from the great hall in the dungeons. Soon Rafe would be executed, and I had to get out if I was going to prevent that from happening. The thought of Rafe gave me strength; I had to help him.

I searched for light magic and understood more of what Abraxas was trying to teach me. It was a culmination of all my fae powers. Knowing how it worked made it easier to access. I pushed away all doubts from my mind, gathered all the threads of my magic, and plunged inward, deep inside myself, where the source of my magic lay. The Dawnstar was there waiting to be called forth, shining like a beacon within my very soul. I opened myself to it and let it rise within me.

"Good," said Abraxas, *"now infuse the darkness in the iron with light, just as you did with the cuffs; that will nullify its power. Mind you,*

you will need much more power to achieve this. It will not be easy, but it should work."

I grinned. It was good to know Abraxas was there. If I was doing anything stupid, he didn't have any qualms about popping into my head and telling me so. And if he thought I could do this, I knew I could.

I pushed my magic into the walls, and the darkness pulsated beneath my fingers. I could feel the veins of blackened iron around me as the darkness clung to my magic like a leech.

Erien watched me, his eyes as wide as saucers. "What is she doing?"

"What she's doing—" Tristan drew his swords and threw a quick glance at Erien, "—is getting us out of here."

I gathered more light magic and pushed it into the walls, guiding it through the stone, surrounding the blackened iron. Power seared through my veins as the light of the Dawnstar engulfed the blackened iron, which seemed to scream and pull away like a trapped beast, but I strengthened my will and held on, pushing more and more power into the walls around me.

The darkness that surrounded me seemed endless. My hands became clammy, and my body began to vibrate with the pressure. There was so much dark magic here that it threatened to engulf my light completely, gnawing at it like a ravening beast. But still I held on. I couldn't let go, not yet. Rafe's life depended on it.

I braced myself and reached deeper into the well of light that now lay wide open for me to use, drawing up immense power as my whole body started to glow. I pushed the magic into the walls and the tunnel lit up with white light, causing the darkness to shriek and flee, dissipating into nothing.

Tristan's swords blazed with silver fire, burning brighter than before as he twirled them in his hands. "Nicely done," he growled.

His magic was back, and so was mine.

I smiled at Tristan and flexed my fingers as a ball of silver fire formed in my glowing palm. "We're not out of danger yet."

Erien came over to me. "What you just did was impossible, Aurora."

"Don't ever underestimate the Dawnstar, boy," said Tristan.

"Shield them, Tristan," I said as I released my magic on the blackened iron portcullis.

Tristan threw up a hasty shield to surround the others just as a blast of pure silver fire, hotter than anything mages could produce, burst from my palm and melted the bars as if they were butter.

Vivienne and Erien gaped at me as Tristan ushered everyone out of the dark tunnel and into the ruins of the great arched hall that lay at the end of the dungeons.

Torches flared in the passageways around us. Brandon's mage guards were coming.

Tristan glanced at me. "Create the portal. We need to get them out now!"

Erien put his arm around Vivienne. "Hurry, Aurora, they're coming."

I took a deep breath. I could do this; I was trained by the best. I turned to Tristan. "Keep the guards busy."

The fae prince glowered at me, silver sparks flashing within his twilight-blue eyes. His swords flared brighter with raging silver fire, dispersing the shadows and lighting up the pillars of the great underground hall. "With pleasure," he snarled and lunged for the first guard.

I hurriedly summoned my magic, opening my will to the growing light inside me. After leaving the confines of the tunnel, my magic grew effortlessly. I tried to contain my excitement. I didn't want anyone to know how relieved I was that it was back. Being in that tunnel had scared me, and for the first time in my life I was grateful for everything I had learned—not just an acceptance of my fate, but a sense that I should never take my gifts for granted.

The portal expanded until it was big enough for the children to pass through.

Erien and I herded the children through, and Vivienne stepped into it without even looking at me. I felt a piece of my heart break, but I steeled myself against the emotions that threatened to engulf me. This was not the time to be emotional. I had to be focused.

Erien was the last to go. I clasped his hand. "Penelope will be waiting for you. She will know what to do."

He nodded, disappearing into the portal, and I closed it behind him. It would be a while before I would be able to open one again. Holding it open for so many to pass through had drained my spirit magic considerably, but this time I could manage it better. I knew it could affect the intensity of my other fae powers as well, but I would make do with whatever magic I had left.

I turned to see guards lying face down or flat on their backs strewn all around the hall, Tristan standing over them like an avenging angel. More were coming; I could hear voices in the tunnel.

"Follow me," I whispered to Tristan, moving toward the wall and feeling for the stone that was supposed to reveal the secret passage Rafe told us about. I scanned my memory for the maps to remember exactly where it was.

"Are you sure it's here?" growled Tristan, gathering his magic to face the oncoming guards.

I searched frantically around on the wall. "No."

Finally, a stone in the wall triggered the other stones to shift, revealing the secret passage. Tristan and I got in and closed it as more guards entered the underground hall.

I heard their faint voices. "Where did they go?" Their voices drained away as we moved deeper into the passageway.

"I guess it pays to have a castle as your childhood home," said Tristan as we traversed the damp stone tunnel. "We were lucky Rafe knew about these passages or we would still be trapped down there."

We ran through the tunnels. By now Delacourt would know we had escaped his cell and every soldier in the castle would be on the lookout for us. If we didn't manage to get to Rafe and open the main gate to let the army through, we could lose Eldoren.

The tunnel ended in rough stone steps that led upward to a stone door. There was no handle, so I searched for a trigger stone in the wall beside it. Finally a loose stone clicked, opening the door. We appeared in a shadowy, curtained alcove behind a tapestry in the main corridor, which led to the great hall and the festivities.

I glamoured both of us to become invisible as we stepped out into the brightly lit corridor. My spirit magic was shaky because of the portal I had recently opened, and I hoped the glamour would hold long enough to reach the great hall—and Rafe. We wove our way through the throng of glittering guests and pompous nobles and into the great hall, a vast, cavernous room with a vaulted ceiling held up by stone pillars adorned with a garden of fresh flowers. Massive iron chandeliers gleaming with thousands of candles illuminated the room as the nobility of Eldoren sparkled and danced beneath them.

Brandon was sitting on a raised dais on his throne, the heavy state crown of Eldoren already resting on his blond head. Dark shadows stood behind him. Drakaar! I took in their positions; there were only four of them, but I knew dealing with the Drakaar was going to make this much more difficult than it already was.

I spotted Rafe tied to a pillar nearby, surrounded by at least a dozen guards, with heavy chains resting beside his feet and manacles attached to his ankles. I scanned the room quickly for Brandon's other soldiers and took note of all their positions. A row of great arched doors lined one side of the room, opening out into the courtyard and gardens of the inner bailey, flanked by scores of black-clad guards.

We wound our way through the crowd of chattering nobility

and others who supported Brandon's sudden rise to power, and stopped in a shadowy alcove close to the pillar where Rafe was chained.

It was time. I nodded at Tristan and removed my amulet, which until now had hidden my power from the outside world.

Rafe looked up and scanned the room. I knew he had felt it, felt my magic awakening—and very soon the others would too.

Lilith stood up abruptly from her throne beside Brandon, real fear in her eyes as she hurriedly glanced around. "She's here." The Dark Queen in Calisto's body looked at Brandon, and her voice shook slightly as dark shadows started to form around her like a shield. "The Dawnstar is free."

Rafe smiled at Lilith. "Of course she is. Did you really think your puny dungeon could hold her?"

I was startled by the pride and conviction in his voice.

It was now or never.

I removed the glamour that hid us, and my swords lit up with silver fire as Tristan and I unleashed ourselves on the unsuspecting guards.

The great hall of Caeleron Castle erupted into chaos as we raced toward Rafe. The chain around his wrists was already strangling a guard's neck as I slashed through Delacourt's guards, opening a path forward.

More dark shadows seeped out of Lilith, and she directed them toward Rafe. Shadow Demons sprang up around us as the Drakaar converged, cutting us off. I threw out a hasty shield, protecting Rafe from the shadows as he fought the guards as best he could with restraints still holding him back.

Brandon, emboldened by the presence of the Drakaar, moved toward Rafe.

Tristan glanced at me hurriedly. "Go help him. I will hold them off." He lunged at the Drakaar at the same time I did.

I slashed and swerved, cutting through the arm of one Drakaar who got in my way. He staggered backward as I shot through the crowd—there was no time to kill him. I had to get to Rafe before Brandon did.

Rafe fell to his knees as Lilith's shadows completely surrounded him while her dark magic held him in place. He struggled to free himself. Brandon drew his sword as he advanced on Rafe. A soldier with the chain still around his neck lay dead beside the prince. Rafe's hands were still bound, but he managed to pick up the fallen guard's sword.

This time I didn't even need to think. My hands lit up as I flung out a bolt of white light at Lilith, pushing her back. She screeched and stumbled, falling to the floor. Abraxas had told me the light magic of the Dawnstar would only harm demons, but I didn't want to risk killing her while she was still in Calisto's body. If I could get my hands on her, I might be able to remove the Dark Queen from her host and save Calisto.

The shadows withdrew their hold on Rafe, freeing him and returning hurriedly to their queen. She wrapped herself in a cocoon of darkness.

Brandon brought his sword down on Rafe's head.

Metal clashed as Rafe held up the sword of the fallen guard, blocking Brandon's blow.

I flung a small strike of magic at the chains that held him, and the manacles fell away. Rafe pushed himself up swiftly as Brandon struck again. The fight was short, as Rafe swiftly disarmed his enemy and Brandon's sword clattered away from him. Brandon scrambled backward.

A powerful bolt of dark magic hit me in the back. I cried out, falling to my knees.

Drakaar!

"Aurora!" Rafe shouted and ran toward me.

"Don't let them get away," shouted Brandon from the dais. "Bring me Rafael's head!"

I was winded, but I quickly healed myself and pushed myself up in time to avoid an obsidian sword that came whizzing toward me. Tristan was engaged in battle with three of the Drakaar, but the one I had cut on the arm was targeting me.

I spun and ducked. Magic sizzled in my hands and I unleashed it on my attacker. The Drakaar's mouth opened in a silent scream, sharp canines flashing as a blast of white light hit him squarely in the chest, burning him from the inside out.

Rafe ran up beside me, his gray eyes smoldering as they locked with mine. "I'm glad you made it."

"Don't look so surprised. Did you think I would leave you here?"

"The thought had crossed my mind," he muttered, looking over at Tristan, who was busy dismembering guards and Drakaar alike. Two of the Drakaar were on the ground, their heads severed from their bodies, but one managed to slip away into the crowd.

I smiled faintly as I slashed my sword across an oncoming guard's chest. "We need to get to the gate."

"Go!" Tristan growled and turned to re-engage the guards. Tristan Nightshade on a killing spree was not someone to mess with.

More guards had lined up, blocking our path to the doors. I raised my hand and pushed. My magic erupted in a flash of light, and the guards were thrown out of the way. We dashed through the large arched doors leading out to the gardens.

"Archers!" someone shouted as dozens of arrows released from their bows and came flying at us from all sides. I raised my hands and the arrows stopped mid-flight, dropping like stones around us as we ran.

"Not fast enough," said Tristan, appearing on the other side of me, swords blazing in both hands. "You should have stopped the arrows as soon as they left their bows."

I glared at Tristan as I slashed and twirled, cutting down a guard and flinging my magic at others as they got in our way. "Sorry, I was a bit preoccupied with the dozens of guards chasing us," I snapped as we raced through the gardens and past the gurgling fountains, trampling flowering bushes as the guards pursued us relentlessly.

He glared back at me, cutting down two guards at the same time. "Then you should always be on guard," he growled, always the critic, always pushing me to be better.

Rafe cleared his throat. "If you two have finished, we still have to get through those gates."

Soldiers swarmed around us as we backed each other and fought for our lives, but the guards kept coming. The inner gate was shut, and a heavy iron portcullis barred our path to the outer bailey. Arrows rained down on us from the walls, but I had created a shield to cover all three of us. My hands shook as I struggled with the power it took to hold it and fight at the same time. Beads of sweat had formed on my brow, and I felt my shield flicker. We had to get through the gate—it was the only way out.

Shadow Demons started to appear around us, and my shield fell. Tristan's swords had already started slashing through them as I directed bolts of white light with one hand and kept a grip on my sword with the other.

From the corner of my eye I saw a dark shape, moving faster than an ordinary mortal, come up behind Rafe.

Before I could warn him, the Drakaar had Rafe in a stranglehold, his knife at Rafe's throat. "Curb your magic, Dawnstar, or I will cut him from ear to ear."

I stopped dead in my tracks as a mind-numbing fear pooled in my stomach. One wrong move and Rafe could die.

"Call off your dog." His eyes darted to Tristan.

"Tristan," I snapped.

Delacourt's guards surrounded us as Tristan lowered his sword.

Brandon sauntered up, four more Drakaar in tow. Their black swords seemed to absorb light as they moved toward us.

I kept an eye on Rafe as I faced Brandon. "Hiding behind the Drakaar again, are we, Brandon?"

Brandon smirked. "More of them came as quickly as they could after they heard we had you locked up in the dungeon." He frowned. "I don't know how you got out—the blackened iron should have held you until they got here."

I shrugged. "Well, I guess you don't know me very well, Brandon."

He adjusted his ermine-lined cloak on his shoulders and pretended to flick some dirt off it. "Oh, I know you only too well, Princess." He threw a glance at Rafe, the knife in the Drakaar's hand pressed to his skin. "I know you will never make a move as long as I have a knife to your lover's throat."

My eyes darted to Tristan. He would be ready to fight on my signal. I had come here to help Rafe get this throne back, and I wasn't going to let Brandon win. If I made one wrong move, Rafe could die. There was only one way to end this.

I turned my gaze back to Brandon. "Like I said, you don't know me at all, Brandon."

I gathered my magic slowly, my eyes fixed on Rafe and sent out a silent call. "Abraxas, I need you."

And the ring on my finger started to glow.

Instantly the sky darkened, and a mighty roar shook the castle as the ancient dragon appeared overhead.

It was as if time stopped while everyone halted what they were doing to look up, terror showing plainly on their faces.

"Dragon!" screamed a guard.

The Drakaar holding the knife to Rafe's throat faltered for a moment when the great dragon appeared, but a moment was all we needed.

Rafe spun out of the Drakaar's grip as I unleashed a raging bolt of white light, incinerating the demon sorcerer to dust.

Onlookers shrieked hysterically, and the whole castle fell into chaos.

Tristan roared and pounced on the remaining Drakaar as they banded together to protect Brandon from the dark prince. But we didn't have time to go after the archmage—we had to get to the main gates and let the rest of our army in, otherwise we would not be able to take the castle. We still had to cross the main bailey, a huge open space where the majority of the soldiers were stationed, and they would be waiting for us.

I gathered more magic and let it rise within me before I flung it at the gate. Silver fire, hotter than any man-made construct could withstand, erupted from my hands, burning through the iron gates, melting the portcullis until there was a gaping hole.

The soldiers were waiting for us, but many were taken by surprise at the arrival of the ancient dragon. Some fumbled to pick up their weapons as archers composed themselves and readied their bows, firing a barrage of arrows into the sky. They bounced off the dragon's impenetrable scales like feathers in the wind. Abraxas wasn't doing anything except circling the castle, but it was enough to terrify the life out of Delacourt's army.

"Try not to burn down the castle," I said to Abraxas.

"I shall do my best." The great dragon laughed, and it sounded like a terrifying roar as he swooped closer to the main wall.

We dashed through the melted inner gate.

"I'm going to open the main gate," Rafe shouted as he ducked and spun, his sword embedding in another guard's gut. He pulled his sword out. "Keep those archers off me."

It was still a few hundred feet to the gatehouse, and we had to get there without being killed. I created a wider shield and moved it around Rafe as he ran. Arrows bounced off the shield, but a shield could only protect him from flying objects and magical strikes. I could not protect him from the countless guards who had begun to realize that the Prince of Eldoren was in their midst.

Rafe ran a guard through with his sword.

"Tristan!" I shouted, flinging out my magic and pushing guards out of the way. But I needn't have. Tristan was already there, fighting beside Rafe and cutting a clean path through the guards toward the gatehouse.

Keeping my shield intact, I ran to help.

Rafe and Tristan fought their way through the guards to the gatehouse as arrows rained down from all sides. Finally, they reached the great stone entrance tunnel, but there were too many guards to both fight them off and raise the portcullis at the same time; it required two people to raise it. I had to keep the guards off them so they could open the gate.

"I'm over here, dimwits," I shouted at the guards.

The soldiers who had Rafe and Tristan backed into the tunnel stopped and turned at the sound of my voice. Their eyes widened as they all slowly recognized me, which wasn't that difficult, especially with the massive dragon flying around overhead.

One of the wide-eyed guards said, "Dawnstar."

"Yup! That's me." I flexed my fingers and reached for my magic.

"How can you be here?" said another guard, fear apparent on his pale face. "The archmage had you locked up in the dungeons."

"A futile attempt, obviously," I said as I stood watch over the gatehouse, shielding Rafe and Tristan.

The rest of the guards stopped and surrounded me, but came no closer. More guards were coming for me, so I had to be quick. A few of the guards started flinging magical strikes at me, but they bounced off my shield, useless. Stretching out one hand, I picked up the guards with magic as if they were toys, and with a flick of my wrist flung them against the walls, trapping some there and letting others fall to the ground.

Rafe and Tristan had the opening they needed and started to raise the portcullis. I created two flaming balls of silver fire in my palms. I didn't intend on using my silver fire on human or mage soldiers unless I had no other choice, although the sight of it seemed to keep the soldiers at bay.

I heard shouts and a triumphant war cry behind me as the gates finally finished opening and a white stallion charged past me. Declan Raingate, Uncle Gabriel's captain of the guard, brandished his sword and led the way. I saw a myriad of colors and crests: the Rothguards, Greystones, Foxmoors, Hartfields, and others I didn't recognize. The great noble houses of Eldoren were fighting together with the Silverthornes in service to their one true king. Once they knew their children were safe, they joined together to eliminate Delacourt. The Silverthorne army spilled inward into the outer bailey and a raging battle began.

I fought beside Rafe, my sword flashing as we tore a path through the enemy soldiers. Magic sizzled around me as I held a shield around us both, cutting and slashing as we tried to find Brandon. Slowly the intensity of the fighting lessened, and I heard Captain Raingate's voice over the crowd shouting orders to his soldiers. The last of Delacourt's remaining guards and archers laid down their weapons, surrendering Caeleron Castle to Rafe.

A crowd had gathered in the middle of the main bailey as Rafe and I made our way forward. "What's all the commotion about?" Rafe asked as Eldorean soldiers made way for their king.

The ground before us was strewn with blood and grime, which wasn't surprising given the battle we had just finished. But what was even less surprising was Tristan standing over a cowering Brandon Delacourt, his flaming sword at his throat, while the last four Drakaar lay strewn in the dirt around them, heads severed from their bodies.

Rafe raised an eyebrow as he took in the scene before him and gave me a quick glance. "Well, I, for one, am glad the dark prince is on our side."

I smiled. "Me too."

Captain Raingate came forward, taking Brandon Delacourt into custody.

Tristan moved toward him, his swords still flaming in his hands. "I can execute the traitor right now."

But Rafe stepped between them. "No! Put him in the dungeons. He will be tried by the council."

"He is a traitor. The only punishment is death," Tristan growled. "Why wait?"

Rafe looked at me and smiled. "He really likes using his swords, doesn't he?"

I chuckled. Tristan huffed and sheathed his swords, leaving Brandon to Captain Raingate, who took him away to the dungeons.

"That was quite a feat you and your fae prince pulled off there, Aurora," said Rafe unexpectedly. "Thank you for your help. But I would appreciate it if you could ask your dragon to take a nap somewhere else." He lowered his voice, just in case Abraxas could hear us. Which, in fact, he could, but Rafe didn't know that. "He's making my men nervous."

My eyebrows rose as I surveyed the courtyard. Rafe was right. Abraxas had actually seated himself in the middle of the castle courtyard and proceeded to take a nap. I knew he wasn't asleep, but the guards and soldiers scurried around him as they went about their jobs, one eye fixed on the massive, scaly body that seemed to have taken residence in the outer bailey of Caeleron Castle.

I rolled my eyes and smiled ever so slightly as I tried to hold back laughter. "I'll see what I can do," I offered and strode forward to speak to the ancient dragon.

One big eye opened, the color of burnt honey. The dragon's amethyst scales glistened in the noonday sun as I approached. I was right—he wasn't asleep, just enjoying scaring the life out of the palace guards.

I put my hand on his snout. "Thank you for everything you have done."

"I am at your service, Dawnstar," said the ancient voice in my head. *"But I fear a malignant presence in the castle. You must leave soon."*

"I will," I agreed. "As soon as we get Rafe crowned as King of

Eldoren. We still need their army if we are going to defeat Morgana."

"Be careful," said the great dragon, and much to the horror of everyone around us, Abraxas got up, roared, and bounded into the sky.

THE RIGHTFUL KING

THE CORONATION WAS a grand affair as coronations usually are, and it was held in the ancient throne room at Caeleron Castle, where all the kings and queens of Eldoren had been crowned since the days of Dorian the First. The great hall had been repaired with a little help from Penelope and me. For now, glamour held it together, but it would eventually have to be fixed the traditional way.

Nobility from all over the kingdom had gathered, dressed in their finery. Voluminous skirts in silks and satins, swirled with vibrant colors and embroidered with gold and silver thread, attached to bodices studded with pearls and precious stones. I looked around at the throng of bodies and happy, smiling faces. Each one of these people had been willing to go against their king, and there were very few who had actually helped him. The nobility of Eldoren were fickle at the best of times, putting their own interests above the good of the kingdom. And without Silverthorne here to help and advise, Rafe was going to have his work cut out for him.

I stood on the side of the dais near the throne along with Penelope and Tristan. I had glamoured myself some suitable clothes for the coronation: a demure dress of creamy satin, lightly adorned with snowy pearls on the neckline and waist and along the edges of the long bell sleeves. I wore a delicate pearl and diamond tiara that Rafe had sent for me to wear during the coronation.

Brandon was in the dungeons where he belonged, but Lilith had disappeared. Calisto's broken body was found in the east wing of the castle, devoid of life. Lilith could now be anywhere— or anyone. Tristan, Penelope, and I were on alert in case she tried anything during the coronation.

Getting Rafe secured on his throne was a step in the right direction. His army would be invaluable to us, especially now with the added threat of the blackened iron. I wondered what was going on in Brandor and if Santino had succeeded in convincing the other emirs to shut down the mines.

"Have you heard anything from Santino?" I asked Penelope as we stood watching the procession.

Penelope shook her head. "Not yet, but I am expecting a raven any day now."

Finding and stopping the shipments of blackened iron was a priority. If Morgana got blackened iron to the dwarves and convinced them to make weapons for her, then the fae would face extinction in battle. Morgana already had a good many dwarves working for her, but she still needed their forges in Stonegate to make the truly powerful weapons that could bring down Izadora's Elite.

I looked over at Tristan standing beside me, as handsome and dangerous as ever in a black doublet faintly embroidered with steel-gray thread. I had to glamour his swords invisible because, as usual, he refused to leave them behind in his room. I had given up arguing about it; he never went unarmed. If Morgana could make weapons that could take down Tristan, what chance would the rest of the fae have?

"After the coronation, we will meet with Rafe and the leaders of the rebels to devise a plan to move forward," said Penelope.

The herald announced Rafe's arrival, and a hush fell over the space as he entered the throne room, looking every inch a king. Dressed in the regal coronation robes of purple velvet edged with ermine and with the Eldorean crest embroidered in gold thread as a motif all over the robe, he walked down the crimson-carpeted aisle of the massive room. The crowd cheered for their king, who had been willing to sacrifice his life and his crown to save his people.

Rafe ascended the stairs of the dais slowly and turned to seat himself on the gilded throne. Danica stood in the front row of the guests on the opposite side from me, gazing up at Rafe. I had to admit, when she was dressed up with her long dark hair elegantly styled, she looked beautiful, with sensual curves that filled out her tight blue satin dress better than I could have.

Rafe gave her a quick smile, and my heart sank. He never even glanced at me.

I looked at Penelope, who was watching me out of the corner of her eye. She put her hand on my arm and leaned over to speak softly to me. "The tiara you are wearing belonged to Rafe's mother. It was one of her favorites."

I tried to smile at her blatant attempt to make me feel better, but the truth was that Rafe had probably sent me the first tiara he found. They all belonged to his mother anyway, and it wasn't like anyone else was wearing them.

Two priests from the temple of Karneth were waiting on either side of the throne, dressed in stately white robes lined with silver and pearls. One of them held the heavy crown of Eldoren on a velvet cushion the color of ripe blueberries.

The priests began the ceremony, reciting prayers from their ancient book. They placed the crown upon Rafe's head amid the cheering of Eldorean nobility.

It was done. Prince Rafael Ravenswood was now King Rafael the Seventh.

———◇◇◇———

THE FEAST WAS SPECTACULAR, and I knew how much work had gone into preparing everything for the coronation. Even in this time of war, the preparation had been meticulous. Footmen brought out gleaming silver trays of Eldorean delicacies and circulated glazed honey tarts and fragrant meat-stuffed pastries. The tables were piled high with trays of flaky breads and berry-glazed poultry cooked in figs and rosemary, along with roast pork, summer berry pies, and delicious-looking buttercream cakes.

The nobility danced the night away, happy in the knowledge their children were safe and the rightful king had been restored to the throne.

One happily drunk noble tottered over to our table with some of his friends, who were also quite intoxicated. "Who let this monster into the palace?" he slurred, glaring at Tristan. "You fae scum should not be allowed into our lands."

Tristan slowly pushed his chair back. As he got up to face the drunken lord, his midnight-blue eyes started to swirl with silver sparks. I knew from experience that was never a good sign.

I got up from my chair and stood in front of him, facing the young lord, who I recognized as Viscount Steele, the same lord I had danced with at my first royal ball at the Summer Palace. It now seemed like a lifetime ago, and I had changed a lot since then. "I think you should leave, my lord," I said politely, keeping my voice even. I didn't want to cause a scene at Rafe's coronation.

"You want me to leave?" he spat, his eyes red and puffy as he looked at me with contempt. "You are the one who brought this monster here. Do you even know what he did to our people?" He grabbed my hand. "Come away from him, you are one of us. Stay away from the filthy fae."

I didn't move as I held his stare. His eyes moved downward and widened as he looked at where his hand was, probably only just realizing what he had done.

My eyes narrowed, and my hand lit up with silver fire—only a spark, but it was enough to reduce the insipid lord to a blubbering idiot. He let go immediately, squealing in pain as his flesh sizzled. He stumbled backward, cradling his charred hand as I stalked toward him and caught him by his collar.

The throne room was so quiet you could hear a pin drop. The nobles didn't move as they watched the scene unfold. Rafe did not interfere.

"You call Tristan a monster," I growled, my voice reverberating around the room, "because he fought a whole garrison of soldiers in fair combat and defeated them. The real monsters are the mage soldiers who brutalized, raped, and murdered a defenseless fae woman just because they could." I let go of his collar and he stumbled backward, the new leather soles of his boots slipping on the polished marble floors. "If I were there, I would have killed the whole group myself."

The lords and ladies started arguing among themselves as Viscount Steele backed away into the crowd, surrounded by his minions.

"Enough," said Rafe, standing up from his throne, and the crowd went quiet. "Prince Tristan is our guest here at the palace, and if anyone has a problem with that—" his eyes narrowed, and his voice was pure steel, "—you are free to leave now."

Everyone bustled about, whispering and going back to their seats, but no one left the throne room except the viscount and his motley crew.

Tristan came up behind me and whispered in my ear. "Thank you for standing up for me. You didn't have to, you know. I can take care of myself."

I turned to face him. "I know, but I didn't want you splattering the viscount's remains all over the new carpet," I said with a grin.

And the dark prince smiled back at me for the first time since we had reached Eldoren.

I was about to sit back down and finish my dinner when I finally spotted Vivienne in the corner of the room. She moved to the entrance and slipped away from the festivities.

"I'll be right back," I said hurriedly to Tristan. I had to try to make things right. I couldn't bear the fact that she wouldn't even speak to me, and I missed my best friend. I followed Vivienne out of the room.

Vivienne scurried through the brightly lit corridor as I called out to her. "Viv! Wait."

She didn't look back. She turned a corner and kept on walking at a fast pace down a more dimly lit corridor lined with arched windows, one of which was open, letting in a chill. Thunder rumbled outside as lightning flashed over the castle, lighting up the passage in an eerie white light. Pelting rain beat against the windows as I followed her, my heart beating wildly. I had to explain why I had left without saying goodbye. I wanted her to know I would be there for her. There had to be a way to make this right.

"Viv, please. Just hear me out."

She stopped abruptly, her back toward me as I hurried forward, putting my hand on her shoulder. "Viv, please, let me expl—"

She turned.

There was a flash of red light that temporarily blinded me. I raised my arm to shield myself. An agonizing pain burst through me, and I felt as if the cold wind had seeped into my very bones. A void opened within me, and I felt a wrench, as if some sort of cord had snapped inside. I staggered backward, dread chilling my heart and pooling deep within me.

Vivienne stood before me with a dagger in her hand.

She had attacked me.

Terror gripped me when I saw the amount of blood running down my arm, a gash that exposed the flesh all the way down to the bone. The pain hadn't registered yet, but my dress was soaked in blood. I looked at her in horror. "Viv . . ."

But it wasn't Vivienne who looked back at me. Her eyes were gleaming black coals devoid of white.

"Lilith," I gasped, gritting my teeth as the pain hit me. I clutched my arm, trying to get my bearings and heal myself. "What have you done to Vivienne?"

"There is nothing you can do for your friend now—she's gone," the Dark Queen sneered, her voice raspy and otherworldly. "If you kill me, she will die."

She had cut me all the way down my forearm. If I hadn't moved in time, she would have gotten me in the stomach. I opened myself to the magic around me to heal myself. Nothing happened—the pain only got worse. I tried harder to reach for my magic, but there was no fire, no ice, no light, nothing.

"No!" I gasped. I was no longer looking at her but at the curved Dagger she held in her hand, a huge red ruby flashing on its hilt. There was no mistaking it—the Dagger from my nightmares, the Dagger I had been searching for.

"The Dagger of Dragath," I said slowly, cold dread flashing down my spine.

I scrambled for some power and shot a weak push strike at her. At least some of my mage magic remained. But it was not enough to fight the Dark Queen.

My fae magic was gone.

Lilith laughed, a cruel, sinister sound, as she stalked toward me in Vivienne's body. "Your magic will enhance the Dagger's powers a hundredfold. Our plans have finally come to fruition. The general will be very pleased. Now no one will be able to stop him from raising the demon lord."

"Lilith," I ground out through gritted teeth, staring at the

Dagger as a blinding horror took hold of me. "What have you done?"

I couldn't lose my magic, not now. Not when I had so much to do. I was the heir of Illaria Lightbringer, I was the Dawnstar, and my fae magic was my power. My grandmother said I could touch the Dagger without being pulled inside. But she never said what would happen if I was cut with it.

Had she known?

The pain intensified, and the corridor seemed to tilt as I fell to the ground, too weak from the loss of blood to do anything more. My fae strength was gone, and my senses dulled as the world swam before my eyes and darkness threatened to swallow me whole.

I heard a shout at the end of the corridor. "Aurora!" It was Tristan.

Lilith growled when she saw the dark prince, but she didn't advance on me. Instead, she took out a small stone from her pocket and flung it at the wall. To my astonishment, a portal opened.

Witchstone, I thought through the haze. Marcus had told me about these rare stones in the Night Bazaar in Sanria.

"Till we meet again, Princess," sneered Lilith as she stepped through the portal, just as Tristan's sword clashed with the stone wall as it closed behind her.

"Aurora, what happened?" Rafe appeared behind Tristan and knelt beside me.

His face swam before my eyes. "Rafe, I, she, Lilith . . ."

"Shh, you can explain later," Rafe said, gently picking me up in his arms.

A crowd had gathered, and Penelope ran over. "Get her to her room now," she ordered.

Tristan had both his swords drawn and threatened anyone who came near us, making way for Rafe to carry me quickly through the castle corridors.

"Rafe." I could barely get the words out as I held on to his neck, resting my head on his shoulder. "I'm sorry," I mumbled as my eyes closed.

He probably thought I couldn't hear him, and it may have been a hallucination, but I could have sworn he whispered, "I know, my love. I know."

When I woke up, I was lying in a blue-and-gold canopied bed under a confection of satin pillows and blankets. A light fragrance of lavender and vanilla filled the room. Penelope was at a table mixing and grinding powders and speaking to Kalen in hushed whispers. They hadn't noticed I was awake.

"Is there any hope?" Kalen asked his mother.

Penelope shook her head. "I've examined her thoroughly. All her fae magic is gone."

"But she will be all right. Won't she?"

Penelope nodded. "Yes, she will live."

I winced. Her answer didn't seem very encouraging.

"How was she not pulled into the Dagger like her mother and the other fae?" Kalen asked, pacing in front of the table.

"Her mage blood protected her essence, but it could not protect her fae magic." Penelope looked as distraught as I felt. "As soon as the Dagger touched her blood, it extracted her fae magic, drawing her power into it like a sponge."

I coughed as I tried to sit up, catching their attention. The pain in my arm had dulled but was still there, the wound heavily wrapped in muslin bandages.

Kalen ran over to the bed. "Aurora, you're awake."

I smiled faintly. "Kalen." I was always glad to see my old friend. He was a breath of fresh air in a world that had gone completely mad.

He held my hand, his violet eyes shining. "I'll get Rafe." He ran off and came back moments later with the King of Eldoren.

For the first time since I came back, Rafe fully smiled at me, but only for a moment. It was so fleeting I could have imagined it. His face took on the bored, regal look he was so good at portraying, so different from his worried expression when he was carrying me back to my room.

"Ah, good! You're awake." His tone was flippant. "At least now Prince Tristan will stop questioning and threatening everyone in the castle. The nobles have been asking to have him locked up."

I groaned at the thought of Tristan prowling the corridors of Caeleron Castle in a bad mood. I could well understand the nobles' fear for their lives. An angry Tristan was not someone you wanted to mess with.

The door burst open and Tristan stalked into the room. "Why didn't anyone inform me she was awake?" He spoke to Penelope and ignored Rafe.

Rafe rolled his eyes. "See what I mean?"

He was about to say something more when Penelope stepped between them. "We were just about to call you, Tristan."

Tristan moved past Penelope and came to my bedside with a scowl. "What happened?"

I told them everything.

Rafe frowned. "So all your magic is gone?"

I nodded. "I can't even speak to Abraxas," I said numbly, looking at the ring, which now rested cold and dull on my finger.

"Everything fae about her has been stripped away," Penelope replied. "Which includes her fae strength and her powers as a Dragonlord."

"And the Dawnstar?" asked Tristan.

Penelope shook her head. "Her fae magic is the basis of her Dawnstar powers, a culmination of them, if you will. She can no longer summon the light of the ancient queens."

"It's only her fae magic that's gone," said Rafe, trying to look on the bright side. Not that there really was a bright side to this. "She will still be able to use her mage magic."

"Not that it's going to be of any use to us," Tristan growled.

Rafe raised his eyebrows and looked at me. "Cheerful fellow, isn't he?"

Tristan glowered at Rafe and was met with the famous Ravenswood smile.

"So let me get this straight," Rafe continued. "Lilith has now taken over Vivienne Foxmoor's body?"

I nodded.

"And what happens when she decides to change bodies again?" said Rafe.

Everyone looked at Penelope.

"Lilith will take her essence to strengthen herself," Penelope replied.

"Which means?" I asked. I had to know if there was anything we could do.

"Which means when Lilith decides to leave Vivienne's body, Vivienne will die."

My mind flashed back to Calisto's broken body, and I pictured Vivienne in its place. "There must be something we can do. Some way to remove Lilith from Vivienne's body without killing her."

Penelope shook her head and looked at me. "Only the Dawnstar can do that."

I hung my head. I had failed her. I had failed everyone. I thought I was invincible, but I was wrong. I was so wrong. Now I was being punished for my hubris. Without my fae powers I was no longer the Dawnstar; I no longer had the power of Illaria Lightbringer within me. I was a failure. A queen without a throne. Now it looked like I would never be able to defeat Morgana, or this general Lilith spoke of. Dragath would rise again and enslave the whole world because I was too weak to stop him. Morgana had won, and there was nothing I could do about it.

"Erien is going to be so upset," I mumbled. My thoughts were an absolute mess. How was I going to get through this? There were so many people counting on me.

"Then he mustn't know," said Penelope sharply. "In fact, no one outside this room must know that you have lost your fae magic. It will only weaken your position to retake your throne."

"I agree," said Rafe. "But we must find out more information about this general Lilith mentioned. Who is he?"

"She implied he was the one calling the shots, not Morgana."

"If that is so, then whoever he is, he is a master strategist," said Penelope. "We didn't know he existed until now. I must consult Izadora. She will know what to do."

"Are you going to tell her what happened with Lilith?" I asked.

What would my grandmother do when she found out I didn't have my fae magic anymore? Would she dismiss me as her heir? Would she still help me retake my throne?

"I must," said Penelope. "Without you being able to contact Abraxas, Izadora is the only one who can tell us if there is any way to get your powers back."

My eyes lit up. "You think that's even possible?"

Penelope's eyes narrowed. "I certainly hope so. Without the Dawnstar, our world doesn't stand a chance."

A FALL FROM GRACE

PENELOPE WENT to speak to my grandmother through a mirror portal. I had been looking forward to learning how to use them, but now that option was gone. I had spent so much time being upset that I was different and had so much power to control. But now that it was gone, I would do anything to get it back.

"Get some rest," said Rafe, his eyes briefly meeting mine. "I will speak with the rebels about this general and see what we can find out about him."

I nodded, too weak to argue. What was the point? I was no use to anyone anymore. I was just another mage with inadequate training.

Tristan stood guard outside my door.

I hoped my grandmother would come up with a plan. She had warned me against coming to Eldoren, even though she had finally sent me here herself. Saving the children from Brandon's dungeons was the catalyst to me coming here. But I saw now it was not the only reason, however much I may have tried to deny it.

The truth was that I wanted to see Rafe, and I wanted to be the one to help him, to show him what I could do. Somehow, I thought if he realized I could be an asset to him he would see me differently. Once more I had jeopardized everything because of my feelings. I saw now I couldn't save everyone individually, however powerful I was. My purpose was bigger than myself. I was a symbol of hope for the people of Avalonia, a promise that things would be all right. Now I had given that up, and I had failed the world.

Penelope finally returned. "I have spoken with Izadora," she announced, clasping her hands in front of her as soon as we were alone.

My eyes narrowed. "Did you tell her I lost my magic?"

Penelope shook her head and gave me a meaningful look. "I didn't have to say anything; she already knew. When the Dagger took your magic, Izadora and some of the Elders felt it. The transfer of such formidable magic doesn't go unnoticed by those who are powerful enough to sense it."

"Did she know this would happen if I was cut with the Dagger?"

Penelope shook her head. "She was not sure. But she did hope it was not so."

"So much for hope," I said darkly.

Penelope cleared her throat. "The fact remains that you can still touch the Dagger without being pulled into it. The other fae cannot." She lowered her voice, and I could feel her pulling a magical shield around us to prevent us from being overheard. "Your grandmother wants you to be the one to find the Dagger. And she doesn't want the mages involved. The Dagger must not fall into the wrong hands again. Whoever possesses the Dagger of Dragath will have the power to wipe out the fae. You are the only one she trusts to have such power and not abuse it."

"Rafe would never use the Dagger against the fae," I said, automatically defending him. But now I wasn't so sure I even knew him anymore.

"He may not, but the other mages cannot be trusted," said

Penelope. "Racial prejudices run deep in Avalonia. There was a time when all the kingdoms were at constant war with each other. It is only in the last hundred years we have had peaceful relations with our neighbors. An object as detrimental to the fae as the Dagger of Dragath can never be trusted with the mages."

I nodded. She was right. We had to be careful.

"Did my grandmother say if there was any way to get my magic back?"

"She is working on it," Penelope said. "Without the Fae Codex it will not be easy. I will contact her again once we have met with Rafe and the Eldorean Council."

THE DAYS WENT by slowly as I curled up in a ball in my blue-and-gold canopied bed feeling extremely sorry for myself. We had still not heard back from my grandmother, and I still didn't know if it was possible to get my fae magic back. Every minute that passed dragged me deeper into a well of despair and hopelessness. Now I would not be able to protect myself from Morgana or this general, whoever he was. I could not lead an army, not without my powers.

My arm was already getting better. Penelope was a gifted healer, but I had lost all confidence in my abilities, and I could not face the world. Penelope had told me to keep this a secret, but I was sure someone would see through the deception and expose me as the fraud I really was. What use was I to anyone? It was better to just lie here in my bed and let more capable people handle it.

On the third evening after my injury, Tristan stormed into my room. "Get up, Aurora." He came over to me and pulled my blankets off. "Stop wallowing in your own misery."

I glared at him and replaced my blankets. "Go back to Elfi, Tristan. There's no point in you being here anymore. I'm of no use to anyone; there is no need to protect me now. I can't go up against Morgana, not without my fae magic. Let my grandmother lead her own army. I can't do it. I give up." I turned over in my bed and shut my eyes tight, as if I could block out the world and all the horrible things that had happened.

"Rubbish," said Tristan, pulling me up. "Just because you lost your powers doesn't mean you don't still have a job to do. Your powers don't make you Queen of Illiador. Your bloodline does. Have you forgotten your parents? Or how your mother gave up her immortal life so you could live to save the world?"

"That's not fair," I complained as I got out of bed and punched him on his arm.

Tristan didn't flinch. "Who said life is fair?"

My anger abated. "I'm sorry. I know you lost your mother too."

Tristan's jaw tightened. "If there were any chance I could get her back, I would scour the ends of the world. With or without my magic."

I moved closer and put my hand on Tristan's shoulder. "I know. But without the Dawnstar, I can do nothing. I cannot protect the ones I love, let alone save them. I will only succeed in getting more people killed. That's all I seem to be good at doing these days."

Tristan's eyes flashed with silver stars, and he held me gently by the shoulders. "You can do something. And you will. I know you, Aurora. You are brave and kind, and you care about people. Where is the girl who came to the fae kingdom and defied the Queen of Elfi? Where is the girl who stood up to the Prince of the Day Court when no one else would?" He lowered his voice. "It is your spirit, not your magic, that will make you a great queen. You are the true Queen of Illiador, and your people are suffering." He moved back and opened the door to leave. "Do you intend to let the world be swallowed into darkness because you were too scared to face what is coming?" He closed the door behind him with a definitive click.

I walked over to the windowsill and leaned against it, taking in a deep breath of fresh spring air as my head cleared. The moon shone its splendor over the valley beyond as I gazed out at the small town that lay at the base of the castle, its little lights twinkling from fires and hearths. I realized Tristan was right. Lilith had stripped me of my self-confidence as well as my powers. Without my magic I felt exposed, vulnerable. But giving up was not an option. I would not hide in the shadows, weak and afraid. I would not go down without a fight.

I put on the green velvet robe that had been laid out for me and left my room in search of Rafe. I had to clear things up with him if we were going to work together. As I made my way through the moonlit corridors of Caeleron Castle I almost turned back. The memory of Lilith still lingered, and my heartbeat sped up when I heard a small sound up ahead. I stopped, hesitating, but was relieved to see it was just a guard. Rafe had soldiers stationed at regular intervals all over the castle after my attack, and that made me feel a little better even though there was no guard who could protect me if Lilith came back. I cringed at the thought of what I had become—afraid of my own shadow.

I hurried to the king's chamber after getting directions from one of the guards. I knew Rafe was very busy during the day, especially during such a crisis, and this was the best time to catch him alone. I had hoped he would have come to see me, but he hadn't. So I would have to go to him and explain everything. I knew he would not forgive me easily, but I had to try.

As I neared his room, his door opened, and Danica stepped out. I backed into the shadows and held my breath as my heart raced. Why was she in Rafe's room at this time of night?

Rafe stood at the door shirtless, his dark hair tousled and his muscled torso glistening in the moonlight, as Danica ran her hand down his arm. She went up on her tiptoes to kiss him as he bent his head slightly to meet her lips, his hand tightening around her waist. She ran her fingers through his dark wavy hair and deepened the kiss.

He pulled away eventually. "It's been a long day. I'm tired, Danica."

"I'll let you rest," she said in a low, throaty voice. "You know where to find me."

Rafe smiled at her, and in that moment, I felt my heart break all over again. It was strange, because I thought I didn't have anything left to break. Turned out I was wrong.

I moved through the shadows and hurried back to my room, crawling into my bed and stifling the tears. There was no point in explaining anything now. Rafe had obviously moved on. I knew Danica and he seemed to be close, but I never thought he would take her to his bed. I shook my head at my own foolishness and laughed, a bitter sound even to my ears. Of course he would take her to his bed! Rafe was a grown man, and an extremely attractive one at that. He wasn't attached, so why wouldn't he? Especially with girls like Danica throwing themselves at him. There was no place for me in his life anymore. I had to accept that and hope that time would heal the wound he had ripped open again.

THE NEXT MORNING, I got dressed in my fae leathers and tunic, Dawn strapped at my waist, and met with Penelope and Tristan in the antechamber to Rafe's council chamber. He was in a meeting with some of his nobles about Eldorean matters, and we were told he would see us as soon as he was done.

It would be hard being in the same room with Rafe again, especially after what I had seen last night, but I had to push my feelings aside and concentrate on the task at hand. We needed his army to join us; the Eldorean mages were powerful warriors who would be invaluable to our cause. I pushed my shoulders back as the council chamber doors opened and we were ushered inside.

The mood was somber as we entered the large, rectangular room. Huge latticed windows framed two sides of the council chamber, looking out at the gardens beyond. Rafe stood at the head of the massive table as the nobles of Eldoren milled around talking and arguing while pointing to parts of the map that lay in the center. He was talking in a low tone to the Earl of Rothguard and the Marquis of Greystone, my father's old friends who were also part of the resistance against Morgana.

Everyone looked up as we entered, and to my surprise, they all started clapping. Earlier during the coronation, they had been focused on Rafe, but word had spread about what had really happened. One by one they came up to me and bowed, expressing their lifelong gratitude to me for helping to rescue their children. At that moment all doubts of whether I should have done it disappeared. I had saved the lives of the children. I may have lost my magic because of it, but seeing the relief and happiness on the faces of all these people made it worth it.

Tristan was right. Maybe I wouldn't be stronger and more powerful than everyone else anymore, but I was still the rightful Queen of Illiador, even without my magic. And it wasn't as if I had lost all of it. I still had my mage magic, which due to my bloodline was stronger than most, and for now that would have to suffice.

The rest of the council thanked me and left the room until only Rothguard and Julian Fenton remained. Rafe explained that after Silverthorne's execution, Fenton had become the leader of the Silver Swords.

I was grateful my father's friends still supported me, but I wondered how long that would last if they found out I had lost most of my powers.

Captain Declan Raingate entered the council chamber. Danica was with him. After asking around, I had come to discover Danica was Captain Raingate's niece. She used to live at Silverthorne Castle after her parents died, and Captain Raingate was her guardian now. It made sense that she was part of the resistance since her uncle was a member of the Silver Swords.

"Danica has a request," said Captain Raingate.

Danica bowed stiffly to me, but her eyes held no warmth in them. "We could use your help with the wounded, your highness. We have heard of your amazing healing powers. Surely you can spare some time to help those in need. There are some who will not live unless you do something."

I stared at her in shock. What could I say? I couldn't tell her I had lost my ability to heal. And if I refused to help, they would think I was cold and callous.

Penelope stepped in. "Aurora has just recovered from a very dangerous magical battle that has taken a toll. I don't recommend she does any healing magic until she recovers."

Danica's eyes darkened. "But what about the wounded?"

"I am a skilled healer; I will tend to them," said Penelope. "Give me a few moments, and I will be with you."

She bowed to Penelope with obvious relief in her eyes. "Thank you, my lady." With that, she left.

"Did you find out anything, Declan?" asked Rafe.

He nodded. "It's not good."

Rafe threw a quick glance at Penelope. "I sent Captain Raingate to find out information on this general Lilith mentioned."

"And what did you find?" Penelope asked the captain.

"Not much, except that he commands the Drakaar."

"Does he have a name?" Penelope asked.

"If he does, no one knows of it. They simply refer to him as the general." Captain Raingate moved closer. "And he is moving his army south." He pointed to an area in Illiador.

I looked at the map on the table. "But I thought they were busy attacking the dwarven fortresses."

Captain Raingate gave me a sharp look. "Well, it looks like he decided there is something more valuable here."

Tristan, who had kept quiet so far, came up to stand beside me and crossed his arms. His dark eyes flashed, and Captain Raingate, who was usually unfazed, seemed to take a step back. Everyone had seen what the dark prince could do, and there was no one here who was brave or stupid enough to get in his way. I was glad Tristan was here; after my experience with Lilith, I felt safer with him around.

Rafe continued looking at the map. "And where is Morgana?"

"My spies tell me her army is amassing in the plains and will meet with the general's forces here." He stabbed a finger at the map, pointing to the Valley of Flowers, not far from Oblek's castle. "More forces are said to be entering through a pass in the Silverspike and meeting in the Darkwood. They have been marching ever since the winter snow cleared."

"Their destination?" Rafe's tone was clipped.

"Eldoren," said Captain Raingate gravely.

Rafe looked over at Rothguard and Fenton. "Ready the army. We must march northward at the earliest. We must fortify the fortress at the Eastern Pass in the Cascade Mountains and meet Morgana's army before she reaches Eldoren."

"I will dispatch riders immediately," said Fenton.

Fenton and Rothguard took their leave and left us alone with Captain Raingate.

The captain's jaw tightened. "My reports suggest Morgana's army is ten times the size of ours. She has the whole Illiadorian force of warrior-mages from Nerenor, the royal army, Andrysian foot soldiers, and another even larger army led by the general advancing onto the plains. Along with the Drakaar and their shadow creatures, our warrior-mages will not stand a chance."

"More and more people are rising up against her," said Rafe, "and many more are flocking to the resistance."

"Even so," Captain Raingate replied. "With all our nobles and their private armies, along with Eldoren's full force, we will still be sorely outnumbered."

Rafe turned to Penelope. "What about the fae army?"

Penelope shook her head. "They are not coming."

Rafe was quiet for a moment. "Then we will have to face them alone." He ran a hand through his dark hair and let it rest on the nape of his neck. "We need more information, Declan."

"I will find out what I can," said Captain Raingate, and he took his leave, closing the big council room door behind him.

I turned to Penelope. "I need to speak to my grandmother myself."

Penelope studied me, flicking a glance at Rafe and Tristan. "I will open a mirror portal in the antechamber. I saw one that would suffice."

Rafe left to speak with the other captains in his army. We followed Penelope out of the main council chamber and into a smaller adjoining room.

Penelope stood in front of a full-length oval mirror that lay in the corner of the room. She wove her magic and my grandmother came into view, seated on her throne.

Her gold eyes flashed when she saw me, but she didn't say anything and instead turned her gaze on Penelope. "Have you any news?"

Penelope nodded and explained the situation as it stood now. "Morgana has set her sights on Eldoren. If the fae do not help, the Eldorean mages will be massacred."

The fae queen raised an eyebrow. "That is not my concern."

"Once they create the weapons they need, they will turn on the fae." My voice was sharp.

Izadora's eyes narrowed as she assessed me, but she addressed Penelope. "What is the situation in Brandor?"

Penelope took out a note a guard had brought to her during the meeting. "For now, Brandor is still embroiled in civil war." She shook her head. "There is no more news from Santino."

Izadora's knuckles turned white as she gripped her throne. "Then there is no time to waste." She turned her golden eyes on me. "You must leave Eldoren immediately and find Morgana. Your first priority now is to retrieve the Dagger. Everything else is secondary."

"That will be impossible," said Penelope. "Morgana is traveling with an army. We would have to sneak into her camp to get to the Dagger."

Izadora's eyes flashed. "Then do it."

"I won't leave Eldoren to fend for itself," I said, crossing my arms. "It is the last kingdom that stands against her. Once she conquers Eldoren she will bring her army to Elfi."

Izadora's hard eyes narrowed, flashing with an eerie light. "Haven't you ever wondered why the Dagger only traps but does not kill the fae? If killing was Dragath's only motivation, then why leave them alive inside the Dagger?"

I pondered this. "You are right. I never thought of it that way."

"What are you getting at, sister?" said Penelope.

"Dragath is not the only threat to our world," the fae queen explained. "This is something only those who have read the Fae Codex know. When Auraken Firedrake locked the *Book of Power*, he warned us of a greater threat, should the book ever be opened again. According to the codex, the original purpose of the Dagger was not to wipe out the fae."

My eyebrows scrunched together. "It wasn't?"

"No, it wasn't." The fae queen shook her head. "When Dragath was summoned to this world by the Ancient Fae lord, the lord thought he could control Dragath."

I nodded. "Yes, I know this part. Dragath overpowered the fae lord, took the book for himself, and created the Dagger to entrap the fae and gain more power."

Izadora nodded. "Yes, but that is not all he wanted. When Dragath came to this world, he came alone, summoned through a portal that remained open for only seconds. Dragath may have been a powerful demon lord, but he was only one, cut off from his demon army. What you have encountered here, the Drakaar and the Shadow Demons, are mere shades of his true followers, the ones still trapped in a dying world of fire and ice." The queen paused, letting her words sink in. "After accessing the *Book of Abraxas*, Dragath realized that by creating the Dagger he could trap the spirit-fae within it and combine their power to create a permanent portal powerful enough to let his demon army through. Once his whole army comes, even if your powers are restored, you will not be able to stop them."

A shudder snaked down my spine as I stared at her in horror. There was an army of Dragath's demons from another world with magic far greater than any of us could understand. If it took all Auraken's power to contain just one demon lord, what would a whole army of them do? It would be impossible to fight them.

"But I thought he trapped only the fire-fae in the Dagger," I said, trying to remember the story as I had heard it before.

"The fire-fae were Illaria Lightbringer's trained warriors, and he had to go through them to get to the spirit-fae. But Dragath never managed to amass enough power in the Dagger to open such a portal, until . . ." She trailed off, her gold eyes boring into mine.

"Until Lilith took my magic," I finished, the words leaving a bitter taste in my mouth.

I had sentenced the world, albeit unknowingly, to a terrible fate.

DESTINY AWAITS

"Do you think we will get there in time?" I asked Penelope as we rode through the valley northward along the river road that led to the mountains that lay beyond Silverthorne Castle.

Penelope nodded. "For now our main aim is to find Morgana and the Dagger. She will not use it until she has the book and all the keys in her possession. If we can get into her camp and steal the Dagger before she or the general has a chance to use it, we may have a chance. Without it they can't move ahead with their plans."

I nodded gravely. We had to get to Illiador as quickly as we could, and the fastest way was through the fae portal in the Cascade Mountains. It was the same portal Rafe had used when he first followed me from Pixie Bush to Silverthorne Castle. He was the only one besides Duke Silverthorne who knew where it was. He had agreed to lead us to it, after which he would ride east and meet his army near the Eastern Pass. If the Eldorean army could hold the pass, they might be able to stop Morgana's forces from entering Eldoren.

Captain Raingate and Erien also accompanied us, as Erien had to return to Silverthorne Castle as the new duke and ready his troops for the upcoming war. I was not pleased Danica had accompanied us as well, as she wouldn't leave Rafe's side. She even feigned exhaustion halfway through the journey so she could ride on his horse with him. She ended up sitting demurely in front of him, his hard chest pressed against her back, his strong arms encircling her. I tried to act like it didn't affect me, but I would be lying if I said it didn't. In fact, at that moment all I wanted to do was claw her eyes out.

When the sun started to set, we stopped and made camp in a shady glade on the outskirts of a little village. It was better to remain unnoticed until we crossed over into Illiador. Morgana's spies were everywhere. I sat on a log staring into the fire while Penelope and Danica laid out the food. Rafe and Tristan went to check out the area. After we ate, Danica set out her bedroll next to Rafe and lay down.

I tried to ignore them. I definitely wasn't going to be able to sleep, so I sat near the fire for a while longer. I glanced over at Rafe, and my heart tightened in my chest. I quickly looked away. It was no use thinking about what we'd had together. He had forgotten about it and moved on. Mentioning what happened would only reopen old wounds. Once Rafe showed us the way to the portal, he would return to his castle with Danica, and I would probably never see him again.

The forest was quiet at night, with the occasional hoot of a lone owl breaking the silence. I was lost in my own thoughts when I heard a twig snap and looked up. Rafe had gotten up from beside Danica, who was still sound asleep, and come over to sit beside me.

"Couldn't sleep," he mumbled, poking the fire with a stick.

I looked away and pretended to concentrate on the fire. "Me too." I kept my voice low so as not to wake the others, who were all motionless under the twinkling night sky.

He turned slightly to look at me. "I want to apologize," he said abruptly.

My heart fluttered as I turned my head to gaze into his devastatingly gorgeous gray eyes. "For what?"

He ran his hand through his dark locks, tousling them a little, and he'd never looked so handsome. I had to look away. "I shouldn't have let you get involved in retaking my throne. If you hadn't come, you would still have your powers."

I put my hand gently on his arm. Even that slight touch sent thrills coursing through my body. "It's not your fault, Rafe." I smiled. "You couldn't have stopped me anyway," I added, trying to lighten the mood. I didn't want him feeling guilty for my failures. But at least I now knew he still cared.

He shook his head and moved his arm away. "No, I probably couldn't have." He shot a dark look at me. "It's better you are with Tristan anyway. He seems better suited to the task."

My eyes narrowed. "What's that supposed to mean?"

"We are too different, you and I."

"And I suppose Danica is a perfect match," I said tartly.

He shrugged. "Maybe."

I stared back into the fire. "Then there's nothing more to talk about, is there?"

"I suppose." He got up and went to lie down next to Danica.

The leaves rustled as I got up from the log. I spotted Tristan leaning against a tree, watching me. I had forgotten Tristan was on night patrol, since he never seemed to need sleep. He looked me straight in the eyes, turned, and disappeared into the woods.

Great! I thought. Now Tristan was also upset with me. It seemed I couldn't win either way.

THE NEXT MORNING, warm sunlight filtered in through the canopy of trees. The leaves rustled gently in the spring breeze as we packed up our things and headed for the mountains that lay beyond Silverthorne Castle.

We rode swiftly though the Willow Woods, stopping only to sleep and eat. Rafe never spoke to me alone again. He stayed beside Danica, who looked as smug as a cat that had gotten all the cream. In four days, we were cresting the hill that overlooked the flower-filled valley beyond.

Silverthorne Castle rose up amid the rolling hills, meadows, and colorful fields that encompassed the valley. Tall white towers glistened in the midday sun as they rose effortlessly upward, spearing the sky. The town of Fairlone stretched out around it, protected by high stone walls. Beyond it lay the Cascade Mountains, a vast range that separated Eldoren from Illiador.

Rafe rode forward to speak to Penelope and me. "We will stay the night at Silverthorne Castle."

"We need to press on, Rafe," said Penelope. "Time is of the essence."

"It is too dangerous to camp in the woods so close to the Cascade Mountains, and we cannot go through the portal at night," Rafe answered. "We have had reports that there are gorgoths patrolling these mountains for a while now, and we have to pass the castle anyway to get to the portal. In the morning I will lead you to it. Once you get to Illiador, meet with the Silver Swords. They will help you infiltrate Morgana's camp."

Penelope nodded. "Maybe you are right. We need to pick up supplies as well. Heavens know what we have in store for us when we reach Illiador."

"I will make the arrangements," Rafe said as we rode through the gates of the town with our hoods up. We were most easily recognized here, and the fewer people we trusted the better.

We passed through wide stone archways and whitewashed buildings, through the cobbled streets and toward the castle gates. I was immediately struck by the stark difference in the town from what it was just last year. Once a prosperous, bustling place, Fairlone was more like a ghost town now. Shuttered windows and closed doors met us at every turn. Shops were locked, and no one walked the streets except for lone soldiers and guards keeping watch over the town. They saw Captain Raingate and bowed, not asking anything about the people he had brought with him. With Silverthorne gone, the town had fallen to ruin. Many had moved away to the south of Eldoren, where there was less chance of war reaching them. But here, so close to the Illiadorian borders, the people were afraid for their lives.

The castle was as I remembered it from the outside. We entered the enclosed courtyard and got off our horses. Footmen scurried forward to take Captain Raingate's horse and to tend to the others.

"We will need fresh horses for tomorrow," said the captain to one of the guards. "We ride out in the morning."

"Yes, Captain," said the guard, leading the horse to the stables.

We climbed the massive stone steps that led into Silverthorne Castle, and my heart constricted at the thought that I would never see Uncle Gabriel again. Without him, the castle seemed cold and distant, a shadow of its former self. The heart of Silverthorne Castle was gone, and even though I'd wanted to return here because of all the memories, I didn't want to stay long. There wasn't anything left for me here anymore.

My room was the same, but this time I wasn't filled with wonder at everything around me. Sleep evaded me, so I went to see Penelope in her room.

"Did you know?" said Kalen as soon as I walked in.

"Know what?" I turned, arching a brow at Penelope, who was sitting on a chair near the fireplace, her back ramrod straight, her delicate hands clasped in her lap.

"That Tristan and I are brothers," Kalen elaborated.

I nodded. What else could I say?

"You should have told me."

"Penelope wanted to be the one to tell you."

A knock sounded at the door and Tristan came in. "You sent for me, Penelope."

Kalen looked at his mother. "Does he know too?"

Penelope nodded.

Kalen's eyes narrowed and a cold smile curled his lips. "So clearly I am the last to know."

"It was for your own good, Kalen," said Penelope, getting up from the chair and moving to put her hand on her son's shoulder.

He shifted away, but Tristan stepped forward, blocking his path. "You will need to be trained in the ways of the High Fae, Kalen. You must learn control of your powers."

Kalen threw his hands up in the air. "What powers? I don't have any."

Tristan raised an eyebrow and looked pointedly at Penelope, then back at Kalen. "That is not possible. You are the son of the most powerful Grand Duke of the Night Court. Your magic must be formidable."

Penelope cleared her throat. "I may have had something to do with that."

"I thought so," Tristan growled.

Kalen looked wide-eyed at Tristan, and his eyes narrowed to slits when he turned to look at his mother. "What did you do, Mother?"

She looked down, and it was the first time I had seen Penelope look embarrassed by something she had done. "I may have tampered with your powers slightly."

"Slightly!" Kalen raised his voice. "I have no powers at all. I don't even have enough air magic to be an archer. And that is the most basic fae magic there is." Kalen stormed off, slamming the door behind him.

"Air magic," Tristan scoffed. "I suspect he has a lot more than that." He looked pointedly at Penelope. "The darkness of the Night Court bloodline cannot be contained for long. He must learn to control it before something happens to make him lose control. And Goddess help us when he does."

Penelope nodded. "I will remove the spell that contains his powers, and you can begin training him immediately."

Tristan nodded and left the room.

I crossed my arms and looked at my mentor, who was now staring out of the big bay windows of her room. "Why did you do it, Penelope? Kalen had a right to know who he really was and what he can do. I know from experience being kept in the dark about your powers never ends well for anyone."

"I know," said Penelope, her regret showing plainly on her face. "I thought I could keep him safe. Being the son of the Grand Duke of the Night Court comes with its own dangers. I may have been in love with Kildaren, but I am not blind to his faults. He can be cruel and selfish at the best of times."

"Tristan is not like that," I said, suddenly feeling the need to defend my betrothed.

"Oh, but he was," said Penelope. "Tristan has changed over the centuries. You've only known him for a few months, Aurora. He is an immortal and has been around for a very long time. On the surface the enmity between the Night and Day Courts seems frivolous, but it was not always so. Night Court magic is dangerous. Those of the royal bloodline of the Night Court are sometimes born with powers so dangerous they cannot be controlled." She looked away. "I wanted Kalen to have a normal life, before he got caught up in the problems and machinations of the High Fae court."

"I understand you did it to protect him," I said. "But I'm not sure Kalen sees it that way."

"Maybe he will listen to you."

I nodded. "I will go speak to him now."

I left Penelope's room and went in search of Kalen. Stray beams of moonlight lit up the corridors as I hurried through them, my heart racing; the memory of Lilith's attack was still fresh in my mind. Somehow, knowing Uncle Gabriel wasn't here made Silverthorne Castle seem more dangerous and eerie than I remembered it.

Kalen wasn't in his room, and I ended up outside Uncle Gabriel's study. I stood before the big oak door and felt my heart constrict. I missed my granduncle's gruff presence. In this time of turmoil, I would have given anything to be able to talk to him and ask his advice. He would have known what to do.

I opened the door and entered the study. Everything seemed to have remained untouched since he left. Moonlight streamed in through the immense bay windows, hung with richly embroidered crimson curtains trimmed with gold, illuminating the numerous but slightly faded tapestries that covered the cold stone walls. Scenes depicting lush green forests filled with a host of different fae creatures stared back at me as I walked farther into the room, the sound of my boots muffled by the exotic carpets blanketing the floor. A sudden noise startled me, and I spun around to see a dark shape move out from behind Uncle Gabriel's large mahogany desk.

I let out a gasp, my heart beating rapidly in my chest, as a light appeared. I didn't even know I had been holding my breath. "Rafe! You scared the daylights out of me." I put my hand on my chest to calm myself. "What are you doing here, skulking around in the dark?"

"I was going to ask you the same thing." His tone was sharp, abrupt. He was holding something in his hand—an old worn scroll.

"What's that?" I asked, jerking my chin toward his hand.

"Nothing of importance," he said, and slipped it into his doublet. "You should be in your room. It's late."

I put my hands on my hips. "I'm not a child."

"Well then stop behaving like one," he snapped.

I furrowed my brow. "I know you're upset with me, but—"

"Upset!" He smiled, a sardonic look on his face as he ran his fingers through his hair. "You could say that."

"I told you I'm sorry! I never meant for it to happen like this. I didn't know. I thought you were married. My grandmother, she tricked me." I knew I was rambling, but I had to explain. "She—"

"Save your breath, Aurora!" he said, stepping forward and pulling me toward him. I didn't stop him as desire burned through my traitorous body. His hard body pressed against me as he leaned in, his breath hot on my ear. "Are you telling me you never meant to get betrothed to someone else? Or are you just upset I found out before you could spin another web of lies?"

"Rafe! I have never lied to you." I put my hands on his chest and looked up into his eyes, which appeared as if a storm were roiling inside them just waiting to be released. "Please, just listen to me. I didn't have a choice."

"You always have a choice, Aurora," he whispered. His voice was rough, bitter. "And you have made yours." And just as abruptly, he let me go, turning toward the door.

The door banged open before he reached it and Penelope barged in. "I thought I would find you here," she said hurriedly.

Rafe composed himself. "What's wrong?"

Penelope was wringing her hands, which was never a good sign. "It's Kalen. He's gone."

"Gone?" Rafe's eyes narrowed. "Kalen wouldn't leave. He knows to stay within the safety of the castle."

"He's upset," I interrupted, and then I told Rafe everything.

He threw a glance at Penelope. "And you didn't tell me this because . . . ?" He left the words hanging and waited for Penelope to reply.

"I couldn't, Rafe," she said. "I told no one except my sister. If the fae court found out there was another Night Court prince—a Nightshade, no less—they would have tried to get rid of him when he was just a child. Even Tristan only found out recently that Kalen is his brother."

I looked toward the door. "Where is Tristan?"

"He's out looking for Kalen."

I turned to Rafe. "Tristan doesn't know these woods. And Kalen hardly knows Tristan. He will only listen to you, Rafe."

"We will find them." I could almost see the wheels turning in Rafe's head as he quickly assessed the situation. "You both stay here in case he returns."

I shook my head. "No! I'm coming with you."

Rafe shrugged. "Suit yourself."

WE RODE out into the woods that lay beyond the town walls. A thick mist rolled in from the mountains, shrouding the trees and undergrowth. A lone owl hooted in the distance, and the leaves of the massive willow trees were still. There was no breeze, and the woods felt eerily quiet, devoid of life. Rafe didn't say a word as he scanned our surroundings, his senses on full alert. These were not the same woods I had ridden through with Erien just last year. Evil had been here—I could feel its malignant presence in the air.

A twig snapped, and we wheeled our horses around. Rafe's sword was already in his hand as he jumped off his black stallion. I followed suit, tightening my grip on Dawn.

I heard a sudden screech and then a cry.

"Kalen," I called out and ran toward the sound.

Kalen was on the ground, surrounded by at least a dozen gorgoths. For a moment my heart stopped, but I sighed in relief when I saw Tristan was already there, fighting the gorgoths, defending Kalen. His twin swords blazed as he systematically took down one gorgoth at a time, sometimes two. They circled around the two fae princes, growling and attacking, but couldn't get past Tristan.

Rafe raised an eyebrow. "Your fae prince doesn't look like he needs any help."

Just then, another growl sounded behind us.

My spine went rigid and I spun around. A whole pack of gorgoths had started to emerge from the trees behind us.

Rafe lifted his brows. "Friends of yours?"

"We've met before." I shot a dark look at him as I readied myself to meet them, my heart beating erratically. I wished I had my fae senses, strength, and magic that could take down a bunch of gorgoths in one blow. But I didn't. I was no longer a match for them, and whoever sent them knew that.

I remembered how the last bunch of gorgoths had managed to defeat Tristan and my palms started to sweat.

"Go for the wings," I shouted to Rafe as I raised my sword. The gorgoths attacked. "Once they are down, cut off their heads—it's the only way to kill them."

"Good to know," Rafe muttered, slashing his sword and injuring one gorgoth as another flew at him from the trees.

I gathered my magic and blasted the gorgoth with everything I had. The blast managed to push away the gorgoth from Rafe. I raised my sword and slashed at it, tightening my grip on Dawn as I ran forward, slashing through another gorgoth's wing and making my way closer to Rafe.

The gorgoths now turned their attention on Rafe and me. They were advancing on us from all sides. Without my fae powers I could not kill them; mage magic could not kill gorgoths like fae magic.

"Aurora!" Kalen shouted, finally noticing us.

He pushed himself up and ran toward the gorgoths. Among all the confusion I noticed something was different about him—he moved faster than I had ever seen him move before. Kalen's violet eyes flashed silver, and dark shadows started to form in his hands as he ran, snaking out from his fingertips. I stifled a gasp as he reached out his hand and one of the shadows uncoiled like a snake, wrapping itself like a noose around the closest gorgoth's neck. It sank to the ground, struggling and thrashing in its deathly bonds.

Searing pain slashed across my back as a gorgoth took advantage of my distracted state. I screamed as I fell to the ground, and the gorgoth pounced on me. There was a time when my magic could have killed all of them, but now I couldn't even get one gorgoth off me.

"Aurora!" Rafe shouted, and slashed the gorgoth's wing with his sword, kicking it away from me.

It sank to the ground, its eyes glazed over.

I pushed myself to my knees and looked at his sword; it was glowing with a faint silvery sheen. Dwarven-made, I thought, just like my own sword, Dawn, that Rafe had given me what felt like a lifetime ago.

A gorgoth loomed behind Rafe. Without thinking, I pulled out the dagger from my boot and flung it straight at the creature. It buried itself in its chest, and the monster staggered back. Rafe turned swiftly, raising his sword and severing the gorgoth's head from its body.

He held out his hand to pull me to my feet. "Your sword and dagger skills have improved considerably," he said unexpectedly, glancing over at Tristan. "I suspect a certain fae prince might have had something to do with that."

I couldn't help but smile and nod. My attention turned to Tristan, who stood with a pile of severed gorgoth heads at his feet. His twin swords blazed with silver fire in his hands, and his dark hair framed his face as his stormy midnight-blue eyes glittered with silver sparks. He looked like an avenging angel, like when I first saw him in Brandor when he saved me from the Drakaar. And in that moment, even with Rafe standing beside me, a part of me was proud to be Tristan's betrothed.

"I guess the legends about him are not so far-fetched after all," Rafe said, and I could see admiration in his beautiful gray eyes.

There were still many gorgoths surrounding us, but they had stopped advancing. To my astonishment, it wasn't Tristan they seemed afraid of. It was Kalen, who was standing in front of them, his hands outstretched as tendrils of darkness moved menacingly around the closest gorgoth, smothering it completely until the creature was nothing but a pile of dust.

The remaining gorgoths, recognizing Kalen's power, bowed their heads and moved back into the shadows of the trees, disappearing into the darkness of the misty night.

Kalen collapsed at Tristan's feet.

RETURN TO PIXIE BUSH

TRISTAN CARRIED Kalen back to the castle. He was still unconscious and lay limp in his brother's arms.

Penelope was waiting for us at the entrance, wringing her hands. "What happened?"

"Gorgoths," Rafe answered quickly, as he helped me walk with his arm around my waist. The gash on my back had soaked my tunic with blood, and the pain made me feel lightheaded. I really missed my fae powers.

"They must have been tracking us," Penelope confirmed. "Those gorgoths were waiting for you." She gave me a quick glance. "We must leave at the crack of dawn and get through the portal before anyone realizes we have left. They will be waiting for us in the mountains, but we will be long gone."

We took Kalen to his room, and Penelope proceeded to check him while Tristan explained to her how his powers had manifested in the forest, causing him to collapse after using them.

"Will he be all right?" I asked, sitting down on the bed beside him.

Penelope nodded. "He just needs to rest. Using his powers for the first time has taken a toll. He will slowly adjust to having them."

"I told you something like this could happen," Tristan said. "He has to learn to control his powers. He used too much when it wasn't necessary."

"Yes, you are right," Penelope agreed. "He will be fine by morning." She looked me over. "But your back seems to be in worse condition. Lie down on your stomach and let me take a look at it."

"I'm fine," I muttered, as Penelope went to her table and started mixing ingredients to put on my back.

Penelope shooed Tristan and Rafe out of the room before inspecting my wounds. I lay still and let her do her work, relieved that Penelope was here to heal me. I needed all my strength for the days ahead.

I barely had a nap before it was time to leave. Sleep was out of the question.

We were in our saddles riding into the forest as the sun started to light up the morning sky above the trees. Kalen was much better, and Penelope had healed my back. It was still uncomfortable, but there was no pain. Luckily, the gashes had not been deep. We had gathered supplies for our journey ahead, and we could not waste any more time.

"What you did last night with the gorgoths was amazing," I said to Kalen as I rode beside him.

"Maybe, but I had no idea what I was doing." He shrugged, staring into the distance. "I guess my mother removed the spell that contained my magic. I could sense the feelings of the gorgoths, and in a way I could communicate with them through thought. I could feel their internal struggle—they would not willingly attack a member of the royal Night Court. They are being controlled by a powerful spirit-fae."

I nodded. "Andromeda."

He shook his head. "No, the image I got from them was of a young fae girl around our age with golden hair."

I sucked in a breath. "Skye!" I couldn't imagine my friend being the cause of so much destruction and pain. But she was Andromeda's daughter, and the power she must possess to be able to control so many gorgoths made her a dangerous enemy.

"I don't understand," I said to Penelope, maneuvering my dappled gray mare closer to her horse, which plodded along behind the others. "Why is Kalen's magic so different from anything I have seen before? I have never seen anyone control gorgoths like that."

"This is exactly what I was afraid of," said Penelope. "Kalen may have gotten his shadow powers from his Night Court bloodline, but he has spirit magic because of me." She adjusted her reins and brought her horse closer to mine. "The Day Court spirit-fae have an affinity for all magical creatures, giving them the ability to control them depending on the power of the fae who wields it. You know how unpredictable spirit magic is at the best of times. But coupled with the royal bloodline of the Nightshades, Kalen's powers may evolve into something we have never seen before. There hasn't been a Night Court prince with spirit magic for centuries. The last Nightshade to have spirit powers was Rhiannon, Tristan and Kalen's grandmother. But even she could not subdue a pack of gorgoths like you said Kalen did last night. Once Kildaren hears about this he will want to train Kalen himself. He will want him to return to Elfi and join his court."

"Then we will have to keep him away from Elfi," I decided. I didn't want Kalen to fall into Kildaren's clutches. I knew what a snake Kalen's father could be. He was cunning and callous and would just as easily replace one son for the other if he thought it suited his purpose.

Penelope nodded as she rode forward to talk to Tristan.

"I guess we can't take the horses with us through the portal," I stated to Rafe, who had just ridden up to join me.

Rafe shook his head. "I'm afraid not. The passage to the portal is small, but it will save days of travel over the mountains."

It was noon by the time we got to the base of the mountains. We got off our horses and tied them to a tree, proceeding deeper into the forest on foot. Rafe would send his guards to retrieve the horses later.

He led us to a densely wooded area and moved some bushes apart to reveal a small cave. "The portal is through there." Rafe pointed to the cave. It wasn't a big opening; we would have to bend to get inside. "It will take you straight into the Goldleaf Forest. From there you won't have any problem finding your way." He looked at Penelope. "The Silver Swords will know where Morgana's army is camped. They are your best chance at getting into her camp. We have our own people stationed as spies within her army; they will assist you."

"Thank you, Rafe," said Penelope. "We will stop in Pixie Bush. I have friends there who will help us acquire fresh horses for the rest of our journey."

"Be careful," Rafe warned. "You are walking right into Morgana's territory. Pixie Bush may not be as you remember it."

Penelope nodded.

A lump formed in my throat. "Protecting the Eastern Pass will be dangerous too. Be careful."

He flashed me his charming Ravenswood smile. "Aren't I always?"

I shook my head. "No, not really."

He chuckled as Tristan inspected the cave entrance and unexpectedly turned to Rafe with his arm outstretched. "Thank you for taking such good care of Kalen for so many years. My brother and I spoke at length last night, and I can see why he holds you in such high regard. He told me of everything you have done to help the fae, and that even though you are a mage, you are not like the rest of them. You didn't have to come looking for us yesterday, but you did, at risk to your own life, and for that I am grateful."

Rafe smiled. "I don't think you or your brother needed my help last night. But I was glad to be of assistance." He grasped Tristan's forearm. "Train him well. I've seen what you did for Aurora, and if you can train her, I'm sure Kalen will be a breeze."

"Hey!" I said, my hands on my hips.

Rafe grinned and Tristan scowled at me before they turned back to each other.

"I should be the one thanking you for your help in restoring my throne." Rafe inclined his head. "I am forever in your debt, Prince Tristan."

Tristan smiled, his midnight-blue eyes sparkling. "And I in yours, Prince Rafael."

"Seriously?" I said, standing beside them staring with my mouth hanging open and my hands still on my hips. "You two are going to be friends now?"

"Maybe," said Rafe, winking at Kalen. He bowed to me. "Goodbye, Princess Aurora," he said formally, and my heart constricted in my chest. "I'm quite sure we will meet again. It seems I can't avoid you, however much I might try." He turned and disappeared into the trees, just as he had done so many times before.

"Nice fellow," said Tristan, turning toward the cave entrance.

I glared at Tristan, and Kalen suppressed a chuckle. This was just great! Now the two of them seemed to be getting along swimmingly, but neither of them wanted anything to do with me. Although if Tristan was warming up to Rafe, it was some progress at least.

We entered the small cave in the mountainside. It narrowed into a passage that resulted in a dead end. As we neared it my hand lit up, illuminating the rock face within the mountain.

"You can see the part of the rock that holds the portal if you look closely," said Penelope, pointing to the wall, which shimmered when the light hit it. It was an artfully concealed fae portal created by a powerful Ancient Fae. Without knowing it was there, it would be easy to miss it. "There are very few of these permanent portals left in Avalonia. Only the ones created by the strongest Ancient Fae have survived the test of time."

I nodded. Rafe had explained this to me when I first came to Avalonia, but I had never seen or used one of these portals before. Except for the tapestry in Redstone Manor, through which I had come into this world.

"I'll go first," said Tristan, stepping up to the wall. He took a confident step forward and disappeared into the mountain.

We waited a few moments and followed.

Time stopped, and for a second that felt like a lifetime, it seemed like I was floating in nothingness. I blinked, and when I opened my eyes I was standing at the mouth of a small cave in a clearing, surrounded by an ancient forest. This was no longer the Willow Woods in northern Eldoren. We had crossed over the Cascade Mountains in seconds, into the Goldleaf Forest in the kingdom of Illiador. Usually the journey through the mountains would have taken us days, maybe even weeks.

I looked around at the massive oak and hawthorn trees towering above us toward the sky, the tops of the huge branches swaying in the spring breeze. On the surface everything looked the same.

But something was different.

Once a cheerful, bright forest with sunlit groves and sparkling waterfalls, the Goldleaf Forest was now eerily quiet. No birds chirped in the tall trees; no animals rustled in the bushes or peeked out to greet us as we passed. There weren't even any butterflies, and the Goldleaf Forest always used to be awash with them.

Tristan had already sensed something was wrong. He had his

swords out and was scanning the surroundings, his razor-sharp senses attuned to the forest. I missed having my fae senses and strength. I used to be able to connect with the earth, the air, and all the elements of this world, using them to shape my magic as required. Now it was gone, and I had to adapt.

I had started practicing my mage magic on my own, but there was so much I didn't know about it. I had only finished a few months at the academy, and a fully trained mage took four years of intense study and training to reach the level of a warrior-mage. I needed a mastermage to teach me, but without professor Dekela and my granduncle, there was no one who could train me.

"This way," said Penelope, appearing beside me and starting down a path deeper into the forest.

I followed Tristan, Penelope, and Kalen through the decaying trees, along a path toward Pixie Bush. The forest was still. Dried leaves crunched beneath our feet and twigs snapped as we made our way deeper into the Goldleaf Forest.

I thought back to when I had first come here, and how warm and kind Uncle Gabriel was to me, taking me into his home and giving me a family. Without him I was lost, and the world didn't make sense anymore. He was the only one who had my best interests at heart. Everyone else had an agenda, something they wanted from me, or something they needed me to do for them. Uncle Gabriel only ever did what was best for me. It took losing him to realize how important he was to my life. Even in the few months that I had known him, when he was around, I felt safe, at home.

Penelope let out a gasp, snapping me out of my reverie. I looked up to see a sight that brought tears to my eyes.

Pixie Bush was gone.

The once-prosperous fae village was a charred mass of blackened leaves and rotting wood. The tiny cottages were reduced to heaps of burned wood and ash. The once beautifully flowering underbrush was now just mud and dirt.

I saw something black and shiny glitter when the midday sun forced its way through the towering trees, and I bent down to pick it up.

"What is that?" asked Tristan, coming over to me.

I held it up and dropped it as soon as I realized what it was— an arrowhead made of blackened iron.

Tristan bent down to inspect it but was careful not to touch anything. "There are more of these littered all over the village. Morgana must have been working on these weapons for some time."

Penelope nodded, her face a mask of pure anger as she gazed at the destruction all around her. "They came for me," she said, almost to herself. "They knew I once lived here. They must have wanted information on my whereabouts." She ran her hands over her face. "Now all these poor innocent fae have suffered because of me. And I wasn't here to help them."

My blood boiled at the thought of Morgana's soldiers storming into Pixie Bush and torturing and murdering the fae. Her words ignited within me a burning desire to rid Avalonia of Morgana and her evil. This was no longer about me taking back my throne, or making my parents proud, or even avenging their deaths. This was much more.

I had been brought into this world for a higher purpose, and it took losing my fae powers for me to realize I was made the Dawnstar for a reason. It was meant to be used for the greater good; it was meant to save this world from destruction. It didn't matter that I was not stronger or more powerful than everyone else. It didn't matter if I ever sat on the throne of Illiador. The only things that mattered were stopping the darkness from engulfing this world and preserving the light from being destroyed forever. There had to be a way, and if it took everything I had, even my life, I would find it.

I went over and put my hand on Penelope's shoulder. "Have faith, Penelope—all is not lost yet. We will make this right."

She shook her head. "All those innocent lives . . . gone. We will never get them back."

"I know, but we can make sure this never happens again."

Kalen's eyes flashed with determination as he looked at his mother and turned to me. "We will find a way to get the Dagger back, Aurora. And when we do, we will make them all pay for what they have done."

"Well, you will have to get a move on," said Tristan, his swords lighting up with silver fire. His eyes scanned the trees as his fae senses picked up something I did not. "Someone has betrayed us. We're surrounded."

The forest was still; no one moved. It was as if time itself held its breath.

From all around us, dark forms started to emerge one by one from behind the trees. Shadowy figures in black robes took shape with elongated canines and dark black pools for eyes.

My blood chilled as I recognized who they were, or rather what they were.

Drakaar! And along with them, a host of uniformed soldiers wearing the crest of the black rose—Morgana's minions. All of them had bows in their hands with black-tipped arrows pointed directly at us from all angles. Even the immortal fae couldn't withstand an onslaught of this many arrows. A fae shield would not stop them.

A familiar face, large with a patch over his eye, stepped forward and away from the group. His hideous scarred face grinned at me, showing his blackened teeth. "You just don't die, do you, Princess Aurora?"

How did he find me?

"Sorry to disappoint you," I said through clenched teeth. My hands balled into fists, but I dared not move. One word from him could release those arrows. "What do you want, Oblek?"

"Is that any way to greet an old friend?" Oblek said.

"I'm quite sure your concept of friendship severely differs from mine," I said tartly.

"I'm sure it does." Oblek waved his hand as if dismissing me. "But it's not me you have to worry about. The general wants to see you."

"And who is this general?" I asked. We needed more information. We were completely in the dark about him and his plans. My mind raced as I glanced around. There seemed to be no escape—we were completely surrounded. Who could have betrayed us? No one knew we were here except Rafe and Captain Raingate. I didn't want to believe either of them could have given us up to Oblek.

Oblek laughed. "You will find out soon enough."

"Why not just kill me here and get it over with?" I said, putting my hands on my hips. Without my magic I would not escape this time. And with my friends' lives in jeopardy, Oblek knew I would give myself up to save them.

Oblek rubbed his bearded chin. "As much as I would love to kill you, I can't. It seems the general has a use for you. And I am to bring you to him alive." He looked at Penelope, Kalen, and Tristan and raised his chin to them. "They are not needed, so we will have to get rid of them."

Tristan smiled but didn't put down his weapons. "Is this general such a coward that he cannot face us himself? He sends you to do his dirty work?"

"Ah! Prince Tristan. The general is not foolish enough to go up against the Dark Prince of Elfi on his own." Oblek smiled. "That's why he sent them." He nodded at the trees, and two warriors stepped forward.

I gasped and Tristan's eyes narrowed. These were not Morgana's mages nor Drakaar; they were unmistakably fae. Dressed in black fae leathers with long dark hair secured by a band at the nape of their necks, they had eyes that glowed red like the demons with which they were allied.

"Dark fae," Tristan growled under his breath.

I had heard of such creatures, the offspring of a fae and a demon as powerful as a High Fae warrior and just as deadly. But every book I read had told me they were extinct, and even before that time, they rarely survived past childhood.

Oblek laughed. "You weren't expecting that, were you, Prince Tristan? The general has found a way to breed a whole legion of these dark fae soldiers especially to take care of you and the fae queen's scanty band of Elite warriors. With you out of the way and Princess Aurora's powers gone, no one will be able to stop the general's plans."

Demon-powered fae. Great! As if we didn't have enough people to fight. Tristan would have his work cut out for him if he was going to fight those two.

"Rafe will stop you," I said, trying to sound as positive and unafraid as I could. "And so will Santino."

Oblek's lips formed a cruel sneer. "I don't think so, Princess Aurora. It was your dear King Rafael, or should I say the Black Wolf, who betrayed you."

"Well, that wouldn't be very nice of me, would it?" said Rafe, sauntering through the trees, his black cloak billowing around him as he walked slowly and steadily toward us.

A bunch of archers trained their arrows on him.

What was he doing here? How did he know?

Rafe held up his hands to show he was unarmed. "It astounds me how easily you can tell a lie, Oblek. But your little spy doesn't seem to have your abilities. Danica confessed she works for you."

"Danica," I hissed. Why wasn't I surprised? I looked at him out of the corner of my eye, not wanting to look away from my attackers.

Rafe paused, his eyes taking in all our positions. Penelope was standing beside me, and Oblek had arrows positioned on her too. If we made one wrong move, one of us could die. I had seen the destruction weapons of blackened iron had wreaked on the fae in the village of Pixie Bush, and I wasn't going to take any chances with my friends' lives.

"You can't help them this time, Rafael," said Oblek. "That is, unless you brought an army with you."

Rafe raised an eyebrow. "Who says I didn't?"

Oblek laughed. "I'm onto you, Black Wolf," he spat. "This whole area is surrounded; we know you came alone."

"That would be quite remiss of me, wouldn't it?" Rafe quipped, his tone flippant. He was toying with Oblek and enjoying it.

Had he really come alone? Rafe was not stupid—he must have a plan.

While he was talking, he moved slowly closer to me.

"Rafe," I said softly, "what are you doing?"

"What I always seem to be doing since I met you, my dear," said the King of Eldoren, his lips curved up in a half-smile. "Getting you out of a tight fix."

I glared at him. "I'm handling it."

"Enough talking," Oblek said and pointed his finger at me. "Kill the others and take the girl," he ordered. "The general is waiting."

It took only seconds for the arrows to be loosed from their bows. I heard the sharp twang of bowstrings as the arrows flew at us from all angles. I called forth my mage magic and threw up my hands, engulfing all of us in a mage shield. At the same time, Rafe created another shield that covered mine and took the brunt of the attack. Our shields merged together as one and held. The arrows stopped in midair, falling to the ground.

Oblek raised his eyebrows. "Your mage magic seems to be as strong as ever, Princess."

A second set of archers emerged from behind the others, bows ready and black-tipped arrows nocked. The dark fae bared their teeth at Tristan, sharp canines flashing in the light of their swords, which were now lit up with red fire.

Oblek raised his hand, readying the archers to fire again. "It was a good show of resistance, but your mage magic will only hold for so long, and I have an abundance of archers and arrows."

From the corner of my eye I could see Kalen moving toward the trees. Black shadows had started to snake out of him and wind around the closest tree, spreading to the others.

My eyes widened and my blood chilled when all around us the trees suddenly started to come to life. Brown and green shapes emerged from the tree trunks, separating themselves from the bark.

"Impossible," Penelope gasped as she beheld the incredible spectacle. "Hamadryads. They haven't awoken outside of Elfi in centuries."

A scream pierced the air.

My head whipped around to see a hamadryad—a fae spirit of the trees, strong beyond measure with razor-sharp teeth and claws that could kill with a single swipe—pounce on one of the Drakaar. The Drakaar screamed in pain as the brown-skinned maiden crushed its neck, twisting it and severing its head with her claws.

The Drakaar and Oblek's soldiers looked startled as they began to realize what was happening. Some fumbled for their bows while others dropped theirs, drawing their swords instead.

Shadows started to form around Tristan as his magic took shape. Tristan rarely used the magic of the night, but when he did, anyone could sense the power of the High Fae prince. It was only now that I finally realized why he was the most feared of Izadora's warriors. This was a magic I didn't understand, reserved only for the royal Night Court bloodline, a darker magic than most of the fae would dare to use. The magic of the night was a darkness that flickered on the outskirts of fae magic, an ancient calling passed down through Tristan's bloodline to keep darker forces in check.

Tristan roared as his twin swords lit up with silver fire, and he charged at the scattered, confused soldiers. Half of them turned and ran before the fury of the Prince of the Night Court, as the Drakaar tried to get the warrior-mages to stay and fight. The dark fae ran at Tristan, swords flashing as they clashed with the Dark Prince of Elfi.

He blocked their blows easily and grinned at his enemies. "You are going to have to do better, dark fae," he said, twirling his swords effortlessly in his hands and attacking again.

Rafe drew his sword, and mage soldiers went down like stones as the King of Eldoren released his magic upon them. He fought with his sword in one hand and a ball of magic in the other. Heads rolled and magic crackled all around us as Penelope shielded Kalen while he worked his magic.

I unsheathed Dawn from the scabbard on my back. I may not have fae magic and strength, but I did know how to fight, and I had my mage magic. Taking Rafe's cue, I gathered my magic in one hand and flung it at an approaching mage soldier. Lightning sizzled and struck as I called forth my powers. This was no time for push strikes and shielding; it was kill or be killed. However many times I had been put in this situation, it was hard for me to bring myself to do it, but I knew I had to—our lives depended on it.

Metal clashed against metal as I braced my sword for an attack from the side. I whirled around and swung my sword in a wide arc, slicing through my attacker's arm. My hand sizzled with mage fire as I let it loose, engulfing the screaming mage in a torrent of fiery death. The stench of burning flesh made me nauseous, but there was no time to think or stop as I braced myself for another attack.

Tristan was still fighting the dark fae, silver and red fire shooting back and forth between them as their swords clashed and flickered faster than the human eye could see. They were strong, the dark fae, and powered with demon blood, they were ferocious fighters with all the strength and fire Tristan had.

Two Drakaar moved toward me from the trees. Before I could shield myself, one reached out his clawed hand and a Shadow Demon emerged, snaking in my direction. My mage magic could not withstand a Shadow Demon, which I had learned the hard way back in Brandor when one had first attacked me.

The shadow creature pounced upon me, its dark claws choking my throat. I tried to pull it off, but I was not strong enough.

"How does it feel to be helpless, Dawnstar?" sneered the Drakaar, moving closer, his hand outstretched, controlling the Shadow Demon. "Without your fae-fire you are noth—" His words were cut short as two hamadryads emerged from the trees behind him and embedded their claws in his throat.

The Shadow Demon disappeared with the death of its master, and I gasped for air. Black blood stained the undergrowth while the tree spirits finished their work.

I looked at Tristan, who was standing over the bodies of the two dark fae. They lay lifeless on the ground, their heads severed from their bodies. I smiled. I guess they underestimated the Prince of the Night Court.

Out of the corner of my eye, I saw an arrow whiz toward Kalen. It tore through Penelope's shield and embedded itself in his arm.

"Kalen!" I screamed. If I had my fae speed, I may have been able to stop it.

He grimaced and pulled out the arrow. Penelope ran to him to check the wound.

I breathed a sigh of relief. He was lucky the arrow had only hit his arm. Tristan had told me that if an arrow of blackened iron hit a vital organ, it could be deadly even to an immortal.

The Drakaar were shouting to each other to retreat as more hamadryads broke away from their trees and ambushed the soldiers and Drakaar. They tore out throats and strangled others in a fury, resulting in bloodshed and carnage the likes of which I hadn't seen since the werewraiths in the temple in Elfi.

Suddenly, a roar sounded above—a creature I could not recognize. It wasn't Abraxas; my magic could not reach him to summon him or speak to him. I craned my neck back and saw a flash of white wings through the trees.

Chaos erupted all around me.

Magic flashed and crackled in green and blue hues above the treetops.

A musical voice spoke in my head. *"Do not fear, little one. I am here. And I brought help."*

I knew that voice, and my heart lifted with hope. "Snow!"

My beautiful white pegasus came soaring through the trees.

Behind her flew huge white snow leopards with massive wings. They came tearing through the branches and settled themselves in a circle around us. On their backs rode towering warrior women, resplendent in full battle armor that flashed in the midday sun.

"The warrior witches of Rohron," Kalen whispered in awe.

The warrior women were beautiful and incredibly tall with braided hair, holding wooden staffs topped with shining jewels. A few of the witches' staffs had more than one jewel shining on their apex.

One of the witches calmly aimed her staff at a Drakaar near me while still astride the winged leopard. Blue light shot out of one of the jewels and hit the Drakaar in the chest. He went down like a stone, and Tristan severed his head before he even touched the ground.

My legs nearly gave way in relief when I saw who was at the head of the witches of Rohron.

A familiar figure jumped off my pegasus, as agile as a young man. His long white hair was plaited like the warriors with whom he rode, and a familiar sword flashed in his hand. He looked thinner than I remembered, and with his short beard shaved off, his face appeared gaunter than before. But his blue eyes twinkled when he saw me, and he smiled.

There was no mistaking who it was.

I could hardly believe it. I felt my heart lift and fill with hope as a beam of sunlight fell through the trees, illuminating the clearing and the man who stood before me.

Gabriel Silverthorne was alive.

AN OLD ENEMY

THE WITCHES, hamadryads, and Tristan cleared the forest of the threat, and Oblek was bound and tied to a tree, unconscious.

Uncle Gabriel spoke privately with Rafe, then joined us.

"We will need him for questioning," said Uncle Gabriel after he hugged me tightly.

"We thought you were dead," Penelope said plainly.

"I almost was."

"Then how?" I asked, my heart still bursting with joy. I felt as if everything was going to be right again. Uncle Gabriel was here.

"All in good time, my dear." Uncle Gabriel put his hand on my shoulder. "There are some things we need to deal with first."

He went up to the hamadryads, who had gathered in a group. "Thank you for your help," said the Duke of Silverthorne, bowing to them.

One of the hamadryads stepped forward and inclined her head. Her hair and eyes were a dark green like the leaves of the tree she inhabited, and her skin was crusty and brown, resembling the bark of an old oak. Up close they seemed more human than when they were tearing open Drakaar throats, but they still made me nervous. "We came at the behest of the Prince of the Night Court."

Silverthorne looked over at Tristan, who shook his head.

"Not Prince Tristan," said the hamadryad, and she turned to Kalen and bowed. "Prince Kalen summoned us."

Uncle Gabriel narrowed his eyes and looked at Penelope. "So my suspicions were correct. Kalen is Kildaren's son?"

Penelope nodded as Kalen shifted uncomfortably beside her.

"Interesting," Uncle Gabriel said, rubbing his chin and turning back to the hamadryads. "Thank you for responding to the summons," he said formally.

The hamadryad nodded and unexpectedly turned to me and bowed as well. "It is an honor to serve and protect the Dawnstar."

I had read about the hamadryads at the library in Elfi. They were different from ordinary dryads in that they were the spirit of the oak trees specifically and the ancestors of dryads. Their life force was tied to the trees they came from. The older the oak tree, the more powerful the hamadryad was. They were ancient creatures and almost impossible to control. That was why Penelope was shocked to see Kalen summon them.

I thanked them and smiled faintly. I knew powerful fae creatures could sense my fae magic even when it was shielded by the amulet. But if my fae magic was all gone, how did they know I was the Dawnstar?

The hamadryad came closer and put her clawed hand on my shoulder. I stood very still, not wanting to make a wrong move. Magical fae creatures were temperamental; any slight could cause them to attack. She spoke softly in a musical, ethereal voice only I could hear. "You were destined to be the protector of this world, Aurora Firedrake. The magic of the Dawnstar was meant for you and you alone. There is no one else who can wield the magic as it was meant to be wielded."

"But my fae magic," I whispered back. "Lilith stole it."

"Your fae magic doesn't define you, and neither does your mage side," said the Ancient Fae creature. "You are the Dawnstar, the light that fills this world with magic. You are here for a reason. Your destiny is still to unfold. Find your true purpose and path; do not waver in your faith. Only then will you be able to find your power."

Those words. *The light that fills this world with magic.* It was the same thing Abraxas had once said to me. I missed him and his advice. His powerful ancient voice had kept me going at the darkest of times. But now I couldn't even contact him. The ring on my finger lay dull and lifeless.

"I have no idea how to do what you ask," I said softly, looking at my ring. "I'm not as strong as everyone thinks I am."

"You are stronger than you know, Dawnstar," said the hamadryad, and she turned to disappear into the tree from which she came.

Once the hamadryads had returned to the forest, Uncle Gabriel smiled, patting Kalen on his back. "That was quite a feat you pulled off back there, young Kalen."

Kalen grinned, a twinkle in his eyes. "Not as big a feat as you managed to pull off, Your Grace."

Uncle Gabriel laughed. "Yes, I suppose."

"Are you ever going to tell us how you managed to escape when everyone thought you were dead?" Kalen asked my granduncle, wincing as he tried to move his arm.

"All in good time, my friend," said Uncle Gabriel, throwing a fleeting but pointed look at Penelope. "I think you should let your mother take a closer look at that arm."

Kalen nodded and went over to his mother.

Uncle Gabriel turned to the witches, who stood slightly apart, the great white leopards prowling impatiently behind them.

One of the witches, with sparkling eyes the color of burnt honey and long dark plaited hair falling over one shoulder, came forward. Her caramel-colored skin was heavily tattooed with strange symbols that ran down her neck and arm. She held her head high as she stalked toward me. Her body was all muscle, and I could see she was a warrior through and through by the way she carried herself.

"This is Ashara, war leader of the northern witch tribes," said Uncle Gabriel, introducing us.

I stepped forward to clasp her forearm in the universal greeting. "Thank you for your help. If you hadn't come to our aid, we would not have survived."

Ashara smiled warmly. "It is an honor to come to your aid, Aurora Shadowbreaker," she said formally.

I glanced at my granduncle. "How did you convince them to help us?"

Uncle Gabriel huffed a laugh. "I didn't. It was you who convinced them."

I put my hand on my chest. "Me? How? I've never even met them."

"Yes, Aurora, you have," said Uncle Gabriel, his blue eyes twinkling as he spoke to me. "It seems the slave girl you rescued in Neris was none other than the witch king's granddaughter and heir."

I gasped. "Rhea!"

The Duke of Silverthorne nodded, a smile on his face. "She had been taken a few months ago while out visiting a sick friend. They have been searching for her ever since. When she returned to Rohron, safe and sound under your protection, she told her grandfather everything about the young queen who rescued her—the Shadowbreaker who was going to save the world."

I shook my head and looked at Penelope and Tristan. This was unbelievable.

Ashara spoke up. "What the duke says is the truth. Our kingdom never gets involved in mage or fae disputes. But when

Rhea told us of the young queen from the west who saved a seemingly inconsequential slave girl at great cost to her own life and safety, we knew a high queen who was worth fighting for had finally arrived. Our king has granted full support of his witch warriors to assist you in your battle against Morgana. So far, forty-two tribes have answered the summons." She bowed to me. "We are yours to command, my queen."

I was speechless. This was much more than we had hoped for. The witches of Rohron might be few in number, but there were some among them who possessed the powerful magic of their ancestors, and they were formidable allies to have when fighting demons.

Oblek, who was still tied to a tree, regained consciousness.

He opened his eyes, and they widened when he saw who was standing before him. "You!" he spat at the Duke of Silverthorne. "You're supposed to be dead."

"Well, I'm not," said Uncle Gabriel calmly. "But what I would like to know is the name of your general."

"Ha! You can tear me to pieces, but I will never tell you." He grinned a maniacal grin. "You don't have any idea what is coming for you. You'd better run now, Silverthorne, while you have the chance."

Uncle Gabriel sighed and looked at Rafe. "He's never going to tell us what he knows this way. I will have to take him back to Silverthorne Castle if we are to get any answers out of him."

Rafe gave a brief nod, his arms crossed in front of him. "Take him."

Tristan stepped forward, drawing his sword. "I can take care of this right now. Based on the stories I've heard from Aurora, this mage doesn't deserve to live."

Rafe looked at me. "We need him for questioning. But if you want him dead, I will allow Prince Tristan to execute him right here."

My old enemy was tied up before me, and all I could feel was remorse. I didn't want him dead, even after everything he had done to me. It was not up to me to pass judgment on his life, even though I had the power to end it.

I shook my head and put my hand on Tristan's arm, restraining him. "Take him to the dungeons at Silverthorne Castle and find out what he knows," I said to Uncle Gabriel. "There has been enough bloodshed here tonight."

Tristan scowled at me but put away his sword.

Uncle Gabriel came forward and clapped his hand on my shoulder, his blue eyes twinkling with an emotion I had not seen before—pride. "Spoken like a true queen, Aurora Shadowbreaker."

My eyes welled up, but I forced back the tears as I had learned to do and hugged my granduncle. I was so glad he was back.

Uncle Gabriel scrutinized the area. "We need to get out of here. It is too easy to get ambushed in this part of the forest." He turned to Ashara. "If your witches can take Oblek back to Silverthorne Castle, Captain Raingate will take care of him."

Ashara nodded. "It will be done." She turned to instruct her warriors.

The relief was palpable all around. The Duke of Silverthorne always knew what to do.

"I know a place where we can rest and decide our next course of action," Rafe said. "Hopefully the people of Pixie Bush took my advice and have gone into hiding."

"Do you think any of them are still alive?" Penelope asked.

Rafe nodded and led the way. "If they left when I told them to, yes."

The Goldleaf Forest was still and quiet as we traveled through it. I fell into step beside Rafe. "Why did you come after us?" I asked finally. "Don't you need to be with your army?"

Rafe ran a hand through his dark hair. "I shouldn't have come, I know. But it was my fault Danica found out where you were going in the first place. I had to warn you, but I was too late. I should have been more careful."

I raised an eyebrow and looked at him from the corner of my eye. "Maybe you should be more discerning about who you take to your bed."

He shot me a dark look. "Maybe you should have thought of that before you went running off to get betrothed to someone else."

"Does it always have to come back to that?" I sighed and peeked at Tristan in my peripheral vision. "I told you, it was my grandmother who . . ." I shook my head. I was done explaining myself. I had told him the truth. If Rafe chose not to believe me, then there was nothing I could do about it. "You shouldn't have come, Rafe. I can take care of myself."

His tone softened. "I know." He added stiffly, "I just wanted to make sure you were all right."

I nodded, but I didn't meet his eyes. I didn't want him running back to save me every time he felt guilty. I wanted him to be with me because he wanted to, because he loved me and nobody else.

Behind us, Tristan and Ashara were arguing.

"Leave him alone, witch," Tristan growled. "Penelope is a fae healer, and she has already looked at it."

"Whatever you say, fae," Ashara said, holding up her hands in mock surrender and rolling her eyes.

I stopped to talk to Tristan. "What's wrong?"

He scowled. "Nothing."

Ashara stalked up to the Duke of Silverthorne and pointed at Kalen. "That young fae has been hit by an arrow of blackened iron." She then pointed at Tristan. "And that insufferable brother of his refuses to let me look at the wound."

"Why do you care?" Tristan growled at her and looked at my granduncle. "I don't want any filthy witch magic touching Kalen. She could make it worse."

Penelope stepped in and put her hand on Tristan's arm to calm him. "What is your concern, Ashara? The wound is not deep, and the arrowhead has been removed. Is there something I've missed?"

Ashara nodded. "I'm no healer, but witches can sense demon magic a league away. I can still sense a shard of blackened iron in his blood."

Penelope wrung her hands, and her eyes darted to Silverthorne, whose face adequately portrayed the gravity of the situation. "Let's get to the cave, and then I can have another look at it." She turned to Ashara. "Your help is greatly appreciated, Ashara."

Ashara nodded, and we continued on the path through the trees.

I looked at Penelope's furrowed brow and lowered my voice. "He will be all right, won't he, Penelope?"

"I hope so." Penelope's expression was grim. "Let me check him first so we know how severe it is."

We walked the rest of the way in silence and thankfully reached the safety of the cave by nightfall. The entrance was small and overgrown with foliage; we had to cut aside branches with our swords to get to it. A small arched opening and steep stone steps carved out of the rock descended into darkness. Rafe went first, his hand lighting up with a ball of mage light. The rest of us did the same and followed him down into the depths of the ancient caves that lay below the Goldleaf Forest.

When we reached the cave floor, which was almost two hundred feet underground, I was stunned by the absolute silence that greeted us. We trod carefully over the slippery, moss-covered stones and entered another cavern, an immense cave with stalagmites and stalactites over a hundred feet long.

"The caves stretch out under the Goldleaf Forest and part of the mountains all the way to the town of Royn on the western coast," Rafe explained.

I was not the only one stunned by the massive size of these caves. Penelope was also in awe as she looked around. "I lived in the Goldleaf Forest for so many years but never knew these caves existed. How did you find them?"

Rafe shrugged. "I stumbled upon them a few years ago."

Penelope created balls of light that hardened and floated upward, illuminating more of the immense cave. The air around us was cool, and a light mist seemed to hover above us as the rest of the cave came into view.

Scores of rimstone pools dotted the cave floor, and one was almost as big as a small lake. Through the mystical underground landscape meandered a river that ran the length of the cavern and disappeared into the unknown darkness of the other caves that branched out from the main one. A light mist rolled over the surface of the water, creating an eerie preternatural feel. But the biggest surprise was a massive forest growing undisturbed deep in the heart of the cavern.

We followed Uncle Gabriel toward it. "Sections of this cavern have collapsed," he explained, pointing to places in the cavern ceiling through which we could faintly see the moon. "In the daytime, sunlight can penetrate the darkness, allowing these ancient trees to survive here."

Ashara and Penelope started to weave protective spells around the cavern to ward us against intruders. Fae and witch magic intertwined to form a stronger barrier.

But Tristan stiffened. He had heard something. I was sure of it when he swiftly drew his swords, lighting them up with silver fire.

"What is it, Tristan?" I asked, alarmed. Had they followed us here?

But Penelope gasped and stepped toward Tristan, putting her hand on his arm and restraining him. "Wait."

I squinted to see what their fae eyes saw clearly, as small shapes started to emerge from behind the massive trees within the cave.

Penelope's face lit up when she saw who it was. A small bedraggled brownie came into view.

"Fitzbean!" cried Penelope as she ran forward to hug the stunned brownie. He didn't seem to recognize her because she had changed her appearance since she lived in Pixie Bush. But he did recognize Kalen.

"You're alive." Kalen came forward, his eyes lighting up as more figures started to come into focus around us—dryads, with little children, brownies, pixies, and tiny flower fairies.

"You're all safe." Penelope rushed forward to hug a dryad lady, whom I recognized as her friend, Mrs. Herbchild.

Mrs. Herbchild nodded and hugged her back as Penelope explained her change of appearance.

"How?" asked Penelope, so happy she was at a loss for words.

"The Black Wolf," said Mrs. Herbchild simply. "He came to Pixie Bush last moon tide and told us to leave the village. He said war was coming. We found this place by accident and have been living in these caves ever since."

"All of you?" Penelope smiled, looking at Rafe, who watched quietly. They still didn't know he was the Black Wolf, and it was better to keep it that way.

Mrs. Herbchild shook her head. "Not everyone listened to him. Many stayed behind. Have you seen them?"

Penelope's face fell. "Oblek's men attacked the village. I'm afraid there were no survivors."

Mrs. Herbchild nodded, her face grim, the realization that many of her people would never see their loved ones again stark in her sad brown eyes. "I will inform the others." She went off into the trees to speak to the remaining fae about the fate of their village and loved ones.

Penelope turned and unexpectedly hugged Rafe. "Thank you," she said softly.

Rafe looked Penelope in the eyes and nodded. "I knew Oblek's men had been causing trouble around here, so when I got back from Elfi—" he glanced at me briefly and back at her, "—I went to Pixie Bush and told them to leave the village. I hoped they managed to stay hidden and safe, but I didn't have any way of knowing for sure."

Penelope nodded and squeezed Rafe's arm. "You did what you could, Rafael. And I will be forever grateful for the many times you have helped our people."

I smiled at his quiet way of helping others. Rafe was always the one who watched out for the fae of Pixie Bush, and even in the midst of his own problems he found time to go there and warn them, without asking for anything in return. I shouldn't have been surprised; it was one of the many reasons I loved him.

Tristan smiled too as he sheathed his swords. And I could see how his opinion of Rafe had shifted significantly since they first met.

As I helped start a fire, my thoughts returned to the ones who didn't get away from Oblek's men: families with children, innocent lives lost because they believed they would be safe in their homes. And they should have been, not hiding in forest caves unsure where they would go next. I could stop this. I could stop all of this. I knew I had to save my people from a life of destitution and fear. But without my magic, I didn't know how I would ever succeed.

Penelope sat down with Kalen on a log beside the fire and took a look at his arm. When she looked up her face was grave.

Tristan hung his head. "I should have protected him."

I went over and clasped Tristan's hand. "You were busy fighting the dark fae. There was nothing you could have done—he was too far from you. If it is anyone's fault, it is mine. If I had my fae speed, I could have gotten to him in time." I looked down at my feet.

"Stop it, you two, it's nobody's fault." Penelope wrung her hands. "This is not looking good," she said, shaking her head. "These arrows have been forged in dwarven forges and spelled with a dark magic I don't recognize. Usually an arrow like this is not fatal to a High Fae, unless it pierces a vital organ." Penelope gave Silverthorne a meaningful glance. "But Ashara was right—a piece of it has broken off and entered Kalen's bloodstream. That is the demon magic Ashara sensed still clinging to him." Her eyes were wide, confused by this new danger. "It's sentient. Alive. A darkness that now runs in his blood. My magic cannot remove it. Fae healing will not work."

Silverthorne's face was somber. "Mage healers are not capable of dealing with this sort of darkness."

He looked over at Ashara, who shook her head. "We are warriors, not healers."

"What happens if we don't take it out?" I prodded. I needed to know.

Penelope took a deep breath. "It will slowly leech his magic until there is nothing left." She ran a hand over her face as if to dispel images she could not deal with. "Once the shard reaches his heart, Kalen will die."

I gasped as my hand flew to my mouth. "No!" It didn't seem possible.

Penelope's eyes glistened with tears; she glanced at her son, who was sitting beside her, and put an arm around his shoulders. "Kalen is strong, so we may have some time."

Kalen was silent through her explanation. Only his eyes indicated that he had just heard his death sentence.

I threw my hands up in the air. "Time for what? You just said your magic cannot remove the shard and neither can Ashara's. The mages cannot do it." I looked down, my voice breaking. "The magic of the Dawnstar could have removed it." It wasn't a question.

But Penelope confirmed it and nodded. "Yes."

I sank to my knees beside Kalen, tears forming and threatening to spill at any moment. "I'm sorry. I'm so sorry, Kalen. I should have never dragged you into this."

He smiled his usual cheerful grin that I had come to treasure. "It's not your fault, Aurora. I wanted to help."

"There may be another way," said Silverthorne, stroking his chin. "The druid monks of Andrysia are skilled healers and ancient scholars. They may be the only ones with enough knowledge of ancient magic to save Kalen's life."

"Marcus Gold said the druids are long gone from Avalonia." I looked at my granduncle. "They never taught us anything about them at the academy."

"That's because Marcus is right," said Uncle Gabriel. "Once there were quite a few druids in Avalonia, powerful magic users, scholars, and healers who came to these lands from beyond the great western sea and landed on the shores of Illiador and Andrysia. They were a peaceful people and resided in monasteries or traveled around, helping and healing in the villages and towns along the coast. Because their magic was strong and they could fight demons, they came to be revered among the common folk, who couldn't depend on mages to help them when a stray demon creature attacked a citizen.

"But the mages grew jealous of the druids' healing powers and knowledge of ancient magic, so they turned the people against them. Over the years, the druids were run out of the southern kingdoms. They settled in northern Andrysia, in the areas surrounding Redthorn Forest, and built monasteries hidden away in the Silverspike Mountains. Fewer and fewer druids were born with magic, and their race eventually died out."

"But if they have died out, how do we find one?"

"Stories emerge from time to time of druid sightings," Penelope answered, drying her eyes, "or people being miraculously healed by a druid. But even these stories have become rare in the past twenty years or so." She looked at Silverthorne. "I just hope we can find them before it is too late."

Rafe furrowed his brow and stared into the fire as if he were trying to recall something. "I know an old sailor, Captain Jarvik, who lives in the town of Royn on the coast not far from here. At the tavern he would always boast that he had met the druids. The townspeople believed him to be an old drunk making up stories." He met Penelope's eyes. "If there is anyone who has an idea where to start looking, it would be him."

Silverthorne nodded. "Then in the morning we will go to Royn and find this drunken sailor."

IN SEARCH OF DRUIDS

THE MOOD WAS somber as Ashara passed around some bread and dried meat. Everyone ate to sustain themselves, but no one was really hungry or took any enjoyment in it. In the morning we would set out to find the druids, and I would not rest until Kalen was healed. He seemed okay for now, and Penelope gave him a potion for the pain.

An uneasy feeling had settled on my shoulders. It was hard to believe there was anything that could kill the immortal fae. But apparently there was, and Morgana was equipping her whole army with it.

Once we were settled around the fire, Uncle Gabriel told us what had happened to him. It was quite a fantastic story. Apparently, it was Maggie, the Alkana, who changed his form and snuck him out of the dungeons, putting someone else in his place.

"But how did no one see through the glamour?"

It was Tristan who answered. "The Alkana's magic is more powerful than any spirit-fae, so it cannot be detected by anyone, mage, fae—" he glanced over at Ashara, "—or witch."

Uncle Gabriel smiled and nodded. "True. Maggie managed to

glamour one of the prisoners to look like me. He was the one who went to the block in my place."

Tristan glared at Uncle Gabriel. "You let someone else die in your place?"

I knew Tristan valued courage above all, and what Uncle Gabriel had done would seem cowardly to him.

Uncle Gabriel looked calmly at Tristan. "The man she glamoured to take my place was a child rapist. He had raped and mutilated twenty children in the past year alone, but the magistrate only gave him a ten-year sentence in prison because the children were servants or commoners."

Tristan's midnight-blue eyes shone with silver sparks. "So justice was done."

"He will never hurt another child again," said the Duke of Silverthorne, his eyes pure steel.

Tristan nodded, satisfied by the outcome.

"But why didn't you tell us you were alive earlier?" I asked.

"It is far easier to get things done when people think you are dead," said Uncle Gabriel. "I've tried to teach you to always have a second and third plan in place."

My eyes narrowed. "I don't think the plan was to get yourself thrown in the dungeon."

He raised his eyebrows. "Wasn't it?"

Kalen laughed at this. "And what was your second plan, Your Grace? Getting yourself executed?"

Uncle Gabriel smiled at Kalen. "Exactly!"

My jaw dropped. "You couldn't have possibly planned for that too."

My granduncle looked me straight in the eyes. "Couldn't I? Didn't I say that it was far easier to get things done if everyone thinks you're dead?"

My hand flew to my mouth. "You did plan it!"

He rubbed his chin, and his blue eyes twinkled when he nodded.

"How?" asked Penelope.

"I sent word to Maggie as soon as you came to me with the news about Lilith taking over the king's body." He turned his knowing gaze back on me. "I instructed Rafe to get Serena, Erien, Penelope, and Kalen out of the castle. If I had left as well, they would have hunted us all down."

"So you sacrificed yourself for us," said Kalen, his eyes wide as saucers.

Uncle Gabriel chuckled. "Not exactly. I knew Maggie would come and get me out. And I needed all of you to be safe so I could do what needed to be done."

"Which was?"

"The Alkana told me it was of utmost importance to journey to Rohron and meet with the witches. She tasked me to convince the witch king and his witches to join us. At the time it seemed like an impossible task. But Maggie assured me they would listen." He looked over at Ashara, who was sitting on the other side of me listening to the story. "The witches are known for staying away from mage wars; they do not normally interfere or help. And I was right. When I first got there, the witch king refused to help—that is, until I mentioned we would be fighting for you."

I looked at Ashara, who smiled and nodded. "The witch king also agreed to send more witch warriors to Brandor to assist Prince Santino in shutting down the mines and rescuing the slaves."

"Thank you," I said, genuinely grateful for their help.

Ashara crossed her powerful arms in front of her. "Many of the slaves are our own people. Justice will be swift—the witches take no prisoners."

"Good," said Tristan nodding, suitably pleased with Ashara's brand of justice.

Uncle Gabriel continued his story. "I accompanied them to Brandor to meet with Santino and to let my daughter know I was alive."

"Aunt Serena must have been so happy to see you," I said, thinking back to the state my poor aunt was in when I left Brandor. "She was distraught, to say the least, when she heard what had happened to you."

Gabriel Silverthorne nodded. "I know it was hard for her, but it had to be done. I couldn't stay long, but I was there long enough to meet with Santino and make some plans regarding the war."

"Witches and Brandorians don't really get along, Gabriel," said Penelope. "How can you be so sure they will listen to Santino?"

Uncle Gabriel's eyes twinkled. "It seems our pirate prince is not all he seems."

My eyes narrowed. "What do you mean?"

Uncle Gabriel shot a glance at Ashara. "As you know, Santino is the son of the emir and a slave that resided at the palace."

I nodded. "Yes, he told me."

"But what he didn't know," said Uncle Gabriel, "is that his mother was from Ashara's war tribe and is her youngest sister."

"In return for our help against the Detoris, Prince Santino has agreed to free all the slaves in Brandor," Ashara said.

Penelope's eyes widened and her eyebrows rose. "All of them?"

Silverthorne smiled. "Every last one."

"And the mines?" Penelope asked.

Silverthorne rubbed his chin. "Santino is still fighting the Detoris. If he succeeds in securing the east, only then will he get a chance to shut them down and free the slaves." He furrowed his brow. "But the fae army can still pass through Brandor."

Penelope shook her head of golden hair. "Izadora has made it very clear the Elder Council will not send the fae army to fight a war against an army that possesses weapons of blackened iron and the Dark Dagger. The fae will be wiped out and could face extinction. Until the Dagger is in our possession and the mines are shut down, the fae army will not come. Elfi has been sealed off with the most powerful wards they can muster. No one goes in or out."

Silverthorne's blue eyes narrowed. "So we are on our own."

Penelope bowed her head. "I'm afraid so."

I got up from my seat and started pacing. "What was the point of helping all those ungrateful fae? When we need their help, they run away and shut themselves up in their kingdom."

Uncle Gabriel rose and put his hand on my shoulder. "Doing good should not come with any expectations or rewards, young Aurora. You do it because you want to. True goodness reflects our inner selves. You don't need the approval of others to help people. Your destiny is much greater than any ordinary mage or fae can understand. You are the Dawnstar, whether you like it or not."

I knew he was right, but it still hurt to know after everything we had done to help, the fae were not willing to sacrifice anything to help us. Most of them didn't even understand if we lost this war, their world would be destroyed as well.

Penelope stood up. "We haven't lost this war yet. If we can get the Dagger out of Morgana's clutches, it will halt all her plans. The last we heard, Morgana's army is amassing in the plains, and the general's forces are on their way to join her."

"They are headed for Eldoren, Gabriel." Rafe paced in front of the fire with me. He turned to look into Duke Silverthorne's eyes. "Any idea why?"

Silverthorne shook his head and looked around at our grave faces. "I know what you are thinking: that they are after the key. But the last key to the *Book of Abraxas* is not in Eldoren."

Penelope glared sharply at my granduncle. "It isn't?"

"No, and it's better none of you know where it is. For now, it is still safe. We must concentrate on getting the Dagger back and stopping Morgana's army from entering Eldoren."

Rafe gave Uncle Gabriel a pointed look. "If the Brandorians and fae don't come to our aid, we will never be able to stand against them." He flicked a glance at me, and his eyes looked troubled. "I have to return to lead my soldiers into battle. I have wasted enough time as it is."

Uncle Gabriel put his hand on Rafe's shoulder. "I will return to Eldoren and mobilize the army. You are the only one who can find the druids and help Aurora get into Morgana's camp. No one knows this area better than you." He looked at Penelope. "I will take the army to the Eastern Pass. If we can hold it until you steal the Dagger and Santino shuts down the mines, then we may stand a chance. Once we get the Dagger back, will you make sure Izadora sends her warriors to fight?"

"I will do my best." Penelope held his gaze. "Getting the witches, Brandorians, mages, and fae to fight together will be a task in itself. They will want to see the Dawnstar on the battlefield, Gabriel."

"Then finding the druids should be our top priority," said Uncle Gabriel, turning his azure gaze on me. "Besides being able to help Kalen, they may have more answers about your magic. Ashara will accompany you. Going up against Morgana and the general without all your powers is a chance I would rather not take."

"You know what Lilith did to me?" I asked Uncle Gabriel, not looking him in the eyes.

He nodded.

I didn't know why I'd foolishly hoped he wouldn't know I had gone and lost my magic.

I could see the disappointment in his eyes. "The Alkana had a vision. It was she who sent me straight back to Illiador to find you —to warn you to stay away from the Dagger." He looked into the flames. "But I was too late."

"Do you really think these druids will be able to do something to help?"

"I hope so," said Uncle Gabriel, stroking his chin, probably expecting his beard to still be there. "Or the world will be overrun with darkness, and there will be nothing any one of us can do about it."

CHASING LEGENDS

I AWOKE to the sound of birds chirping high above, nestled within the branches of the ancient trees that grew in the forest under the ground. Stray beams of shimmering sunlight forced themselves through the holes in the cavern ceiling, through the dense foliage, illuminating the lush green undergrowth that covered the cave floor. Butterflies fluttered about the little bushes and flowers that grew around me, and insects danced at my feet. A light mist hovered on top of the meandering river that made its way through the underground forest and into the darkness beyond.

I had been so tired I fell asleep as soon as my head hit the mat. Not having my fae strength and healing was something I was going to have to get used to again. I had pushed myself more than my body could take and didn't even realize it. Until now.

Penelope came over and crouched down beside me. "Good! You're awake."

I groaned and sat up. My limbs were stiff, and my back was in agony. I rubbed my eyes and looked around. I was the last one to get up. "Where's everyone?"

"Getting ready to move out," said Penelope, helping me gather my things.

Kalen was sitting nearby on a rock, cradling his arm. Penelope had made him a makeshift sling so he could be more comfortable.

"How is he?" I kept my voice low.

Penelope's eyes were hard as steel. "The veins in his arm are starting to turn black. I'm afraid we may not have enough time."

I put my hand on her shoulder. "We will find a way to heal him, Penelope. We will do everything we can."

She nodded and gave me a forced smile. "I know."

Uncle Gabriel was talking to Rafe when we approached them. "I need you to go with them, Rafael," Uncle Gabriel was saying, his voice low. "You are the only one who knows this sailor. And if anyone can find the druids, it's you."

Rafe ran his hand through his hair. "I can't do this anymore, Gabriel. She's not my responsibility. I should go back and help my people. They need me. She doesn't." His eyes darkened. "She has Tristan."

Uncle Gabriel gave Rafe a steely look. "If you don't get Kalen to the druids, he will die." His tone softened. "I will handle Eldoren. But I need you to go with them."

Just then, Ashara and Tristan joined us.

"The tunnel is clear," said Tristan, sheathing his sword. They had done a quick sweep of the surrounding caves and tunnels before we set out.

Uncle Gabriel had decided it was better for Rafe to lead us through the tunnels to the town of Royn. It was much safer than traveling through the forest, where more of Morgana's soldiers would be waiting for us.

Rafe looked up and saw me. He didn't smile.

Silverthorne gestured at Penelope. "Has there been any change?"

She glanced at Kalen, her eyes troubled. "The shard is moving quickly. The faster we find a druid, the better. There is no time to waste."

"If we can find them," Rafe interrupted, coming over to me.

"Don't get your hopes up. The druids haven't been seen in years. No one is really sure if they even exist anymore."

"There are still a few left in Avalonia," said Uncle Gabriel in a tone that brooked no argument. "You just have to know where to look."

"If you say so," Rafe shrugged. "But I wouldn't hold my breath."

Penelope's eyes narrowed. "This is Illiadorian territory. Morgana's kingdom. We will have to be extra careful."

"I will accompany you until we reach the end of these caverns. From there, Penelope can create a portal for me back to Silverthorne Castle," Uncle Gabriel announced. "If they have fae tracking the portals, it will throw them off your scent and give you more time to find the druids.

"Penelope will glamour you in the town," he added, addressing the rest of us. "But be careful, get the information you need and get out fast. Powerful Drakaar and certain mages can see through fae glamour, and, of course, there are the dark fae to watch out for." He threw us a warning look. "Once you find the druids, get the information you need to heal Kalen and find out what they know about the Dagger and Aurora's magic. Then we will go after the general. In the meantime, I will gather what forces we have and try to form some semblance of an army."

"It's settled then." Penelope clapped her hands together. "Let's move out."

The tunnels within the cavern were quiet and eerily still. Occasional sounds of rushing water from the underground rivers and waterfalls faded as we moved deeper into the cavernous maze, which existed as a separate world, hidden underneath the Goldleaf Forest. Some of the caverns we passed were completely filled from top to bottom with stalagmites and stalactites hundreds of feet in length and interlocking like the teeth of a monstrous creature. Droplets trickling into puddles filled the air with noise as we walked deeper into the labyrinth.

"I have a question," Tristan said to Uncle Gabriel as we

traversed a large cavern with a steep drop on one side leading into the darkness underneath. A valley spread out before us, and the steep rocks climbed high around us like massive underground mountains.

"Ask away."

Tristan lowered his voice. "I would like to know why the Alkana chose to speak to you."

"It is a long story," Uncle Gabriel answered.

Tristan scowled. "It's not like we are busy at the moment."

Uncle Gabriel laughed. "No, I suppose we are not, Prince Tristan."

My ears perked up. I, too, wanted to hear what Uncle Gabriel had to say. I knew that the fae revered the Alkana; they were powerful seers and ancient guardians of this world. For an Alkana to speak to a fae, let alone a mage, was the highest praise.

Duke Silverthorne began his story as we walked. "When I was a young boy, I got lost in the Willow Woods outside Silverthorne Castle. Maggie found me and revealed to me who she really was. She told me Dragath would rise once again, within my lifetime, and in response, so would the Dawnstar. She also told me I had been chosen to be the guardian of the Dawnstar."

"She did?" I repeated, wide-eyed, falling into step just behind them so I could hear more clearly.

He nodded and continued walking. "Yes. At the time I had no idea what the Dawnstar was. But Maggie trained me in the ancient arts and taught me the Dawnstar would need someone to guard it until the time came for it to reveal itself to the world."

We entered another, wider tunnel. Rafe seemed to know where he was going, so we followed. He was the only one who knew the way out.

Tristan's eyes narrowed. "You didn't know the Dawnstar was a person?"

"Not at first, because the magic that protected it—" he glanced at me out of the corner of his eye, "—protected you, prevented the

Alkana from telling me who or what it was. But when I turned eighteen, she did tell me the Dawnstar would be born into my family."

I fell into step beside my granduncle. Ashara and Rafe were up front. "So you knew I was the Dawnstar even before I did?"

He shook his head and flicked a glance at me. "Again, not at first. When your father was born to my sister, Fiona, I thought he was the Dawnstar. It was only when he died I realized my mistake, but it was too late—you were already gone, sent through the portal into the other world. I knew Penelope had been sent here by Izadora to find you, so we worked together to prepare for your coming."

I raised an eyebrow and looked back at Penelope, who was walking behind us with Kalen. "You knew who Penelope really was?"

But it was Penelope who answered, her fae hearing giving her the advantage of eavesdropping easily. "Yes. Gabriel was the only one who knew my secret."

I stopped to wait for her to catch up. "You said no one knew."

Penelope looked down. "It was the Alkana who told me to work with Gabriel." She glanced at him, but Uncle Gabriel didn't look surprised. "It seems she has been guiding us all together."

Silverthorne nodded. "Some Ancient Fae creatures have knowledge of things beyond what we perceive."

It took us the whole day of walking through the tunnels and caverns that lay under the Goldleaf Forest to reach the exit.

Penelope quickly went about glamouring all of us to look like poor farmers in worn brown cloaks that covered our heads for extra protection. She hadn't changed all our features completely, as that would require a lot more magic.

"I'll go first," Tristan said and disappeared out of the cave.

"I will see that he doesn't get into trouble," murmured Ashara as she hurried after him.

Penelope created a portal for Uncle Gabriel to return to Silverthorne Castle.

Uncle Gabriel hugged me and patted Rafe on his back. "Find the druids, Rafael," he said softly. "There is too much at stake."

Rafe nodded as Uncle Gabriel stepped into the portal. Penelope closed it behind him.

I exited the cave with Penelope and Rafe. Though the sun was setting, it took a few seconds for my eyes to adjust to the onslaught of sudden light after the dim, eerie world of the caverns.

We were in a small clearing, and there was the distinct sound of swords clashing near the trees. My head whipped around to see Tristan engaged in a fight with over a dozen masked outlaws. Ashara was fighting the rest and had knocked out a few of the bandits. Tristan had disarmed three men already, and two were lying on the ground clutching their stomachs. But there were more coming. Two archers had emerged from behind the trees, and arrows came whizzing toward Tristan.

Rafe waved his hand and the arrows fell to the ground. He drew his sword and charged into the fray to help Tristan.

I drew Dawn and ran after him.

"Stand down!" came a voice as a hooded man made his way toward us from behind the trees. The masked men stopped fighting and backed away from us.

The leader of the bandits removed his cowl, revealing a worn face with dark shaggy hair that covered his head like a mane.

"Fagren!" I gasped, my eyes darting to Rafe.

Rafe's eyebrows rose. "I didn't expect to see you here."

"Neither did I," said Fagren, raising one bushy eyebrow, bowing briefly, and clasping Rafe's forearm. "What are you doing so far north, Rafael? I thought the rest of Avalonia had abandoned us. Morgana's army is on the move, and they are headed for Eldoren."

Rafe nodded. "I know."

Fagren chuckled. "You choose to travel with a strange group, my friend."

Rafe ran his hand through his dark wavy hair. "This is personal."

Fagren's dark eyes scanned the unglamoured faces of our motley crew, paused on Tristan and Ashara, and finally settled on me. Fagren raised an eyebrow. "I can see that."

My spine bristled as I stared him down. Finally, I couldn't take it anymore and stepped forward. "You can't trust him, Rafe."

The leader of the Eldorean underworld narrowed his dark angular eyes at me, shadowed by his bushy eyebrows. He came closer, his worn brown cloak fluttering in the wind. He was wearing brown fitted pants and a green doublet covered by a leather vest and a short, hooded cape. Very different than what he usually wore when he frequented the taverns of the Eldorean underworld. "And it is a pleasure to see you again too, my dear princess." With a smirk, he gave me a sweeping bow.

Rafe turned to me. "Fagren can help us, Aurora. Forget about who he once was; I'm only interested in what he can do for us now. Illiador is crawling with Morgana's guards. It will be impossible to get into town without some assistance."

I crossed my arms. "He hates mages. Why help us?"

"Well," Fagren answered, stroking his thick beard, his dark eyes boring into mine as he assessed me. "You aren't exactly just a mage anymore, are you, Princess? You are something else completely, are you not . . . Dawnstar? In any case," he shrugged, "I owe Rafael a favor."

I raised my eyebrows. "Another one."

"One of many, I am afraid." He turned his gaze on Tristan, and his eyes seemed to sparkle with delight as he bowed. "It is an honor to serve the High Fae prince, though."

Tristan smirked at me. "Clever fellow. I like him."

"I'm sure you do," I said tartly, then glared at Fagren. "You know who he is?"

"Of course!" said Fagren, a smile flickering on his lips. "Everyone knows the dreaded Prince of the Night Court." He shrugged. "Plus, the Silver Swords can't stop talking about him."

I raised an eyebrow and flicked a glance at Rafe. "Fagren is part of the Silver Swords?"

"Yes," Rafe confirmed. "He joined the resistance a while ago." Rafe looked around at the band of men and, I noticed, women too. He lowered his voice and gave Fagren a pointed look. "Is there somewhere we can talk?"

The leader of the Eldorean underworld nodded. "Come with me."

We followed a path skirting the edge of the forest and soon came to a cave, dimly lit and separate from the maze of caverns we had just come through. A few warriors stood guard around the entrance, swords strapped to their waists, one with a bow and a quiver of arrows hanging on his back.

The cave was cut into a hill, and the ceiling of the cave was only about ten feet high, its walls black and glistening with the occasional drip of water, creating puddles where they pooled. Small intermittent fires dotted the damp space, surrounded by a raggedy bunch of people who huddled around them for warmth. Children clung to their mothers as the old sat still, gazing into the flames in remembrance of a time that once was.

Fagren smiled as he looked around and, with a flourish of his hand, said, "Welcome to the resistance." His tone changed. "Or what's left of it."

I was shocked as I looked around at the once-great resistance —the rebels called the Silver Swords were now merely a band of refugees who had escaped Morgana's guards only to die here in a dark cave, forgotten and alone.

Rafe explained to Fagren that we were looking for Captain Jarvik and we needed to get into the town of Royn.

"That old goat!" Fagren sneered as we sat around a fire that night, nibbling on stale corncakes the ladies had made a few days before. "Full of tall tales."

"But he's here?" Rafe confirmed. "In the town of Royn?"

"Seems like it," Fagren nodded. "His vessel docked here just a few days ago, last I heard."

"We need to talk to him urgently," Penelope interrupted.

"Now?"

Rafe threw a fleeting look at Kalen. "The sooner the better. Can you get us into Royn tonight, Fagren?"

"I don't know. Royn is teeming with guards. They have ransacked all the towns and cities along the coast and put the citizens to work to supply the growing needs of Morgana's army. Blacksmiths, tanners, and all the other useful artisans are now making clothes and weapons for Morgana. She has raised taxes, bleeding the kingdom dry to a point where the citizens are paying more than they are making. It's a mess here. Anyone who rebels against her or her guards is quickly silenced or shipped away to the mines. Others who have managed to escape the dungeons find safe haven here."

Rafe leveled him a steely look. "We still need to find Captain Jarvik urgently, Fagren. Can you get us into Royn or not?"

The leader of the Eldorean underworld stroked his dark beard. "I will see what I can do."

Two young girls came up to me and tugged at my belt.

I looked down at their pale dirty faces and hollow eyes staring up at me with wonder.

"Mama says you are the true Queen of Illiador," said one girl with fair hair; it once could have been a rich gold but was now caked with ash and blood. "She says you are the Dawnstar."

"Mama says you came to save us," said the other. Her dark eyes narrowed. "Have you come to save us?"

I had never felt the loss of my magic as much as I did at this very moment. Every time someone called me the Dawnstar I felt a sinking feeling in my stomach. Aurora Firedrake the Dawnstar was gone. All that was left in her place was an imposter, a powerless husk of the so-called Shadowbreaker.

My eyes welled up at the hope in their faces, and my heart constricted as never before. I could have helped them once—I could have burned Morgana's soldiers to a crisp and given these people back their homes and their town. I could have united the kingdoms and defeated this general. But that was before the Dagger took my magic from me. It was like a gaping hole within me, and I felt the loss of my magic every waking moment.

I shook my head at the twisted turn of fate. The Dawnstar had been their only hope, and I had taken it from them. Even though they didn't know I had lost my magic, one day they would, and their last shred of hope would die along with a kingdom I could not save.

A fire rose up inside me, born not of magic but of anger and despair all intertwined in a fiery mass that seemed to choke me. I knelt before the girls, put my hands on their frail shoulders, and said the only thing that gave me solace in the darkest of times. "Have faith." I tried to keep my voice from breaking as a wealth of emotions stormed within me. "A very wise dragon once told me if you have faith, nothing is impossible."

The girls' eyes grew wider. "You know a dragon?"

I stood, pulling myself up to my full height, and surveyed the room. "Of course," I said, smiling at the two girls, my course set, my mind clear as to what my path was. "His name is Abraxas. And he is the mightiest dragon who ever lived."

The fair-haired girl's lips trembled. "Will he come to save us too?"

I gazed around the cave once more at my people, the world I was meant to save. "I certainly hope so, my dear." My voice was low. "I certainly hope so."

But the ring on my finger lay dull and lifeless like any other ordinary ring.

STARS TWINKLED OVERHEAD as we skirted the edges of the forest following Fagren to the town of Royn on the coast of Illiador. As midnight neared, we reached the little walled town.

I really hoped this Captain Jarvik, whoever he was, could help us find the druids. If we didn't get to them in time, Kalen would die.

Fagren had agreed to keep an eye on the movements of Morgana's army and find out more about her whereabouts when they made camp. Once we found the druids, if we found them, eventually we would have to return here and try to sneak into Morgana's camp to steal the Dagger.

Penelope glamoured us while Fagren paid the guard at the gate. The guard carefully ushered us in through a side entrance. The resistance had men positioned at key places in different towns, gathering information and helping others escape the guards.

The town was surprisingly busy at this time of night. Closely packed wooden houses with thatched roofs were separated by a maze of small cobblestone streets that all seemed to lead to the docks, which were the main trade and hub of the town. A salty sea breeze carried with it the smell of fish as fishermen haggled at the docks with multiple buyers, trying to get the best deal for their daily haul. The sizzle of metal cooking and the sounds of stone banging rang in my ears as blacksmiths toiled away on their anvils. The leather tanners and carpenters seemed to be working through the night making weapons and armor.

"Why are they all still at work?" I asked Fagren as we hurried through the streets toward the docks. An array of Illiadorian warships and Brandorian merchant galleons lined the port. Smaller Andrysian fishing boats bobbed about in the restless sea between them.

"Morgana is depleting the resources of all the conquered

kingdoms to equip and clothe her soldiers," Fagren replied. "Your people are starving, Aurora. Everything we make, even the produce that grows in the farms all around Illiador and farther north, goes to feed Morgana's growing army."

I shuddered at the thought of what Morgana had done to my kingdom as we turned into a small dark street leading to the docks. Wooden warehouses ran the length of the rickety quay, and sailors, merchants, and traders were busy loading ships to supply the army.

According to Fagren, floggings and hangings were an everyday occurrence here. Morgana's black-uniformed soldiers roamed the streets like dark shadows, instilling fear in the residents and watching for any miscreants. Anyone even hinting at supporting the resistance was immediately taken into custody. Most of the people were too scared to do anything else but surrender to Morgana's rule. As long as they swore allegiance to her, she allowed the town of Royn and its citizens to continue their work and trade.

We reached the quay and boarded a sleek-looking Andrysian sailing vessel.

"Here we are," said Fagren. "Captain Jarvik's ship." He scrunched his nose as he scanned the old boat. "If you could even call it that."

It wasn't as big and grand as the pirate prince's galleon, the *Starfire*, but it looked fast. I just hoped Captain Jarvik had some idea where to find the druids.

The crew recognized Fagren immediately and ushered us across the wooden deck to the captain's cabin. It was a small space with a bunk along one wall and a big wooden table along the other, covered with ledgers and charts and whatever else captains used for navigation of the seas.

The captain was sitting at his desk, scribbling away on a piece of parchment. When he saw Fagren, he jumped up. The wooden cup he had been holding crashed to the ground, its contents flying all over our feet. The room smelled of stale sweat and alcohol.

He backed away, his small eyes wide and a bit glazed. "Your men already collected my debts, Fagren." He straightened his worn leather tunic and smoothed his messy gray hair, shot with silver. "I don't owe anything till I get back from my next haul."

Fagren grinned, showing his rotting teeth, some of which had been recently replaced with silver, I noticed. "It's your lucky day, Jarvik. I haven't come to collect."

Rafe raised an eyebrow. "You've been keeping busy, I see, Fagren."

"A man has to make a living." The leader of the Eldorean underworld shrugged, his hands in his pockets. "I offer protection from Morgana's guards. For a fee, of course," he added.

"Rafael, my boy," said Captain Jarvik, smiling once he realized who Fagren had brought with him. "Or should I say King Rafael." He gave a short bow, nearly falling over.

"Rafe will do, Jarvik," said the King of Eldoren, an amused look on his face.

The number of people Rafe knew never failed to amaze me. During his time as the Black Wolf helping the resistance, he had traveled all over Avalonia. But I was not convinced this drunken captain was going to be any help to us.

Jarvik's eyes trailed over Tristan, Ashara, Kalen, and Penelope, slowly widening and finally settling on me. "The Dawnstar," he said in awe and started to bow again.

I smiled faintly and looked down.

Rafe cleared his throat. "We need some information, Jarvik."

His eyes immediately lit up, and he ushered Penelope, Kalen, and me into chairs. Fagren lounged on the bunk, while Tristan and Ashara stood guard at the door. "How can I help?"

Rafe leaned against the desk in front of Jarvik as he scanned the maps on them. "You once told me you had met the druids."

"Aye," said Jarvik solemnly.

"Is that what this is about?" Fagren laughed, interrupting. "I could have saved you time if you had told me earlier what you were after. The druids are long gone. There aren't any left."

Jarvik shook his head stubbornly. "There is still one monastery left on an island in the Sea of Pearls."

"Those islands are uninhabited, Jarvik," Fagren insisted. "The waters around there are treacherous and many a ship has been lost trying to get to them. I have heard reports of ships simply disappearing, never heard from again."

Rafe gave Jarvik a half smile and crossed his arms. "I have heard of the mysterious mists that surround those islands, Jarvik. And Fagren is right: no sailor in his right mind would take his ship close to those islands. Everyone knows to navigate the Sea of Pearls only along the coastline."

"Can you create a witchstone to the islands?" Penelope asked Ashara. "There is some kind of magic that protects those islands. Fae portals don't work there; they never have. Many have tried, but no one has ever succeeded."

Ashara shook her head. "That would not work. I have never been there before, so it is impossible. But I may be able to make one to get us out of there if needed."

Penelope turned her azure gaze on Captain Jarvik. "How can you be so sure the druids are there?"

Captain Jarvik's eyes narrowed. "I've been there before. I've seen the druids myself."

Fagren rolled his eyes as he got up from the bunk. "Well, good luck to you then." He shrugged. "Your confidence is commendable, Jarvik. But no one has seen a druid in over twenty years. And no ship has ever made it to those islands and come back."

Rafe smiled, the charming princely smile he saved for when he was trying to convince people to do what he wanted. "I have faith in you, Jarvik. I know you, of all people, can get us there."

The old captain's eyes shone at the prospect and the praise. "I could." He puffed out his chest, which only succeeded in making his stomach protrude more than normal. "There are mists that shroud the islands, but I know they can be parted by magic. I've seen it done before," Jarvik insisted.

"When?" Penelope asked.

"Years ago, I took an injured soldier there. A mage. He parted the mists with magic and showed me a safe cove to anchor in."

Penelope clasped her hands together as she flicked a glance at Kalen, whose arm was steadily worsening. Time was slipping away, and we didn't know how long we had left. "Then it's settled. We leave immediately." Her tone brooked no argument.

"Well, I hope you make it there." Fagren threw a dark glance at Rafe. "Provided the dear captain can stay sober enough for the length of the journey."

A PATH FORWARD

THE NIGHT TURNED stormy as the crew untied the ropes and hoisted the sails. Fagren procured us some supplies from the town before we left. It would be a short but precarious journey across the Sea of Pearls, where all sorts of sea creatures lurked. The cerulean-blue coastline of Illiador gave way to a churning sea, and the ship rocked dangerously over swells and strong currents as we left the coast behind, heading into the open sea.

Captain Jarvik positioned himself on the upper deck, shouting instructions to the sailors who adjusted the rigging and sails. "We will need more wind if we want to get there faster."

Penelope stood up. "Get some rest," she said to me. "I will man the sails." Her eyes narrowed as she braced her legs and gathered her magic, and a gust of salty sea breeze caught the sails. The wind picked up as Penelope guided it, propelling the ship faster over the open sea. If I had my fae magic, I could have assisted her, but for the moment there was nothing I could do to influence the elements. Once the air and sea had called to me, and I could feel the magic pervading each and every part of them. I could summon it and guide it, shaping it into whatever I wanted. Now all I had was mage magic, which wasn't going to help us out here on the open sea.

We were lucky—the weather brightened the next day. The small ship glided across the water, leaving the coast of Illiador until we reached the darker, more treacherous waters in the middle of the Sea of Pearls. Captain Jarvik expertly guided us toward the islands that lay in wait in the deepest waters of the sea.

The day went by slowly as Rafe and I helped the sailors with the ropes. Penelope spent most of her time with the captain, trying to make sure we remained on track. She could control the air to an extent, but the ocean was fickle and water-fae were rare. I was the only one of us who could have forced the sea to obey if we were to fall on rough waters. Now all I could do was pray we got to the islands safely.

In my free time I alternated practicing mage magic with Rafe, as he taught me things I had never learned before, and sparring with Tristan, as he insisted on continuing with my training even though I didn't have fae magic to back it up. Still, something was better than nothing, and I needed to be stronger and more resilient if I was going to get through this alive.

Kalen lay on his bed below deck, wasting away as his strength began to leave him. His arm had started to form a rot, and his fingers had turned black. Once it spread to his chest it would be a matter of time before it reached his heart. The problem was, we had no idea when it would happen.

Spending so much time with Rafe onboard this small vessel made my heart ache. He was polite and restrained, and even when he spoke, he only discussed our plans or training, never anything personal. After our practice sessions, he would busy himself with other chores aboard the ship.

I could tell he was avoiding me.

The next evening, when Tristan and I finished sparring on deck, I stole a quick glance around the ship and spotted Rafe helping the men tie off some ropes. He had been staring at me and looked away as soon as he caught my eye. His shirt was open, and his chest glistened with sweat as he worked. It was hard to imagine him growing lazy and content with sitting on his throne and dealing with insufferable nobles. He was a warrior and an adventurer, but I had to keep reminding myself he was also a king. Soon he would have to return to his kingdom, and I would return to mine, if I got out of this alive.

Tristan seemed amused with Rafe's behavior and didn't waste time telling me so. "Your beloved doesn't seem to want to let you out of his sight," he snorted.

I shrugged casually, a hint of a smile tugging at my lips. I didn't want to reveal my feelings about Rafe anymore, especially in front of Tristan. Rafe had made it clear he had no intention of being with me, and I didn't know what more I could do to convince him that what happened between Tristan and me was a mistake.

But Tristan wasn't scowling like he usually did when we spoke about Rafe. His attitude toward the other man had changed considerably since we came to Illiador, as he had come to realize how much Rafe had done over the years to help the fae.

Tristan raised an eyebrow. "I presume he hasn't forgiven you yet?"

My eyes narrowed. "No," I said flatly. "And I don't think he ever will."

Tristan's mouth quirked to one side. "Oh, he will. I've seen the way he looks at you when your gaze is elsewhere. He's still in love with you, without a doubt."

My eyes darted to Rafe as I tried to keep my face passive. Tristan was right—he was watching us again, and his eyes were like storm clouds when he saw me talking to the fae prince.

Tristan chuckled. "I almost feel sorry for him. I wouldn't want to be in his shoes."

I smiled at Tristan's change of attitude. "So," I ventured, smiling up at the big fae warrior, "I think it is safe to presume you are not still upset with me?"

He shook his head. "No. I understand why you did what you did. And if it weren't for my oath, I wouldn't have agreed to it in the first place."

I laughed and hugged Tristan. "I can live with that." And in that moment, I knew we would always remain friends. "But I am glad you don't find me irritating anymore." I grinned.

He scowled, but his midnight-blue eyes danced with amusement. "Oh, you are as irritating as ever, Princess," he drawled. "But I don't mind putting up with it as long as we are not bound in wedlock."

Someone cleared her throat as I wriggled out of the hug. I turned to find Ashara standing behind me, her arms crossed and legs apart as she regarded us. "If you two are finished with your . . ." She paused as if trying to find the right word. ". . . training." She put her hand on her sword and looked at Tristan. "We had a sparring match scheduled, did we not, fae?"

Tristan's eyes started to swirl with silver stars and narrowed as he regarded Ashara. "Yes, witch. I haven't forgotten. I thought I would give you a chance to back out."

Ashara smirked. "I was giving you time to do the same." She tossed her plaited hair over one shoulder.

Tristan's jaw tightened. "Not likely," he said, unstrapping his sword belt and removing his shirt. He drew both his swords, and his muscles glistened in the evening sun.

Ashara smiled, a gleam in her dark eyes as she regarded the Prince of the Night Court in all his glory. She picked up her staff. "Trying to distract me is not going to work, fae," she said, flushing slightly as she took on a fighting stance, her hands tightening around her staff. "I'm still going to best you."

Tristan smirked as he twirled his swords effortlessly in his hands and faced her. "We shall see," he said and launched himself at Ashara as I moved out of the way.

Twilight had started to set in as the sun disappeared past the horizon, and everyone gathered around to watch the fight.

The warrior witch was just as fast, and nearly as tall as the big High Fae warrior, with reflexes like a jungle cat and speed that seemed to reduce her to a blur at times. They circled each other as they each looked for an opening. Ashara's staff was more than a match for Tristan's blades—the end of the staff opened to become a spear with a deadly sharpened tip and serrated jagged edges. The wood was magically enforced to withstand the blows of a sword. She wielded the staff as an extension of herself, just as Tristan did with his blades. They were a pleasure to watch as they danced around the deck of the ship, neither one giving in to the other at any point.

"Looks like your fae prince has met his match." I didn't even notice Rafe coming up behind me. His tone was flat, guarded.

My lips curved upward. "So it seems," I concurred.

Just then, Tristan ducked a blow from Ashara's staff and, dropping one sword, caught her staff with his free hand. At the same time, he sliced her cleanly on her leg. It wasn't a dangerous cut, just enough to end the match.

Ashara leaned on her staff, her chest heaving from exertion, as did Tristan's. It hadn't been an easy fight for him, I could tell. Normally he would have drawn out a sparring match like this, toying with his opponent to assess their weaknesses. But with Ashara he had ended it fast. So far, she was the only one I had ever seen make Tristan break a sweat.

Tristan held out his hand to her. From the expression in his eyes, I could see Ashara had finally earned his respect. "Not bad," he said. "For a witch."

Ashara laughed, obviously not angry at being bested by Tristan. Not many people could stand against the Dark Prince of Elfi without paying for it with their lives. There was a reason he was a legend among the Drakaar.

"It was a good match, fae," said Ashara, clasping his forearm. "I look forward to getting another chance to best you."

Tristan raised his eyebrows, but his eyes held a hint of amusement. "You could try."

"I most definitely will," said Ashara, flipping her braid over her shoulder as she spun and sauntered off.

As NIGHT BEGAN to advance on us, I stood on the quarterdeck, the sea breeze brushing my face as I inhaled deeply, grateful for the fresh air. The cabins were stuffy and smelled faintly of fish. I was worried about Kalen. We were sailing to a destination we knew nothing about, and there was no guarantee the druids would even be there.

It seemed I was not the only one who couldn't sleep. Rafe stood at the railing scanning the horizon, while the stars in the night sky twinkled above like lanterns lighting our way. The memory of the things he'd said to me earlier burned through me as I made my way toward him, the timber beneath my feet creaking softly. His brow furrowed at the intrusion, but he didn't say anything as I rested my hands on the railing beside him. We both gazed out to sea, silent except for the slap of the waves on the side of the ship.

"Rafe," I said, finally breaking the silence. "We need to discuss our relationship."

"There is nothing to discuss, Aurora." He turned to me, his face a mass of emotions as he ran a hand through his dark tousled hair. "You were the one who ran off and became betrothed without telling me." He laughed harshly. "I don't even know what I am doing here. I should be in Eldoren with my people. Instead I'm here helping you chase after ghosts again."

"You don't have to, you know." I sighed and looked out to sea. "You could go back. I don't need you to protect me anymore. I can protect myself."

"I know." He came closer, pulling me toward him ever so

slowly. "But that's the thing." His breath grazed my ear and my heartbeat sped up. "I can't help myself." He trailed his lips along my jaw. "Why is it I can't stay away from you?"

He kissed me, his arms tightening around my waist. He pulled me closer, his hard body pressed against mine, and I melted into his arms. His kiss was urgent, hard, and insistent, as if it were our first, or our last.

When he finally broke away, his breath was as ragged as mine. We just stood there looking at each other, our foreheads touching and breath intermingling.

"Tell me everything that happened," Rafe said finally, holding my hands in his, his storm-gray eyes gazing into mine. "Don't leave anything out."

We spent the rest of the night in his cabin talking. I told him everything that had happened to me since I left him all those months ago and went to Elfi. So much had changed, and both of us were different people now. I explained the relationship Tristan and I had down to the last detail, and what it was like to live with my grandmother and her fae court. I explained what I had heard about him and Katerina as well.

He listened quietly, but he did have questions, and I tried to answer them.

Rafe's forehead creased and his eyebrows drew together as he tried to make sense of it. "So you are not in love with him?"

I shook my head. "No, silly." I ruffled his hair and kissed him full on the lips. "I've only ever loved you."

Rafe smiled and kissed me back, pulling me into his arms as we lay down on the small bunk, my head resting on his chest.

"Rafe," I ventured. "Now that you know everything, what does this mean for us?"

He looked straight into my eyes. "I know now this is not the way you intended it to be," Rafe said slowly. "But in the eyes of the fae court, you are still betrothed to Tristan. We cannot just ignore it and hope it will go away. At some point we will have to face it."

I didn't want to meet his eyes. "If we get out of this alive."

He lifted my chin with a fingertip. "Things have been hard for us, Aurora," he said, bringing my fingers to his lips. "But I have always loved you. I still do." He drew my face toward him once more, his lips grazing my jaw. "And I suspect I always will."

"What about Danica?" I asked tentatively.

He shook his head. "Danica was a distraction. To keep my mind off you." He gave me a sheepish smile, but his tone was low and serious. "I don't think it worked."

I looked straight into his eyes. "But you did take her to your bed."

His eyes were like storm clouds that seemed to be subdued. "No. It never went that far," he clarified.

"But I saw you kiss her when she left your room that night at Caeleron Castle."

"And that's all I did." Rafe's eyes narrowed. "I am not a saint, Aurora."

I nodded. "I'm sorry for doubting you."

He kissed my forehead, and his gaze softened. "And I you."

THE NEXT MORNING was dark and gloomy as the sun refused to show itself and hid behind a cloud like a shy bride. A strange mist seemed to blanket the sea beneath us and wound its way around the ship. Captain Jarvik was at the wheel, steering our vessel expertly toward it. The mist crept on deck, weaving itself around poles and sails as the wind died down and everything went still.

"We are close," Captain Jarvik said, coming down to join us on the main deck.

Penelope raised her hands and pushed at the mist with her magic, but it only crept closer. "I have never encountered mist like this."

"I have." Ashara stepped forward and raised her staff. The

jewel on its apex glowed as a light blue magic halted the flow of the mist, pushing it back.

Tristan raised an eyebrow as he stood on deck watching Ashara, his arms crossed. "Not bad, for a witch."

Ashara smirked. "You haven't seen anything yet, fae."

A dark shadow seemed to pass through the mist as a second jewel on Ashara's staff lit up. I tensed, my heart hammering as my eyes darted around the eerie thick mist. What else was out there?

"It is as I thought." Ashara threw a quick glance at Penelope. "Demon magic. There is something else within these mists. We need to move. Now."

Penelope raised her arms above her head and summoned a strong wind. She directed the wind at the sails as Ashara held her staff aloft, two stones glowing brightly and pushing back the encroaching mist.

The tip of an island came into view, and I released a breath I didn't know I was holding. The ship moved silently forward, slicing the water as Captain Jarvik steered us toward a small cove.

We anchored close to the coast, and the crew rowed us ashore, landing on the beach at the edge of a lush overgrown forest. The island looked massive, with hills and valleys that surrounded us and a landscape that seemed untouched for centuries.

We followed Captain Jarvik through a small overgrown path into the hills. The mist seemed to lift once we reached the island, and the sun lit our path through the forest. It was strangely quiet here; no birds chirped high in the trees, and the forest seemed deep and primeval. "What is this place? Why do the druids live out here, so far away from civilization?"

"These islands have been this way as long as anyone can remember," explained Penelope. "But I have no idea why the druids are here. I heard the last druid monastery burned down somewhere in the Silverspike Mountains, which is where all their monasteries used to be."

"What if the druids refuse to help us?" I had to ask.

"They might," said Rafe, lifting a dark brow. "The druids have shut themselves away for centuries. They don't trust mages, fae, or witches for that matter."

Penelope nodded. She glanced over at Tristan, who was carrying Kalen in his arms. There was barely any time left. Kalen had fallen unconscious on the ship. He was still breathing, but his strength was failing; soon, it would be too late to help him. "Rafe is right. The druids are an order unto themselves, and their knowledge of the ancient world is vast. Their magic is powerful, and the secrets they guard so closely make it worth trying to find them."

We walked the rest of the day, only stopping to eat a few chunks of bread and cheese we had brought with us. Captain Jarvik led us farther and farther into the depths of the mysterious island. The setting sun's rose-pink hues lit up the trees around us as we walked up a winding path through the hills, inward to the heart of the island where Captain Jarvik said the monastery was situated.

The mist started to creep around us again, and a cold wind blew down from the mountaintops.

Captain Jarvik hurried forward. "It's just over this hill in the next valley."

We crested the hill, stones slippery as we scrambled forward, eager to get out of the cold. But when we reached the valley, there was nothing there.

Rafe turned to the captain, our guide in this misty land. None of us had ever been here before, and Captain Jarvik was the only one who had ever seen the monastery of the druids. "Jarvik, you said you knew where they lived. There is nothing here."

Captain Jarvik scratched his scruffy white beard. "It was here —I've seen it. Twenty years ago, I brought a wounded soldier here. He knew where it was and showed me the way. He had been badly injured in the war, so I had to help him from the boat to the monastery."

"Twenty years is a long time, my friend," said Rafe, coming up to put his hand on the old mariner's shoulder. "Maybe it was another valley?"

The captain shook his head. "Nay, it was here. I saw it. A huge giant of a fortress. Like a castle, it was."

A shriek rent the air. It was coming from within the mist.

I looked up, and a dread colder than ice raced down my spine. A black shadow that looked like a Drakaar formed entirely out of mist and darkness came flying at us from the trees.

"Drakwraith," growled Tristan, drawing his sword as it lit up with silver fire. He could only use one sword as he slung Kalen over his shoulder, holding him with his other arm.

Ashara aimed her staff at the Drakwraith, and the creature screamed as witch-fire slammed into it. The Drakwraith dissipated but immediately started to reform.

It gave us the seconds we needed.

Rafe took my hand. "Run!"

"What is it?" I shouted. My heart raced and fear pooled in my stomach. My legs burned as we ran across the valley, slipping and sliding on wet rocks, but there was nowhere to hide. If we could make it back to the forest and the safety of the giant trees, we could hide ourselves. But there was no time—the Drakwraith was gaining on us.

"Soul eater," Penelope shouted back. "Shield yourself!"

Penelope and Ashara were behind us, with Tristan and Captain Jarvik following after.

A scream!

I turned to see the Drakwraith pounce on the old mariner.

"It gets stronger with every life it takes," yelled Penelope as the Drakwraith devoured him, sucking out his soul. His life force was gone as the soul eater reduced him to a husk of skin and bones, his eyes a dark pool of black.

Rafe had turned back to help the mariner, but it was too late. The wraith looked up, fixating on him.

Rafe blasted the Drakwraith with mage fire, but it wasn't enough. He slashed the Drakwraith with his sword, but it only hissed and attacked again.

Falling backward, he scrambled for his sword, which had dropped beside him.

"Rafe!" I screamed as I ran to his aid.

Tristan handed Kalen over to Ashara swiftly, rolled his eyes, and turned to help me.

His swords lit up as he slashed through the Drakwraith. It hissed and faltered with the power of the dark prince's silver fire.

Rafe and I scrambled out of the way.

"The Drakwraith cannot be killed, only sent back to the dimension it was summoned from," Penelope shouted as she shielded Kalen and Ashara.

I gathered my mage magic and flung it out in a large arc, creating a shield between the Drakwraith and us. Pain seared through my skull as the Drakwraith tore through my shield, ripping at my defenses and magic. I fell to my knees.

The Drakwraith turned its burning-red eyes on me. "Dawnssssstar," it hissed. The gleam in its eyes was enough to confirm it was here for me. It flew toward me, a dark and evil cloud, ready to suck out my soul and destroy the Dawnstar forever.

Seemingly out of thin air, a brown-robed monk appeared beside me.

A druid!

He held a sleek wooden staff in his right hand, the top glistening with a large crystal that changed color. He banged it on the ground, his left hand stretched out toward the Drakwraith. The earth shook as a shield formed around us all, shimmering with a bluish-white light. The Drakwraith hissed and tore at the shield, shrieking its fury at the druid who stood beside me, his old weathered face a mask of calm. I could see no fear in those fathomless brown eyes, eyes that seemed to have seen all of time.

"Victor," he said as another monk appeared next to him, again seemingly out of thin air. "Could you take care of this? My hands are full at the moment."

"Of course, Brother Sebastian," said Victor, as calm and unruffled as the first druid.

The bottom of Victor's staff emitted sparks of red fire, and he used it to create a rune on the ground. "Remove the shield."

The first druid, Sebastian, lowered his hand, and the shield fell. The Drakwraith screamed with delight and rushed toward Victor. Victor held up his hand and banged his staff into the middle of the rune. The Drakwraith screeched with rage and tried to get away as a force more powerful than I had ever felt before emerged from the rune and pulled it into the ground.

The rune disappeared.

The Drakwraith was gone.

Silence filled the air as we all caught our breath. If the druids hadn't come when they did, we would have been dead like Captain Jarvik.

The druid called Victor stepped forward, pushing back his hood to reveal a craggy face and deep, coffee-colored eyes that had seen lifetimes come and go. His brown woolen robe was simple, as expected of a monk, and tied at the waist with a thin rope.

"Come," he said to me, and started walking toward the middle of the valley.

"Just like that?" I raised my eyebrows and ran after him. "Aren't you going to ask who we are and why we are here?"

The old druid turned his eyes on me. "We know who you are and why you have come, Dawnstar. We have been expecting you." He looked at Ashara holding Kalen. "Get the young fae inside, and we will tend to him. He doesn't have much time left."

I looked around. "Inside? Where?" All I could see was a lush overgrown valley blanketed in mist.

Victor banged his staff lightly on the ground and muttered

something under his breath. Through the mist, lights materialized before us as a massive stone structure appeared out of thin air, just like the druids had.

I gasped. Captain Jarvik had been right. The monastery had been here in this valley all this time, hidden by druid magic, which from what I had just seen was far older and more powerful than the magic of the mages or even the fae.

Victor and Sebastian walked forward, and the big wooden doors of the monastery opened. Tristan took Kalen from Ashara as we followed the druids into the gray stone fortress. The doors shut behind us with a definitive thud.

Victor turned to the door and wove his staff in the air. "The monastery is now secure and hidden by magical wards. You are safe here."

DESTINY CALLS

THE ENTRANCE HALL WAS MASSIVE, with two enormous stone staircases that curved upward to the second floor. It was warm and dry inside the monks' home, and wooden torches burned in sconces on the walls. Two more monks appeared silently from a door on the left, their forms hidden under the loose brown robes they all wore.

We followed the monks, and Tristan carried Kalen to a room at the far end of a gray stone corridor. Kalen's skin had turned the color of ash as his blood and magic were slowly consumed by the darkness that moved within him. His arm hung limp at his side, black veins protruding as the surrounding flesh rotted.

The monks directed Tristan to lay Kalen on a large wooden table in the center of the room, while they bustled about mixing herbs and potions at the worktables on the side wall.

Brother Sebastian held up his staff and ran it through the air over Kalen's body. The crystal flared when it reached his chest. He put down the staff and turned to us as he rolled up his sleeves. "There is still a chance. I must work fast."

Penelope let out a cry of relief and leaned on me, tears streaming down her face. I put my arm around her as my own heart beat faster with hope. Kalen still had a chance. I couldn't begin to imagine the pain Penelope was going through. No mother should have to see her child like this.

"Come," said Victor. "Let Brother Sebastian do his work. We have dealt with this kind of darkness before."

I tightened my grip around Penelope's shoulders. "You need to rest, Penelope. You said yourself the druids will know what to do. Let them heal Kalen. There is nothing you can do for him right now."

Tristan's eyes softened. "Go. I will stand guard and let you know if there is any change."

We followed Victor down long stone corridors and up the western staircase, all warmly lit with sconces on the walls. The druid monks might not have lived in lavish surroundings, but the rooms were clean and warm, with big stone fireplaces piled high with wood. I chose to stay in the same room as Penelope since I didn't want to leave her alone. The beds were small but comfortable, covered with soft linens and warm furs. After a quick sponge with the hot water the druids had sent up from the kitchens, Penelope and I changed into the warm and dry woolen robes the monks had given us and sat down in the old faded armchairs before the roaring fire.

Victor came to our room to check on us, which was a comfort in itself. It had been such a long time since I was warm and safe and with people who knew what to do. Kalen's illness, if you could call it that, had taken a bigger toll on me than I cared to admit. If I had not dragged him along in the first place, he would be safe at home. Instead, he had risked his life and nearly died. I hoped the druids knew what they were doing. Kalen was my closest friend, the one who was always by my side.

"Will Kalen be okay?" I asked Victor as he opened the door to leave.

The old druid nodded. "Yes, I believe he will be. You got here just in time."

THE NEXT MORNING, I opened the thick curtains to gaze out at a land of trees and mist. Beautiful on a grand, sweeping scale, the magnificent landscape stretched out before me as far as the eye could see. Penelope was already dressed in her own clothes, which had been washed and dried, and waited while I hurried to put on my own.

We walked quickly along the long stone corridor and down the staircase. I hadn't noticed the beautiful banister last night when we came in, shaken as I had been with the appearance of the Drakwraith and worry for Kalen. I ran my hand along the intricate carvings of ancient creatures, fae, and, surprisingly, demons as well.

Victor was waiting for us by a set of big doors that led out from the main foyer.

"How is Kalen?"

The old druid clasped his hands in front of him. "He will live, but he is not awake yet. The shard was deep inside his veins, and it took a great amount of power for Brother Sebastian to stop it from moving closer to the heart. We just caught it in time—another day and he would be dead."

Penelope's shoulders sagged in relief. "When can we see him?" Her tone was weary.

"Soon," said Victor. "Brother Sebastian still has to remove all traces of the shard from his blood. It is hard and tedious work, but no one is a better healer."

I nodded, relief apparent on my face as I smiled at Penelope and turned to the large doors. I could hear the murmur of voices and the clink of plates and cutlery. We followed Victor into a vast hall with tall wood-framed windows and rectangular tables. I hadn't realized how many monks lived in this monastery—there must have been over a hundred. I was glad to see the druid monks were not extinct as everybody thought they were.

We sat down for breakfast next to Rafe, who was already finishing up. Tristan came to join us. He had stayed with Kalen the whole night, and now Ashara was standing guard. The food was simpler than palace fare, but it was a lot better than what I had eaten at taverns.

Sliced loaves of freshly baked bread lined the tables in baskets, and around them were little clay pots filled with creamy white butter, a tart berry jam, and thick dollops of cream, which of course I couldn't resist. Slices of cured meats and boiled eggs were set up across all the tables, and I noticed some of the monks were eating an oatmeal porridge that they topped with dried fruits, nuts, and fresh honey. I sipped on my cup of hot milk brewed with cinnamon and wondered how to approach the druids to help me with the information I needed.

After breakfast was over and the other monks filtered out, Penelope got straight to the point. "Victor—" she lowered her voice, "—you know why we are here?"

Victor nodded slowly but let Penelope continue.

"It is imperative we find the Dark Dagger before Morgana or the general use it to wake Dragath."

The old druid looked at Penelope, his features solemn. "Child," he said to the three-hundred-year-old High Fae, shaking his head. "As the fae queen's sister, you should have been able to read the signs in the stars."

Penelope's blue eyes turned steely as she arched an elegant eyebrow. "What do you mean?"

The old monk sighed as if he had come to the end of the road. "The general cannot wake Dragath—" he glanced sidelong at me, "—because Dragath is already awake."

An eerie silence fell over the group as everyone tried to process what the old druid had just revealed.

"How?" Penelope asked while the others came to terms with this news.

The druid looked around at our worried faces. "He is not yet fully awake. He has found a way to move his consciousness into another's body, and so his powers are still limited. That is why he needs to complete the ritual—to release his body and all of his powers."

Penelope clasped her hands together, and her eyes shone with understanding. "The general is Dragath."

"Precisely."

Penelope's face tightened. "Then all the more reason to make sure he doesn't get the Dagger."

Victor nodded. "Yes, but the Dagger is not all he needs to raise his true form and powers. There is still one thing that has eluded him."

Penelope leaned forward and whispered, "Once they have the *Book of Abraxas* and the keys to open it, they will have everything they need. We must stop them."

The old druid shook his head, and a shadow crossed his aged face. "When Auraken Firedrake and Illaria Lightbringer sealed Dragath in his prison in Mount Khatral, they used blood magic to do it. Opening the *Book of Abraxas* and wielding the Dagger is only part of what the general will need to raise Dragath."

Dread inched down my spine; I knew instinctively I wasn't going to like the answer, but I asked anyway. "What more could he need?"

"The blood of his jailers," said Victor slowly, turning his fathomless brown eyes on me. "The blood of the Firedrake line."

My face paled. "My blood."

Victor nodded. "Indeed."

Penelope's eyes narrowed. "And you know who the general really is?"

I held my breath.

"Come." Victor got up slowly from the bench. "It is better that you see for yourself."

The old druid led us into what was unmistakably the library. Shelves upon shelves of old scrolls and ancient tomes no one outside this monastery had seen in centuries lined the walls. Wooden ladders on wheels were attached to every wall, and a number of monks were hanging precariously on them, trying to find elusive titles.

Victor opened a small door at the end of the library and we all stepped inside. All the room contained was a table made of a natural crystal, its surface polished to a smooth sheen. But there was a fog beneath the surface, constantly shifting and swirling.

Penelope raised an eyebrow. "A scrying table?"

Brother Victor nodded. "The only one left in existence." He looked over at me. "It is how we knew you were coming. We have been keeping track of you ever since you came back into this world."

I swallowed, my voice rough. "How does it work? Can you show us who this general is?"

Victor raised his staff and waved it over the table. The fog in the table parted, revealing a small legion of soldiers camped at the base of a mountain.

"I don't recognize the area," Penelope said. "Can we get closer, Victor?"

Victor nodded and moved his staff over the table; the magic within it hummed and the scene changed. The general was in his tent in the midst of a small encampment of soldiers. But he was not alone. Andromeda was there, and so was Skye.

The general was speaking, his back toward us and his hand held out. "Give me the book, Andromeda. I will not ask again."

She clutched it to her as I had seen her do before. She didn't intend to give it up. "We had a deal, General," Andromeda spat out the words. "You and Morgana were supposed to make me Queen of Elfi." She lifted her chin. "Do you see a throne?"

The old druid raised his staff and the scene shifted until we were staring right into the general's face.

Penelope's hand flew to her mouth but could not stifle the gasp that escaped. Her face turned white as she leaned forward to get a better look. "Joreth!" Her voice cracked slightly. "This is impossible—he died twenty years ago in the last mage wars. I was there, I saw it with my own eyes."

I looked at her and Rafe and back at Victor. "Who is Joreth?"

Penelope's tone was low and serious. "Don't you remember your history lessons at the academy, Aurora? Joreth was a traitor, the leader of the Black Mages. He and Lilith tried to take the kingdom from your grandfather."

My stomach dropped to the floor. I did remember her telling us about the Black Mages and the army of traitors my father defeated over twenty years ago. "But isn't he supposed to be dead?"

Penelope nodded. "Your father faced him in battle and killed him."

"Unfortunately," the old druid interrupted, "Joreth didn't die. Watch and you will understand."

We all turned back to the scrying table.

Joreth smiled at Andromeda, as sinister as a deadly snake about to strike, and a chill scuttled down my spine. His obsidian eyes glistened as he regarded the Grand Duchess of the Day Court, who, despite the circumstances, stood with her head held high, not cowering before him. I respected her for that, but I also knew it was a vain stance. Joreth would get what he wanted eventually. Dragath would not let one High Fae stand in his way. And I was right.

Out of the pocket of his robes he drew forth the Dagger. I gasped. He already had it. It wasn't with Morgana as we had presumed.

The blade glistened with an eerie sheen, and the ruby on the hilt shone the color of blood as he turned it over in his hands. The blade, curved and twisted, was made of a metal that seemed to absorb all the light around it, a black pit of darkness that consumed everything it touched. Even so far away, seeing the dreaded Dagger caused my heart to beat fast, and I shuddered involuntarily as I remembered what it had done to me. How it had made me feel powerless and alone, as if there would never be any light left in the world. It had stripped me of my magic as if it were no more than a piece of clothing. If I hadn't had my mage magic tethering me to this world, I would have been trapped in the Dagger with my mother and all the other fae-warriors of Elfi.

Andromeda's eyes widened in shock, and I could see real dread in them. No fae could stand before the Dagger of Dragath and not experience fear.

Like lightning, he struck.

Before Andromeda realized what was happening, the Dagger sucked her in. In a flash, she was gone. The book in her hand thumped to the floor where she had been standing.

Skye screamed, "Mother!" But it was too late.

Joreth turned to her and held out his hand as Skye bent down and picked up the book. "I hope you have more sense than your mother." His voice was cruel, mocking.

She stood before him, her face showing a multitude of emotions. My stomach twisted as she handed him the book.

"Now all he needs is the key," Penelope said softly.

"And a Firedrake," said Victor, shooting me a quick look as he waved his staff and the table went dark.

Everyone was quiet as we tried to process what we had just seen. We took a seat in the library on benches around an ancient oak table piled high with dusty leatherbound tomes and haphazardly strewn scrolls. The monks were not exactly a tidy bunch.

Finally, Penelope spoke. "I think we need more of an explanation, Victor. How is Joreth still alive?"

"Captain Jarvik brought him to us on a night just like this twenty years ago," Victor explained. "At the time we did not know Dragath, or rather his consciousness, resided in this man's body. We have always helped those in need, and he was close to death.

He shouldn't have survived, but Dragath's dark powers somehow held his body together until he could be healed."

"Go on," Penelope urged.

"We healed him, and he stayed with us for a few months. He showed a lot of interest in the knowledge of magic, so we permitted him to stay and learn with us. We trusted him because we had no reason not to. He began spending a lot of time in the library, and when we finally realized why, he had already fled with the scroll."

"What scroll?" I asked.

"The scroll that gave him the names of the Guardians of the Keys to the *Book of Abraxas*," said Victor, shaking his head.

"And he gave the names to Morgana?" Penelope prodded.

"Yes."

Penelope's eyes narrowed. "I think you'd better start from the beginning, Victor. We are completely lost here."

The old druid nodded and got up from the bench. "Come with me." He gestured for us to follow. "There is something else I need to show you." He looked at Tristan. "You too, Prince Tristan. We are going to need your help for this."

My brows furrowed as everyone got up and followed Victor out of the library. "Where are we going now?"

"You'll see," he said cryptically and started climbing the steps to the tower. "Once we found out what Joreth had taken and who he really was, it was too late," Victor went on. "Dragath cast a curse over this whole island so that we could never leave or warn anyone about him."

"That's why the druids disappeared twenty years ago," said Rafe, almost to himself.

"We didn't disappear, King Rafael," said the old druid. "We were always here. Dragath's dark curse also kept people away from the island, and the Drakwraiths were left here to make sure no outsider ever made it to the monastery alive."

Finally, after climbing a long winding staircase that led

hundreds of feet up through the monastery, we reached the top of the tower.

The room itself was magic; I could feel it in the air as we walked through the large wooden door at the top of the stairs. The tower was built in a square and so was the room. Opposite us on the far wall hung a massive, intricately woven tapestry.

"It can't be!" Penelope gasped aloud. "Is that the Thirteenth Tapestry?"

"Yes." Victor nodded. He moved forward to touch it, almost in admiration. It reminded me of the tapestry in Redstone Manor through which I had entered this world.

"How?" Penelope's eyes were as wide as saucers as she took in the elegant weave of the ancient tapestry hanging on the wall in front of us.

"For centuries we have searched for the missing pieces of the tapestry, and when we found them, we wove them back together. Brother Sebastian and I have been working on this for over two hundred years."

I was used to people being unusually old in Avalonia, but I had to ask. "How old are you really?"

"Older than everyone in this room, young lady," said Victor, a small smile playing at the corner of his lips, wrinkling his worn face.

Penelope stepped closer to inspect it. She hesitated, and I could see fear in her touch. "Does it still work?"

I stepped forward. "Sorry to interrupt, but can someone please tell me what the Thirteenth Tapestry is?"

Penelope turned to me, her eyes stern. "There was a time when the Ancient Fae enjoyed traveling to other worlds. For their convenience, they created twelve different magical tapestries that acted as portals or gateways into the most frequented worlds."

I nodded in understanding. "Like the tapestry in Redstone Manor."

"Exactly!" said Penelope. "The tapestry you came through was one of the twelve. It was thought to be the last one left, as all the other tapestries have been destroyed over the ages."

Rafe's eyebrows rose. "And the Thirteenth Tapestry?"

Penelope drew a deep breath. "The Thirteenth Tapestry was created out of dark magic by the same fae lord who used the *Book of Abraxas* to bring Dragath to this world."

"What does it do?"

"It is the only tapestry that doesn't lead to another world but to our own," said Brother Victor. "Through it one can travel through time."

"Why would he make such a dangerous thing?" asked Rafe, his eyes stormy.

"When the Ancient Fae lord realized his folly and the fact that he could no longer control Dragath or send him back, he used the knowledge in the *Book of Abraxas* to create a thirteenth tapestry, one that would take him back in time to erase what he had done. But before he could use it, Dragath killed him, shredded the tapestry, and took the book."

I shook my head at this story. "Who was this power-hungry fae who caused all the problems in this world?"

The old druid looked confused, and something flickered in his eyes as he glanced at Penelope. "They don't know?"

Penelope looked away. "No."

"Penelope?" My eyes narrowed as I turned to her. "Are you keeping something from us again?"

"Why am I not surprised?" said Tristan, his arms crossed.

Penelope turned to look at the tapestry, her back toward us, finally resigned to the fact she could not keep this secret anymore. "The Ancient Fae lord who summoned Dragath to this world was a Nightshade." She turned back to face us, and her gaze settled on Tristan. "Dresdaron Nightshade, the first Grand Duke of the Night Court. Kalen and Tristan's ancestor."

Everyone was silent. No one had expected that, even though it had been quite obvious now that I thought back on all I had learned so far. Now I realized what she meant about the Nightshade bloodline. Why she was so worried about letting Kalen meet his father. They were all descendants of the Ancient Fae lord who was so hungry for power he brought Dragath into this world. To do what he had done required a powerful magic, a darker magic than most fae would dare to wield. That magic ran through Tristan's blood as well as Kalen's, and that kind of power was best left forgotten.

Victor cleared his throat. "But there is one part of the story that is not common knowledge." He looked at Penelope. "This tapestry was created by blood magic." His eyes flicked to Tristan. "Only the blood of a Nightshade can make it work."

Penelope backed away from the tapestry. "No, Victor! It is too dangerous. If we travel back in time and something goes wrong, everything can change. The Dawnstar could cease to exist."

"I am well aware of the risks, Penelope," said the old druid. "But it is imperative the Dawnstar has full knowledge of what she is up against if you want to have a chance to defeat Joreth and Morgana." He turned his fathomless gaze on me. "If you fail, Dragath will rise again, and this time he will bring his army with him."

Tristan stepped forward. "What do I have to do?"

"All we need is a little of your blood, Prince Tristan, and for you to accompany us into the tapestry. I will create a shield so no one will see or hear us. But you still have to be careful. Stay close and don't make any sudden movements. I will do the rest."

"I don't like it, Victor," said Penelope, clasping her hands in front of her. "Are you sure it will work?"

Victor looked sheepishly at Penelope and shook his head. "I told you it has taken over two hundred years to create. We didn't have time to test it as well."

"It will work," said Brother Sebastian from the doorway. "I'm sure of it. All we need is the blood of a Nightshade."

We turned toward the druid who had shielded us from the Drakwraith, and I immediately ran toward him. "Is Kalen okay?"

Brother Sebastian nodded and looked at Penelope. "He is recovering. We finally managed to remove all the darkness from his blood."

Penelope went up to him and grasped his hand. "I cannot thank you enough for all you have done for us, Brother Sebastian. I am forever in your debt."

Brother Sebastian smiled. "There is no need for thanks. It is what we do."

I heaved a sigh of relief, as if a great weight had been lifted from my shoulders. It wasn't a victory in battle, but it was a victory nonetheless: a victory over darkness, a sliver of hope. Kalen was going to be all right. "When can I see him?"

"The witch Ashara is standing guard; she barely let us work on him." Brother Sebastian rolled his eyes. "I don't think anyone is going to disturb him any time soon. But he will be better by morning. You can see him then," he added, moving past me to inspect the tapestry just as Victor had done. He rubbed his hands together, and his eyes lit up like a child's as he spoke to Victor. "Are we going to use it? I've been waiting to see if it works."

"Well, there is only one way to find out," said Victor. He drew a knife from his robes. "If you would, Prince Tristan." He held out the knife.

Tristan took the weapon from the druid and, quick as a flash, sliced his palm.

Victor nodded. "Good. Now place it on the tapestry. It will recognize your Nightshade blood."

Tristan placed his bleeding hand on the tapestry, which absorbed the blood as if it were never there. Suddenly the tapestry sprang to life, shimmering and moving like a living thing.

"Brother Sebastian, you will have to wait here to make sure we return," Victor said over his shoulder.

The old druid's face fell. "Why can't I go in and you stay here?"

Victor raised his eyebrow, and it was obvious who was in charge. "You shall have other opportunities to test it, Brother Sebastian."

He nodded. "Of course. Go, I will stand guard."

Victor drew a rune in the air with his staff and then touched it to the tapestry. A ripple started to form inside it, moving outward. "Follow me."

One by one, we followed Victor into the tapestry.

THE THIRTEENTH TAPESTRY

THE DARK FORTRESS loomed above us, an obsidian giant which seemed to be carved out of the massive mountain itself.

"That's Mount Khatral," said Victor, "also known as the Black Mountain. This is the place where your ancestors trapped Dragath so many centuries ago."

The name itself sent a shiver down my spine. The air felt dead, and nothing seemed to grow for miles around. Black rocks and an even darker mountain absorbed all the light around it. I looked down. Centuries-old bones lay by the wayside, fallen and forgotten, while a mage in a dark robe climbed the carved stone steps to the base of the fortress. I recognized the crest on the robes. He was a mage of Evolon.

Penelope gasped. His hair was short and dark, not peppered with white as it was now, but there was no mistaking who it was. "That's Joreth."

Victor nodded. "Yes, before he came to work at the palace in Nerenor. His thirst for knowledge and power led him here, to the Darklands. But it was fate or a power far greater that led him to Dragath's tomb."

We followed Joreth into the fortress, through dark corridors, and into an underground cavern deep within the bowels of Mount Khatral. I knew he couldn't see or hear us, but every time he looked back, my heartbeat sped up.

We came to a dark chamber within the cavern. The only thing in this room was a stone tomb where Dragath lay, bound by Auraken Firedrake's magic. The floor around it had deep grooves etched in the shape of druidic runes, and I knew the druids had helped my ancestors in their war against the demon lord.

Joreth touched the tomb with a reverent finger, then placed both his hands flat against it. I saw him grimace in pain as dark veins forced their way through his body. He looked like he was trying to pull away, but he couldn't—the darkness was latching on to his soul. I wished we could stop him from doing this, but Penelope had warned us of the dangers of tampering with the past. It could change the course of everything, and it rarely ever ended well.

Finally, Joreth let go, but when he turned toward us his eyes flashed demon black. In the center of the obsidian iris glowed an ember of red evil soullessness. Joreth left the chamber with part of Dragath's consciousness firmly embedded within him.

Victor turned to me, speaking softly even though the shield around us created a sound barrier. "The bonds around Dragath's prison had weakened over the centuries, allowing him to latch on to Joreth and invade his mind."

He drew a rune on the ground with his staff and the scene in front of us changed. We were standing in a magnificent white stone palace with marble pillars and gold leaf furnishings.

"The Star Palace," Penelope whispered.

My breath hitched in my throat. This had been my home, the place where I was born, where I lived with my parents for the short time we were together. I could barely remember it except in my dreams, and now I was here. I didn't expect to feel this way.

"Joreth joined the palace mages," Victor explained. "He was soon appointed military advisor to your grandfather, Ereneth, who was king at the time. Guided by Dragath, his aim was to find the Dagger, which was rumored to be buried in the vaults of the Star Palace and protected by the Firedrake line. But even with his high post, he could not get into the vaults, so he seduced Lilith, the king's new wife."

My heartbeat sped up, but Rafe silently took my hand in his as we walked through the long white corridor to what looked like the throne room. We stopped outside one of the rooms, the door of which was slightly ajar, and slipped inside. Joreth was already there, looking very different from when he'd been in the Darklands. He was dressed in a fine, emerald-green doublet and dark pants with highly polished boots that singled him out as a nobleman of the realm. He had his arms around a woman, dark-haired and beautiful, with upturned eyes and lips the color of fresh blood.

The woman broke the embrace. "We cannot do this anymore, Joreth," she said, moving back. "It is too dangerous. If my husband finds out, he will have us both executed for treason."

Joreth held her hands in his, and his dark eyes grew darker still as Dragath spoke softly. "Lilith, I love you. No one has found out."

"It's different now." She shook her head. "You don't understand, Joreth." She paused and took a deep breath. "I am with child."

Joreth's eyes widened, but he produced a smile that didn't reach his eyes. "It doesn't matter. They will simply think it is the king's child."

She withdrew her hands and moved back. "No, they won't. Ereneth and I have not been together in that way for years now. If someone sees us together, then they will suspect the child is yours."

Joreth grabbed her by the arms, his eyes eerie with shadows that seemed to swirl around behind them. "Then we must take the throne for ourselves."

Lilith gasped. "You are talking treason, Joreth."

He nodded solemnly. "It is the only way to ensure we can be together." He put his hand on her belly. "And the only way to make sure our child is safe."

Lilith stopped resisting, her stance changing, and she looked down, her hand over Joreth's on her still-growing belly. "What do I have to do?"

My mouth fell open. "The child. It can't be . . ." I whispered.

Victor's eyes darted to me, and he nodded solemnly. "The child is Morgana."

I was staggered by the implications as I looked around at Rafe's, Tristan's, and Penelope's faces. Slowly the pieces started to come together in my confused mind. Morgana was not really King Ereneth's daughter and my father's half sister. She was the daughter of Joreth and Lilith and not related to my father by blood in any way.

I glanced at Penelope, my voice a strained whisper. "This was her big secret, the one she was trying desperately to hide. Lucian knew her true identity. That was what he held over her. Morgana is not truly a Firedrake."

"It seems so." Penelope's lips were a thin line when she nodded. "Lilith must have passed her off as the king's daughter, when in actuality it is Joreth who is Morgana's real father."

"Yes, that is why they are working together," said Victor as he drew a rune on the ground with his staff and the scene changed. We were in another part of the castle, in a dark courtyard.

"Where are we now?" I inquired, looking around.

The courtyard was empty, shadows forming in the corners as clouds flitted across the moon, veiling its light.

"We are now twenty years after the last scene," Victor confirmed. "Joreth convinced Lilith to join him in overthrowing the king, making her believe he did it for her and the child. But his real motivation was getting to the Dagger. All Dragath's plans rested on it. So together, they formed the Black Mages when Morgana was still a baby. They attacked the palace and fought a long battle for the throne of Illiador. But your father, Azaren, led your grandfather's army to victory, killing Joreth and saving his father's throne—the throne that would one day be yours."

"So that's when Joreth came to the druids to heal?"

Victor nodded and held up his hand. We turned to see two figures come into the courtyard.

Morgana! She was young and beautiful and not much older than I was now.

I involuntarily moved farther back into the shadows.

The man beside her removed his hood. It was unmistakably Joreth, older and scarred with a short white beard and salt-and-pepper hair.

"Why are you here again?" Morgana spat. "I told you, you can't be my father. I'm a princess of the royal house of the Firedrakes." She turned to leave. "I'm going to tell my brother about you, and he will get rid of you for good."

Joreth caught her arm in a viselike grip. "You are no more a Firedrake than I am," he snarled.

Morgana snarled back at him, and I could see a faint resemblance, not in their looks but in their attitude. "You are a liar," she spat, pulling her arm free and lifting her chin. "I even look like a Firedrake."

Joreth laughed. "A simple spell conjured up by your mother when you were born," he said.

Morgana stood rooted to the spot at his words.

He softened his voice. "What do you think your dear brother will do when he realizes you are not really of his bloodline? He will throw you out and take everything from you. And that is the best-case scenario."

Morgana's brow furrowed, and she rubbed her arm. "What do you want?"

Joreth smiled, sinister shadows moving around him in the dark courtyard. "It's not what I want that's important. I'm your father, Morgana. I only want what's best for you. I can give you what you always wanted. Power beyond your wildest dreams. I can make you undisputed Queen of Illiador and beyond."

"How?" Morgana looked skeptically at her father. "Azaren will be king for a long time, and after him, his daughter Aurora."

"But we can change that." He put his hand gently on her shoulder. "Kill Azaren and his brat of a child, and you shall have your crown."

Morgana's eyes widened, and she took a step back. "You want me to kill my brother and niece?"

"Haven't you been listening, Morgana? He is not your brother, and she is not your niece. I am the only family you have left."

She shook her head and straightened her shoulders. "No! I cannot kill him. I will not do it. I will tell Azaren the truth. He will understand it is not my fault my mother had an affair." She turned from him and started to walk away.

Joreth raised his hand, and his magic grabbed Morgana and spun her around to face him. "Foolish girl," he hissed. "He will kill you as soon as he learns the truth. He will not give you time to explain. He killed your mother and tried to kill me. Why do you think he will treat you any differently? He will think you are a spy, or worse, a traitor."

I could see the confusion in Morgana's eyes. She was still young, her fate still undecided. It was the moment that would change everything for my family. I wished I could have said something to stop her from taking the wrong path. But I just stood there, unable to interfere, unable to do anything but watch Joreth turn his daughter into the monster she was today.

Morgana raised her eyes to her father's, a determination in them that wasn't there before. She echoed her mother's words unknowingly. "What do I have to do?"

Joreth smiled. "Go to the Firedrake vaults and find the Dagger of Dragath. If you want to kill Azaren and his child, you will have to get rid of the fae-warrior first."

"Elayna?"

Joreth nodded. "The fae queen's daughter is an elite fire-fae warrior of Elfi and too powerful to defeat without the Dagger. She is an immortal, and she will protect her child with her life. Elayna is almost impossible to kill. The only way to get rid of her is to trap her within the Dagger of Dragath."

Morgana clasped her hands in front of her and raised her chin. "It will be done, Father."

Victor drew a rune with his staff and the scene shifted again. Morgana and Joreth were in a room at the palace. In her hand was the Dagger I recognized so well, curved and twisted with a massive ruby on its hilt. They had managed to find what no one else had. Just seeing it again, even though it couldn't hurt me now, brought a bone-chilling fear I could not control. How would I be able to face it again? When the Dagger had cut me, I'd felt its magic. It was strong, powerful—too powerful, in fact. It had stripped me of my magic so easily, and there was nothing I could do to stop it.

Rafe, alert as always, took my hand and squeezed it. His ability to read what I was feeling was uncanny, and his presence always made me feel safe.

Joreth spoke, grabbing my attention. "I have sent for the Drakaar assassins to assist you. They will take care of Azaren while you get rid of Elayna and bring the child to me."

Morgana's eyes flashed. "But you said yourself the child has to die for me to be queen."

Joreth clamped his hand around Morgana's arm. "The child must not be harmed. I have a use for her yet."

"But the throne—"

"—will be yours," Joreth finished.

Morgana nodded.

Victor looked at me. "This is the final part. Are you sure you want to see this?"

I nodded. I had to know the whole story. I straightened my shoulders. "I'm ready."

Victor drew a rune with his staff and the scene shifted one last time.

I could smell something burning, and a flash of light blinded me. The curtains were enveloped in a blaze, and the acrid smell of smoke filled my lungs. I had to remind myself we were shielded and safe.

We were in the nursery. A child cried in the corner. My mother was there, her beautiful blonde hair flashing golden in the light of the fire. Two dark terrifying shapes loomed up behind her, swords glinting red in the light of the roaring flames. Drakaar. I wanted to warn her, but it was unnecessary—she already knew they were there.

Elayna Firedrake whirled around to meet her attackers, and her hands started to glow, flashing with silver fire. Twin swords blazed in her hands as she attacked. Steel clashed and fire sizzled as she fought with the strength and grace of the fae, her swords a fluid extension of her arms. The Drakaar fell before her, their heads severed, eyes lifeless.

She looked at her child. "Run, Aurora." Her voice was strained. "Run now. I am right behind you."

I looked over at my little self, and all the feelings I had suppressed for years came crashing down around me. This was my dream, the one I had relived again and again for months before I came into this world. I longed to rush over and help, but I could not do anything but watch my destiny unfold before me.

My childhood self obeyed my mother and ran as fast as her little legs could carry her, coughing and trying to breathe through the smoke as the flames grew closer. My heart broke as we followed her, unable to do anything but watch a whole family and royal line be extinguished in one night.

I heard a terrified scream and stopped. I looked up. A wooden beam was poised to come crashing down on the child's head. But in a flash, my mother was beside my past self, her fae strength and speed the only reason I was alive today. She scooped the child

Aurora up in her arms and darted out of the burning room. Part of the room crumbled behind us as the ceiling caved in. Wafts of billowing black smoke chased us, flames licking at our heels.

Young Aurora clung to her mother's neck as they ran into a vast stone corridor with massive windows and statues lining the walls. The winter night was void of moonlight, and half-burned torches flickered and died. From within the darkness, sinister black shapes moved toward them, cutting off their escape.

We stopped, backs to the wall, watching helplessly as I relived my parents' last day.

A shadowy figure emerged from the group, holding the curved Dagger with the huge red ruby flashing on its shining golden hilt. It was a woman. Her crimson robes swirled around her like a shroud of blood as she moved toward my mother.

I would know her anywhere. Morgana!

"Give her up, Elayna," she said, her voice no more than a whisper that carried on the wings of a shadow. Her bright, emerald-green eyes flashed with triumph.

"Never, Morgana." My mother set me down beside her, still holding my hand. "Stay still, Aurora, and do exactly as I say."

Little Aurora nodded her head quickly, understanding only that it was very important to listen to her mother.

"You cannot escape me, Elayna," said Morgana. "Give me the child."

Morgana was advancing on them, but my mother made no move to run. I wanted to shout at her to escape, not to send me away.

My childhood self pulled at her hand frantically, trying to do the same thing, to run as fast as we could, but stood rooted to the spot as per my mother's instructions.

Morgana's crimson robes fanned about her as she glided forward, her feet barely touching the ground. She raised her arm, clutching the gleaming Dagger in her clawed fingers.

My mother closed her eyes, and I knew what she was doing. She was preparing the portal, gathering her magic.

Suddenly, my mother's eyes snapped open, flashing silver. She raised both her arms over her head, bringing them down in front of her in one sweeping motion.

The power she unleashed was immense, ancient.

My mother moved to shield her child from Morgana, the Dagger still coming for her heart. But an invisible force held little Aurora in its grip; as the portal opened, young Aurora was pulled backward.

"Nooo!" screeched Morgana, flying at them, and plunged the gleaming Dagger into my mother's heart.

A flash of blinding light. My mother disappeared.

I hung my head and closed my eyes. It was more painful to watch than I had imagined. I turned to Victor. "Let's go. I've seen enough."

Victor put his hand gently over my arm. "There's more."

My eyes flew open. This was where my dream had ended.

"What have you done?" Joreth snarled, hurrying down the corridor toward Morgana. "Where is the child?"

Morgana spun around to face her father. "I couldn't help it. Elayna sent her away through a portal before I could get my hands on her."

Joreth raised his hand, and his eyes flashed in fury. "Idiot." He slapped Morgana across her face. "Luckily, I made other arrangements." He adjusted the sleeves of his robe.

Joreth snapped his fingers, and the Drakaar assassins dragged a man down the corridor.

He looked up.

My voice choked on the word. "Father!"

I recognized him from the portraits I had seen in Silverthorne Castle. He was bleeding and barely conscious as ropes of dark magic held him in check.

I took a step forward, but Victor kept his hand firmly on my arm.

"What is he doing alive?" spat Morgana.

My father's face was scarred, and deep gashes had split his arm and leg. His lip was split, but he raised his chin and spoke in a clear voice. "How could you betray your own brother, Morgana?"

"You are not my brother," she said and looked away. "Kill him and be done with it."

Joreth smiled, looking as sinister as the demon that resided within him. "Not yet. I still need at least one Firedrake alive for what I plan to do. I was intending to keep the child because she would have been easier to control. But now you leave me no choice."

"How can I be queen if he is still alive?" Morgana snarled. "He has to die."

"And he will, but not right now," said Joreth. "As far as anyone is concerned, Azaren and his whole family died in the fire at the Star Palace today. You are now Queen of Illiador."

He turned to the Drakaar. "Take him away."

I gasped and my hand flew to my mouth as my knees threatened to buckle under me. "My father is still alive?"

Victor nodded. "It seems so."

Joreth stopped as if he had heard something and turned to look straight at me. His eyes shone dark as night. He grinned, and a single word escaped his lips. "Dawnstar."

Victor's face paled. "He's seen us!" His voice sounded panicked. The old druid waved his staff in front of us and the Star Palace disappeared.

Penelope's face was white. "What happened?" she said as soon as we reappeared out of the tapestry. "How did he see us?"

"Who saw you?" Brother Sebastian interrupted. He had been waiting for us in the tapestry room in the tower.

"Dragath," said Victor.

"Did your shield fall?" Sebastian asked.

"My shield never falls." Victor gave Sebastian a warning look. "Somehow the demon lord saw us through Joreth's eyes. The longer Dragath resides within him, the stronger he grows." He turned to me. "He now knows where you are, and his creatures will come for you. You must leave immediately, there is no time to waste."

I grabbed Victor's arm, and my brows drew together. "Wait! What about my father? I want to see where they took him. We have to go back into the tapestry." My eyes lit up with the possibilities. "If he is still alive, I can find him."

Victor shook his head. "Absolutely not! It is too dangerous. I never expected the tapestry to work like this. Dragath's power has grown within Joreth—he has become more powerful than before. It will no longer be possible to go unnoticed."

Penelope moved past me and blocked Victor's path. "You should have told us." Her eyes flashed dangerously, sharp as steel. "So that we were prepared."

Brother Victor sighed. "I would have if I knew how it worked. He shouldn't have seen us. No one else could except Dragath himself." He gave me a pointed look. "And it is important the Dawnstar has all the necessary information needed to defeat the Dark Lord."

"But now you must go," Brother Sebastian interrupted. "You need to take back the Dagger before Joreth has a chance to use it."

"How can I if I don't know where he is?"

Victor looked at Brother Sebastian as if trying to make a decision. "We will try the scrying table again. Come."

We descended the stone tower, and Victor led us back to the library and to the room at the back where the scrying table was located.

"Joreth must be somewhere in the center of his army. Getting to him will be extremely difficult," said Rafe.

"But not impossible," I added.

"No, not impossible." Penelope wrung her hands. "But when

we saw him earlier with Andromeda, he didn't seem to be with his army—only a few soldiers and Drakaar. If we can figure out where he is, we may be able to get to the Dagger before he rejoins his army. We need to see the area where he is camped."

Victor waved his staff and the fog in the scrying table shifted slightly and reformed. It showed us a small encampment at the foot of a gigantic mountain range, a twilight glow blanketing the valley.

"That is dwarven territory," gasped Penelope, inspecting the rocky landscape that lay before us. "Those are not the Cascade Mountains. They are the Silverspike Mountains."

Rafe put his hands on the edge of the table, his sharp eyes scanning the scrying table. "Stonegate."

Penelope rubbed her hand over her face. "What could be so important he would leave his army and go so far into dwarven territory?"

Victor waved his staff over the table, and the fog changed.

Joreth was still in his tent when the tent flap opened and a guard came in. "You have a visitor, general."

Joreth nodded. "Send him in."

A short, squat man with a broad chest and clipped brown beard came into the tent.

"A dwarf," said Victor, his eyes narrowing. He rested his hands on the edge of the table and peered carefully at the scene within it.

"That's Drimli, Ranthor's cousin," Rafe said, recognizing the newcomer. "What's he doing there?"

"Maybe he has come to negotiate?" offered Brother Sebastian.

Penelope shot a dark look at the druid. "Ranthor would never negotiate. He knows Stonegate can't be breached."

"I think we might have a problem," said Victor, his gaze fixated on the events unfolding hundreds of miles away.

We looked back to the table. "Wait for the signal by the western gate," Drimli said. "You can enter from there."

Joreth smiled. "And you are sure Ranthor has Silverthorne's key?"

Drimli grinned. "The old mage believed this to be the best place to hide it. Once I get rid of my cousin, Ranthor, you shall have the key you seek."

Joreth and Drimli shook hands.

"I think you will make a perfect new king for the dwarves, Drimli."

Drimli nodded briskly and left.

I drew back as if I had been slapped. "The last key to the *Book of Abraxas* is in Stonegate."

"And Joreth found the only way Stonegate can be breached," said Rafe, his eyes sharp as he drew back from the table. "Betrayal."

Penelope turned to Rafe and me, her eyes like ice chips. "We have to warn Ranthor. There isn't much time. We need to leave now."

Rafe's eyes narrowed and he shook his head. "We will never reach them in time, Penelope. You cannot create a portal over such a distance." He looked at me. "Aurora could have done it, but that was before . . ."

I put my hands on my hips and glared at him. "Before what?" I snapped. "Say it, Rafe, everybody else does."

Rafe shook his head. "I wasn't blaming you, Aurora, I was merely stating a fact. If you had all your magic, you could have portaled there immediately."

I hung my head, disgusted with myself at my sudden and unruly outburst. I knew he wasn't blaming me, but every time someone reminded me of what I had lost, a great sadness and pain welled up inside me in the place where my magic had been.

"Because of Dragath's curse you cannot portal off this island anyway," Victor interrupted. "You would have to return to the mainland by ship and then portal from there. And now that he knows where you are, all the Drakwraiths left here to keep trespassers off the island will be looking for you. They will be waiting for you near the harbor and along the coast. Your ship will not have any survivors."

Penelope flashed a worried look at me. "If Drimli lets Joreth into the fortress, all will be lost. Once he has the last key to the *Book of Abraxas*, there will be nothing stopping him from raising the Dark Lord. And now that we know he has Azaren, he doesn't need Aurora's blood to break Dragath's bonds. He will kill Azaren and raise the demon lord along with all his powers."

"We have to get there somehow." I clenched my hands into fists. "I am not going to let him kill my father."

"Once Dragath rises, he will use the Dagger to open a portal to the demon world and let his whole army through," said Penelope to the druid. "We need to retrieve the Dagger, whatever the cost."

The old druid did not look surprised. "I know of the true use of the Dagger of Dragath, but I never believed we would come to this. And now with your magic within the Dagger . . ." He shook his head and never finished his sentence.

My eyes narrowed into shards of steel as I addressed the old druid. "There has to be a way to get my magic back from the Dagger before he can use it to open the portal."

Victor raised both his eyebrows. "There is, but you will not like it."

I felt a chill scuttle down my spine, but I squared my shoulders nonetheless. Whatever it was, I would deal with it. "Tell me."

Victor held my gaze without blinking. "The only way to retrieve your magic from the Dark Dagger is to be stabbed by the Dagger itself."

Silence pervaded every breath of air in the room. It was as if the world stood still.

Rafe spoke in a whisper. "There has to be another way."

The old druid rubbed his neck and looked up at the ceiling, as if searching for answers from some higher power. "I'm afraid there isn't." Victor turned his eyes on me, and his tone softened.

"While the Dagger is embedded in your body, theoretically, it may be possible for you to pull your magic back into yourself." He paused. "Mind you, it won't be easy. The Dagger will fight you for the magic. It was created to absorb fae magic, not give it back, and it will not give it up freely. You will have to fight for it. But it can be done."

"And what if Aurora fails?" Penelope asked.

I leaned forward, holding my hands tightly together to stop them from shaking.

Victor's eyes narrowed. "Then the Dawnstar will die."

THE SIEGE OF STONEGATE

I TOOK a deep breath and steeled myself. "I can do it."

I could not allow the general to use my magic to open such a portal. Even if it meant giving up my life so the world would be safe, I was prepared to do it. Although I wasn't really sure how I would find the courage to face the Dagger when the time came.

"But we still need to get there in time," said Penelope. "He already has Azaren and the Dagger. Once he gets the key, he will waste no time starting the ritual to raise Dragath. We must get the Dagger back before that happens."

I looked at Penelope. "Maybe we could contact my grandmother through a mirror portal and tell her to send the griffins."

Penelope shook her head. "That won't work. I've already tried. No kind of fae portals work on this island. Joreth made sure of that."

Ashara entered the library where we were gathered. "Kalen is awake."

My shoulders sagged with relief.

Ashara gave me a sharp look. "He wants to see his mother."

I sat down, my hands in my lap, my spine stiff. "Go to him, Penelope. We will handle this."

Sebastian got up. "I will go with you. I need to check on him anyway."

Penelope nodded, her eyes brighter than I had seen them in days. She rose and followed Sebastian to the infirmary. I was glad Kalen was going to be all right, but we still had a long road ahead of us.

Victor rubbed the day-old stubble on his chin as he eyed Ashara, who had just joined us. "Maybe no fae portals can work on this island. But Joreth never imagined the witches would get involved." He addressed Ashara. "Could you create a witchstone portal to Stonegate?"

"Yes, I have been there before," she said with a nod. "But it will take some time."

"Do it," said Victor. "Time is the one thing we don't have."

"Ashara, are you sure you can create such a powerful witchstone?" Tristan questioned.

"Of course I can," Ashara scoffed, her eyes narrowing. "Do you doubt my abilities, fae?"

"Frequently," said Tristan, turning back to Victor. "How do we get into Stonegate and warn Ranthor?"

"Leave that to me," said Rafe. "I know a secret way into Stonegate. It is magically protected to only open for the Ravenswood bloodline."

"Blood magic." Victor nodded.

Rafe glanced at the old druid. "Yes, it is from an old alliance my family has with the dwarves since Dorian the Great was king." He flashed me a half smile. "Why do you think they agreed to make me your sword?"

I ran my hand over the hilt of Dawn and smiled back at him. My dwarven-made sword, which Rafe had gifted me while he trained me in sword fighting during my time at the academy, was once a perfect conduit for my fae-fire. But now there was no silver fire left in me to infuse the sword with, and it hung at my side like any ordinary weapon.

"Then it's settled," said Victor. "Once Ashara makes the witchstone, I will take you to an area where you can open the portal outside the wards."

Sebastian returned to the library.

I put my hand on his arm. "How is Kalen?"

"Still weak," said the old druid. "You can see him now, but only for a moment. He needs to rest."

I nodded and followed Brother Sebastian. Kalen had been moved to a small room near the infirmary. He was lying on a small wooden bed in the corner of the room, propped up by pillows. Penelope was sitting on a stool by his bed, holding his hand.

He smiled when he saw me. "Aurora."

I smiled back at my old friend and hurried over to hug him. "I'm so glad you are okay, Kalen."

Rafe came over and patted Kalen on his shoulder. "You gave us quite a scare."

Kalen winced. "I can't even remember how we got here. Mother has been filling me in." He looked up at Tristan, his violet eyes shining. "Thank you. Mother told me you carried me all the way here."

Tristan came over and squeezed Kalen's shoulder softly. "And I would do it again, brother."

Kalen's eyes shone with tears. He looked away. "I'm tired."

Sebastian bustled forward. "I think that's enough for today. Kalen needs to regain his strength."

I nodded and looked at Penelope. "As soon as Ashara creates the witchstone, we can leave."

Penelope turned her gaze on Brother Sebastian, who was busy checking Kalen. "Will Kalen be well enough to travel?"

The old druid shook his bald head. "No, it is too soon. He needs at least a fortnight or maybe two until he is strong enough to leave."

Penelope stood up, her eyes steely blue as she regarded her son. "Kalen will be safer here with the druids. We have no idea what we will encounter once we get to Stonegate."

Rafe and Tristan nodded simultaneously. Protective as they were of Kalen, there was no way I could see either of them willingly dragging him along on a quest such as this.

Penelope kissed her son's forehead. His eyes were already closing. "Now get some rest."

She glanced at us. "How long will Ashara take to make the witchstone?"

"She said she will have it ready by morning," Tristan huffed.

Penelope arched an elegant eyebrow. "So soon? Witchstone portals can take months for an ordinary witch to make. Is Ashara that powerful?"

Tristan shrugged. "She believes she is."

"Well, I hope she knows what she is doing," Penelope said as she ushered us out of Kalen's room. "I will stay here with Kalen tonight while you make preparations to leave in the morning."

THE NEXT MORNING, Ashara had the witchstone ready as promised. Rafe had spent hours with her poring over a map of the area around Stonegate so she could create the portal to take us exactly where we needed to go.

Tristan took the witchstone from Ashara to look it over. It was a small green stone the size of a marble with a strange mist swirling inside it. "Impressive," he said as he turned it over in his hand and scowled at it. "Does it work?"

Ashara rolled her eyes and took it back. "We will just have to wait and see, won't we, fae?"

Tristan did not look amused.

We said our goodbyes to Kalen and the druids.

Victor led us through a secret passage out of the monastery that led to the woods behind it. "We cannot open the witchstone portal anywhere near the monastery," said Victor, waving his staff in front of him and removing the wards. "But we must be quick."

Outside the magical wards of the druid monastery, the mist was thick and menacing. It crept over the ground and through the trees as if waiting to swallow us up. Tall firs rose above us as we raced toward the hills. Our feet slipped on treacherous wet rocks as we ran, our breath fogging before us. We had one chance to make it through the portal before the Drakwraiths realized where we were. Twilight had started to set in, lighting up the sky in a burnished pink sheen. The mist-covered hills rose all around us, like sentinels at the gateway of a lost world.

Sounds of shrieking pierced the air.

The Drakwraiths were here.

Victor pointed to two large fir trees. "Create the portal there."

We pushed ourselves faster and ran for the trees.

Victor had stopped. He drew a rune on the ground with his staff, preparing to meet the wraiths. "Go! I will hold them off."

I glanced back. The Drakwraiths were not alone. "Dark fae," I gasped and ran faster.

"Victor might be able to stop the Drakwraiths," shouted Rafe, "but not dark fae."

Tristan stopped and turned to meet them. "I will make sure they don't pursue." His swords lit up with silver fire, fierce and unyielding like the warrior who wielded them. "Go, I'm right behind you."

I faltered. We were so close, but I knew Victor could not fight the Drakwraiths as well as two dark fae on his own. Ashara stopped as well. She threw me a dark look and pressed the witchstone into my hand. "Go!"

She turned to stand beside Tristan, the stones on her staff coming to life as she woke her magic.

Rafe took my hand. "We have to go, Aurora. If those things

follow us through the portal, we will never make it to Stonegate in time. They have to be stopped."

I nodded and ran, pumping my arms as we raced for the trees. I threw the witchstone at the largest tree. The air before us shimmered as we neared. I let Penelope go first, then Rafe and I followed. Just as we touched the bark of the tree, we were transported by the witchstone portal to the very heart of the Silverspike Mountains that lay in eastern Avalonia.

The portal closed behind us. I hoped Tristan and Ashara were okay.

The air was chilly as an icy wind blew down from the northern mountains. The dwarven fortress of Stonegate lay beneath us, situated within the mountain itself.

"The secret entrance is close by," said Rafe as he started inspecting the path before us.

"Drimli is planning to let Joreth in through the western gate, which is on the other side of this mountain," said Penelope. "The Drakaar will be guarding all the entrances. Be careful."

We climbed down a rocky side of the mountain. "Shh . . ." Rafe crouched behind a rock and pulled me down near him along with Penelope.

My heart leapt into my throat—just a few feet away, two Drakaar were inspecting the area. "I don't know why the general sent us to guard this side of the mountain. There is nothing here," one said.

The other nodded. "I would much rather be ripping out dwarf throats."

I looked over at Rafe, my eyes showing my distress. How were we going to get past these Drakaar? Without Tristan, we wouldn't stand a chance.

A shadow loomed behind us. "What have we here?" said a raspy voice.

I whirled around, drawing my sword.

A Drakaar stood before me, soulless black eyes and serrated

teeth flashing as Dragath's henchman regarded me. His smile was vicious as he reached out his hand and shadows formed around us, rooting us to the spot.

"The general did say we might have visitors," he said to the other two Drakaar, who had just noticed us and hurried over. "But we weren't expecting the Dawnstar herself."

He looked the three of us over. "I don't see the dark prince." He grinned, flashing his razor-sharp teeth. "Finally, you are at our mercy, Dawnstar. The general tells us you have lost your fae magic." His clawed fingers curved into a fist, and the shadows that wound around us tightened. I gasped for breath, my sword falling from my hand and clattering to the ground.

Rafe and Penelope struggled with their bonds, and Penelope's magic flashed dangerously as the shadows around her broke and reformed. It was not enough. Only the fire-fae were any match for the Drakaar.

"We will take great pleasure in killing you, Shadowbreaker," he sneered. "We will—"

His words were cut off as a flaming sword appeared out of nowhere and the Drakaar's head was severed from his body.

I looked up.

Tristan stood over the fallen Drakaar, twin swords blazing in his hands and eyes flashing with silver stars. He eyed the other two Drakaar, who had already started backing away at the sight of him. "Why don't you ever learn?" Tristan scowled. "If you want the Dawnstar, you are going to have to go through me."

Ashara stepped up beside him, the jewels on her staff glowing dangerously bright. "And me too, apparently," she scoffed and flipped her braid over her shoulder, flicking a glance at Tristan. "Do you want to deal with this, or should I?"

Tristan grinned, the smile wholly genuine. "Be my guest," he said, and stepped out of the way.

Ashara launched herself at the Drakaar, who turned to run as soon as they saw the warrior witch coming at them. But they were not fast enough. Ashara made quick work of the Drakaar, while we watched in awe of her strength and power.

Tristan sheathed his swords and threw a look at Rafe. "So where is this secret entrance?"

Penelope arched an eyebrow. "How did you two get here so fast? The portal closed behind us while you were fighting the dark fae."

Tristan's mouth twitched upward. "It seems Ashara was not exaggerating about her powers. She made two identical witchstones, just in case."

Penelope's jaw dropped. "Two at the same time?"

He flicked a glance at the warrior witch. "Apparently so."

We followed a steep mountain path down to a section of rock covered by shrubs and bushes. Rafe parted the foliage and searched along the rock with his hand.

"Have you used this entrance before?" I asked Rafe.

"No, but my father explained where it was. This is the place, I'm sure of it."

"So you have no idea if it will actually work?" Penelope asked.

"No," said Rafe, his voice clipped as he drew his dagger and sliced it across his palm, drawing blood. He placed his bleeding hand on the rock.

The rockface started to shimmer. Rafe drew in a sharp breath. He raised an eyebrow and smirked at me. "Who wants to go first?"

Tristan stepped forward and glanced at Ashara. "I will make sure it is safe." He stepped into the rock and disappeared.

Ashara rolled her eyes and followed.

"After you," said Rafe.

I stepped inside.

I got a sudden feeling of claustrophobia as the rock closed around me, but in a moment I was standing in a vast hall deep within the mountain. Tristan and Ashara were already scanning our surroundings, the jewels on the witch's staff giving off an eerie glow and illuminating the cavern.

As my eyes adjusted to the light, I willed my heart to calm while I caught my breath. My hand lit up with mage light as I looked around. We stood in a large, rectangular room with massive carved pillars holding up the stone ceiling. The walls of the cavern were polished to a smooth sheen and carved with dwarven symbols that rose into the darkness. We walked through the hall toward an arched opening where light streamed in, and I stepped out of the smaller cavern onto a ledge overlooking the biggest cavern I had ever seen. There was no sky visible here, but the top of the cavern seemed to glitter with sparkling light globes that floated around aimlessly, illuminating the whole place in a dim glow.

"The ancient city of Stonegate," Penelope breathed, her eyes taking in the expanse that lay before us.

Terraced levels with stone houses and opulent buildings were built on the different levels encircling the sides of the cavern. The walls looked like a labyrinth with roads and steps and small stone bridges that connected the city dwellings. My mouth fell open in awe as we traversed the small steep steps down through the different levels.

An ancient underground complex, Stonegate was an architectural marvel. Each level had numerous carved passageways, chambers, and pillared halls like the one we came through, which disappeared into the darkness of the mountain beyond. According to Penelope, the upper levels housed the mansions of the nobility and rich merchants, and they traveled among their levels via slender bridges, ornate arches, and wide steps made of carved stone and secured by dwarven magic. The lower levels of the workers and miners led into another whole network of twisted tunnels and dark passages that changed to primordial caverns where light never reached and nameless creatures lay in wait. I shuddered at her description of the darker parts of Stonegate as we reached the cavern floor.

Penelope pointed opposite us in the distance, at a monstrous structure of stone pillars and arches created seemingly for giants. "The palace is there. We will have to go through the city to get to it."

Rafe scanned his surroundings. "I just hope we are not too late."

We followed the road through the city, where shops and houses dotted the area, leading off into smaller arched entrances and dingy streets. A river ran along the side, disappearing into the mountain beyond. The city was quiet, although a few of Stonegate's citizens hurried through the streets, giving us scared glances and dashing off. Shutters closed and doors slammed as we passed. The city, which I had presumed was full of people, seemed more like a ghost town at this time of night.

We stopped as the sound of booted feet thumped toward us. The main road leading to the palace was cut off by a legion of dwarven guards, heavily armored with weapons at the ready.

"Who goes there?" said a booming voice. "How did you get into the city?"

Penelope stepped forward. "We need to see the king."

"The king sees no one without an appointment," said one dwarven guard, his spear held firmly in his hand. He was of average height, about five feet tall. I quickly glanced around at the others whose beards were trimmed and short, framing stout faces with weathered skin. Tough-looking, the dwarven guards stoically stood their ground. "You can petition for an audience with the king tomorrow."

My eyes narrowed. I didn't want to waste any more time. I pushed my shoulders back and stepped forward. "My name is Aurora Firedrake, and I have to see the king."

My name had the desired effect. The guards darted hasty, alarmed looks at their leader, whose eyes widened in recognition. His gaze moved from Rafe and Penelope to Tristan and Ashara standing behind me. He bowed once, then thumped his spear and one booted foot as he turned. "Follow me," he said and led us through the main street to the palace.

"Where is everyone?" Penelope asked the guard as we passed the marketplace, which was empty except for unused stalls and dilapidated stacks of crates. We'd passed numerous little shops all over the city, but they were all shut down.

"Curfew," the dwarven guard answered, not looking back.

King Ranthor's palace rose up above us, a huge stone fortress carved out of the very rock of the cavern. Enormous iron gates opened to let us in as we followed the guards. They led us through vast halls with massive pillars and curved arches that held up the domed ceilings. Intricate silverwork was embossed into the stone, and precious gems, the likes of which I had never seen before, decorated the arches above. The same eerie glow lit up the halls— hovering globes that gave off a faint light. It wasn't like the warm glow of the fae magic that lit the halls of the Crystal Castle in Elfi, but a darker, more sinister magic.

Four guards had to pry open the big stone doors that led to the throne room. Entering a cavernous vault with carved stone pillars and walls smooth and polished, we walked down a long crimson carpet to where the king sat.

As we neared the throne—a monstrous seat of iron—Penelope stopped, her hand on my arm. "That's not Ranthor."

The dwarf on the throne got up. "No, it's not." I recognized him from the scrying table. He was the same one who had met with Joreth. It was Drimli, the traitor.

Rafe and I drew our swords. Tristan and Ashara moved to flank us.

"Where is Ranthor?" Rafe demanded.

"Dead," spat Drimli. "My useless cousin didn't deserve this throne. I do."

Penelope gasped as a shadow stepped through the doorway beyond the throne and removed his hood.

Joreth! He was already in the fortress.

Joreth clapped his hands together, a big smile on his face. "Ah! Dawnstar. I knew you would come, but I wasn't expecting you so soon." He walked forward. Two young girls followed out of the shadows: Andromeda's daughter Skye, who also happened to be my fae cousin, and my best friend Vivienne.

"Viv!" I took a step forward but stopped, remembering she wasn't herself—the Dark Queen resided within her. Lilith sneered at me from behind thick lashes, her stark black eyes sinister in the eerie light. I looked over at Skye. Her blue eyes were crystal clear, but she served the Dark Lord all the same.

They stopped a few feet away.

"Oh! Your friend is long gone," Joreth said, stroking Vivienne's hair as she stood docilely beside him. "I think I like this new body of yours, Lilith. Maybe we should keep it."

Vivienne smiled, but I only saw the Dark Queen swirling behind her eyes, a predator. She smoothed her hands over her new body. "Yes, I think so," she purred. "Much better than Calisto's body. She required too much upkeep."

An image of the beautiful Calisto lying dead and mangled in the palace after Lilith left her body flashed before my eyes. I shook my head to dispel the images.

It didn't work.

Joreth's eyes were now completely black; no iris and no white could be seen anymore. Dragath had taken over his mind and body completely. He drew the Dagger of Dragath from his robe, the ruby on its hilt flashing as if in warning. "We have what we came for."

Vivienne opened her hand. The last key to the *Book of Abraxas* rested within it. He wasn't lying—they already had everything they needed. Well, almost everything.

From behind the pillars and the shadowy arches, more shapes emerged. They surrounded us, and I recognized who they were instantly: dark fae, over a dozen of them. We were completely outnumbered.

I straightened my shoulders. I needed answers. "Where is my father?" I demanded. "What have you done with him?"

Joreth raised an eyebrow. "Yes, I realized you had been poking around in the past. It's a wonder that foolish druid Victor managed to get the tapestry to work in the first place." Joreth traced the Dagger in the air beside him, and a portal started to open. "It doesn't matter where your father is. He won't be alive for long." He paused and looked at me. "Soon my true form will be restored, and my demon army will join me. I don't need you anymore." He glanced at the dark fae. "Kill her. Kill them all."

Tristan stood in front of me, his swords flashing with silver fire. Ashara was on my other side, her staff steady in her hands, the jewels on top glowing, ready for battle.

Rafe drew his sword and took up a fighting stance beside me.

Joreth raised an eyebrow. "It won't do you any good. I have already won." He sneered. "How do you like my latest creations?" He gestured toward the dark fae. "Not even you, Prince Tristan, can defeat so many dark fae on your own."

"Maybe." Tristan's eyes narrowed, and his ears twitched. I could tell his fae hearing had picked up something the others had not. His lips turned up in a sardonic smile as he looked at Joreth. "But it seems I'm not as alone as you think."

Two dark fae heads rolled toward us out of the darkness, eyes hollow, mouths open in silent screams.

"No, you are not alone, Tristan," said a High Fae warrior stepping out of the shadows. Cade and Farrell flanked him on both sides. "The Elite never are."

"Aiden." Tristan's lips curved upward. "Good to see you."

The Prince of the Day Court stepped into the light, his fair hair glinting and twin swords blazing in both hands. Aiden and I might not have seen eye to eye, but I was more than relieved to see him. The blond-haired High Fae was an exceptional warrior, nearly as powerful as Tristan, and part of Izadora's elite band of fire-fae warriors, the scourge of the Drakaar.

Joreth's obsidian eyes widened when he saw the Elite fae warriors. "Kill them!" he shouted and quickly stepped through the portal with Vivienne and Skye. The portal shut behind them.

"With pleasure," Tristan growled, flashing the dark fae a wolfish grin. His muscles rippled, magic of the night rolling off him in waves, a darker magic reserved only for the royal Nightshade bloodline. I remembered what Penelope had said about the original Nightshade prince, the fae lord with exceptional powers who summoned Dragath to this world. I shuddered at the thought of the power that ran through Tristan's veins. The dark prince's swords burned brightly, lighting up with a silver fire hotter and more potent than I had ever seen him produce.

There was a reason Tristan Nightshade was a legend, as he demonstrated when he pounced on the nearest dark fae and the battle for Stonegate began.

The dark fae swords lit up, casting an eerie red hue on the great stone hall, and a burning smell of fire meeting fire filled the air as red and silver swords clashed, sending out sparks of magic. The air around us was charged with power, as any remaining dwarven soldiers scurried out of the way, huddled in a corner with no way out, protecting their traitorous leader.

"Don't let Drimli get away!" shouted Penelope.

Rafe rushed to assist her.

I followed, but a dark fae with serrated teeth like those of a gorgoth came at me, sword raised. Although the dark fae looked like High Fae, they were abominations, and their magic felt wrong, like it wasn't meant to be. Made by dark magic and raised by the Drakaar, the dark fae had nothing of the High Fae in them. Their demon side was dominant, but they had the magic of a fire-fae warrior. I swung Dawn upward and braced my legs. My arms shuddered, but my dwarven-made sword stood firm against the dark magic of Dragath's servant. But the dark fae had the same strength as a High Fae, and he pushed me back. I staggered and my grip loosened, my sword clattering to the ground. Dark eyes glowed red as I reached for my sword, but it was too far. The creature raised his weapon, but before he could lower it, a sword of flashing silver severed his head and his body fell at my feet.

I looked up at a mop of red hair framing a familiar face. "Miss me?" Cade grinned as he bent down and pulled me to my feet.

I smiled at my old friend. "Always, Cade." I lunged for my sword. It was always good to see Cade, but this time I was more grateful than ever before to see him. If they hadn't come, we might not have made it.

The dark fae were no match for Izadora's Elite Guard; they might have had the same strength and magic, but that was no replacement for the centuries of experience, battles, and victories Tristan and the Elite had been through. Soon the throne room of the palace at Stonegate was littered with the bodies of Dragath's minions.

Aiden had the traitor Drimli by the throat, his short legs flailing about as the massive fae warrior lifted him up like he was a rag doll. Aiden shot the dwarf a disgusted look. "What do you want me to do with him?" he asked me.

For a moment I was stunned when all eyes turned on me. The Prince of the Day Court had made it clear he supported me as Izadora's heir and looked to me for orders. Aiden might not have liked me, but he was always loyal to the crown of Elfi.

Tristan came forward, his sword still flashing silver fire. "There is only one punishment for a traitor."

Ashara nodded. She, too, was bloodthirsty when it came to doling out punishments.

The guards brought out King Ranthor's body and laid it reverently on the table in the grand hall. Rafe stepped forward and inspected the body. "It's him," he confirmed.

Drimli struggled in his bonds. "I told you he's dead," he spat, struggling as Aiden tightened his grip on the traitor's throat. "I'm the rightful King of Stonegate now; you cannot do this to me."

Rafe stalked over to the traitor, his hand on his sword. "You are not king yet, Drimli." His eyes narrowed as he regarded the situation. "Drimli is Ranthor's cousin and not first in line to the throne. Ranthor has a son, Prince Mirin. He is now the rightful King of Stonegate and all the dwarven cities." He shot Drimli a disgusted look. "Where is he?"

Aiden dropped the dwarven traitor to the ground so he could speak. He clutched his throat, hidden by his long beard, and sneered at Rafe. "Also dead!" he spat. "And you all will be too, once the Dark Lord is done with you."

Aiden punched him in the stomach, and he doubled over.

But one of the dwarven guards stepped forward. They had all surrendered and had been disarmed. "He lies. The boy king lives. After Drimli killed King Ranthor, Mirin slipped out of the palace before he could kill him too."

"Shut up!" growled Drimli, shooting the guard a wild look. "The boy's a coward. He's not fit to be king. He ran at the first sign of trouble. That throne belongs to me!"

Rafe glanced at me and scowled. "He will kill the boy when he gets his hands on him. I have seen his kind before."

It was still hard for me to sentence someone to death, even though I knew this was war. We could not allow a traitor like this to turn the tide. He had already cost us dearly. I had to think like a queen, and that meant making tough choices.

I pushed my shoulders back and nodded once to Tristan. "Do it."

He raised his sword and severed the dwarf's head from his body.

I turned my head away. Sometimes the right decision was the hardest one to make.

Penelope turned to Cade. "Find the boy-king Mirin and secure the fortress until help arrives. We must go after the Dagger."

"That might be difficult," said Aiden. "No help is coming. The war has already begun."

My eyes widened in shock. "But Joreth was just here in Stonegate."

Penelope shook her head. "Joreth has his own agenda, it seems."

Aiden nodded. "I'm afraid I don't have good news. Morgana's forces have amassed in the Valley of Flowers. Silverthorne's forces have blocked the Eastern Pass in the Cascade Mountains, but they won't hold it for long. The general had a second, much larger force hiding in the Darkwood. Morgana's forces outnumber us ten to one, and her army is still gathering." He shook his head; I had never seen Aiden look so defeated. "There are too many of them. Without help, we cannot win this war."

"What about the Brandorians and the witches?" I asked, horrified at what had already occurred. "Is Santino all right? Have the Council of Five agreed to send reinforcements to Eldoren?"

"Santino is fine," said Cade, stepping in. "The Council of Five does not exist anymore. He has invoked the old title of Sultan and has taken over Brandor."

Penelope's eyes widened. "How?"

"The Detoris attacked the Red Citadel and killed Roderigo Valasis," Aiden explained. "Santino avenged his father and took down the Detori family, killing Darius and Shiraz Detori. The other emirs have surrendered to him. He is now the undisputed Sultan of Brandor and commands all of its armies."

I smiled. I knew Santino would come through. Even without magic, the pirate prince was a force to be reckoned with, and I was glad he was on our side.

"That is good news, at least," said Penelope. "If Santino's forces and the witches join Silverthorne's army, we may have a chance."

Aiden shook his head. "It may be too late."

"It's not over yet." I stepped forward and looked at Rafe. "I'm going after the Dagger."

Rafe shot me a dark look. "Not alone you're not."

My jaw tightened. "You have to go back to Eldoren and defend your kingdom, Rafe. But I cannot come with you. If Joreth has my father, I have to get there before he uses the Dagger on him."

Rafe held me gently by the arms and looked into my eyes. "I will never leave you to do this alone, Aurora. I'm coming with you, whether you want me to or not."

Penelope's eyes looked dull as she regarded me. "We may not make it in time." She wrung her hands. "It is virtually impossible to open a portal anywhere near Mount Khatral. It is protected by the darkest of magics."

"Are you sure that is where he has gone?" I asked.

Penelope nodded. "Yes. Now that Joreth has everything he needs, he will not waste time beginning the ritual. He needs Dragath's tomb in order to start."

I went over the options. "Can we portal close by?"

Penelope nodded. "We can portal to the outer boundaries." She looked over at Tristan. "There will be Drakaar guarding the gates to the Dark Fortress; we will need your help."

"Not a problem," he confirmed.

Penelope turned a stern eye on Rafe. "You must return to the battle and help Silverthorne. You need to protect your kingdom—Morgana must not be allowed to take Eldoren." She shot a glance at Cade. "Take the Elite with you."

Rafe crossed his arms, and frozen rage dulled his handsome features. "There is no way I am letting Aurora do this without me. And have you forgotten? Besides Aurora, I'm the only one who can touch the Dagger without being pulled in."

A shadow crossed my face. I didn't want anyone else to get hurt, yet although I wanted to do this on my own, I knew I would have a much better chance of succeeding if they came with me. I let my gaze settle on Rafe. "Then you must promise me you will rescue my father and get him to safety."

"I will do what I can, but—" he came closer, putting his hand on my arm, "—I'm not leaving you."

I put my hand on his chest. "Please, Rafe, I have to get the

Dagger. But I can only do that if I know someone else is going to protect my father. I've come so far; I cannot watch him die today."

Penelope stepped forward. "I will protect Azaren with my life. You and Rafe concentrate on getting the Dagger. Besides the two of you, none of us can touch it. Tristan and Ashara will handle the Drakaar. But we must leave immediately. There is no time to waste."

I nodded. I had to trust she would do as she said. I had no other choice. Once Dragath had awakened his full powers, he would use the Dagger to create the portal to his world and bring his demon army through to destroy us all.

Just then, I felt an icy wind behind me, and Penelope's eyes widened in shock.

Before I knew what was happening, an arm appeared out of thin air behind me and wrapped itself around my neck.

"Aurora!" shouted Rafe as he ran toward me.

But it was too late.

The last thing I saw was the horrified look on his face as I was pulled swiftly backward through a void.

A flash of light blinded me as the portal closed and I fell back into darkness.

THE DARK FORTRESS

RED FIRE BURNED in the sconces on the wall, bathing the pitch-black stone in an eerie red light. I pushed myself up from the floor and found myself standing in a dark dungeon. Joreth stood before me, the Dagger in his hand. The curved, twisted blade was a black pit of darkness that consumed everything it touched.

Joreth's smile was menacing and lethal. A chill settled in my very bones. His obsidian eyes glistened as he regarded me. There was no more of the man Joreth left. The demon lord had full possession of his mind and movements. "So, you and your fae friends managed to take back Stonegate. Impressive, but it won't do you any good."

My hands tightened into fists as I faced him and tried to gather some semblance of magic to shield me from whatever he had planned. I had no idea where I was, and my friends were gone. There was no Tristan or Rafe to get me out of this now. I was alone.

"How did you open the portal to bring me here?"

He held up the Dagger in his hand, inspecting it with a manic gleam in his eyes. "You would be surprised at the things the Dagger can do now. Your magic was the key to unlocking its full potential. Finally, the Dagger will do what it was created to do. Once I have my body and all my powers back, I will bring my army here and rule Avalonia for all eternity."

I wove a mage shield around myself as dread coiled in my gut. I looked around, but there was no way out. "My friends will come. They will stop you."

Dragath chuckled, the sound grating my bones. "They will not make it in time. No one can open a portal within the Dark Fortress—only the Dagger can. In any case, the whole fortress is surrounded by Drakaar, should your friends be foolish enough to come."

Footsteps scuffed closer, and Dragath turned to the entrance of the dungeon. Lilith was holding a chain and dragging another prisoner in behind her. His hair was matted, and a rough beard covered his features. He looked weak, barely able to walk as Lilith pushed him forward. He staggered to one knee but managed to push himself up. The prisoner's face was weathered, gaunt, and pale. But his eyes shone as they regarded me, focused, clear, and emerald-green—the eyes of a Firedrake.

There was no mistaking it—he was the same man I saw in the tapestry with the druid. "Father!" My heart swelled with the sight of him. It was true. My father was alive. I would know him anywhere.

"Aurora!" His voice was rough, unused.

Tears threatened to fall as I rushed forward to hug my father for the very first time since I could remember. I couldn't believe it as I clung to him. At least I got to see him this one last time. My father hugged me back. His body was frail and weak, but I could feel within him an indomitable will, one that had kept him alive in the most horrific circumstances.

Azaren Firedrake took my hands in his. His face was beaten and bruised. Even after all these years of imprisonment, it looked like he still put up a fight. When he looked at me, his eyes shone with hope. "Your mother would be so proud," he said gently.

My heart constricted at the thought of my mother and the faith she had in me. I had failed her. I had failed everyone.

"Touching," Dragath interrupted as dark shadows snaked out of his hands and pulled us apart.

My father's eyes turned to shards of steel as he regarded Dragath. "Why did you bring her here, Dragath? You have me. Let my daughter go."

Dragath's lips curved upward in a sinister smile. "Oh, but why would I do that?" A whip of dark magic exploded from his hands, pushing my father back and pinning him to the wall. With his other hand his dark power coiled around me as an unbearable pressure brought me to my knees. "True, I don't need both of you, but leaving one Firedrake alive was never the plan. Tonight I will finish what I started. When the sun sets over the mountains on this day, the Firedrake line will be wiped out forever."

I pushed against the magical bonds, but to no avail. We were trapped and absolutely at Dragath's mercy.

"It seems my dear Lilith here has a score to settle with both of you. So I will leave her to it." Dragath shot a dark look at Lilith. "Have your fun, but don't kill them yet." He released the bonds, and I dropped onto the cold hard floor, panting. "I will make preparations for the ritual."

Dragath left the dungeon, his booted feet thumping on the stone floor, leaving my father and me at the mercy of the Dark Queen. Although she looked like Vivienne, the darkness that enveloped her eyes had started to spread in black veins out of her eye sockets and down her face, marring it and giving her a gruesome visage. It was as if my friend's body could not contain the evil of the demon within as it ate away at her soul, piece by piece, until there was nothing left.

I willed myself not to shake as the Dark Queen approached. A sinister silence filled the dungeons as Lilith smirked at me in Vivienne's body and dark shadows reached out, binding me in a viselike grip. The dark bonds writhed around me like snakes and tightened. A blinding pain tore through my body.

With her other hand, Lilith held my father back with magic.

"Don't do this, Lilith," growled my father, struggling against his bonds. "Leave her alone. It's me you want."

She turned her obsidian eyes on my father. "Oh, but I want you to feel the pain of seeing your offspring tortured before your very eyes, Azaren." She clicked her tongue and a lash of dark power speared through me. "You may have lasted through years of torture." She struck again, and her power sliced through me. "But can she?"

I couldn't stop the scream that tore from my throat as the pressure of darkness built all around me. I pushed at her magic with my own, but the Dark Queen was too strong; mage magic could barely harm, let alone kill, a demon as powerful as her.

"Vivienne," I pleaded, trying to get through to my best friend. "I know you are in there somewhere. Please fight it—fight her."

Suddenly Lilith let go. The pressure waned, and the darkness in her eyes flashed momentarily. I could see a kernel of surprise on the Dark Queen's face. Vivienne was fighting her. She was still in there somewhere.

I fell to the ground shaking, panting, trying to gather my strength.

But when I looked at Vivienne again, it was only the Dark Queen who looked back. "Vivienne's gone," Lilith said, smiling as she curled her fingers into a claw. "And she's never coming back."

Her dark power lashed out again, and a wave of blackness enveloped me. An agonizing pain whipped through my body, and I screamed. Wave after wave of darkness washed over me. I writhed on the ground. I heard my father's voice shouting for Lilith to stop, but I couldn't move, couldn't breathe as the crushing darkness shattered my body and I fell back into dark oblivion.

WHEN I AWOKE, I found myself on the floor of a dark chamber.

Burning braziers of red fire flickered menacingly on the walls over a stone altar—Dragath's tomb. Intricate grooves ran through the floor beneath it, carved out in the runes that had helped bind the demon lord so many years ago. The Dark Lord's evil power pervaded every stone, rotting them from the inside. The stench of twisted magic clung in the air. The cavern pulsated with dark power.

My father was chained to the altar. Dragath was standing in front of him, reading from the *Book of Abraxas*, his arm outstretched, the Dagger clutched in his hand.

Skye stood beside him, her eyes fixated on the book. The ritual had begun.

I pushed myself up slowly. I had to get my father away from Dragath.

But a swift kick in my ribs sent me back down to the floor.

Lilith stood over me, her dark power pulsating dangerously as it lashed toward me, lifting me up and pinning me to the wall. "Watch!" she hissed with a hateful smile. "I want you to see Azaren die at last."

Bile rose in my throat, and I gritted my teeth against the pain as I tried to push her off me. But her magic was too strong. Dark spots flashed before my eyes as the pain in my chest grew.

Just then, a blur shot past me and barreled straight into the Dark Queen.

I fell to the ground as her dark bonds dissipated.

I turned to see Rafe holding Lilith by the neck. Magic rolled off him in waves as he held the Dark Queen back. "Go," he growled, and his eyes flashed like a roiling storm.

The sounds of swords clashing filled my ears. Penelope raced toward me.

My relief was evident when I saw her. "How did you get past

the Drakaar?"

"Tristan."

I nodded. It was all the explanation I needed. "We have to save my father," I whispered. "Please."

Penelope's sharp eyes took in the situation swiftly. I could almost see her mind whirling with possibilities. "Whatever magic you have left." She flicked me a quick look. "Now is the time to use it."

I called forth my magic and built up mage fire within me, blasting it at Dragath. I needed to keep him distracted long enough to save to my father.

But Dragath had created a shield around himself and the book.

He looked up, and his eyes flashed in anger at the interruption. His gaze moved over us. "So, your friends came for you. How sweet. Now they can watch me destroy you."

He glanced at Skye. "Kill her."

Skye grinned. "With pleasure," she murmured and stalked toward me, twirling her sword in her hands. In Elfi, Skye and I had been friends; I had trained with her almost every day. She was good, one of the best fae warriors, and I had no fae powers whatsoever.

Instinctively I moved back, creating a shield as Penelope threw me a sword. I knew it would not help me against Skye. She was Andromeda's daughter and a Princess of the Day Court. Even though she wasn't fire-fae, she was a formidable warrior.

Skye's sword flashed as it arced toward me.

Out of nowhere, another sword clashed with hers, pushing Skye back.

Aiden stood before me. A shadow crossed his face as he regarded Skye. "I've been looking for you, sister."

Skye backed away. If there was anyone who could best her in a fight, it was her big brother. I could see something akin to fear flash in her azure eyes. "Aiden. What are you doing here?"

"You took something that doesn't belong to you." He pointed

his sword at her. "And I'm here to take it back to Elfi."

Skye's eyes narrowed and froze to ice as she regarded her brother. "Still the fae queen's loyal dog," she spat and lunged at Aiden.

They crashed together in a fury, both powerful fae-warriors almost evenly matched.

Dragath looked up, his eyes glazed, still concentrating on the magic he was trying to perform. "The ritual has already begun. There is nothing you can do to stop it."

Dragath lifted the Dagger and sliced it through the air before him. To my horror, it cut through the very fabric of the world, creating a portal. The dark portal grew and a hideous creature stepped out of it, twisted and evil with rotting limbs and the eyes of a demon. Shadows coiled themselves around it like a second skin.

Dragath's eyes flashed, and his face spread into a hateful, horrible smile. "There are thousands more where that came from." He waved his hand at his demon minion. "They are all yours."

The terrifying creature smelled of rotting flesh, and its eyes burned with a monstrous bloodthirsty gleam. It ran at me.

I raised my sword and slashed at it, tearing through rotting flesh, and rolled swiftly to the side. Black blood sprayed everywhere.

It snarled, turned, and came at me again.

A blast of raging silver fire came out of nowhere and hit the creature, burning through flesh and monstrous bone, reducing it to ash.

I whirled around to see Tristan racing toward me, Ashara by his side, her staff aloft and glowing in her hand.

Another creature stepped out of the portal.

Dragath raised the Dagger above my father. "All I need now is the blood of a Firedrake." The Dagger made a hissing sound as Dragath sliced it across my father's chest.

"No!" I screamed and ran toward him. No, no, no! I was too

late.

My father's blood dripped into the grooves beneath him and wove around the altar as if it were alive. He struggled in his bonds as the life started to slowly seep out of him, feeding the Dark Lord's power and undoing the magic Auraken Firedrake had used to bind Dragath here.

"You are too late," Dragath said in a voice that was slowly changing, becoming deeper, more otherworldly.

At the altar, tendrils of darkness had started to form, writhing out of the tomb as Dragath's powers began to awake. He reached out his hand toward Aiden. Shadows whipped at the Prince of the Day Court, catching him and flinging him against the wall. Darkness coiled itself around Aiden's body, holding him down and devouring him as he screamed in agony.

The distraction gave Skye an opening.

She raced toward Dragath, grabbed the *Book of Abraxas* from the altar, and shot for the cavern entrance.

Dragath's eyes flashed with fury at the unexpected treason, and he flung a wave of blackness outward, spearing toward Skye. But the Princess of the Day Court was too fast.

She had already disappeared.

Aiden pushed himself up as the shadows dissipated around him. "I will find Skye!" he shouted and raced after his sister.

Ashara's staff glowed dangerously bright as she raised it, directing it at Dragath. She blasted a hole through his shield, breaking the bonds that held my father chained to the dark altar.

I ran faster—I was nearly there.

Dragath raised the Dagger again, ready to finish off my father.

"Penelope, get him to safety!" I screamed as I lunged at Dragath, trying to grab the Dagger from his hands.

The magic around Dragath pulsated with power as the blood in the runes shifted and squirmed. "You are too late."

The Dark Lord struck, plunging the Dagger of Dragath deep into my stomach.

DRAGATH

Pain seared through my body in a wave of agony and I fell to my knees, clutching the Dagger. My blood joined my father's in the runes and splattered on the floor.

"Aurora," bellowed Rafe. But his voice seemed so far away.

He was battling Lilith, but his shield was wavering, and she had him backed up against the wall. I could do nothing to help him.

"No," I whispered as I frantically tried to gather the remnants of my magic, which was slowly but surely flickering out. Faces swam before my eyes as my vision started to blur.

"Tristan," I rasped, slowly bleeding out onto the ground. "The portal."

Tristan's face betrayed his horror as he beheld the Dagger, its blood-red stone glinting on its hilt, slowly draining my life away. He could not help me. No fae could touch the Dagger without being pulled inside. Composing himself, he raced toward the dark portal, facing it to meet whatever came through.

Penelope had reached my father and was helping him up. If she could get him to safety, she could heal him—Dragath's first cut had been shallow in order to prolong the flow of blood into the runes. She looked back at me and hesitated. I could tell she wanted to help, but she could not touch the Dagger without being pulled inside.

"Go! Please," I pleaded. I was going to die here, but at least I could save my father. "Penelope, please! Take him and go!"

But my father was having none of it. He leaned on Penelope, still weak from the loss of blood and years of torture. Determination shone in his eyes as he faced his captor and tormentor. "You dare to harm my daughter, Dragath." He raised his hand and lightning sizzled out of it, hot and alive, slamming into Dragath.

Dragath stumbled back, his expression stunned. He didn't expect my father to still have power like that.

None of us did.

Azaren slumped against Penelope, his use of such magic after so long weakening him considerably. He was injured on top of that, and although the gash on his chest was not a mortal wound, he was losing too much blood, and Dragath's powers were still growing.

Dark shadows whipped toward Penelope and Azaren. Her power flared, creating a shield, but it didn't stop the shadows. They tore through Penelope's magic.

Ashara came between them. All seven of the stones on her staff came to life, creating a stronger shield over them. Dragath's magic slammed into it but couldn't get through.

A wave of gratitude washed over me as I tried not to pass out from the pain. I trusted Ashara would do what she could to keep them safe. At least if they could get my father to safety, I had done something right.

I was losing blood, and the more that flowed into the runes, the more shadows were released from within the tomb, winding themselves around Dragath.

Dragath turned his attention to me slowly, as if he had all the time in the world. Darkness seemed to seep out of his very pores, eating up the magic from my blood. Strengthening him. "Give up, Dawnstar. Your end is near. My army is already preparing to enter this world." He held up his hand in a fist. "Once you are dead, all my powers will finally be restored."

I put up a weak shield around myself, and his sinister magic, evil and twisted, wound tentatively around it, growing more insistent every second. Darkness continued to snake around me, battering at my defenses, shadows that devoured souls feeding on my life-force.

I could barely focus through the pain.

Tristan was guarding the portal, battling a monstrous creature with eight legs that had emerged while Penelope and Ashara protected my father.

Rafe and Lilith were still locked in a magical battle. The Dark Queen's eyes flashed dangerously as she flung out her hands, throwing Rafe across the room. His sword clattered away across the floor as his head hit stone and he fell to the ground.

"Rafe," I gasped. I tried to push aside the pain and reached for my magic again in a last attempt.

Rafe pushed himself up, but before he could find his footing, Lilith pounced on him.

A sword flashed in her hand, the three red rubies smoldering in the firelight.

Dawn! She had my sword.

Lilith raised her arm and plunged the sword into Rafe's chest.

A horrified scream tore from my throat. "Rafe!"

With the last of his strength, Rafe pulled a dagger from his boot and stabbed it into Lilith's neck. The Dark Queen fell as Rafe collapsed on the floor beside her, blood pooling out of his wound as his life slowly slipped away before my very eyes.

"No!" My voice was only a whisper as I tried to push myself up, to go to him, help him, but I had no strength left.

Seeing Rafe lying in a pool of blood, my will collapsed. All hope left me. The darkness threatened to swallow me whole.

This was the end of the road. We would all die here today.

Through the blinding pain, a voice reached me. Strong and unyielding. A command. *"Get up, Aurora!"* said Abraxas in my mind. My ring started to glow. *"You can save Rafael—you can save everyone. The battle isn't over yet; you are needed. Your magic is in the Dagger, just waiting to be summoned back. If you can hear me, then all is not lost."*

I shook my head. "I can't. I'm not strong enough."

"You are the Dawnstar, Aurora, and you always were, even without your magic," said Abraxas, stern and unyielding. *"After five thousand years of lying dormant, the magic of Illaria Lightbringer chose to manifest itself in you. There is no one else who can wield the magic as it was meant to be wielded. You were born in this age for a purpose; you were born to stand against the darkness when no one else could. But you must believe without a shadow of a doubt that this was meant to be. You must have full faith in who you are; you are the light that fills this world with magic! Believe it. Believe in yourself!"*

Through the pain, I tried to concentrate and tried to remember what the druids had said about taking my magic back from the Dagger. In my mind's eye, I could see a thousand tiny sparks, the magic of all who were imprisoned within. I knew my magic was here somewhere, but I could not get to it. I kept searching, and the tiny lights swirled around in a frenzy. I went deeper, sifting through the powerful magic I found inside until I saw it. My power, shining brighter than all around it—the magic of the Dawnstar!

But I still could not reach it. The Dagger was resisting me.

"Your belief is still not complete, Aurora," said Abraxas. *"That is why the magic doesn't heed your call."*

Dragath struck again, and darkness speared through me, ripping, shredding my soul. A shattered scream tore from my throat. I shook my head as excruciating pain lashed down my spine.

"Get up, Aurora," said Abraxas, but his voice already seemed farther away.

I shook my head helplessly, trying not to pass out from the agony. Once I did, it was all over. "I can't!" I cried to Abraxas, throwing the thought out as the last vestiges of strength left me. "I have failed everyone. I am not the warrior everyone expected me to be."

This was the end. I had nothing left.

I looked on in horror as Joreth's body started to distort as more of Dragath's power filled him. His face lengthened, and black horns started to grow out of his head. His body grew in stature, and his skin turned a burnished red. His arms and legs grew as thick as tree trunks. He flexed his clawed hands as his massive presence seemed to fill the cavern. This was the demon lord I had seen in all the books and cave frescoes. This was Dragath at full power.

"Now," the demon lord said, "I will finally get the chance to kill the heir of Auraken Firedrake."

I heard the others screaming as the Dark Lord's power enveloped the whole cavern, devouring, shredding, ripping through their minds and bodies. Evil rose to its full potential, powerful and ancient, a soulless pit of darkness that threatened to swallow the world.

Pain lashed through my body and the world swam before my eyes. It was too much, too much pain. I wanted to drift off in the ball of light that had started to form before my eyes.

The sounds of the cavern and the battle fell away.

A shimmering form stood before me, a form only I could see. Her alabaster skin shone with an ethereal light.

Illaria Lightbringer!

"Be strong, my child," said the Ancient Fae queen, her voice soft and otherworldly. She bent down and brushed her hand across my cheek, and a new strength spread through my body. *"You were*

born to save this world. You are its guardian. Fight! I am with you. I have always been with you."

It was then that something inside me shifted, and I understood what Abraxas had been trying to teach me for so long. My magic was not a weapon as I had once been led to believe. It was a beacon, a ray of hope. It was light, and love, and faith—faith the world put in me. Now I had to become what I was always meant to be. Not queen nor ruler, but protector and guardian of Avalonia and its people.

I reached for my power, which I could see in the distance, far within the Dagger and burning brighter than a thousand stars. With my last bit of strength and an unshakable faith, I commanded it to return to me.

"Come!" I said and opened myself to it.

It was as if the floodgates released, and my magic rushed into me in a great tidal wave of unfettered power, washing over my whole body as it all returned. It was powerful and ancient, a great white light against which no darkness could stand. I pulled out the Dagger and stood up, my whole body glowing with an iridescent radiance as it healed itself.

Dragath's eyes grew wide and he backed away. "No one has ever taken their magic back from the Dark Dagger."

"There's always a first time for everything, Dragath," I said, flexing my fingers. My senses sharpened, my strength grew, and power roiled in my veins, waiting to be released. I faced the demon lord.

"No!" Dragath boomed as he flung out his arms and dark shadows speared toward me. "I will not allow you to bind me again, Firedrake."

A searing pain filled my head as evil magic, dark and twisted, battered at my shield. I gritted my teeth, pushing his magic back. I lifted my hands and blazing white light shot toward Dragath, tearing at his defenses. Sweat formed on my brow as I pushed more magic toward him. Dragath's dark power met mine, clawing at my magic like a ravening beast.

"Finish it, Aurora. This is what you were born to do," Abraxas growled in my head. *"Your magic is more powerful than his. No darkness can stand before the full light of the Dawnstar."*

My hands started to shake as I held Dragath back and gathered more magic.

"Once I kill you, I will kill your father as I always intended," Dragath sneered.

His magic impaled me with a tremendous force. It tore through my shield and a blinding pain ripped through my body, bringing me to my knees.

Dragath's voice filled my head and brought the pain crashing back. It slammed into me, knocking the breath out of my lungs. "It is a shame your mother isn't here to see how useless her sacrifice was to save you. You are pathetic, Aurora Firedrake. You are no Dawnstar."

An image of my mother flashed before my eyes. She'd believed I would save the world. She had faith in me long before I ever did. I had seen for myself how she gave her life to save mine. That kind of selfless love and faith could change the course of fate itself. My mother was still trapped in the Dagger; my work here was not done.

I had a destiny to fulfill.

I plummeted far down into my magic and drew on every last drop I could find within me. A great force of white light surged up, hard and fast, ripping out from the very depths of my power, raw and powerful—a primordial magic older than time itself. It waited for me to command it, to wield it as it should be wielded.

Dragath's eyes widened as he felt the shift.

My body glowed brighter than ever before as I released all my magic on the demon lord.

Dragath screamed in terror. His eyes flashed dark with hatred as white light seared through his skin, tearing through flesh, bone, and magic, scorching him from the inside out. A ravenous, twisted evil fought the light, a soulless devouring pit of darkness, a horrific beast that wanted to consume the world. My head pounded and my mouth went dry as I held on with everything I had. My power tore through him, ripping and shredding away the darkness as the cavern lit up with a blinding light.

My magic exploded.

And the once-dreaded demon lord was reduced to a pile of ash. Obliterated from this world once and forever by the only power that could defeat him—the full light of the Dawnstar.

The dark cavern was still once more, and an eerie silence filled the space as we stared in disbelief at the remains of the demon lord.

Without Dragath, the portal closed. Tristan stood over the headless body of a monstrous creature.

The sound of crying startled me and my head whipped toward it.

Penelope was on the ground, Rafe's head cradled in her lap. The wound on his chest was a deep hole over his heart. His eyes were closed.

Penelope looked up at me with a tear-streaked face. "I'm so sorry, Aurora. I could not save him."

It was a moment out of my worst nightmare.

"No!" I rushed over and fell to my knees beside Rafe. Blood seeped out of the wound on his chest, and his face was pale, so pale. "No, no."

Tears streaked down my face as I searched around with my magic to find a kernel of life to start the healing. It could not end like this. I could not lose him. I could feel Rafe's life force flowing away. I caught on to it just in time and wrapped it in a cocoon of light. "Please, hold on," I pleaded. "Rafe, hold on."

From the corner of my mind's eye I could sense a host of angry souls trying to push past the barrier, to pull him back, to take his place, but I held on with a force I didn't know I had. I clutched onto the last spark of Rafe's life. "Help me, please, someone help me."

Penelope put her hand on my arm and shook her head. "You cannot bring him back, Aurora. He is too far gone. There is nothing you can do." Her hand tightened on my arm, and her voice turned to ice. "Remember Lilith."

I froze and looked over at Vivienne, who lay beside Rafe. He had dealt her a death blow to the neck. Her blood stained the floor beneath her. Vivienne's once-bright eyes were devoid of life, but they were clear; none of the soul-devouring blackness remained. Lilith had left her body and disappeared.

I had done this.

This was the consequence I had to face for saving Snow's life. I had brought Lilith back to this world, and everything she had done since was my fault. All the destruction she had caused, all the lives she had taken—everything, even Vivienne's death, was my fault. Rafe's death would be my fault.

The tears wouldn't stop as I held on to the one small spark of life left in him, hovering just over the threshold of the Otherworld. "Rafe, please don't leave me. Rafe, don't leave me."

"You must let him go, Aurora," Penelope whispered. "It is time."

I shook my head and held on for dear life. "I can't, I can't . . ." My voice broke.

But I knew she was right.

I had been warned of the consequences of my actions, and I had to pay the ultimate price. I was the Dawnstar, the protector of this world. I could not defy the laws of magic for my own selfish gain. I had learned the hard way. All actions had consequences, and I had to accept the price of mine.

My hands shook and the pain in my chest grew as my heart broke over and over again. I had to do it—there was no other choice. I steeled my aching heart and prepared to let Rafe go.

I bent down and kissed him on his forehead. "I'm sorry, my love," I whispered, my tears splashing onto his face. "I'm so sorry."

A shining light filled the space before me.

I looked up through a haze of tears. Illaria Lightbringer appeared, shimmering and resplendent with her crown of pearls atop her head. At that moment, there was something different about her, less otherworldly, more real, as if she were actually here. Behind her more lights started to appear, a line of Ancient Fae queens fanned out around her. My ancestors, queens of the house of Eos-Eirendil—I recognized them instinctively, recognized their magic.

"You have done what no one has ever done before, Aurora Shadowbreaker," Illaria Lightbringer said with a smile on her ethereal face. "Killing Dragath opened the celestial pathways that kept us from this world. Because of you we can return to Avalonia, and so can ancient magic. You have made a great sacrifice and proved yourself worthy of the guardianship of this world." She raised her hand and a ray of golden light seeped out of it in a river of pure power. "But you have already suffered enough."

She directed the golden light at Rafe.

I could only stare with wonder as, one by one, each of the ancient queens directed their light to join hers. The cavern ignited with a blinding glow, and we all had to look away as golden healing light enveloped Rafe in its shining folds. Ancient magic flowed back into Avalonia in waves of undiluted power.

Eventually the light dimmed and went out.

Rafe opened his eyes.

Illaria Lightbringer smiled at me and then looked at Rafe as, one by one, the ancient queens disappeared. "You are now immortal, King Rafael," she said, as her form shimmered and faded. "Use it well."

THE LAST STAND

ALL THE EMOTIONS I had been holding back flowed out in a stream of sobs and tears. Illaria Lightbringer had given me a precious gift —she had saved Rafe's life and given him back to me. And now that he was immortal, she had removed my biggest fear: the people I loved getting old and dying while I remained young for all eternity. Now Rafe would be able to share eternity with me.

So much had happened in such a small space of time—meeting my father, Dragath's defeat, Vivienne's death, and the reality of losing Rafe forever had nearly broken me. But I had survived. I had won. My body shook with relief and sadness as I hugged Rafe fiercely.

We just clung to each other as the others looked on in disbelief.

After everything I had been through, all the years I had spent on my own wishing for someone to love me, I finally realized I had never been alone. I had friends and family who loved me and would risk their lives for me, waiting for me, even though they never knew if I would return. What's more, my parents' love was always with me no matter which world they were in. Now we were finally together.

There was only one piece missing.

My father coughed and snapped me back to reality.

Penelope and I ran over to help him; he had lost a lot of blood, but the wound hadn't damaged any internal organs. Penelope laid him down on the ground, and I knelt beside him, putting my hands on his chest. Slowly, I released healing magic into his wound, joining flesh and muscle until the gash on his chest healed. The skin joined together, leaving a scar over his chest.

Penelope helped Azaren stand, and he clasped me by my arms and gazed at his only child. "No father could have wished for a better daughter," he said, pride showing in his eyes. I let the tears flow as I hugged him, and I knew in my heart everything was going to be all right.

Tristan came over to me and unexpectedly hugged me too. "I'm glad you are all right, Aurora."

I smiled faintly at Tristan, Vivienne's death preventing me from feeling the joy I should have in this moment. "Thank you for always having my back."

Tristan nodded, his face serious as usual. "Always."

I walked slowly to Vivienne's body, my heart constricted with sadness. I knelt beside my best friend and gently closed her eyes. She had tried to fight Lilith, but in the end she was not strong enough. I couldn't save her, and I would have to live with the knowledge that I had failed her, for the rest of my life.

I hung my head and held her hand for the last time. "I'm so sorry, Viv." I turned to the others. "We need to get her back to Eldoren for a proper burial."

Rafe came over and put his hand on my shoulder. "We will."

Ashara walked over to gently pick up Vivienne's body in her arms. The witch warrior was stoic and unfazed as usual, but her gentle handling of Vivienne's body told me she was not as indifferent as she tried to portray.

"The war is not over yet," said Penelope as I stood up. "Silverthorne's forces will be decimated by Morgana's army if we don't do something about it. Dragath has been breeding demon creatures for years expressly for this purpose. Their forces outnumber ours ten to one."

Rafe's face hardened. He checked his weapons. "Silverthorne will be holding the fortress at the Eastern Pass in the Cascade Mountains. As long as we can defend it, Morgana's army cannot get through to Eldoren."

Penelope shook her head. "We cannot defend it for long. The army Aiden described will destroy our forces."

"If Santino's army and the witches can get there in time, we might still have a chance," offered Ashara.

"Maybe," Penelope nodded. "But they are going to need our help."

"And I know just how to give it to them." I picked up the Dagger of Dragath from the floor beside the pile of ash that was once the Dark Lord's body and secured it in a holster in my belt. Dawn was already strapped across my back. "Let's go!"

ONCE WE WERE outside the Dark Fortress, a wave of relief flushed over me. I took a deep breath. A burnished pink glow started to flood the horizon as sunlight touched Mount Khatral for the first time in five thousand years.

Penelope glanced at me. "We need to open a portal directly to the fortress at the Eastern Pass," she instructed.

Tristan scowled. "You do realize we will be opening a portal right in the middle of a war? I would rather summon the griffins to take us there."

Penelope's eyes were set like stone, and she shook her head. "Griffins will take too long. This is the fastest way. If Morgana's army takes the fortress, all will be lost." She turned to me. "Can you do it?"

I gave her a small smile. "Absolutely," I answered, and there was no doubt whatsoever that I could.

Vivienne's death had changed me, and I knew now the consequences of my actions were very real, affecting the ones I loved. But with that realization came a strength I didn't know I had, and with that strength a clear sense of who I was and what I was meant to do. For we create our own destiny with the choices we make, and I had a responsibility to all of Avalonia to make the right one. I had come to realize we live in a world of our own creation, and I was going to create mine.

I gathered the threads of my magic, separating my spirit magic from the rest. In my mind's eye, I could see a clear map of Avalonia. I concentrated on the fortress that defended the pass at the Cascade Mountains. I waved my hand and opened a portal. Mist swirled within it as the magical gateway began to grow.

Ashara stepped forward and glanced at Tristan, inclining her head. "You first."

The dark prince's face lit up as he drew both his swords. "Of course," he said and plunged into the portal.

Ashara went after him, holding Vivienne's body cradled in her arms, her staff strapped across her back.

Rafe followed with my father and Penelope.

As I held the portal open, I glanced at the fortress looming over the Darklands, and my eyes narrowed. It was a place of so much pain and heartache, and had served as my father's prison for the last fifteen years. I had to let it all go, to allow Dragath's memory to fade into the mists of time.

Bending down, I touched my hand to the ground, sending a wave of earth magic through it, powerful and ancient magic that had been long forgotten by this world. A crack appeared in the rock as my power speared toward the mountain.

Mount Khatral shook. A rumbling sound filled my ears as the dark, twisted stone fortress that Dragath had built started to crumble to dust before my eyes. I shot one last look at the Dark

Lord's last resting place, then stepped through the portal after my friends.

The clash of swords rang all around me when I emerged from the portal, shutting it instantly behind me. I had indeed arrived in the middle of a war, and it was still raging.

I swiftly took in my surroundings, my fae senses on full alert.

We were on a balcony overlooking the battlements. The great White Fortress loomed over the valley that lay beyond. Morgana's army had spread out across the Valley of Flowers as far as the eye could see—a massive horde teeming with dark creatures, monstrous abominations with rotting flesh and flashing red eyes. Black-hooded Drakaar led the ranks, an evil writhing mass of darkness that swept across the plains, destroying everything in its wake.

Gorgoths flew over the horde, teeming like an army of locusts as they battered themselves against the wards and shields the mages had created around the fortress. I knew these wards would not hold for long against the combined magic of the Drakaar.

Already some had broken through and managed to make it onto the battlements, causing havoc among the Eldorean ranks. All around me soldiers and warrior-mages shouted, nocked, and fired arrows and magic one after another at Morgana's creatures creeping up the ladders on one side of the fortress walls. Gorgoths flew at them from the skies, ripping out throats and felling soldiers and mages alike. Bolts of mage fire exploded around me as Eldoren's mage-warriors defended the battlements, preventing Morgana's hordes from getting into the fortress.

I spotted Uncle Gabriel on the balcony in full battle armor, swinging his great sword with one hand and blasting Morgana's soldiers off the ladders with the other, all while trying to keep the gorgoths from infiltrating the fortress from the skies.

My head whipped to Ashara and Penelope as I drew my sword. "Keep my father safe."

Ashara nodded, and the stones in her staff came to life.

My father's emerald eyes locked with mine as he picked up a fallen soldier's sword and twirled it deftly in his hands. "Be careful."

I flexed my fingers as magic roiled in my veins, ready for battle, and my sword lit up. Tristan, Rafe, and I rushed into the fray.

Uncle Gabriel's head whipped toward me as I ran to him, and his eyes widened. "Glad to see you made it." He couldn't help the smile that streaked across his face.

I nodded and flashed him a grin. "Right on time, it seems."

Silverthorne blasted a creature back from the massive walls.

Tristan leapt off the balcony and onto the battlements, not even stopping for a moment as he hit the ground in a sprint. Shadows formed around him, and his swords blazed with silver fire as he darted at the Drakaar. The magic of the night shielded him from the enemy. He became a blur, slashing and cutting through oncoming creatures like the angel of death.

"Make sure they don't get through the gates," I shouted to Rafe and leapt off the balcony after Tristan.

I landed in a crouch, sure-footed and nimble. It was a relief to have my fae powers back. Flames erupted from my hands as I blasted the ladders away from the walls. Morgana's creatures screamed and tried to hold on while the massive iron ladders crashed to the ground, crushing a host of scrambling monsters. I continued to burn a whole line of them as I ran along the walls of the mighty fortress.

Soldiers screamed and heads were already rolling as Tristan cleared the walls of threats.

A black-haired fae stepped off a ladder and onto the battlements. Slowly and steadily he turned to me, his eyes red and soulless, canines flashing as he bared his teeth. He raised his sword, and it burned with a deadly red fire.

I held up my hand and pushed him back, my sword flaming in

my other hand. "It's not going to end well for you, dark fae. Your master is dead. You might as well give up."

"You will never win, Dawnstar," the dark fae hissed. "Your army can never defeat Morgana's."

"That's what you think," I said, my tone confident.

The dark fae's soulless eyes widened as my sword flashed with silver fire and quickly severed his head from his body.

As creatures fell, more came to take their place. The horde moved relentlessly against the fortress. Line after line of monstrous creatures attacked, Morgana's mage soldiers in their midst, urging them on. They were like an endless sea of black, twisting and writhing with evil magic.

I sheathed Dawn and ran, calling on a different power, and created a bow and arrow out of glamour. I nocked an arrow as I sprinted across the battlements, infusing it with silver fire. I shot arrow after arrow at the persistent creatures that managed to scale the walls.

Tristan continued fighting, swiftly and efficiently slashing through the enemy, unleashing himself on any creature that managed to get up the ladders. Many ran at the sight of the dark prince, his swords flashing as he decimated Morgana's minions.

The majority of the warrior-mages were at the gates, holding them with magic as the Drakaar battered them from the other side. A few witch warriors who had come to Eldoren with Silverthorne helped hold the wards in place. But even they could not hold it for much longer.

I spotted Rafe helping them and shouting orders to his warrior-mages. "We need more magic to reinforce the wards; they are not going to hold!"

The wards fell. Dark magic ripped through the shields and a host of gorgoths burst through, flying straight at Rafe.

My heart nearly stopped, but I did not. I dashed toward him, weaving magic in the air around me, sealing the gaps in the wards and reinforcing them as I ran.

Rafe turned swiftly to meet a gorgoth, his sword drawn. Lightning flashed in his palm as he slashed his sword across the monstrous creature's wing, exactly as I had taught him. It screamed and fell to the ground, momentarily stunned as Rafe hit it with a bolt of lightning. Rafe raised his sword and sliced the gorgoth's neck.

More gorgoths battered at my shield. I blasted them away from Rafe. They fell out of the sky amid screams and cries as my magic hit them, incinerating them on contact. I could keep going, burn a hole in their ranks again and again, but eventually I would tire and so would everyone else. No one could keep this up forever. And Morgana's army was endless; they just kept coming.

A horn sounded in the distance.

I grabbed Rafe's hand, and we scrambled to the stairs and back up to the battlements to look out at the valley.

A wave of soldiers on horseback thundered down the plain toward the demon army. Pointed helmets flashed as the vast cavalry smashed into Morgana's unsuspecting troops, shattering their ranks.

Leading the charge rode the pirate prince on a white stallion, his golden crown flashing in the sunlight.

Santino had come!

Above the Brandorian cavalry flew a cloud of white snow leopards, growling with fury. Staffs lit up above them in multicolored hues. Magic crackled and streaked overhead as the warrior witches of Rohron crashed into the gorgoths, felling hundreds from the sky.

The drums sounded, Morgana's army calling for a retreat.

Cheers and excited shouts went up from the White Fortress as we paused to watch Santino's massive army drive the demon creatures away from the pass.

I heaved a massive sigh of relief. The battle wasn't over yet, not by a long shot, but at least we would live to see another day.

OLD SCORES SETTLED

ONCE THE FORTRESS WAS SECURE, we all gathered in the great hall as night approached. Fires burned in the oversized hearths. The white stone walls, scuffed and dulled with time, were covered with faded tapestries from another age, showing weapons and crests of Eldorean noble families who supported the kingdom with their personal troops.

Beyond the keep walls, Morgana's horde regrouped. They would be back in the morning, of that I had no doubt.

Uncle Gabriel paced in front of the flickering hearth. He looked up, and his eyes flashed in the firelight, which illuminated fresh scars on his face from the battle. His gaze settled on my father, who walked in beside me, and his mouth fell open. "It can't be."

My father smiled. "It seems I wasn't so easy for Morgana to get rid of after all." He glanced at me. "I guess it helps to have the Dawnstar as a daughter."

I blushed.

Uncle Gabriel's stoic face burst into a wide smile, one I had not seen in a very long time. He strode up to my father and enveloped him in a big bear hug, completely oblivious to the shocked faces all around him. "It's so good to have you back, my boy."

"It is good to be back, Gabriel," said Azaren Firedrake, returning the embrace.

Santino joined us in the great hall after he had settled his troops. They were now camped outside the fortress guarding the pass. Santino greeted Silverthorne and clasped forearms with Rafe and Tristan.

He turned to me and gave me a hug. "I'm glad to see you are still alive, Princess Firedrake."

I smiled at the pirate prince and hugged him back. "Thank you for coming, Santino." I took a step back and raised an eyebrow as I studied him. "Or should I say, Sultan Santino?"

"Santino will suffice." Santino chuckled, his amber eyes crinkling at the corners. "And I couldn't very well ignore a summons from my father-in-law, could I?"

Silverthorne shot his son-in-law an amused look and clapped him on the back. "Your timing is impeccable, Santino."

"Isn't it always?" Santino said, completely stone-faced.

Penelope cleared her throat. "We don't have much time." She clasped her hands in front of her. "Now that we are all here, we must discuss how to proceed."

"Most of the mines have been shut down," Santino offered. "Morgana will not get any more supplies of blackened iron to her army."

Penelope nodded. "Good. But I suspect they have already managed to forge a good number of weapons from what they have."

"Have you spoken to Izadora?" Silverthorne asked.

Penelope nodded. "Yes, and the Elder Council has finally relented. They have agreed to send the fae army to assist us. They have already started to march."

Tristan stepped forward. "Even with their fae speed, it will take the army of Elfi days to get here. A few may be able to make it faster on griffins, but they are not enough. Even if we summon all the griffins from the keep, their numbers are scant at best."

"We will have to hold the pass until then," said Rafe, running his hands through his hair.

"The fortress will not hold until then," my father said softly. "This is no ordinary army. Those creatures have been bred out of dark magic." He shot a look at Silverthorne and Rafe. "Your warrior-mages cannot win against the Drakaar." He glanced at Penelope and Tristan. "The fae have become weaker over the centuries, and the army Izadora will send is not strong enough to defeat this one. I spent enough time with Dragath to learn all I could about his plans. Today's battle was just scouts trying to assess our weaknesses. There is a whole legion of dark fae armed with blades of blackened iron waiting within their ranks to destroy the fae army when they come. Once she unleashes her whole army, this fortress will fall, that is certain. Only Izadora's Elite stand a chance against them, and there are only—" he looked at Tristan, "—seven Elite fire-fae warriors?"

"Eight," the dark prince replied, jerking his chin in my direction.

My father gave me an indulgent smile and nodded. "Yes, eight it is. But even the Dawnstar cannot defeat them all."

I stared into the flames as I sat quietly by the hearth and let them talk. My father was right. Even though Dragath was gone, it sounded like we were going to lose the war.

I turned the Dark Dagger in my hands, inspecting it from every angle. It pulsed with dark magic, still infused with the evil power Dragath had used to create it. Ever since I took it from him, its darkness called to me like a living thing, shrouding my mind with dark thoughts and trying to coax my magic back into the Dagger, even though it could not forcefully take it anymore. Having it with me all the time was proving to be harder than I had imagined. I wanted to be rid of it.

But I couldn't get rid of it, at least not yet. My mother was still trapped within it, and along with her so many other fae that Dragath had taken over the many centuries of his rule. I pushed magic into it from every angle, trying everything I could think of, but nothing seemed to work.

I sent a thought out to Abraxas. "Any idea how I can break the curse on the Dagger?"

"It won't be easy," the dragon responded immediately.

"Obviously, Sherlock," I murmured, running my fingers over the dark, twisted blade.

"Who is this Sherlock?" said the great dragon, a note of puzzlement in his deep voice.

I rolled my eyes but couldn't find it in me to laugh. "Never mind."

Lights seemed to swirl within the blade when I touched it, but I could not get to them. I had no idea how to get my mother out. The Dagger held on to the lives and the magic it had taken. It was not going to give them back easily.

I heard a commotion in the corridors as the doors of the great hall burst open and Aiden came in dragging Skye with him. Her face was battered and bruised, and her golden hair was matted with dirt and blood from a gash on her head. It was painfully obvious Aiden had not gone easy on his sister. I almost felt sorry for her.

"How did you find her?" Penelope asked, taking a tentative step forward.

"I caught her opening a portal and I followed her through," spat Aiden. "Little vixen was not easy to catch."

"And the book?" said Penelope.

Skye hung her head and didn't answer.

"Where is the *Book of Abraxas*, Skye?" Penelope asked again.

"She told me she already gave it to Morgana," Aiden replied.

My eyes narrowed. "Why would she . . ." I froze. "That's not Skye."

Cold calculating eyes looked back at me, black as obsidian. She grinned.

"Lilith!" I gasped.

Before Aiden realized what had happened, Lilith grabbed a dagger from his belt. "Azaren must die!" she screamed and flew at my father.

My father's eyes widened as Lilith raised her hand to strike a killing blow.

"No!" I sprang to my feet. My magic exploded without so much as raising my hands, flinging Lilith against the far wall and pinning her there.

She thrashed and writhed in her bonds, and in a flash, Tristan had a sword to her throat.

"Wait!" my voice boomed across the room.

Tristan stilled his hand. "She has to die. It is the only way for a traitor like her."

"No," I said as I stalked toward her. "Skye may be a traitor, but she doesn't deserve to die."

Lilith had occupied Skye's body for her magic, to make her more powerful. She would keep changing bodies until someone stopped her. She had taken Vivienne's life when she left her body, and I was not going to let her take any more.

"This ends today," I said and placed my hands on her chest.

Tristan and Aiden held Lilith pinned to the wall as I plunged my magic deep into her. The Dark Queen screeched in fury; her rotting magic clawed and tore at mine, a hateful, twisted darkness that devoured souls and fed on power. I gritted my teeth against it and pushed harder. Light magic streaked through Skye's body, drawing a shriek from her lips as Lilith swore and raged curses at my father. Wave after wave of pure, shining white light shredded apart the darkness and shadows that lurked in the deepest recesses of Skye's body, incinerating the Dark Queen from this world forever.

I removed my hands from Skye's chest. She stared back at me, eyes wide but blue as Mermaid Lagoon.

Aiden shook his head. "I'm sorry, Aurora. I didn't know Lilith had taken over her body."

I put my hand on Aiden's shoulder. "It's all right, Aiden. No harm done." I turned my eyes back to Skye. "You will be tried by the Elder Council for your crimes."

Aiden nodded. "I will make sure she is delivered to Elfi."

Skye spoke up. "I can help you get the book back."

My eyes narrowed as I studied her face. There was no more of the Dark Queen left in her, but Skye had willingly betrayed the fae and helped her mother steal the *Book of Abraxas*. "Why would you do that? You were the one who helped steal it in the first place."

Skye's azure eyes glinted dangerously. "Dragath took my mother. She is trapped in the Dagger." Her eyes softened as she lowered them. "I just want to get her back. And you are the only one who can do it."

Now that was something I understood. But I had no idea how to get my own mother out of the Dagger, let alone anyone else's. Still, Skye didn't need to know that. Maybe we could use her to turn the tide of this war.

"I could," I said noncommittally and ran my fingers over the hilt of the Dagger, which was now secured at my belt. "After everything you did, why would we trust you?"

"You can't." Skye crossed her arms. "But it's your best option."

"I will go with her," Aiden said, his tone flat. "I can convince Morgana I have turned sides."

I shook my head. "No, Aiden, it is too dangerous. Her camp is teeming with Drakaar."

"Not to mention dark fae." Tristan arched an eyebrow. "She will never believe one of the Elite would betray Izadora."

"I will tell Morgana that Skye convinced me to help her." He threw her a disgusted look. "She is my sister, after all." He turned back to me. "If I can get close enough to Morgana, I can kill her and end this wretched war."

"And it's common knowledge how much he hates you, Aurora." Skye smirked. "Morgana might actually believe he betrayed his queen just to get rid of you."

Aiden opened his mouth to say something, but I held up my hand. "It's okay, Aiden."

"If she finds out you are lying, she will kill you," Penelope added.

Silverthorne, who had remained quiet so far, spoke up. "Aiden is right, it is the most practical plan."

I nodded. It did make sense—provided Skye kept her word.

"You will go tonight," Silverthorne continued, "while her army is regrouping. We only have a few hours. They will attack again at dawn."

"Be careful," I added.

Aiden nodded and caught Skye by the arm. His boots clomped on the stone floors as they left the hall.

I fiddled with the Amulet of Auraken, which rested around my neck. I did not need it anymore, and it could no longer contain my magic.

Penelope held out her hand. "I will hold on to the amulet for safekeeping. We do not want it lost in battle."

I nodded, taking the Amulet of Auraken from around my neck and giving it to Penelope. "Do you think Skye will betray us again?"

Penelope's eyes were unreadable as she gazed out the great arched window. "I don't know. But I think we may need to come up with another plan, just in case."

THE FINAL BATTLE

THE MONSTROUS ARMY stirred as dawn approached.

We had run out of options, and we had run out of time.

I hadn't slept a wink. I had sat on my makeshift bed in the great hall staring into the fire, waiting to hear from Aiden. There had been no word. I hoped he had succeeded in killing Morgana and ending this war. But it looked like there was going to be no such luck.

The fortress was packed to bursting, with all the rooms and beds full of casualties from the last battle. Soldiers slept on the floors and in the various halls and corridors, preparing themselves for what was to come. They offered me a room they had made available, but I had no interest in sleep. I preferred to remain in the great hall and wait for word from Aiden.

The thud of drums began as Morgana's horde began to march again. Today the fate of Avalonia would be decided, and we would need a miracle to win this time.

"Aurora." Penelope's voice was strained.

I looked up. "What's the matter?"

"I think you'd better come and see."

I followed Penelope to a wide balcony that overlooked the

blood-soaked valley. Morgana was standing at the front of her army with a crown on her head.

She addressed the fortress, her voice amplified by magic. "Come out, Dawnstar. I know you are in there."

An eerie silence followed.

"So, it seems you need a little persuasion." Morgana shrugged and gestured for someone to join her.

My hand flew to my mouth as Skye dragged forward a barely conscious Aiden, bound in chains of blackened iron. She pushed him to the ground at Morgana's feet. Six dark fae surrounded them, in case the Prince of the Day Court were to get free.

Skye had indeed betrayed us, but I never thought she would betray her brother like this.

"Hear me, Dawnstar," Morgana warned. "If you come out and face me now, I will allow the others to live." Her voice rose. "People of Avalonia," she addressed my army. "Give up the Dawnstar and you shall all return to your homes tonight. If she doesn't face me, you will never see your families again, and every one of you will die here today."

Penelope put her hand on my shoulder, giving it a little squeeze. "You don't have to do this. Every soldier here will fight for you with their dying breath."

I shook my head. "I can't let them do that while there is another choice." I squared my shoulders, and my eyes narrowed. "I will meet with Morgana, and if I can get close enough to her, I can end this."

My father stepped up first. "I will go with you."

"No, I can't let you. It's me she wants. Once she has me, she will withdraw her army."

"She will never do such a thing," Tristan snarled.

Rafe walked over and put his arm around my waist, pulling me to him. "I am never letting you go alone, and that's not up for discussion."

"I, for one, have been waiting to get my hands on those dark fae." Tristan drew his sword and threw a quick glance at Ashara. "What about you, witch?"

Ashara smiled, and the jewels on her staff started to glow. "Only if you let me go first, fae."

The dark prince's face lit up. "Fine, but just this once."

Penelope clapped her hands together. "Now that that's settled —" she gave our little band a once-over, "—let's go."

The Duke of Silverthorne's voice bellowed over the battlements as he called for the gates to be opened. I drew Dawn and walked out onto the battlefield, flanked by Rafe, Tristan, and Ashara. Penelope, my father, Silverthorne, and Santino followed close behind.

My heart hammered in my chest. I ran my fingers over the Dagger at my belt. I had one chance to end this war.

"Lay down your weapons," Morgana warned as we strode toward her. "If you accept me as your queen, you will be pardoned. Fight me, and all of you shall die here today." Her voice grew, reaching a crescendo; she seemed to love to hear herself speak. "Surrender, Dawnstar, and your friends can return to their mundane lives."

My father stepped out from behind me and faced her. His raven hair was neatly cut, although now generously peppered with silver strands. His beard, which had grown quite unruly in captivity, had been trimmed. He looked every inch the king he once had been. "That's my crown you're wearing, Morgana."

A gasp went up from both sides, and everyone stilled. Azaren Firedrake was their true king, and everyone knew it.

Morgana reeled back at the sight of him. "It can't be."

The demon army became restless behind their queen. Drakaar and dark fae looked on with ravenous eyes, Shadow Demons swirling around them. Gorgoths hovered above, shrieking and waiting to pounce on us.

"Oh, but it is." I smiled at my enemy. I called out to her army. "Soldiers of Illiador, you fight for a usurper. Azaren Firedrake is your king, and he is very much alive. Join me now, and fight for us, fight for Avalonia!"

A cheer went up from within Morgana's army as the mages of Illiador realized what was happening and that what I said was true.

I raised my arm, the Dagger of Dragath flashing in my hand as I held it up for all to see. "The general is dead, Morgana." I paused as her eyes betrayed her horror. "And so is Dragath."

Another gasp from the army.

"Impossible!" yelled Morgana.

I grinned. "You always say that, Morgana. But I think I have proved to you time and time again that nothing is impossible."

I felt a shift in the air around me as two brown-robed monks appeared beside me, the tops of their staffs glowing with a pure white light.

"Druids!" hissed Morgana. "I thought the general got rid of your pesky kind."

"He tried," Victor nodded. "But now he is gone, and the curse has been lifted." His spine straightened as the old druid pulled himself up to his full height and pointed his staff at Morgana. "We came to assist the Dawnstar."

"Surrender, Morgana," I urged. "Give up this foolish pursuit of power, and I will spare your life."

"Never!" growled the usurper queen. Skye raised a sword to Aiden's throat. "If you make a move, your High Fae minion will die." The blade in Skye's hand gleamed obsidian. If his throat was cut with her blade, Aiden would surely die.

Morgana smiled, reached into her cloak, and took out the *Book of Abraxas*.

"You think you have won." Her eyes strayed to my companions. "But I still have the book, and I know how to use it."

Tristan growled at the sight of it, and a ball of silver fire hurtled toward Morgana. She held up her hand and a shield formed around her. The silver fire hit it with such force that it raced over the shield in a wave of fury, scorching the ground around her. But Morgana remained unharmed, protected by magic from the ancient book. Only Abraxas could destroy the *Book of Power*, and the book seemed to protect itself as well as its bearer.

Morgana laughed hysterically. Wind whipped around her, churning up the earth as she read from the *Book of Abraxas*. Beside her, a portal started to open. "With this book, I can summon others like Dragath." Her eyes gleamed with the prospect. "I will summon an army of them."

I held out my hand, unleashing a wave of scorching white light at her, battering her shield, but the magic of the *Book of Abraxas* was too powerful. Even my magic could not get through her shield. "Don't do it, Morgana. Something worse than Dragath could come through that portal."

"That's what I'm counting on," Morgana sneered. "I will be Queen of Avalonia, whatever it takes." She raised her hand in the air and dark shadows wound around the portal. Something was forcing its way through.

Tristan and Ashara moved forward to meet whatever it was.

I blasted more magic at her shield, this time aiming for the portal, but the magic of the *Book of Abraxas* protected it.

"We must get her to drop the shield. The book is protecting itself. If I can get past its shield, I can destroy it once and for all," said the great dragon, his voice tense. *"Have faith in yourself, Aurora. You can do this."*

I nodded as three demonic creatures, eyes dark as night, ravenous with the need to devour souls, stepped out of the portal.

Tristan's sword lit up, and Ashara's staff glowed.

Sebastian and Victor drew runes on the ground beside me. The army at my back tensed.

"No one can stop me now," Morgana shrieked as her demonic creatures shifted toward us, ready to pounce.

In that moment I instinctively knew what to do.

"I was born to stop you, Morgana." My resolve was clear—this time I would not fail.

I held up the Dagger of Dragath and gathered my magic. We needed more warriors, and if my grandmother could not send the fae army in time, then I would summon my own.

I bent my knee and swiftly plunged the Dark Dagger into the ground, into the very heart of Avalonia itself, sending out a call of ancient magic, the power of summons, a call of light.

"Warriors of Illaria, hear me now! Cast off the veil of darkness that keeps you from this world. Rise and fight! Defend Avalonia." My voice rose to a crescendo as the ancient magic of Illaria Lightbringer arose once more. "The Dawnstar summons you!"

Both armies stilled.

Over the horizon where the sun crested the hills beyond the plains, a mighty force reared its fearsome head. Magic crackled and the sky lit up as a power older than time itself awoke.

I looked to the east. Sunlight glinted off the shields of an ancient army, swords flashing with silver fire.

The fire-fae warriors of Illaria Lightbringer! Thousands of them!

At the helm, her white-and-gold cloak spread out behind her like wings billowing in the wind, stood my mother in full battle regalia, resplendent and shining like the morning sun.

Morgana wavered at the sight of Illaria's immortal warriors, and her shield fell.

She dropped the book.

"Abraxas!" I screamed, summoning the great dragon.

Abraxas roared, a sound that could be heard at the very ends of the world.

Morgana shrieked in terror as dragon-fire engulfed her and the *Book of Abraxas* in a flaming ball, burning brighter than the sun itself. Everyone shielded their eyes as the great dragon appeared. Morgana and the *Book of Abraxas* were reduced to ashes where she stood.

With the book gone, the portal closed.

A burst of silver fire erupted near Skye as Aiden broke out of his bonds, grabbed the obsidian blade from Skye's hand, and plunged it into his sister's stomach.

Elayna Firedrake raised her sword, and it flashed silver with a fire deadly to demons and darkness alike. "For Avalonia!"

"For the Dawnstar!" shouted the mages, the witches, and the Brandorians.

"For the Dragon Queen!" shouted the fae army as a massive wave of ancient fire-fae warriors crashed into Morgana's demon horde, swords blazing.

They cleaved through the darkness, making way for the age of light.

THE RETURN OF THE DRAGON QUEEN

THE BALLROOM at the Star Palace in Illiador glittered with a thousand stars, magically floating around the great arched ceiling.

I smiled. This was definitely Penelope and my mother's doing, I could tell. It was made to look like the throne room at the Crystal Castle.

My father sat on his throne, regal and happy, with my mother, the love of his life, at his side. Tristan stood close by with Ashara. They had become rather attached to each other recently.

I stood at the foot of the stairs leading to the dais and looked over at my parents. Of course Rafe wasn't here. He had to return to Eldoren and deal with restoring his own kingdom. But he did promise to return, and this time I had no reason to doubt he would. But in that moment in time, there was nowhere else I would rather be. My heart swelled with a feeling I wasn't very familiar with—happiness.

Magic shimmered in the ballroom, and a portal opened. My grandmother stepped out, followed by Tristan's father Kildaren and his grandmother Rhiannon, the Dowager Duchess of the Night Court.

Everyone stilled. The Queen of Elfi never left her kingdom,

and she had certainly never traveled to Illiador before. Not even for her daughter's wedding.

Queen Elayna Firedrake got up from her throne. "Greetings, Mother."

The fae queen's golden eyes flashed as she regarded her daughter. "I almost didn't believe it when Penelope told me," she murmured. "I had to come and see for myself." And for the first time in over a hundred years, the queen of the fae let a single tear fall from her eye. It vanished as soon as it appeared, of course, but I had seen it. She held out her hands. "Come, my daughter. Let me look at you."

My mother glided down the stairs gracefully and clasped her mother's hands in hers. They regarded each other silently, and then my grandmother turned to me.

"You have done well, Aurora," said the queen of the fae. "You have achieved the impossible, and for this, you deserve to be happy. I may have made a mistake with your mother. But I won't make the same mistake with you."

I smiled at my grandmother. "So you don't intend to force me to marry Tristan?"

My grandmother shook her head. "No. I don't." She clasped her hands together. "But it seems it's not in my hands anymore."

My eyes narrowed. "What do you mean?"

Kildaren stepped forward, a cruel smile on his lips. "What she is trying to tell you, dear daughter-in-law-to-be, is your betrothal to my son was magically binding. It cannot be dissolved unless it is proved that the betrothal was done without your consent." He smiled at me, his white teeth flashing in an unkind grin. "And you did agree to it at the time, did you not, Dawnstar? Or should I call you Dragon Queen now?"

I ignored his jibe about my latest title. "Yes, I did agree, but . . ."

Kildaren held up his hand. "It doesn't matter why you said yes, the fact remains that you did." He turned to my father. "King Azaren, I'm sure you are aware of the protocol for these things."

My father, who had been watching quietly, got up from his gilded throne and walked down the short set of white marble stairs to stand beside my mother.

He looked at me sternly. "Aurora, did you agree to this?"

I nodded. "I was tricked, and Tristan is bound by an oath, so he had to say yes." I had to be concise before someone interrupted me again. I couldn't believe my family was really going to force me to marry Tristan on a technicality when neither of us wanted it.

My father shook his head. "It doesn't matter why you said yes. The grand duke is right. If you willingly agreed to the betrothal, you cannot break it without a very good reason."

"I have a very good reason," I said, throwing my arms in the air. "That's what I've been trying to tell you. Tristan and I don't love each other. I am and always have been in love with Rafe. Everyone knows that. Even Tristan."

Rhiannon stepped forward to stand beside her son, Kildaren. I saw her eyeing Tristan and Ashara in her peripheral vision. I could tell she was not happy about his association with a witch. "Love is not enough. Why don't you young ones ever listen?"

Kildaren sneered at me. I knew all he wanted from me was to breed a more powerful line of magic into the Night Court bloodline, giving him more powerful heirs.

"Let me get this straight," said my father, rubbing his short beard. "Prince Tristan doesn't want to marry you either?" He looked at Tristan, who came to stand beside me.

"My father may wish for me to marry Aurora," said Tristan, "but I do not." He narrowed his eyes at my grandmother and his. "Izadora's oath keeps me from following my true feelings." His eyes strayed to Ashara, who was standing behind my parents, tall and proud, a powerful warrior in her own right.

Then my grandmother did the most unexpected thing. "I release you from your oath, Tristan. You have more than paid your dues." I could feel the power pass between them, severing the magical binding.

Tristan's eyes widened. None of us had expected her to break their bond.

I smiled and so did Tristan as he bowed to his queen, gratitude visible in his midnight-blue eyes.

Kildaren's dark eyes swirled with silver sparks as he regarded his son. Sinister shadows seemed to twist around him. "It doesn't matter if his oath has been fulfilled." He eyed my father. "They both agreed to it, and you cannot break a magical contract, mage," he spat. "Do you really want to make an enemy of the fae, King Azaren?"

I stepped in front of my parents, my voice deceptively calm as my magic started to roil up inside me. "Are you threatening my parents, Kildaren?" My hands started to glow with ancient magic, and a shadow passed across the room. The castle rumbled as Abraxas settled himself on the highest tower and roared.

For the first time, I saw a spark of fear in Kildaren's eyes as he took a step back. "You cannot break a betrothal without a good enough reason," he repeated.

My father gave me a wry smile. His voice was stern, but there was a twinkle in his emerald-green eyes, so similar to my own. "Aurora, please tell your dragon to be careful. This is a very old castle, after all."

I smirked, nodding as I crossed my arms in front of me.

Rhiannon stepped in. "My son, Kildaren, is right. You agreed to it. Now it must be upheld."

My mother clasped her husband's hand, her beautiful blue eyes wide with worry. "Azaren, you cannot let them do this. Our daughter deserves a chance at happiness. She deserves to have a choice."

Azaren patted his wife's hand. "Don't worry so much, my love." My father turned his attention to Kildaren and Rhiannon. "If the betrothal is not valid in the first place, then that is another matter altogether. Is it not?"

Kildaren's eyes narrowed and he sneered. "You can't prove that."

"But I can," said Rafe, as the great double doors to the throne room opened, and the King of Eldoren strode in. He looked dashingly handsome as always, especially with his midnight-blue cloak swirling around him. His storm-gray eyes flashed with anger.

My heart skipped a beat like it always did when Rafe walked into a room. What was he doing here? When we parted after the battle, Rafe returned to Eldoren. He had said he would be back, although I hadn't thought he would come so soon. But it didn't matter why he had come. He was here, and that was all that mattered.

My brows furrowed. Rafe was accompanied by none other than the Duke of Silverthorne. They were all up to something. I couldn't help but smile then. If Silverthorne was here, then he must have a plan. My granduncle always had a plan or two up his sleeve. It's what earned him his newest title of kingmaker.

My father ignored Kildaren and smiled at Silverthorne. "Do you have it, Gabriel?"

The Duke of Silverthorne nodded. He looked solemn, but there was a spark in his azure-blue eyes. I knew that look; it was the same look he had when he could see all his plans falling into place. I wondered how he was going to fix this mess.

Rafe held up an old worn scroll and handed it to Silverthorne.

I stepped closer and my eyes widened. I recognized the scroll. It was the same one Rafe had been searching for that night in Silverthorne Castle when I found him in my granduncle's study. I wondered what could be so important about it that Rafe had gone looking for it in the middle of a war when the world was falling apart around us.

Kildaren stepped forward and snatched it out of my

granduncle's hand before he could give it to my father. "What's this?" He opened the scroll and read it, his eyes widening as his mouth fell open.

"That, I believe," said my father, stepping in, "is a contract. One that was made a very long time ago. The year Aurora was born."

My eyes widened like Kildaren's. I wasn't expecting that. I looked at Rafe. "What contract?"

Rafe glanced at my father and back at me. His eyes softened. "Shall I continue?"

My father waved his hand. "Please do."

"This contract," said Rafe, gesturing to the scroll clutched in Kildaren's hand, "is a betrothal contract made by King Azaren of Illiador and my father, King Petrocales of Eldoren. The contract between Tristan and Aurora has never been valid, since Princess Aurora Firedrake of Illiador was betrothed from the day she was born—" he paused, a mischievous glint in his eyes as he slipped his hand through mine, and announced, "—to me. Prince Rafael Ravenswood, now King of Eldoren."

My mother's face broke into a smile, and Penelope sniggered as she caught my grandmother's eye. I couldn't help the wide grin that had started to spread across my face.

Izadora smiled faintly at her sister and moved forward, holding out her hand. "Let me see the contract."

Kildaren handed the fae queen the scroll, resignation in his eyes as he came to terms with his defeat.

The queen of the fae spoke. Her gold eyes shone as they regarded Rafe and me. "This contract between Azaren and Petrocales is binding." She glanced at Kildaren. "Aurora's betrothal to Tristan was never valid." She turned to her daughter. "If I had known about this earlier, I would never have forced her to become betrothed to Tristan."

"I would have told you, Mother," said Elayna. "But we weren't really on speaking terms after my marriage."

Izadora's lips turned up into something resembling a smile as she clasped her daughter's hand in hers. "Well, I'm glad we are now."

"Me too," said my mother, flashing me a smile.

I looked up at Rafe, squeezing his hand. "Why didn't you tell me about this?"

He drew me toward him, brought my hand to his lips, and kissed it. "I wanted you to be sure this was what you wanted, Aurora. I didn't want to force you into anything."

I raised an eyebrow. "So if I wanted to marry Tristan, you would have let me?"

He nodded, his gray eyes stormy as I gazed into them. His brow furrowed. "Yes."

I smiled at this and raised my hand to his cheek. "Well then, it's a good thing I've only ever wanted you."

Rafe grinned and pulled me to him, tucking me in the nook of his arm. With his arm around my waist, we faced my parents.

But it seemed Kildaren was not yet done. "I've heard a rumor," he said, striding over to Penelope, "that I have another son."

Penelope's eyes flashed with fury as she threw a glance at her sister, who looked away. My spine bristled as I glared at my grandmother. She must have been the one who told him, just as she had threatened to do. But it could just as easily have been Rhiannon, Tristan's grandmother, who told her son about Kalen.

"Is this true?" Kildaren pushed. His gaze stole over all who were gathered, finally fixating on Kalen. There was no way Kildaren would not recognize him. Anyone who saw them together could see he had the same features as Tristan and the Grand Duke of the Night Court.

Kalen fidgeted. I could tell he was nervous, and I didn't blame him. He had only just found out along with the rest of us that he was Kildaren's son. But I also knew Penelope had tried to keep him away from Kildaren until he had learned to use his powers. If she had reservations about him, I did too. Penelope did not scare easily, but I could tell how uncomfortable she was when Kildaren was around. I had had my fair share of run-ins with Tristan's father, and I knew how cunning he was. He valued power above all else, and if he thought he could get his claws into another son who he could shape and mold in his image, he would not let it go.

Kildaren walked over to Kalen slowly and assessed his son. I could tell he was searching, probing to assess what kind of magic Kalen possessed.

I held my breath. The whole room seemed to still. No one said anything while we waited for Kildaren to announce he would be taking Kalen with him. I tensed. My magic started to rise within me.

Rafe squeezed my waist tightly and shook his head; he knew me too well. He knew if Kildaren tried to take Kalen by force, I would not let him. "Wait," he murmured in my ear.

Kildaren raised an eyebrow and turned to Penelope, a disgusted look on his face. "I expected more from you, Penelope. Your son has hardly any magic. He's not even worth mentoring."

I was startled, and for a moment I couldn't understand what had happened. But then I saw my grandmother and Penelope exchange a fleeting glance, and I knew. They had planned this. It was probably Rhiannon who told Kildaren about Kalen. But my grandmother, as always, was one step ahead of everyone else. Penelope knew the grand duke would be coming for Kalen, and the only way she would know was if my grandmother had warned her in advance. I smiled at Penelope and finally understood why she took the Amulet of Auraken for safekeeping. If it could suppress Kalen's powers and help him escape his father's clutches, then I was all for it. I let my magic settle down.

Kildaren turned to leave. "Come, Mother. Our business here is done."

Rhiannon opened a portal.

Kildaren's eyes narrowed as he shot a glance at Tristan. "I presume you will not be returning to Elfi any time soon?"

Tristan shook his head and took Ashara's hand. "No, not for a while, Father," he drawled. "Aurora still needs someone to train with. I think I will stick around here for a while."

"Have it your way," snarled Kildaren. "I tried to help you. What can I do if you prefer to waste your time with rabble?" He flicked a dark look at Ashara and stepped into the portal.

Rhiannon flicked a glance at Ashara, but she had the sense to look embarrassed by what her son had said. "Give him time; he will come to terms with it eventually." She smiled at Tristan. "I will speak to him and see what I can do."

Tristan nodded at his grandmother as she turned and stepped through the portal to return to Elfi.

My grandmother's golden eyes flashed as she regarded the room, a lion surveying her pride. They settled on my father. "It is because of your bloodline that Aurora bears the mark of the Dawnstar. You are of the Ancient Fae line of Eos-Eirendil, even though you are—" she paused for a moment, "—a mage." The word sounded distasteful on her lips. She inclined her head to my father in the only gesture of respect and acknowledgement he was going to get, but it was a start. "Considering this," she went on, "you are welcome in Elfi as our guest, should you wish to visit."

My father nodded and gave his mother-in-law a short bow out of respect. He was chivalrous and a gentleman through and through. "I would be honored, Izadora."

A smile tugged at the fae queen's lips as she looked over at my mother. Still stern, still the fearsome, unyielding fae queen, but her eyes shone with a light that could only be described as happiness as she gazed at her only daughter. "You are all invited to Elfi for the harvest festival feast." She glanced at Rafe, who stood beside me, his arm still around my waist. "You too, King Rafael," she added, using his title. "Aurora can portal you there." Her gaze settled on me. "It is expected for my heir to attend. Don't be late!" she snapped. The queen of the fae stepped into the portal, shutting it swiftly behind her.

I turned to Kalen, who sheepishly pulled out the Amulet of

Auraken from beneath his shirt, the only thing that could have hidden his powers from Kildaren. This way, Kildaren would never suspect Kalen's magic was stronger than that of most High Fae and steadily growing. With the proper training from Penelope and Tristan, he would become a formidable warrior one day. Then Kildaren would find out about him, but not before.

Kalen took off the amulet from around his neck and handed it to me. "Thank you for letting me borrow it."

I closed my hand around his, the amulet still clutched in his palm. "Keep it, Kalen." I smiled at my oldest friend. "At least until you have adequate control over your powers."

Penelope stepped forward and put an arm around her son, who didn't pull away this time. "Izadora warned me Kildaren was coming for Kalen, and I knew the only way to get him to leave Kalen alone was to make Kildaren believe he had no magic. The spell I had put on him earlier to hide his magic will not work anymore now that he has accessed and used it. Only the Amulet of Auraken could have hidden his powers from a High Fae as powerful as Kildaren."

I smiled at Penelope. "It was a good idea. But you could have told me why you needed it."

Penelope raised her eyebrows, but she was smiling. "You are not the best person when it comes to keeping secrets, my dearest Aurora."

My eyes narrowed, and I scowled as Tristan solemnly nodded his head at this, as did Kalen, while Rafe chuckled beside me.

My father came up to me and put his hand on my shoulder. "Now that this unpleasantness is over—" he looked at Rafe, "—we can announce your betrothal to Rafe at the harvest ball in Elfi, if you wish."

My mother came forward, clasping my father's hand in hers. "Even now, you still have a choice, my darling. We will not uphold the contract if you don't want to wed. We always intended for the two of you to be together." She eyed Rafe warmly. "But it seems you beat us to it."

I looked up at Rafe. "The harvest ball is a good time to announce the betrothal," I said to my parents. "But there will be no wedding just yet." I squeezed Rafe's hand and he understood. We had already decided we were not going to marry immediately. We were still young, and there was so much for us to do. Rafe had to sort out his kingdom, and I had to help my parents rebuild mine. Morgana had destroyed whole parts of our world, and it would take time and effort to restore and heal. And now that Illaria Lightbringer and the ancient queens of Elfi had made him immortal, we had all the time in the world.

My father beamed from ear to ear. He seemed happy he wasn't going to lose his only daughter just yet, especially since we had all just found each other again. We needed to be a family again, to spend time together. There were so many years to make up for, and I wasn't going to waste another moment.

I knew Rafe and I would be together eventually, of that I was sure. Whatever happened and wherever I went, in this world or any other, my heart would know.

And I would always choose him.

Every single time.

ACKNOWLEDGMENTS

It has been a long journey to reach the end of a series that I have been working on for nearly ten years. I couldn't have done it without the help and support of so many wonderful people.

I would like to thank the extraordinary Kate Tilton, who has been a pillar of support throughout the whole process, and without whom none of this would have been possible. I am so grateful for her unflagging enthusiasm and tireless work to bring this series to its completion.

To my superb editors, Amanda Rutter and Christie Stratos, for their keen insight, patience, and guidance, which have helped me grow as a writer and produce the best possible version of this book.

To the awesome team at Wise Ink Creative Publishing, especially Laura Zats, for believing in me and my books. Thank you for all the work and expertise you have put in to bring this series to readers and for helping me realize my dreams.

To my amazing cover designer, Steven Meyer-Rassow, for capturing the essence of the book and creating two spellbinding covers.

To the talented Joshua Stolarz for creating a beautiful, detailed map of the world of Avalonia.

I would also like to thank the talented team at Findaway Voices for helping me create the audiobooks for this series, and the wonderful Fiona Hardingham for bringing my characters to life with her incredible performance.

And finally, a big thank you to all my wonderful readers and fans who have supported The Avalonia Chronicles from the very beginning. You are the reason I write.

ABOUT THE AUTHOR

Farah Oomerbhoy is the international bestselling author of The Avalonia Chronicles. Her first book, *The Last of the Firedrakes*, was originally published on Wattpad where it gained over two million reads and a Watty Award. Since publication, *The Last of the Firedrakes* and book two *The Rise of the Dawnstar* have gone on to win numerous awards, including matching silver medals in IBPA's Benjamin Franklin Awards. Wielding her master's degree in English literature and her love of the fantastical, Farah spends her creative time crafting magical worlds for young adults. She lives with her family in Mumbai, India but can often be found checking closets for magic portals to Narnia.

FarahOomerbhoy.com
Farah@FarahOomerbhoy.com

facebook.com/FarahOomerbhoyAuthor
twitter.com/FarahOomerbhoy
instagram.com/farahoomerbhoyauthor